THE GOLDEN GLOW DREW NEARER

"Robswerran," Dolph said tightly with a nod toward the light and laughing in a curiously humorless way, and Jerico wondered if the Plackers were in fact members of one of those obscure religious sects whose tenets required the periodic sacrifice of a total stranger. It would explain the red clothes, the stolen truck, and perhaps even the elephant. What it didn't explain was the frequent explosions within the golden glow, as if a great battle was taking place beyond the next hill.

"I'm retired, you know," Jerico said at last. The glow now reached into the cab, and Jerico stared at it, rubbed a fretful hand across his forehead and stared again.

It wasn't a glow at all.

It was a wall.

And Dolph wasted no time driving right through it.

Also by Lionel Fenn
published by Tor Books

**AGNES DAY
BLOOD RIVER DOWN
WEB OF DEFEAT**

LIONEL FENN

THE SEVEN SPEARS OF THE W'DCH'CK

A TOM DOHERTY ASSOCIATES BOOK
NEW YORK

THE SEVEN SPEARS OF THE W'DCH'CK

Copyright © 1988 by Lionel Fenn

A TOR Book
Published by Tom Doherty Associates, Inc.
49 West 24 Street
New York, NY 10010

Cover art by Jill Bauman

ISBN: 0-812-53791-2   Can. ISBN: 0-812-53792-0

Library of Congress Catalog Card Number: 88-50989

First edition: December 1988

Printed in the United States of America

0 9 8 7 6 5 4 3 2 1

This one is for Craig,
the Godzilla of Cambridge

How many spears could a W'dch'ck chuck
If a W'dch'ck could chuck
Spears.

—from *The Book of Ralph*

1 When Jerico Dove bumped into the elephant, fell sideways into the gutter, and a mere second or two later was nearly shredded by the bristles of a street-cleaning truck, he knew instinctively that things weren't going to get any better anytime soon.

Hell, he thought as he hauled himself up by a lamppost and looked with a grimace at the muck damply clinging to his shirt and trousers; and *hell* again when he turned around and saw that the elephant was gone.

The street was empty, the storefronts were dark, and the air had turned a good ten degrees cooler.

He ran to the corner and looked left, looked right, and barely managed to stifle a moan. Now he was seeing things, and bumping into them to boot.

And it was all the fault of the man with the white cane and the toothless German shepherd.

Being a hero had never been easy. Quite beyond the fact that it was occasionally dangerous, there was, surprisingly, not much call for it. Not that there had ever been anything like an overwhelming demand for his somewhat specialized services. Or even, for that matter, ebbs and flows. It was, if he was going to be honest with himself, mostly ebbs. Mud flats, to be precise. Low tides of such monumental proportions that heroically shouldering his despair of ever making a decent go of his chosen profession was about as busy as he ever got.

Not, he thought as he limped up the street, that he wasn't qualified.

His attitude, for example, was impeccable. And it helped that his family was wealthy enough to indulge him; it helped further that there was nothing left of his family, save the odd cousin or two, to stop him when he converted everything but the mansion in Nevada to hard cash and moved East, where, he had been assured by the media, things were really rotten and in definite need of a hero.

And physically he was, modestly, nigh unto perfect —an inch or two over six feet, his weight proportional to his height, and his musculature of a sort that, when he wanted to be impressive, permitted him to split his shirt down the back and sides just by taking a deep breath. Of course the shirt had to be altered somewhat in advance, and it didn't do much good if he was wearing a jacket, but the point was, he was strong, looked it, and could prove it whenever he got the chance.

He glanced behind him. The elephant was still gone.

He wasn't that bad-looking, either, if his photographs weren't lying. On the other hand, not everyone cared for the length of his blond hair, or the smoothness of jaw and cheek that sometimes gave him the appearance of an adolescent just waiting for experience to happen; and there was something rather unsettling about the heavy concentration of black eyebrows which resisted all attempts at plucking, not to mention the extraordinarily dark blue eyes which, in certain lights and with the shadows of his brow, made it seem as if they were black with rage.

Nevertheless, he did cut a rather dashing figure, and certainly hovered close enough to the heroic stereotype to quicken the grateful hearts of those who required safe passage through the white-water straits of the paranoiac urban sea.

Chance was where the fault lay. Too much of his business relied on chance, on prowling the dark streets, seeking people who needed rescuing. Unfortunately, a lot of them didn't. A lot of them were only going to and from the movies, or the theater, or dinner, or a hockey game. A lot of them traveled in packs. A hell of a lot of them refused to be threatened by the punks who accosted them; and the punks, being punks, merely shrugged and moved on.

The problem was, he reflected as he absently flicked a cigarette wrapping from his sleeve, that he couldn't fly and he didn't have superhearing, thereby preventing him from locating cries of alarm and speeding there before the crime was completed.

Not being Superman was sometimes a real bitch.

He wasn't a total failure, however; far from it.

There had been several times in the last decade when he had been at the right place at the right time. And he smiled when he recalled the robberies and muggings he had foiled, the one attempted murder and two near maimings he had turned into routs in the cause of Justice. And there had been several times when his picture had been in the paper, the commentary at first mocking when he announced his heroship, then praising his intentions, then wondering snidely if he wasn't really out to turn a fast dollar by selling his story to magazines and the movies. He protested, and the newspapers finally believed him when he refused offers of millions for his official biography.

They believed him, and they ignored him because he wasn't news anymore.

Heroes weren't news unless they moved on to better things.

A gust of wind snapped his disheveled hair across his eyes. Another gust plastered his sodden silk shirt against his chest. And a third made him jam his hands into his tailored trouser pockets, duck his head, and stare at the tips of his soiled English shoes.

Those very same shoes which had carried him to the mouth of the alley at the lower end of Manhattan not more than ten minutes ago, the alley in which he had heard the muffled grunts and groans of desperate combat.

He had looked in and had seen three brawny youths struggling with a man with a white cane while, on the outskirts of the group, a brawny German shepherd danced and snarled frantically, grabbing at and missing arms, legs, and anything else that came within momentary reach of its powerful jaws.

It was obviously a job for Superman, or the next best thing, considering the odds.

So he had set his shoulders and strode in, declaring loudly that the meeting was over. When no one paid him any attention, he clucked at the futility of crime, grabbed one of the youths by the collar of his leather jacket, and yanked him effortlessly back. The kid growled his displeasure and whirled to face this new antagonist, saw a fist instead which further dimpled his jaw and sent him crashing into a pile of garbage. The others heard the noise, saw him, and let out with a series of obscenities and curses which only served to make the dog more frantic. It charged him, grabbed a

hunk of his trouser leg, and tried to pull him deeper
into the alley.

"No!" Jerico commanded.

No sooner had the word passed his lips than the
embattled man turned his attention from his assail-
ants, and the white cane came down with astonishing
weight across his shoulder. He yelped and went to one
knee, blinking in astonishment when the dog shifted
its attention from his leg to his hand. It was then that
he realized the beast had no teeth, though its gums
were nothing to sneer at once they had gotten hold.

Another blow brought him to his other knee, and
the three youths fled.

"Son of a bitch," the man with the white cane said
angrily. "Do you have any idea how much money
those preppie punks were carrying? Do you have *any*
idea? Jesus!" Then he spat in disgust, whacked Jerico
once in the side for good measure, and called his dog
off.

"Glad to be of help," Jerico wheezed, slightly
confused as to which shoulder he should rub.

"Help? Help? What are you, some kind of crazy? I
didn't need any help, you stupid bastard. I was doing
just fine on my own."

"But those creeps—"

The shepherd growled deep in its throat and bared
its monstrous gums.

"Christ," the man muttered. "How the hell am I
going to pay the rent now? Damn."

Jerico swiveled painfully as the two headed for the
street. The dog looked back and growled again; the
man looked back and spat again before wandering off,
the echoes of his cane tapping the sidewalk forlorn
against the deserted buildings, the empty street, the
silent October night.

That was when Jerico Dove decided to swallow his
pride and retire.

And it was not two blocks and five minutes' walk from the alley when he bumped into the elephant.

It isn't fair, he thought glumly. A man has his standards, and no one cares.

He sighed, plucked an orange peel from his collar, and thought less about the disappearing pachyderm than he did the cost of replacing his clothes, which never in his life had he ever bought off the rack since God knew he had to maintain an image, if not for the media then at least for the people he served in his capacity as a full-fledged, more or less full-time, all-American hero.

At the next corner, since there were no taxis in sight and why not since it had started to drizzle, he slumped wearily against the display window of a closed all-night delicatessen and gingerly probed his side where the cane had thumped him. His left wrist wasn't doing all that well, either, and it was while he was examining it for signs of gum marks that he heard the footsteps to his left.

He cocked his head and frowned.

Their cadence was odd, they bespoke great weight, and when he peered around the corner of the building, he saw the elephant again, plodding its solitary way down the middle of the street, until it stopped at a red light at the intersection and scratched its head with its trunk.

Jerico gaped. He closed his eyes. He opened them. The light turned green, and the elephant started around the corner, its form blurred by the drizzle which raised islands of shifting fog from the drains and gutters.

"No," Jerico muttered. "I am only dazed by my failures. There is no elephant here."

Unless, he thought suddenly, there *was* a circus, and said circus had somehow misplaced one of its star attractions.

He straightened.

He smiled.

He ran down the pavement, head high and arms pumping, disillusionment shunted aside as he realized that by returning the beast to its rightful owners he would not only be following his calling, but he would also spare thousands of children the agony of loss.

It would be perfect—the best of all conceivable ways to end his career with dignity and retreat to his Nevada mansion, where he would try to figure out what to do with the rest of his life, and all that damned money.

Midway down the block he slowed.

There was a problem.

Making a citizen's arrest of a felon was one thing; stopping a determined elephant was something else. There was obviously going to be more to it than standing in front of the thing and telling it to halt. And he didn't think he'd be able to find a convenient position from which he could leap onto its back and ride it, much less control it. And he doubted as he reached the corner that he'd be able to convince it that he meant no harm. All things being equal, a determined elephant was something he seldom counted on when he set out on his missions of justice.

The elephant was at the next intersection, and turning right.

But that very element of sublime chaos, he thought as he sped up again, was what made his job so exhilarating, so filled with suspense—one just never knew, did one?

He crossed the street, his shadow racing ahead of him as he leapt the curb and swung around the corner in the elephant's wake.

He understood perfectly that speed was of the essence if he was to be spared the sight of children's mournful tears; he understood that he would have to play things by ear once he had actually caught up with the creature; and he understood full well that once the animal was corraled and ready to be returned to its circus, he would have to find some way to clean off the gutter's debris hanging from his clothes if he were going to present the proper image to the police.

What he didn't understand was why the elephant had stopped in the middle of the street, nearly causing him to once again ram into its hindquarters. Except that it wasn't its hindquarters he nearly collided with because the thing had turned around and was facing him now, trunk half-curled, great ears slowly flapping, and its pair of long yellow tusks aiming straight at his chest, which had managed to halt itself a mere inch from their devilishly filed, glinting tips.

Nor did he understand why, out here in the rain, which was going to be hell on his English shoes, there was an old man sitting on a wicker rocking chair on the sidewalk, smoking a pipe and talking to a younger man standing beside him.

And he definitely didn't understand why the elephant decided at that moment to wrap its trunk around his chest and begin, ever so gently, to crush him to death.

The children, he thought as he began to black out, are going to be awfully disappointed.

2 The light at the end of the tunnel was no mere cliché, Jerico discovered when consciousness returned; nor was it the sole property of those who had undergone certain metaphysical experiences on their solitary journeys to the very threshold of death. Had he been unconscious when he noticed the light, he might have been curious; since, however, he found himself otherwise, he could only wonder why he felt as if he were increasingly seasick.

The nausea was possible, of course, he thought as he struggled to sit up—he could very well have been shanghaied, bound and gagged, and dumped into the hold of an eastward-sailing freighter which was, at this very moment, on its way to some disreputable foreign port where he would be sold into slavery, to spend the rest of his life serving the unnatural whims of a powerful potentate.

But there was the inescapable fact that oceans

didn't have car horns blaring every few seconds as far as he knew; and there was, as well, the light.

It was right up there, dead ahead and not one hundred yards away, and, despite the stomach-wrenching tilts and drops which knocked its perspective dizzyingly out of kilter, it was also damned familiar.

Unfortunately, he was unable to say the same for the compartment he was in; it was definitely not a ship's hold. It was, as a matter of fact, little more than six feet on the long sides, comfortably padded with multicolored pillows, hung with exotic-looking thick carpets to either side and behind him, and far enough off the ground to provide reassurance that he wasn't about to be smashed into the rear of the automobiles he had spotted just ahead. And as he examined the conveyance more closely, he was puzzled to note how much it resembled the howdahs of the rajahs he'd seen in old movies.

But howdahs belonged on top of elephants.

Well, I'll be darned, he thought.

Carefully he gained his knees against the pitch and roll of the great animal's gait and crawled to the large opening in the front wall. A look down; there was indeed an elephant carrying the contraption. A yellow-tusked one. The very same beast which had, only minutes ago, embraced him to the point of unromantic swooning. And immediately ahead, moving slowly to accommodate the creature's own less than scenery-blurring speed, was a large trailer truck on the back of which garish lettering proclaimed to those traveling in the other lanes the passing of the Great And Wondrous Adolph Placker Circus And Extravaganza.

Not, Jerico thought after a moment's rifling through the files of his mind, one of the big ones.

Mindful then of his stomach's increasingly delicate

condition, he crawled to the rear of the howdah and
lifted the nearest carpet. The wall was solid. As were
the sides and roof when he checked them.

And a good thing, too, he decided as the room
suddenly canted back and he was thrown against the
wall with a thud that lay a brace of pain across his
shoulders when the pillows, thrown up and back by
the same motion, evidently thought he was going to
hit the ceiling instead.

He gasped, he groaned, he batted the pillows aside
and looked ahead long enough to understand that the
creature was now climbing what was clearly the
spiraled Bergen Viaduct.

As I thought, he thought, sagging to the floor again;
they had traversed the Lincoln Tunnel and were now
heading into New Jersey. While he had no idea why,
he was comforted by the fact that they were not
heading for Philadelphia since, once they had regained level ground, the entrance to the New Jersey
Turnpike was ignored, and they proceeded at an
alarming speed directly westward.

It occurred to him, as he was flipped from side to
side, that perhaps the Great Adolph Placker was
attempting in some way to atone for the manner in
which his animal had treated him; it also occurred to
him that he might be the victim of an elaborate
kidnapping plot.

I think, he decided then, I'd best escape—a plan
instantly derailed when the pachyderm swerved
sharply to the right to avoid a pothole. The movement
was magnified by the roll of its great shoulders, and
the resulting turmoil was such that Jerico once again
discovered that portion of the rear wall which was not
protected by either carpeting or pillow.

He blacked out a second time.

He blacked out a third time when he regained
consciousness and tried to scramble to safety outside,

tripped on a pillow rather smaller than its fellows, and struck his brow on the edge of the opening.

When he awoke yet again, it was full daylight.

There were hills when he looked out over the elephant's bobbing head. Lots of hills. And lots of trees on those hills, many of which were resplendent in their autumn finery, lending the air not only an Impressionistic tint of gold and red, but also a tang that only their yearly transformation could achieve.

What there weren't lots of, he noticed when he pulled himself up and peered out to check the road, were cars. Or people.

In point of fact, the elephant and the truck were the only two things moving on the road, which itself was a not terribly impressive two-lane highway.

His temper began to flap a bit at the edges.

"Enough," he muttered. "This has gone far enough."

After all, wasn't it bad enough that he'd been duped into making a fool of himself by the man with the white cane and the toothless German shepherd? Hadn't there been sufficient humiliation heaped upon him on the last night of his chosen career? My god, hadn't he endured enough jeers and mudslinging, epithets and laughter, without having him lurch into the sunset on the back of a goddamn elephant?

Wasn't it bad enough, he cried silently, that a man's boyhood dreams have died in the gutters of an uncaring city?

"Damn right," he said angrily. "Damn right!"

So saying, he knelt at the opening and willed himself to become accustomed to the animal's undulations, for only after that was accomplished would he be able to effect some sort of action which wouldn't knock him out again.

An hour later he succeeded, and slipped out of the howdah to perch precariously on that relatively narrow portion of the elephant's neck directly behind the ears, whose flapping seemed determined to bat his knees off. The truck was still ahead, there was nothing behind but highway, and he told himself that he need only be patient from now on. Sooner or later the trees were going to fall away from the rocky verge and reveal a plot of ground grassy and wide enough for him to leap upon. Then he would run like hell to the nearest town, call the police, and have Adolph Placker tossed into the clink without so much as a thanks for the goddamned ride.

And then, seeing an abrupt image of himself atop the beast, howdah behind, circus truck ahead, Jerico laughed aloud.

If only his mother, rest her ashes, could see him now. Her only child, gleefully riding a full-blown elephant as if he were in a circus parade. Somewhere in the wilds of the Garden State.

"God, this is great!" he shouted in temporary delight.

The air was warm despite the season, and the scenery was such that there was little save his own situation to distress him. It was incredible, unbelievable, a remarkable experience, and not really all that terrible once he'd gotten the hang of not letting the thing below toss him off on his head.

What the hell, he could always escape later, this was too much fun.

And he laughed again until a disturbing thought crowded out his merriment—from experience, he knew that the wilds of the Garden State were, if they were still heading west, a good fifty miles from New York City. And judging from the current pace of the truck, it should have taken them at least three or four days to get that far, three or four days during which someone surely would have noticed, some policeman certainly would have stopped them to demand a permit or explanation, some fool would have ridden by leaning on his horn loudly enough to send the elephant screaming into the woods.

And if they weren't in the wilds of the Garden State, where in hell were they?

And if they *were* in the wilds of the Garden State, how the hell did they get here so fast?

He placed his palms on the twin bulges of the elephant's broad skull and attempted to look down at its face, to find a clue perhaps in the expression of its eyes. Which he was unable to find because he was nearly pitched headfirst onto the road when the animal picked up enough speed to match that of the truck.

Shaken, he sat back and decided that, for the time being, he was in no mortal danger. If whoever was driving up there had wanted him dead, they'd had plenty of opportunities. And they surely could not believe he wouldn't attempt an escape from such a slow-moving conveyance. And if all that was so, it might, he thought further, be interesting to find out what was going on before he jumped ship.

After all, what did he have to go home to but a lot of money and a mansion in a desert?

With a rueful sigh for his plight, he studied the land around him and saw a sign which noted tersely that he'd better turn left at the next intersection or he was going to miss the only road within reason that would take him straight to the charming ski lodges of deepest Sussex County.

Christ, he was farther along than he imagined.

And when the next sign passed so rapidly that he was unable to read it, he realized that the elephant had managed to defy all laws of Nature, and a few of the more esoteric ones of Mans, by moving along at such a clip that the wind was actually bringing tears to his eyes.

Jerico, he said to himself, you are in trouble.

With more skill than he knew he possessed, he managed to creep back into the howdah, where he was at least spared the sight of trees moving by far faster than he wanted to see. And when he lay down among the pillows and clasped one of them to his chest, he discovered that as long as he kept his eyes closed and pretended he was merely in a suicidally fast car, his stomach kept its rebellion to a minimum.

He grunted.

He pondered.

He supposed it was the street-cleaning machine. He had tripped into the gutter, had struck his head, and was now in the midst of a hallucination the meaning of which would come to him as soon as his senses were restored.

It was, in short, a sign.

He snuggled the pillow closer and smiled briefly at the faint roselike scent that squeezed out of its fabric.

And when push came to shove, he also supposed that having all that money wasn't really all that bad. It had enabled him to live out a dream, no matter how tattered that dream had become; and it had provided him with the wherewithal and the English shoes to keep him comfortable while he learned rather painfully that adults were in bad shape when their childhood finally died; and finally, it would most certainly allow him to sue the ass off the driver of the street-cleaning machine, not to mention the city, the mayor, and anyone else he could think of, thereby adding to his fortune and forcing him to spend more in order to keep his misery at a controllable level.

The elephant slowed.

He hugged the pillow more tightly to him and squeezed his eyes shut as hard as he could.

The rocking became less pronounced.

He took deep breaths.

The rocking almost stopped.

He opened his eyes and looked down between his feet to the howdah's entrance.

The rocking stopped.

He could see the sharp blue sky, the branches of trees, a single large cloud so white it was nearly transparent. He could feel the breeze, an Indian summer breeze that touched his cheek sadly and as much as told him he wasn't dying, nor was he hallucinating, nor was he still asleep in his bathtub.

Damn, he thought.

And sat up just as a man's face popped above the ledge and grinned at him.

"Hey," the man said. "You the hero?"

3 In such life that Jerico understood to be real, clarion calls were few and far between. Once in a great while, however, a man heard the triumphant ruffles and flourishes, calling him to action, to glory, to the performance of deeds soaringly above the summons of ordinary obligation. It was exhilarating to those few who were called; and it was terrifying because those same few knew that their lives would never be the same again, especially if that performance resulted in their heroically premature demise.

But such consequences were beneath consideration; it wasn't death that mattered, but the manner in which death was achieved. Heroism, in deeds large or small, carried its own brand of sanctification, one usually found only in specialty shops of an obscure nature.

Nevertheless, those trumpets made their call, and Jerico, as he stared at the man staring back at him, heard them.

Tentatively he nodded.

The stranger grinned even more broadly and beckoned with a blunt-tipped finger. "Wonderful! Superb! Come on out and let's have a look at you."

Jerico, without completely casting aside his instincts for self-preservation, was grateful for the interruption of the elephant's lurching progress and scrambled out of the howdah before the invitation was withdrawn. A rope ladder was affixed to the howdah's side, which he used to reach the ground. Where he collapsed when the ground didn't roll, or pitch, or attempt by stealth and strength to knock him off his feet.

The stranger laughed heartily and offered his hand.

Jerico shook his head. For now he was thankful just to be on something that didn't move.

And while he sat, he glanced up and down the road, seeing nothing but trees and leaves and rocks and other natural things not usually found either in Nevada or New York City. Then he looked at the stranger and saw a man approximately a head shorter than he, with long black hair gorgonlike in its complex tangles, and a round and ruddy face which matched the round and red-dressed body beneath it. Every stitch of clothing was red, for that matter, from the billowing shirt to the snug trousers to the knee-high boots whose heels added yet another two inches to the stranger's height.

Jerico nodded at the truck. "You're Adolph Placker, right?"

The man nodded and hunkered down in front of him, idly slapping aside the elephant's trunk, which had been poking around in a voluminous hip pocket. "Right on one, my friend. And you're Jerico Dove."

Jerico admitted it with a modest smile.

"You're the hero?"

A melancholy sigh coupled with a yearning glance down the road was the answer.

Placker sighed as well. "Right. A bitch, I guess, trying to save people who don't want to be saved."

"Tell me about it," Jerico said.

"You do good work, though. I read the papers, I know these things."

"I try."

"A bitch," Placker said again, and lowered himself until he sat cross-legged on the shoulder. "You want to give it one more shot before you quit?"

Immediately suspicious, Jerico parried the question with one of his own: "How do you get that thing to move so fast?"

"It has an accelerator."

"No, the elephant."

"Oh." Placker glanced over his shoulder. "I don't know. It's just something he does, like being able to pat your head and rub your stomach at the same time."

Slowly Jerico pulled his legs under him and rose; when he didn't fall, he inhaled deeply and rubbed at the small of his back, his upper arms, and his stomach in an effort to ease the subtle aches and pains the ride's jolting had given him.

"What were you doing in New York?" he asked as he walked along the verge toward the truck's red-and-chrome cab.

"Looking for you." Placker hadn't moved.

"Really? May one ask why?"

The elephant, having somehow divested itself of the howdah, sidled off the road and began testing the underbrush for lunch. From the way he tossed it over his back, it was apparent he didn't think much of the local cuisine.

"Because you're needed," Placker told him.

Jerico turned and put his hands on his hips. "Oh really?"

Placker nodded.

"I think not, Mr. Placker, if that is your real name. I am not a trapeze artist, I am not a lion tamer, I do not know a damn thing about elephants, and I am certainly not a clown, which you obviously think I am if you think I'm going to believe that your thing there can run as fast as a truck."

"Do you always talk that way?" Placker asked.

Jerico straightened. "In what way is that, may I ask?"

"That way."

At that moment the cab's passenger door opened, and a woman climbed out.

Jerico, temporarily forgetting his breeding, stared.

She was no taller than the man, but her roundness was reserved for those parts of the female anatomy which cry out for such topography and, he thought, must be screaming like hell about now considering the tight fit of the red outfit she wore. It was an embarrassingly long second before he was able to look at her face, at the startling grey eyes and the deep black hair and the tilt of a nose that shrieked out for kissing.

He put a hand to his chest and ordered his heart to stop its unseemly pounding.

She smiled politely, and turned to Placker. "This the hero?"

Placker nodded.

She held out her hand and Jerico took it gently, held it for a moment he would never forget, and did his best not to sigh when she lowered her arm.

"Are you really in the business of heroing and things?"

A swallow to stop his voice from cracking. "I was."

She frowned. "Are you on vacation?"

"Retired."

Instantly the frown became a scowl, and she whirled on Placker. "A good one, Dolph," she said. "You've done it again. Of all the heroes in the goddamn world, you had to pick a retired one."

All the heroes? Jerico thought; now what does she mean by that?

Placker stood and adjusted the wide black belt around his ample middle. "We're in a hurry, Rhonda. Or had you forgotten?"

"What do you mean?" Jerico asked her. "What other heroes by profession are there? Is there a club or something?"

"How much of a hurry can we be in that we can't at least pick one who's still working?"

Jerico, seeing the disappointment in the woman's stance, and fearing suddenly that he might well be throwing away the chance of a short lifetime, cleared his throat twice. "Well," he said, "I actually only retired last night."

"Does it really make a difference?" Placker asked her. "As it is, we may be too late anyway."

"Another day wouldn't kill us," she said in disgust.

"I'm not actually wedded to retirement," Jerico said. "I may even think it rather boring."

"Poor choice of words, my dear," Placker said, and whistled at the elephant, who snorted and turned, and reached up to open the back of the truck.

"Honest to god," Rhonda said. "There are days when I think I have to do everything myself." A look over her shoulder at Jerico. "You ever have days like that?"

"Oh, yes," he said breathlessly. God, if those eyes looked at him one more time he knew he was going to do something stupid.

The truck's rear doors swung open, a ramp clanged to the ground, and the elephant rumbled in. Placker had just reached up to close the doors behind it when, from somewhere near the front, there was a terrified shriek.

"Dammit, Rhonda," Placker said angrily, "I thought you'd gotten Father out of there."

"He wanted to finish his settee," she snapped as she leapt back into the cab.

Jerico started toward the back, intending to give Placker a hand if it was needed, then whirled and ran back to the front when Rhonda uttered a shriek of her own and launched herself from the cab. He was just in time to catch her, and to feel an arm clamp around his neck, feel her weight settle into his grip, feel a few other things which, under the circumstances, he knew he ought to disregard since they had only just met.

"What's wrong?" he asked anxiously.

"Father," she snarled.

He looked into the cab just as the old man he'd seen in the chair on the street crawled frantically over the seat and out to the ground, where he immediately collapsed onto his back. And if he was indeed Rhonda and Dolph's father, then their hair was inherited from their mother, because the old man's was nearly as red as his shirt.

From the ground the elder Placker pointed angrily at his daughter. "You were supposed to keep that monster out while I was weaving!"

"He wanted in," she said from Jerico's arms.

The old man spat in disgust, forgot he was lying on his back, and wiped his beard with a sleeve. Then he rolled over, stood, and pointed at Jerico.

"Why are you holding my daughter like that? She break a leg?"

"She would have," he said stiffly, "had I not saved her."

"Shit, you're the hero."

"In so many words."

The old man stared at him with one eye closed.
"Hero is one word."

"I was talking about the shit part."

"Point taken."

He held out his hand, Jerico took it, and winced
when he felt Rhonda's weight slipping from his grasp.
His adjustment, however, was less than adroit, and he
ended up on his knees, Rhonda on his lap and the old
man's hand pinned beneath. The resulting confusion
soon had Rhonda on the old man's lap, the old man
on his rump, and Jerico's face firmly pressed to her
bosom since she hadn't yet bothered to release her
hold on his neck. A pause for consideration before
they tried again, and this time made it with all hands
in their proper places, a blush on Jerico's cheek, and
the old man stomping toward his son with what
looked like a dagger in his left fist.

"Is he going to kill him?" Jerico asked fearfully,
thinking his services were about to be tested again.

"No," she said. "He'll cut the belt, Dolph's pants
will fall down, and Father will pass out from laughing."

"Charming," Jerico said, and said it again when she
proved a prophetess and they carried the old man
back to the cab, where they laid him on the seat, his
feet dangling out the door.

Once that was taken care of, Rhonda sat on the step
and shook her head slowly. Jerico knelt in front of her,
sensing despair in her attitude, and seeing it in
Dolph's face as he trudged toward them while thread-
ing a new belt into his trousers.

"I gather you are in some sort of trouble," Jerico
said.

"Damn right," said Dolph, dropping to the ground
so that he could lean back against one of the truck's
huge wheels.

"And I gather that you sought me out in order to give you some assistance in whatever's troubling you."

"Does he always talk that way?" Rhonda asked her brother.

Dolph shrugged.

Jerico ignored them. It wasn't his fault that his parents, while they were living and still paying attention to him, sent him to schools that believed in teaching the Queen's English by way of Thackeray and around the bend from Dickens.

The elephant kicked the side of the truck.

"There goes the settee," Dolph muttered.

Rhonda paid the racket no mind. She looked at Jerico in a way that disconcerted him—as if he were some exotic animal she thought she ought to know but couldn't quite put a name to.

"Tell me the truth," she said quietly. "Are you really a hero?"

"It's how I make my living," he answered.

"Bull. You're rich. You don't need to make a living that way. Besides, it doesn't pay anything."

He lifted a shoulder in a modest shrug. "I don't expect to get paid."

"Because you're rich."

"Because it wouldn't be right," he countered.

Again she stared at him in silence until, "All right." She slapped her palms on her thighs. "All right."

Dolph laughed then and jumped to his feet, grabbed Jerico's arms and pulled him up, hugged him, spun him into Rhonda's arms, which squeezed a surprising amount of lust to the surface before she kissed him soundly on both cheeks and released him.

"Let's move it, Brother," she said. "Dump Father in the back, and let's go!"

"Wait!" Jerico said.

Dolph ran around the truck, climbed into the cab

from the other side and helped his sister lift the old man through a curtain that divided the cab in half.

"Hold it a minute," Jerico said.

Dolph switched on the engine, its muted roar startling a number of birds into flight and raping the woodland of its autumnal quiet. Rhonda, at the same time, reached down and took hold of Jerico's arms and began to pull as the truck moved forward. Jerico was thus torn between losing a significant portion of his body to the woman he decided he loved, and leaping boldly into the cab with her.

There was no choice.

She yanked him in, slammed the door, and leaned back with her eyes closed.

"Where," he said, "are we going?"

"Oops," Dolph said.

"Is that a place or an exclamation of regret?"

"We're going home," Rhonda said wearily. "At last, we're going home."

Jerico smiled. "And where is that? Shangri-La? In New Jersey?"

"Close," she answered. "You'd be surprised at what you'd find in New Jersey if you looked hard enough."

4 Jerico, watching the landscape blur past him, pondered the woman's cryptic remark.

While it was true that he was not terribly intimate with the Garden State, he did know that it wasn't so large or so wide that it would take all day to get from one end to the other. Especially at the ridiculous speeds Placker managed to get out of the ungainly truck. Yet it was already well past midafternoon, and they were still on the move. To be sure, Dolph kept the vehicle on narrow, two-lane county roads; and Jerico felt that Dolph was exercising what appeared to be a fair amount of caution, since several aspects of the hilly, heavily wooded landscape were becoming increasingly familiar.

Perhaps, then, there was a certain ritual involved before one reached the correct destination. Or perhaps there were enemies the man was attempting to bewilder by pretending to be lost.

He looked across to the driver.

Dolph was scowling.

He looked closer, at Rhonda.

Rhonda was glaring.

"Are we lost?" he asked.

Placker snorted.

Rhonda returned his gaze steadily. "No," she said. "We are not lost. Why? Do you think we are?"

"Well," he said with a glance out the window, "I have seen that barn a couple of times before. The one with the chicken painted on the side."

"I see."

Dolph hunched over the steering wheel and glowered at the road ahead. "He doesn't see."

"I know that," his sister answered glumly.

"But I do see," Jerico said.

Rhonda grabbed his left hand eagerly. "You do?"

He controlled himself at her touch, though not without a certain amount of effort and swift meditation. "Of course I do," he told her gently. "You're either trying to confuse me so I won't be able to find my way back once I have left wherever it is we're going, or you're engaged in evasive tactics. It's really very simple."

He sighed when Rhonda released him.

"He doesn't see," she said to her brother.

"I told you he didn't."

"But I just said I did," Jerico protested.

"We'll have to try again," Dolph said grimly, and wrenched the wheel hard to the left, spinning the cab and its trailer onto yet another road not much larger than a wide trail that climbed the slope of a steep and high hill.

"Try what again?" Jerico asked.

"You'll see."

"But we don't have time," Rhonda protested as she pushed herself away from Jerico.

"Time for what?" Jerico said.

Placker narrowed his eyes. "We must have time, Rhonda. Or it's over for us. For all of us."

Jerico pondered again. Though neither of the Plackers had bothered to explain what his role in this mysterious venture consisted of, it was clear that they were engaged in something deadly serious, so deadly and so serious that they had evidently risked a great deal by slipping into the city with the elephant in order to find him.

To find a hero, he corrected himself glumly; apparently any one would have done.

Then Dolph slapped his hands on the steering wheel. "So. All right." He craned his neck to look at the sky. "Once more, Sis. One more time."

"Time for what?" Jerico asked.

"You'll see," Rhonda told him.

Of course, he thought, propping his elbow on the armrest, his cheek on his palm, and indulging himself in one hell of a pout as he watched the forest abruptly fall away when they broke into the clear on the hilltop, meadows and pastureland on both sides of the road, with absolutely no sign of human habitation.

Midway across, the truck stopped.

Dolph looked at him expectantly.

Jerico, for his part, looked north and east, and was astonished.

The landscape was positively bucolic—gentle hills bunched and rolled to all horizons, and on their equally gentle slopes and in the valleys between were the checkerboard patterns of fields just past their harvest. A glint of water from a wide stream. The colors of the leaves brilliant as the sun set behind a high ridge to his left.

"Incredible," he whispered.

Rhonda stared at him oddly. "You like it?"

"It's . . . it's beautiful. It's stunning. It's—"

"Yes?"

He shrugged at her eagerness, and looked quickly away when he saw how they watched him so intently, almost as if they were trying not to lick their chops.

Not that he wasn't used to being stared at, because his forays into the black underbelly of crime had often produced similar reactions. But he was more interested now in what he had spotted off to the right, above a hill somewhat taller than those around it—a fan of golden light, much in the shape of a trumpet aimed at the moon. It was bright, but did not illuminate anything below it, and it flickered as if something inside were struggling to get out.

"Amazing," he said, pointing. "You know, I wasn't aware there could be a town that big out here that would do something like that."

No one answered; he was struck by the silence that crept into the cab. A *faux pas*, he decided, but didn't know how to correct it.

Then Rhonda looked over to her brother and smiled. "He sees it. He . . . he really sees it."

"Of course I do," Jerico said.

Dolph nodded. "I guess he does."

"You'd have to be blind not to," he said.

"I suppose you're going to gloat," Rhonda said.

"Not me, Sis. I'm magnanimous in victory."

Jerico frowned but did not interrupt the perplexing conversation. Perhaps, he thought, some vital clue as to both destination and ultimate goals might be gleaned from their whispered, almost furtive words.

Dolph touched her arm. "He sees it, right? What more do you want?"

"How about a guarantee he won't screw up?"

Dolph laughed, albeit without a shred of mirth. "Well?"

Jerico feigned indifference.

"He won't," Dolph told her without taking his gaze from the road. And, a few moments later, "He won't."

Jerico's patience finally came to its end. He took firm hold of Rhonda's arm and, steeling himself against the touch of her flesh to his, demanded to know what in god's name they were talking about.

Rhonda kissed him.

Jerico was so startled he hadn't time to close his eyes.

When she pulled away, her own eyes were filled with glittering tears. "You see it," she said reverently. "Thank god. We're saved."

The sun was nearly gone.

Early stars were clustered around the flanks of a bloated harvest moon.

An intermittent breeze brought a winter's chill to the air, and the promise of frost by dawn for those who were fortunate enough to survive the night.

And the romance implicit in the scene only added to Jerico's growing conviction that he had absolutely no idea what was going on. He looked to the brother and sister seated so calmly beside him, and looked to the unnatural golden glow over the distant hill.

He stroked his chin thoughtfully.

He sniffed.

He scratched the sides of his neck and made some small adjustments to the fall of his hair and the line of his jacket, now hopelessly wrinkled. Then he looked Rhonda Placker full in the eye and said, "Is this a joke?"

Rhonda smiled at him, and his heart began to thump as loud as the elephant in back.

Dolph, meanwhile, whistled brightly for a few seconds before restarting the truck, popping the clutch, and jerking them all into swift motion.

"I mean, if it's a joke, it's a fascinating one. The preparation alone must have taken you ages."

Rhonda leaned her head back on the seat, and he congratulated himself for not behaving like a brute.

The gears ground and screeched, and he had another thought: "This isn't your truck, is it?"

Rhonda closed her eyes halfway and breathed deeply.

He considered the Rocky Mountains and how they grew before shaking his head. "It isn't your truck."

The gears begged to be found.

"You really don't know how to drive, do you?"

Dolph waggled his hand side to side.

Rhonda's chest followed suit when they swept into an S-curve and came out the other side with only a few scratches, and a sapling clinging to the right front fender.

"You realize, of course, that this makes me an accessory to a crime and puts a crimp in my reputation."

"You'll live," Dolph said with a brisk laugh.

"I doubt it," he said at the start of another curve.

And was contemplating mutiny when, without warning, Dolph's strained voice said, "Boys and girls, hold on to your hats. I think we have a problem."

Rhonda sat up immediately, Jerico returned his gaze to the road ahead, and gasped when he realized they had plunged off the hill and were back in the woods again. Into a premature twilight that soon turned to midnight as the branches closed overhead.

Placker had not bothered to switch on the headlamps.

And something out there howled.

I don't think, Jerico thought, that's a native to New Jersey.

Another howl, longer and louder.

"Dolph?" Rhonda said, her voice atremble with concern.

"Yeah," he answered stiffly.

"What?" Jerico asked.

"Don't ask," the man answered.

The howl a third time, closer, louder, and of a kind Jerico had never heard in his life. It was high-pitched and, at the same time, hinting at a basso profound with implications more dreaded than dire. It also indicated a creature at least as large as the elephant in back.

Jerico's voice was strained. "Okay. I'm asking."

Rhonda shook her head.

Placker cleared his throat and said, "Xazulla."

Jerico blinked and poked a finger at each ear. "A what?"

"Xazulla," Dolph repeated.

"Never heard of it. What is it?"

"You'll find out soon enough, if that's what it was."

"Oh god," Rhonda whispered.

"What's a xazulla?"

"Dolph," she said then, her face dark with worry, "if one of them has gotten out already—"

"I know, I know."

"I took a smattering of zoology at Yale," Jerico said, "and I never heard of a xazulla."

Rhonda looked at him, her grey eyes welling with sympathy. "Pray that you never do again, Jerico. It isn't nice."

"How nice," he said, "is not nice?"

Rhonda shuddered.

Me, he thought, and my big mouth.

"Think of a bear," Placker suggested at last, leaning over the wheel to catch what slim light there was left on the road. "Cross it with a bobcat only a mother could love. Then add a couple of rows of teeth up and down, a few claws large enough to rip open the trailer with one swipe, eyes that never close once night has fallen, and you'll have an idea of what a xazulla looks like when it's born."

Jerico rolled up the window and waited for the punchline, and when it didn't come, he looked out again, just in time to see a hundred-foot pine tree slam onto the road just inches shy of the rear bumper.

5　The xazulla howled.

Dolph swore loudly and tried to get the truck to move faster.

Another tree fell, this one barely missing the left rear tire.

Then the old man began thrashing about behind the curtain, and his daughter twisted around until she was on her knees, and reached through the break in the metallic cloth, whispering soothingly as she did.

Jerico was amazed at the way her jeans' seams held their position without apparent strain.

The elephant trumpeted plaintively.

Dolph cursed again, in several obscure languages.

"I think," said Jerico, "it's time you gave me a hint about that beast out there. Knowing what it looks like isn't exactly all that helpful."

Placker heeled the truck dangerously around a curve that had no business being on the face of the earth if the laws of physics were to remain at all stable. "You're right."

"I mean, it's rather like fighting blind, don't you think? I am the hero, after all. I ought to have some idea of what sort of danger I'm to face."

"You're right again."

He waited.

Dolph drove.

Rhonda continued to soothe her father.

He glanced to his right and saw something back in the trees, something large and dark and paying little or no heed to the boles and shrubs that got in its way.

It howled.

A nighthawk fell out of the sky.

A possum rolled over on the verge and turned white.

"Adolph," he said, trying not to sound as if he were begging.

Another tree crumpled, and bounced off the front fender.

Dolph sped up, perspiration running from his tangled hair in steady streams.

Rhonda returned to her sitting position and took a deep breath. "I think he'll be all right now. I told him the one about the king, the two ferrets, and the traveling preacher. How's the xaz doing?"

Jerico only pointed.

She grunted, nodded, and suggested that Dolph try not to use the brakes so much since the red lights were obviously attracting the beast, enabling it to continue to track them.

The road leveled and momentarily broke into the open again, flanked by browning fields in which Jerico could see rolled bales of drying hay waiting to be brought back to the barn. He leaned sideways in order to look in the outside mirror, but saw nothing in pursuit.

"I guess we lost it, huh?"

"He'll follow the trees," Rhonda said, pointing toward the woods that marked the farm's boundary and closed again when the road climbed the next hill.

The glow was still directly ahead.

The sun set.

Dolph hadn't yet turned on the lights.

The xazulla howled, this time sounding exactly like a banshee that had cornered its prey.

Shit, he thought.

"Stop the truck," he said calmly.

Slowly Rhonda turned her head and looked at him as one looks at a potential Plague victim.

"Stop," he said again, this time with more authority.

Dolph did, only a few yards shy of the woods.

Rhonda lay a nervous hand to the flat of her chest and said, "Jerico, maybe you don't understand—"

A look silenced her, another look apologized for the bluntness of the first look, and he opened the glove compartment, nodded when he found a flashlight, nodded again when he tested it and found it working. Then, after taking a surreptitious deep breath, he opened the door and stepped down onto the road, shivering slightly in the chilled night air. When Rhonda made to follow, he waved her back.

"But—"

"Hush," he said gently, yet sternly, and walked around to examine the front. As he suspected, there were two headlamps whose wattage far exceeded the legal limits, plus a pair of larger fog lamps mounted below. After a scan of the trees much too close for comfort, he continued on to the driver's side and signaled for Dolph to roll down his window.

"When I throw the flashlight," he said, "I want you to turn on the lights. All of them. On high beam. Do you understand?"

Dolph grinned and nodded.

Recalling the man's remarkable first-time skill in handling the vagaries of the twisting road, he added, "Do you know how to do it?"

Dolph studied the dashboard for a moment before nodding and grinning.

And though Jerico wished much against his nature that he was somewhere else, preferably Nevada, he turned back to face the forest, and starting walking.

If, as he had surmised, the xazulla was irritated by the presence of light, those which the truck carried would probably drive the beast away—or least keep it at a respectful distance until their destination was achieved. Of course it was possible he was wrong and Rhonda was right, in which case the man with the white cane and the German shepherd would seem like as unto nothing compared to what would happen to him now.

Still, he had his obligations.

There was also his duty and pledge.

And there was something back there in the trees, trying to move in on him with a stealth it did not possess.

The moonlight cast his shadow ahead of him.

I'm rich, he thought as he took a step past the first tree; I don't have to do this.

He hefted the flashlight in his left hand, wincing at its lack of weight and declared uselessness in a fight, and took another step.

With his third step he decided that if he got out of this alive, he was heading straight back to Nevada to become a cowboy, who was a hero after all but one who was allowed to get drunk and laid now and then.

The fourth step was never taken.

As he wondered if he could get English boots for his new career, something large and dark exploded out of the trees not ten feet in front of him.

He had no time to scream, or to think about

running, or to consider the best way to use his talents against the thing that panted in the road, the thing with the monstrous body, an incredibly potent odor, too many teeth to bear thinking about, and claws that ripped up the tarmac as it pawed the ground like a bull readying its charge. All he could do was switch on the flashlight and aim it at its eyes before throwing it at its nose. Then he threw himself to one side and covered his head.

The xazulla snorted.

Jerico held his breath.

The xazulla lumbered toward him, grunting as if chuckling to itself.

Jerico raised his eyes and saw its massive, ill-proportioned head, its lipless mouth open and dripping the most unpleasantly thick saliva into its matted fur and onto the road.

And Dolph finally turned on the lights.

There was a scream, a bellowing, a roaring, a scrambling, a shrieking, a volcanic explosion of rage and hatred and contempt and defiance, and a blast of foetid air that knocked Jerico into the underbrush, where he struggled to his feet, only to be knocked down again when the xazulla whirled around and its hithertofor unseen reptilian tail caught him across the chest.

He landed on his back, deafened, blinded by debris raining about him, and positive he would never take another breath of sweet air in his soon-to-be-ended life.

He saw stars, sparks, fireworks, and eventually Rhonda's concerned face as she bent over him, blinking away the dust that filled the night while she expertly tested his limbs for mobility. He gasped, and she sank back on her heels, her hands on her thighs, her face in deep shadow because of the headlamps' glare behind her.

"You made it," she said.

"I did?"

She smiled. "Trust me."

Sure, he thought, and decided to take nothing for granted. With a silent groan he sat up and ran through his own series of examinations before he agreed that he suffered nothing more than a severely bruised rib or two. And when he staggered with her help to his feet, he was surprised to see that he could walk without falling.

He did not ask about the xazulla.

He did not ask why in god's name Dolph took so long in answering his signal.

He did not ask why, when he climbed painfully into the cab, the old man was giggling hysterically behind the screen. He only waited until Rhonda took her place in the center before pointing to the hill and saying, "Drive."

A quarter of an hour later, as they crested the hill, he noted that the golden glow was only a few minutes away.

The elephant kicked the wall of the trailer.

The old man moaned a name Jerico did not catch, though he knew it wasn't Rhonda's.

The golden glow drew nearer.

He tapped Rhonda's shoulder. "I gather we're going there."

She nodded.

"I gather as well that that town, whatever name it may have, is in need of my services."

She nodded again.

"And I gather further that you will let me know beforehand what it is I have to do so that I'll know what to do when I have to do it."

She nodded again, and snored so robustly that Jerico forcibly reminded himself neither a gentleman nor a hero ever hits a lady whilst she sleeps.

"Robswerran," Dolph said tightly as he took another curve and only barely avoided a thirty-foot drop into a dry creek bed.

"I beg your pardon?" he said, leaning forward in order to see the man's expression, and wishing he hadn't when his ribs took a stab at his lungs.

"Robswerran," Dolph repeated with a nod toward the light.

"Ah."

"You ever hear of it?"

"No."

"I didn't think so. Few have."

"I assume you live there?"

Dolph laughed in a curiously humorless way, and Jerico wondered if the Plackers were in fact members of one of those obscure religious sects whose tenets required the periodic sacrifice of a total stranger. It would explain the red clothes, the stolen truck, the circus disguise, and perhaps even the elephant.

What it didn't explain was the frequent explosions of white within the golden glow, as if a great battle was taking place beyond the next hill.

It definitely didn't explain the xazulla.

"I'm retired, you know," he said at last.

Dolph only grunted.

The old man moaned again.

The elephant grumbled to itself.

"I think I told you that before. That I was retired."

The hill they climbed was steep, and the truck shuddered as it took the slope at a crawl.

The glow now reached into the cab, and Jerico stared at it, rubbed a fretful hand across his forehead and stared again.

It wasn't a glow at all.

It was a wall.

And Dolph wasted no time driving right through it.

6 In the well beneath the dashboard Jerico discovered several empty cans of soda, a layer of dust and pebbles, and a length of silver thread he would have examined more closely had not Dolph hit the brakes and slammed him against the seat.

Rhonda woke with a start, stared down at him, and did not seem at all convinced when he said sullenly, "I was looking for the flashlight."

He said no more.

As he reseated himself with a great fussing of lapels and shirt, his mouth slowly fell open, and the aching about his ribs and back were driven into inconsequence.

"My god," he said in a low and astonished voice.

"Robswerran," Dolph told him as he maneuvered the truck into a large parking lot on the lefthand side of the road. The dirt road. The one that led down onto a plain as verdant as any place Jerico had ever seen. To his right he could see the slope of the hill they had just crossed, spring-green and stretching south as far as he could see—a great frozen wave of land thick with trees and shadow. To his left, on the other side of the parking lot, the land was the same. And the view ahead was unbroken by anything even slightly resembling a tree, a city, a fairly large rock, or even another road save the one which aimed straight across it.

The parking lot itself was part of a wide ledge whose eastern lip marked the beginning of a vertiginous drop not even a scream would survive to the valley floor.

The sun was back up.

"Not bad, huh?" Dolph said, opening the door and climbing out with a groan.

Jerico stared.

Rhonda leaned across him, opened the passenger door, and nudged him gently until he grunted, climbed out, and looked more closely around him. He nodded. A parking lot. He knew it was so because of the vehicles of every type and aspect parked any which way in the dozens. Most of them were rusted to their wheels, many were little more than sieves, and a few could be called vehicles only by the grace of a bountiful imagination.

Behind him was the golden wall.

Behind him was also the sounds of Placker allowing the elephant to leave its trailer.

I will not, he thought, ask about the sun.

He looked at Rhonda, who was standing with hands on hips and looking out over the plain. She was breathing deeply, as though starved for the sweet scents a mild breeze brought to her from the east, her eyes glittering in threatened tears. When she realized she was being watched, she turned to him and managed a trembling smile.

"Home," she said simply.

"I see," he said. Then he hitched up his belt, rolled his shoulders to place his jacket more perfectly about him, dusted his shoes on the backs of his trousers, and headed for the road.

"Wait," Rhonda said.

He looked east, he looked south, then he made an abrupt turn west and began walking toward the wall an upward hundred yards distant. He could hear the woman calling to him, he could hear her brother calling to him, he could hear the old man shouting something at the elephant, but he paid no attention. His position was quite impossible. He knew that. In spite of the xazulla, the memory of whose breath made him shudder and miss a step, he knew that this was no ordinary New Jersey valley. He also knew that this decidedly extraordinary valley most likely did not exist on any map in the universe. And he knew as well that if he did not leave this place immediately, he was going to end up believing in it, which he already did in an hysterical sort of way so why was he trying to run away from it?

He paused.

He looked over his shoulder and saw the three Plackers standing in the middle of the road, watching him. That the distance made them appear as three red gnomes looking for a lawn to beautify did nothing for his equilibrium; that the elephant was shambling eastward down the slope toward the valley did nothing for his sense of well-being, especially when he realized the creature had exchanged its ears for forward-aiming horns, its short tail for a long furry one, and its gray color for a faint though not unpleasant puce.

After several long seconds of indecision, he continued on toward the golden wall, stopped in front of it and asked himself if he really wanted to do this.

His right hand reached for the glow, vanished within it, and pulled back slowly.

He could do it, then. He could walk through and not

look back; he could leave these strange people to whatever sorcery they had heaped upon him and hie himself immediately to Nevada and his eight-foot bathtub.

When he took a step forward, he heard Rhonda gasp.

When he took a second step, he heard the old man swear.

When he turned around to apologize for abandoning them, he saw a cloud of dust on the road, sweeping toward them across the plain at a fearsome rate. The elephant was gone. Dolph was waving his arms frantically, as if to say, *How the hell should I know? I'm not the hero.* And Jerico could definitely feel the thunder of hooves beneath his English soles.

Well now, he thought, it's time to fish or cut bait, isn't it, old man? It's time to put to the test all those days and nights of hunting the evildoer, tracking the immoral, sniffing out the vile stench of morality gone awry. A glance at his watch, however, told him it wasn't as late as he thought it was, but a glance at the wall behind and the plain ahead told him it was better to retire in a blaze of glory than strike out the last three times at bat.

His chest swelled, his arms grew stiff with tension, and he strode back down the road, marching to a tune heard only in his mind, glaring at the dust cloud in a solemn dare to do its worst because Jerico Dove was on the scene.

Rhonda grabbed his arm as he passed her. "Where are you going?"

"To meet the enemy," he declared with a nod to the valley floor. "I may have wavered, but I haven't fallen over."

Dolph applauded softly.

The old man, his red hair far darker here than on the outside, shook his head in admiration.

Rhonda stared at him. "You mean that?"

"Of course I mean it," he said.

"You're willing to take on a whole band of Rob-swerran Nessars just to protect us?"

"That's what you brought me here for, isn't it?"

"Well," she said, with a look to her brother Jerico was unable to fathom, "not exactly."

The dust cloud reached the bottom of the slope.

Jerico looked down the road, looked at the Plackers, and said, "And I suppose there isn't time to tell me what you mean by that?"

She shrugged an apology.

The dust cloud separated into a dozen riders, each on a deep black creature that at one time in its life might have been a horse if the mare had decided to have a go with a Gila monster whose beads fell off at the prospect of something he'd only dreamed of as he baked his life away in the hot desert sun. They were striped orange and black, their heads were blunt and held deadblack eyes, and their stumpy legs were tipped with claws that gleamed a gentle emerald in the sunlight.

The riders themselves were cloaked in faded brown, hunched over the stunted necks of their mounts, and carrying what Jerico thought were surely swords of an unconscionable length.

Six remained at the bottom; six began to climb.

"Which," he said as he backed away, "are the Nessars?"

"It doesn't matter," Rhonda answered as she backed away with him. "Kill one and you kill them both."

"Ah," he said. "A symbiotic relationship. Much like a pilot fish and a shark, wouldn't you say?"

They didn't, and with a gesture, he hurried them back to the truck, then took off his jacket, folded it, placed it on the seat, and asked Dolph where the weapons were, since it appeared as if they would soon be actively engaged.

Dolph hung his head. "We don't have any," he answered sorrowfully. "We aren't allowed to take them with us when we go to the Outside."

"I see." Jerico heard the Nessars' panting as they approached the rim of the ledge. "Then we'll just ram them with the truck. That ought to put some mettle into their spines."

Dolph lifted his head. "We can't. Once the vehicle is stopped, it can't be started again. It belongs to the Outside, you see."

Jerico nodded, saw the extremely ugly head of the first Nessar rise over the edge of the ledge, and raced for the nearest and most rusted vehicle. He grabbed a door, pulled, pulled again, and yanked it off its hinges just as the Nessar wheeled off the road and charged him. The Plackers scattered with cries of fear and disgust, but Jerico merely continued with his swing and caught the reptilian beast squarely on the snout with a sickening crunch of bone and rending of flesh. It screamed and stumbled, and he stepped nimbly aside to permit it to crash into the car; the rider was decapitated, and both halves of the thing expired with a loud and dramatic rattling noise.

There was, however, no time to gloat.

He reached into another car and pulled loose a steering wheel with much of its column still intact, saw Dolph and Rhonda following his example, and grinned as he ducked under the ponderous swing of a Nessar's jaws and plunged the jagged column into its throat. It shrieked, Jerico gagged at the riverlike flow of odorous black blood, and Dolph pulled him aside just before the Nessar collapsed atop him.

"Thanks," he gasped.

Dolph merely nodded and speared a rider with a wicked-looking windshield wiper.

A shriek.

The commotion of more hooves as the advance party's fellows began the climb to aid their colleagues.

The cry of victory as Rhonda lured a rapacious Nessar after her, then nimbly leapt aside and watched it plow into the side of the truck. The sturdy vehicle rocked but held; the Nessar rocked backward, staggered in ragged circles while its rider flailed at its head to give it direction, and finally found the lip of the ledge.

When it vanished over the side, it did so silently.

The remaining pair raced from the automobile graveyard at a speed that carried them over the road's abrupt turn downward without pausing for course correction. From the sounds of it, Jerico figured they had met companions head-on midway along, and from the further sounds of it, their rendition of the battle just joined and broken was sufficient to send them all back where they came from.

With a satisfied nod, he moved to stand thoughtfully at the edge of the cliff, not at all surprised to see a swirling dust cloud sweep across the plain, sometimes but not necessarily sticking to the road. "I gather," he said to Rhonda, who joined him a moment later, "we haven't seen the last of them."

She nodded fearfully.

He decided to check the bodies of the slain for a weapon to use, since, he knew instinctively, he wouldn't be able to count on a continuous supply of rusted cars along the way. But when he turned around, he was hard pressed not to lose his gorge, his bile, and every inch of his stomach lining—the Nessars were gone, their sprawled corpses having liquefied into simmering pools of rancid, multicolored tar. Steam rose to curl and vanish in the breeze. The side of the truck was already melting where Nessar blood had touched it at the moment of collision.

"God," he said, looked down and saw that the tips of his English shoes were gone, splashed by the black ichor and no longer in need of a good boot polish. His Italian socks were steaming as well, and he yelped, dropped to his rump, and divested himself of the shoes and socks as swiftly as his fumbling fingers would allow.

"It's hard," Dolph said in solemn sympathy. "Believe me, I know how you feel."

"But it's awful!" he cried. "I can't walk on bare feet. My god, do you have any idea what will happen after only a few minutes on that road?"

"Blisters, running sores, bleeding, scarring—"

"Right," he said with a brusque wave of his hand. He inhaled, exhaled, and beckoned to the old man, just climbing out of the back of the truck. "You know, we haven't formally met," he said when the elder Placker knelt in front of him.

"Don't matter," the old man said. "I know who you are." A wave at the battlefield. "You did good."

"Thank you."

"You'll do better."

"I hope so."

The old man's eyes, as red as his hair, narrowed. "Just keep your paws off my daughter, you hear?"

"Wouldn't think of it," he said.

"Sure."

Jerico closed his eyes, waited a moment, and said, "Now what?"

No one answered for a moment so long it forced him to open his eyes again. Rhonda was busily dragging what looked like knapsacks from the truck; Dolph was trying to think of what else could happen to Jerico's feet without adequate covering; and the old man was picking his teeth with a twig.

"Well?" he demanded.

The old man tossed the twig aside and grunted to his feet. "We go to Kyroppig," he said. And waited.

Jerico raised an eyebrow. "So?"

"So?" Placker looked at his children scathingly. "You mean they didn't tell you?"

"No."

"They didn't tell you what's going on in Rob-swerran? Why we need a hero? They didn't tell you about the others?"

Jerico held up a hand for silence, rose, winced at the dig of earth and pebble into his soles, and leaned forward. "What others?"

"The other heroes."

"What other heroes?"

"Honest to god," Placker said. "Ain't that just like kids? I mean, you work your butt off trying to raise them right, teach them manners and responsibility, and the first time something comes along like this you can't trust them to wipe their own noses. Damn, I hate that."

"Me, too," Jerico said. "What other heroes?"

"I don't know if I should tell you yet," Placker said.

"Tell me," Jerico said. "I can take it."

"Well . . ."

Jerico flexed, and his shirt began to split.

Placker watched the performance wide-eyed. "I'll be damned."

"Yes," he said. "It's a skill."

"So you want to know about the others?"

"Right."

"You're probably going to have to kill them."

7 That section of the road which followed the slope to the plain was not as steep as Jerico had imagined. He did have to manage it by half sliding, half running sideways, but all in all it wasn't as bad as he'd feared when first he approached it and wished he had a pair of reasonably durable wings. And once down and trailing morosely behind the Plackers as they headed without a look back toward the far horizon, he wondered yet again if he might not possibly be better off in Nevada. At least there he'd be wearing a decent ensemble, one more fitting to his station and his stature. As it was, the replacements produced by Rhonda for his ruined English shoes and Italian socks were a pair of high-topped raw leather boots whose faintly yellow tinge didn't do a thing for his tailored brown trousers, the handwoven blue cotton shirt, or the tweed jacket. True, he admitted, the boots were softly comfortable, and true, they did give him the support he required, and true, they promised long wear from the looks and heft of them . . . but really. Being urbane under trying circumstances was difficult enough without having to put up with such tribulation.

The Nessars he ignored in his contemplation of mental injuries—for such fearsome creatures, they were stunningly easy to defeat, and there was the temptation to wonder if the entire episode hadn't been arranged just to prove that he was, in fact, needed.

The real problem was that of the other heroes the elder Placker mentioned.

No reason had been given for the goal of their demise, and no mention was made of how they had arrived in this place of all places in the first place. Who were they? Where had they plied their trade when they were Outside? Why had they come here? How desperate were their circumstances that their death sentences were to be bandied about in such a casual manner?

Jerico was suspicious.

Though the land flowing so grandly about him was lush, green, and speckled with explosions of blossoms whose delicate colors rivaled the greatest palettes of the Renaissance, the very innocent appearance of Robswerran pricked him with doubt. Blue sky, gentle breeze, easy road to walk—what sort of perverted place was this? Aside from the Nessars, what possible complaints could one have, living here? Why, the very idea that there could be trouble—perhaps even evil—in such a paradise bordered on the sacrilegious.

No, he thought; given the reality of the situation, as unreal as it may be, there was something those people were not telling him, and they weren't telling it in such loud silences that he was tempted to scream at them to stop walking so goddamned cheerfully and let the other shoe fall.

He slipped his hands into his trouser pockets.

His eyes narrowed in thought.

His mind spun with a dozen new questions for which he had no answers, and with a dozen answers that fit no questions he could think of. It was frustrating. It was annoying. It was ridiculous that a man of his position should be treated as though he were little more than a servant whose role in the household was on a need-to-know basis.

His temper began to simmer.

His eyes narrowed even farther.

The fists in his pockets produced such unsightly bulges that he could barely swallow for the indignation they caused.

He stopped, spread his legs, and put his hands on his hips.

The Plackers, who were evidently keeping an ear or so tuned to his footsteps, halted and looked over their shoulders. When they realized they were no longer being followed, they exchanged glances of a nature Jerico was unable to determine because of the distance between them, and shrugged.

Dolph came back to him.

Jerico nodded curtly.

"You're not happy, pal," Placker said.

"Clever of you to notice," he responded.

"Guess you feel as if we're taking you for granted, huh?"

"That's one way to put it."

"Taking advantage?"

Jerico nodded.

"Not giving you your due?"

Jerico frowned.

"A bitch," the man in red said. "I kept telling them they ought to lay it out for you, let you make up your own mind, but Rhonda, she's something else, you know? Once she gets it in her head to do something, an earthquake won't change her mind."

Jerico gave him a grunt of understanding and did not object when the man took his elbow lightly and led him forward at, he noted, a much faster pace than they'd previously maintained. The others stayed a dozen yards ahead.

Not a word was said.

Time passed on the back of a breeze that now and then kicked into a brisk wind.

Every so often, flocks of elegantly plumed birds passed overhead, their heartwarming cries drifting to the plain as lightly as their feathers. And there were, in the grass, stirrings, as though tiny creatures of the furry variety were scurrying hither and yon on their mysterious and perfectly natural earthly business.

Jerico watched it all with a faint smile on his lips, wishing he had a camera and knowing that a mere lens would never be able to capture the purity, the innocence, the soul of this place without losing something vital in the translation.

Time continued to pass.

Jerico realized that soft boots do not a walking pair make, but he hoped the others would not notice his limp until he was able to manage it with style.

"Your father," he said at last because the silence was driving him crazy, "mentioned something back there about other heroes."

Dolph nearly stumbled in surprise. "He did?"

"He did. He also mentioned that I might well have to defeat them mortally in combat."

"He did?"

"He did. But he neglected to tell me why such drastic actions would have to be taken."

Placker sighed, sniffed, scratched through his curly hair, and finally shook his head slowly. "Well, the thing of it is, you see, Jerry—"

"Jerico."

"Right. Jerico."

"I have an intense dislike for foreshortened names."

Dolph stared at him a moment before nodding. "Right. Well, as I was saying, the thing is, Rhonda doesn't think you'll believe us when we tell you what's going on."

Jerico couldn't help a burst of giggling, couldn't help another one when he tried to grin an apology and failed, and couldn't help an outright guffaw as he swung his arm around to point at the rapidly receding golden wall atop the hill.

Dolph understood. "I know. But you see, you might rationalize that by saying it's only some kind of meteorological phenomenon. You know, like the Northern Lights or something."

Damn, Jerico thought; I never thought of that.

"I mean, you might think we were still in New Jersey."

Damn.

"Of course, we are, in a way." The man pulled his red shirt away from his chest thoughtfully and stared into the near distance. "It's really a matter of philosophy, if you catch my drift. The tabula rasa effect of parallel worlds congruent to the confluence of civilization and pure nature, the collision of which forces is actually little more than a teasing bump and grind of the scientific imagination."

Jerico directed his gaze to the man's profile, saw no mockery there, and decided that expressing his continued ignorance would only lessen him in the family's eyes.

"Therefore," Dolph continued, "it really isn't quite as fantastic as one might expect, if you catch my drift."

Jerico took a deep breath.

"What boggles the mind, though, is the absolute hell we've been through over the past few months. Jerico, you wouldn't believe it if I told you."

"A shame," Jerico said as he wiped a hand over his face in hopes of waking himself up in a gutter in New York.

"What it all comes down to, naturally, is religion and politics."

"Is that so?"

"Sure."

He released the breath, took another, and noted that the road ahead was widening ever so slightly. There also appeared to be a perceptible break in the monotonous sameness of the horizon beyond, not to mention the ones left and right. As if something was there he could not yet see, yet it was waiting for him, calling to him, luring him from this path into a danger he could not begin to imagine.

Suddenly Dolph stopped, took his arm and said earnestly, "Jerico, what would you say if I were to tell you that some of the most cherished, respected, and valuable works of religious art my people own have been stolen from the very altars which they have adorned since the beginning of time?"

"No!"

"Exactly. And what would you say if I told you, in fairly strict confidence, that those so-called heroes my old man mentioned were the same thieves who have robbed my people of their religious heritage?"

"No!"

"Exactly. And what would you say if I told you that unless those works of unsurpassed art are returned to their rightful places soon, this entire land, all of Robswerran, will vanish, and this valley will revert to what it was in the Outside world and an entire civilization will be lost?"

Jerico staggered back, one hand to his stomach, another to his brow. "No," he whispered.

Dolph, his face flushed with emotion, merely nodded.

Dawn reached Jerico Dove several hours late. "I see," he said. "What you're telling me is that I appear to be a hero who will not betray your confidence, that I seem to be the man who, in conjunction with whatever forces are rallied to his side, has been designated the one to recover said artifacts."

Dolph grinned. "Damn, and he's clever, too."

Jerico found it difficult to catch his breath. "And you place this responsibility on my shoulders?"

"Who else have we got?"

"Who else have you asked?"

"Don't ask."

"I must think," Jerico told him, turned thoughtfully and walked toward the others, who instantly began walking away. He didn't notice. He could only repeat Adolph's words over and over again, sensing the man's deep inner anguish and despair, and not having the slightest idea what the hell he was talking about. It definitely sounded important, though. And the fact that other heroes were involved in nefarious activity set his blood to running cold. If it was true, they were a disgrace to his chosen life's work. There had to be another name for them, for heroes they were not.

And as he walked, his head down in contemplation, he realized that the widening of the road continued until, some time later, he found himself in the center of a broad intersection. The road continued eastward, fell back westward, and branched northward and southward. There was no sign indicating what lay in each direction, nor were there signs that anyone had passed here in the last century or so.

He looked around carefully.

A check of the sky showed him nothing but the

phenomenal blue that was, at this time, shading darker as the sun lowered; a check of the plain showed him nothing but the high grass and pretty flowers; a squint at the horizon showed him the irregularities he'd noticed before, though they were still undefined; and a stare at the Plackers showed them watching him patiently, the old man in the middle and sagging slightly.

He spread his arms and said, "I don't understand."

"Jesus," Rhonda whispered. Then, louder: "Jesus!" She slapped her brother's arm hard.

She strode up to Jericho and poked his chest with a finger. He hoped she wasn't going to stand that close for very long; tailored trousers were no better than any other kind when it came to the sort of male embarrassment he knew he was going to be inflicted with if she didn't back off.

She poked him again. "Look, pal," she said, "weren't you listening back there? Didn't you hear what my brother the idiot had to say?"

"Yes, but—"

Poke. "And didn't you see those creeps who tried to slice us up back there?"

"Well, of course, but—"

Poke. "And I suppose you don't remember the xazulla."

"As I recall—"

"Then what the bloody hell's the problem?" she yelled.

"You!" he yelled back, startling her into stepping away so rapidly she fell squarely on her rump, with an expression he hadn't heard since the day he had saved the Cajun beauty queen from the drunken Marine. "You! Him! And him! That's the problem! You're all behaving as if I'll do this thing without a second thought. As if I've nothing better to do with my life than stumble into a hidden paradise, save the masses from destruction, and then disappear as if I never existed! *That*, young lady, is the problem!"

The old man helped his daughter to her feet, dusted her off, and glared. But Rhonda shook off his restraining hand and strode right back to poke Jerico's chest again.

"So what's the problem?" she yelled, red-faced. "Isn't that what heroes do, or what?"

"Of course it is!" he bellowed.

She raised a fist over her head. "Then . . . what . . . is . . . the . . . problem?"

Jerico reared to his full height, looked down at the beauty so infused with emotion, and screamed, "You didn't ask!"

"So I'm asking!"

"Hey, Sis," Dolph said calmly.

"What!" she screamed as she whirled on him.

Placker pointed toward the eastern horizon.

"Oh Christ, an armacon!" she yelled, and without another word raced off to the south.

Jerico watched her, dumfounded. Watched as Dolph instantly took off to the north, and the old man, staggering a little but still game, took off to the west. Within seconds he was alone in the middle of the intersection.

And seconds later he felt the ground tremble, saw the road begin to split not two hundred yards away, and saw the beginnings of what looked like a terribly unpleasant creature rise into the air.

8 | The creature was stuck.

Jerico had taken several hasty steps in several directions, trying to decide which way to run, when he realized that the thing burrowing up from beneath the soil wasn't burrowing anymore. In fact, it was grunting, rocking side to side, and emitting sounds that reminded him of a child about to burst into tears of frustration.

With a fair amount of trepidation he left the intersection and moved toward the beast, watching in fascination as it thumped the ground, dug at it, rolled its eyes, and sent a high-pitched wail to the sky. Then it stopped, snorted, and started again.

Caution prevented him from getting too close, and curiosity prevented him from bolting.

The thing ignored him.

Jerico sidled up another few feet.

Interesting, he thought.

As far as he could tell, and as much as he could tell anything in this ridiculous place, it was a raccoon. Yet, it wasn't a raccoon at all, for Rhonda had called it an armacon. However, it did have the distinctive black mask, the black nose, the ears, the sharp claws on the front paws; but there was something different about it, something he couldn't quite put his finger on and wouldn't want to even if he could since it was snapping at the air, at the ground, and in his direction with teeth that were considerably larger than an ordinary raccoon's. Probably, he thought, because the beast itself was considerably larger than an ordinary raccoon. Several times larger. Almost as large as a damned big horse, as a matter of fact.

"Hey," he whispered.

The armacon stared at him.

Jerico took a chance on his affinity with animals and smiled. "Hey, fella, you in trouble?"

A black paw rose, fell, and slammed the ground, causing several clumps of grass to leap away from their roots.

Jerico swallowed his nervousness and moved a bit nearer. He had a feeling about this poor creature, one not discouraged when the thing narrowed its soft pink eyes as he approached. Naturally, it would be distrustful. Naturally, if humans in this land hunted it, it would believe that he too was a hunter. And naturally, it would do anything it could to protect itself.

"Hey, pal," he said gently. "Hey, you need a hand?"

The eyes narrowed even farther in suspicion, but its paws rested quietly on the ground. The only movement was an occasional ripple across its heavily muscled back, covered with deep brown scales shaped like blunted triangles.

Jerico circled it warily, hand rubbing his chin. "Looks to me like you can't get out, huh?"

The armacon nodded.

Jerico's eyes widened. "You . . . you understand me?"

It waggled a paw side to side.

He stopped just short of its reach and shook his head. "Will wonders never cease?"

It shook its head.

"Amazing."

It nodded.

Jerico understood instantly that a decision had to be made. This obviously intelligent creature needed his help; this obviously very large creature might very well accept his help and then proceed to rip him to shreds; this cunning beast might only be pretending to need his help, thus luring him into the death that dripped from its long black claws; and god forbid there should be another armacon still underneath it, waiting for its own chance to pounce, rend, and destroy.

"Well," he said.

The creature waited patiently.

"You see my problem," he added.

The armacon bared its teeth in a grotesque smile.

He put his hands on his hips and stepped back, his own eyes half-closed in thought, his right foot tapping the ground, his jaw working as if he were chewing.

The armacon braced its paws and tried to heave itself upward, failed, whimpered angrily, and sagged. Then it wriggled frantically for several seconds before lowering its head to the ground and pulling at its pointed ears. Apparently, it couldn't go back either. It was helpless, and easy prey for any pack of predators which might happen along during the approaching night and knew the armacon's weak spots.

Damn, Jerico thought, and walked decisively up to the beast, looked it straight in one large eye, and said, "Kill me and you'll never get out, right? But if I do get you out, you owe me one, right? And I think you can discharge that obligation by not killing me either now or when I get you out, right? In for a penny, and all that jazz."

The armacon's eyes crossed slightly, but it nodded.

Jerico smiled. He took off his jacket, folded it neatly on the ground, and flexed. Then, after a minute's examination, he reached around its left shoulder and took hold. The armacon seemed to understand, and when Jerico began to lift, it began to push. The scales were slippery, but he maintained his grip, feeling his muscles bulge, feeling the sweat break along his brow, feeling his tendons scream for release when it seemed as if nothing short of an elephant was going to budge the helpless thing from its self-made trap.

There were grunts, whimpers, more grunts, deep breaths, spittings, groans, moans, curses of the sort that neither man nor beast consciously knew until he was trapped in a hole in the ground.

And when it came loose, with a shriek of triumph, Jerico was thrown onto his back some yards away.

He shook his head to clear it, shook it again when the thing lumbered over to him on its six muscular legs and straddled him. Its eyes were wide with gratitude, its puffed brown tail twitched like a nervous whip, and Jerico understood immediately that it was torn between its basic nature and the deal it had made.

He said nothing, but he noted that the scales around its throat were scratched and worn, as though enemies had recently attempted to break through the armor there and pierce the flesh beneath. Slowly he lifted a hand and touched the spot.

The armacon stiffened.

Jerico lowered his hand.

The armacon relaxed, bobbed its head, and backed away, lowering its shoulders in submission and letting its tail droop to the ground.

Jerico scrambled to his feet and dusted himself off, took a slow and deep breath to remind himself he could still do it, and retrieved his jacket before walking over to the hole. When he looked down, he saw what appeared to be a freshly made tunnel through which the beast had traveled, probably using its sensitive nose along the way to check for prey and enemy above. Then, lightning fast, it would dig to the surface, where, all things being equal, it would have dinner.

He looked back at the animal and wondered what had gone wrong.

The armacon shrugged and began preening its scales with its middle legs, the sound much like a dull fingernail on a blackboard. It sighed and rolled its eyes.

A geological freak of some sort, he concluded, and looked to the horizon, wondering which way he should go, since the Plackers had each chosen their own flight routes without so much as giving him a hint as to what he should do next.

So he closed his eyes, stuck out an arm, spun around, and when he finally came to a halt, he found himself facing south. West, of course, would return him to the golden wall and, beyond it, home, so two out of three might be more conclusive. On the other hand, there was clearly some trouble here in paradise and he would be hard put to sleep well at night if he turned his back on it.

South. What the hell, as good as any, he decided, and returned to the intersection with every intention of moving in that direction as far as he could before the sun set, and perhaps he might even encounter the lovely Rhonda along the way.

The problem, as he saw it, was the cloud of dust sweeping toward him across the plain.

When he turned to point out the danger to the armacon, he saw its tail whipping side to side as it vanished into its hole.

When he looked back to the cloud of dust, he saw that it had not moved any closer.

He started south.

The cloud, several hundred yards to his left, stopped its advance and moved with him. When he halted, it halted; when he started again, it kept pace without drawing nearer. When he broke into a testing trot, it maintained the distance and the speed, and did not dissipate; nor did it enlarge itself. Since its thickness prevented him from seeing what caused it, and since experience told him he knew damned well what was inside it, he shifted his trot to a run, one cleverly designed to take him the maximum distance without getting himself unduly tired.

A wind rose at his back.

The grass on either side husked and whispered him along.

Directly ahead, the irregularity he'd noted along the horizon began to resolve itself into the unmistakable skyline of a city. With a smile he lengthened his stride, knowing that there, at least, he would be able to find others of his kind, and perhaps even one of the Plackers. And having once done that, he might even learn more about those other heroes, those cads in heroic clothing who had raped Robswerran of its religious heritage.

His palms itched.

His lungs began to labor.

The boots that weren't made for walking weren't made for running either, and he soon found himself slowing to a limping center, a trot, and finally to a panting walk.

The dust cloud hadn't left him.

His shadow grew longer, and when he checked the

sky he saw an oval moon rising overhead, clustered about with stars that were bright even before the sunlight had withdrawn.

He stopped for a moment's rest.

The dust cloud stopped with him.

He buttoned his jacket against the twilight chill, smoothed the lapels, and took a step toward it.

The dust cloud backed away.

He took another step, this one off the road, and the dust cloud came toward him.

Ah, he thought; as long as I am on the road, I am apparently in safe territory. But once I leave the sanctuary I will probably be slaughtered.

The idea was sobering were he inclined to giggle, and he started out again, noting as he went that the grass was much shorter now, and there seemed to be low walls of greenery that marked off what might very well be pastures or fields. A check of the dust cloud showed him that it had stopped though he continued moving, and he nodded—the Nessars, if that's what they were, were evidently fearful of entering land which clearly belonged to someone else.

He waved.

The dust cloud surged toward him, fell back, and turned into a dervish that made him laugh aloud.

The disappointment he had felt when the armacon deserted him was all but gone now, and he felt as though he could take on an entire army of those hideous Nessar reptiles with their equally hideous riders. He hummed a little. He whistled a little. He moved a little faster when he saw buildings begin to form ahead of him, and houses begin to crop up well back from the road.

By the time the sun had set completely and there was only a wash of pale light left in the sky, he was close enough to realize that he was heading for no ordinary village. A large town it was, whose structures were made entirely of wood gaily painted and several stories high. Though there were no immediate signs of people, windows were lighted, and he could see over each lintel what appeared to be crossed spears engraved into the wood, or the brick, or the cleverly masked adobe.

There was a low distant noise that hinted at some sort of traffic moving about.

Large yellow globes atop tall slender poles burst into glowing as he walked past them, lighting his way and showing him that the houses were now set directly against the verge.

When he drew beyond them, they shut off.

He brushed his hair hastily, checked his jacket, stamped the dust off his boots, and wondered if he ought to prepare some sort of explanation for his presence. After all, he doubted that strangers were commonplace in this community, and certainly one who looked like him couldn't possibly come along every day. He supposed he should ask about the Plackers, though their retreat in the face of the armacon's attack made him wonder; he supposed he ought to locate the leader or leaders of this town and present himself to them as the hero they've been waiting for—unless, he thought, this was the place where the other heroes were, in which case such an introduction was only asking for trouble.

He grinned.

This was a challenge.

And never let it be said that Jerico Dove avoided a challenge.

With lighter step and even lighter head, since he was growing rather hungry, he continued along what he imagined was the main street until he reached what he imagined was the business district. He imagined it because of all the shops lining the road, but couldn't imagine why there weren't any people. He could certainly hear them. And the shops certainly seemed to be open for business. And when he glanced in a window here and there he could see shadows of people wandering among counters and along aisles and sitting at tables in what he imagined were restaurants and bistros.

The trouble was, they were only shadows.

There wasn't anyone inside to cast them.

Impossible, he thought; light plus solid substance equals shadow. Any fool knows that.

He glanced into a cafe—a shadow-waitress was serving a shadow-customer and its companion; he hovered around the entrance to a gaming establishment and saw a shadow-croupier spinning a roulette wheel for a dozen shadow-gamblers; he backed away from a tavern when it proved inhabited by a drunken clutch of shadows singing silently at the tops of their voices.

No one to cast them.

He wondered if perhaps he was looking at things all wrong, but when he cocked his head to one side, all he saw were sideways shadows.

No one.

And he whirled about with hands up and at the ready when a shadow stepped out from under a black awning and said, "Hey, mister, you wanna meet my sister?"

With superhuman self-control Jerico stopped just short of bashing in the shadow's head with the side of his hand. His muscles strained with the effort, the veins in his forehead throbbed, and when the shadow stepped out of the shadows and into the light, the anxiety he'd felt was immediately replaced by a great sense of shame and an even greater sense of outrage.

The speaker wasn't a shadow at all, but only a young lad, no more than twenty or twenty-three, unflatteringly dressed in basic black from ruffled shirt to billowing trousers to high-topped boots with tassels at the toes. Around his neck was a carelessly tied black scarf, and around his waist was a black leather belt from which hung two sheaths lightly strapped to his thighs. He was bald.

Jerico blew softly. "What did you say?"

"My sister," the lad repeated. "You wanna meet her or not?"

There was no one else on the street, unless he

counted the party of shadows lurching out of the tavern and into the gutter.

"Well?" the lad said impatiently. "C'mon, I ain't got all night, y'know."

This, after everything else, was too much. Indignation clouded his judgment. A strange man in a strange town in a world that *strange* didn't even begin to describe, and the first person he meets turns out to be a pimp.

Son, he thought, of a bitch.

So he reached out, took hold of the lad's shirt, pulled the lad toward him, and lifted him effortlessly off his feet.

The young man blinked rapidly in astonishment, kicked feebly, and produced a sheen of perspiration across his wrinkleless, hairless pate that glowed warmly in the streetlight.

"You," said Jerico in a dangerously low voice, "are a disgrace."

The lad tried to respond but was only able to choke and drool a little.

"You," said Jerico, "are an insult to one's confidence and manhood."

The lad, whose hands were gripping Jerico's wrists in a feeble attempt to take some of the weight from his shirt, swallowed and tried to look over his shoulder.

Jerico shook him once, shook him again, and dropped him as if ridding himself of a particularly nasty bag of garbage. The lad fell to his knees, gasping and coughing, but when he attempted an escape, a hand gripped his collar, pulled him to his feet, and held him fast.

"Not so fast, little person."

"Look, pal," the lad began, and stopped himself when he saw the rage in Jerico's eyes. Instead, he did his best to shrink to the size of a baby, a counterploy Jerico knew only too well.

"Do you have any idea where you are?" he demanded.

The lad wiped a hand over his head and nodded. "Fadfy," he said in a frightened voice.

"And do you know who you are?"

The lad sniffed and closed his eyes. "Gramlet, sir. Gramlet Eglantine."

With a sharp knowing nod, Jerico smiled inwardly, pleased that his ruse was thus far working. Now he knew where he was and who his would-be panderer was. All he needed to know next was where all the people were.

"Where is everybody?" he said.

Gramlet stared at him. "What?"

Jerico's free hand waved toward the gambling hall, the cafe, and the tavern. "Where is everybody?"

Suddenly the lad began to laugh. Quietly, to be sure, but of sufficient duration to make Jerico wonder if there wasn't indeed something wrong with his vision, that the people here were visible as shadows only to him. He released Eglantine reluctantly and waited until the young man's eyes were wiped clear of tears and the laughter faded to an occasional hiccough.

"You're a stranger!" Gramlet said in delight.

Jerico saw no reason not to nod.

Gramlet's heavy eyebrows rose and fell in an audacious wink. "Well, you wanna see my sister?"

When Jerico reached for him again, however, he ducked nimbly out of the way, evaded yet another grab, and danced derisively to the corner, where he waited boldly, both hands on his hips.

Jerico debated following. It could be dangerous. The young man might be just an innocent shill for his sibling's crude perversities, but he might also be the point man for a band of robbers who were skulking in an alley, waiting for their next victim.

Still, this disgusting excuse for a man was thus far

the only nonshadow being he had seen since entering town, and it might be wise to go along with him, just to see what more he might be able to learn before taking the kid's head off.

"Well?" Eglantine called.

Jerico looked around him, shrugged, and followed the lad around the corner, into a street somewhat darker than the main thoroughfare. The buildings here seemed to be houses, with only an infrequent shop thrown in for those unable or unwilling to make it to the other businesses. Decorative plaques adorned each high doorway—again with the curious crossed spears—porches were narrow and barely reached to either side of the doors, and the front yards were shallow though bristling with forests of tall flowering plants that filled the air with sweet and tangy aromas.

There were no pedestrians.

There was no vehicular traffic on the street.

Eglantine skipped to the next corner, crossed over, and beckoned to him.

Jerico followed.

The moon was high now and cast such a strong light that the yellow globes were hard put to make themselves useful.

Eglantine stopped four doors from the center of the block, mimed opening a gate in a fenceless yard, and took the four steps he approached at a single leap. There, at the door, he waited while Jerico hesitated on the sidewalk. Though he hadn't yet been waylaid by brigands or thieves, it could still be a trap. The red light over the lintel was bold enough, the tasseled shades in the windows suggestive enough—yet . . .

Eglantine slapped his thigh. "Look, are you coming or not, stranger?"

He sighed. What the hell, it was better than pulling a raccoon out of the ground.

* * *

The foyer was tastefully done in muted scarlet, the narrow staircase ahead carpeted in spring yellow, and the hallway leading off to the staircase's right was a robin's egg blue from its braided throw rugs to the velvet flocked wallpaper. Slender candles burned low in bronze wall sconces. On a table beneath an oval mirror was a silver basket piled high with fresh fruit.

Gramlet offered to take Jerico's jacket and was not put off when he was refused with disdain. He merely bowed without mockery and pushed aside a crystal-beaded curtain on the left.

"After you, stranger," the young man said.

Jerico would not give him the satisfaction of either glaring or smiling; instead, he lifted his chin, settled his chest, sucked in his stomach, and marched into the next room, one furnished so completely in crimson-and-gold Victorian uncomfortable that there was little room to move. Yet move he did, for standing by the fieldstone fireplace on the far wall was a woman whose beauty and sensuality stopped the breath in his lungs and his progress in midstride.

"Good evening, stranger," she said from behind a coyly held ivory fan. "New in town?"

He nodded.

With a deft flip of her wrist she closed the fan to permit him an unobstructed view of the soft planes of her face, the high mark of her brow, the fluttering of her long eyelashes, the depths of her wide ebony eyes, the dimple in her chin, and the expanse of a substantial bosom pushed upward and together by a shocking pink sequined gown whose grip on her lithe frame was nothing more than breathtaking.

She arched a perfectly plucked eyebrow, as fair as the hair curled about her scalp was dark. "Would you care for some refreshment, stranger?"

He nodded.

She flicked the fan against a tiny gold gong on the mantel and Gramlet was instantly at his side.

"The stranger wants a drink, dear brother. Please serve him the best we have to offer."

Gramlet, far from his earlier smug and smarmy self, bowed handsomely from the waist and vanished through the beaded curtain, backward.

Jerico still held his silence, choosing to remain enigmatic while he sidestepped an aquarium and empty bird cage to a couch he asked permission to use with a questioning glance. The woman nodded. He sat back in one corner, one arm draped across the scalloped back, and crossed his legs at the knee.

He cleared his throat.

The woman snapped open her fan.

He surveyed the room with a practiced gaze and decided that this house need never lock its doors. Then he raised his own eyebrow and said, "I gather you are young Gramlet's sister?"

"I am," she said. "I am Dawn Eglantine. And you are . . . ?"

Deciding to withhold that information for the time being, he merely said that she was correct in her assessment of his status in town. He said nothing about the Plackers. He said nothing about his profession. He did not rise to the bait when she flicked the fan closed and, with one hand on the mantel, leaned toward him and asked if he would care for something to nibble on while they waited.

Rather, he said, "Wait for what, Miss Eglantine?"

Before she could answer, however, Gramlet returned with two tulip glasses on a polished pewter tray. He offered one to Dawn, the second to Jerico, and stepped backward again through the curtain without once changing his expression.

Dawn lifted her glass in a silent toast.

Jerico responded with one of his own, and stared into his glass when he realized it was empty.

"The best I have to offer," she said with a slight smile, "is nothing at all, stranger. For nothing at all leaves all to the imagination, and surely there is nothing better than one's imagination, am I not correct?"

The fan opened; all but the seduction in her eyes disappeared behind it.

This isn't getting me very far, he thought as he placed the glass on a marble-topped cocktail table.

Gramlet returned, picked up the glass, wiped it out with a handkerchief he pulled from his sleeve, and left again, again with no expression on his face.

Dawn set hers on the mantel. "And now," she said.

"Yes," he said.

"To business."

He shifted a bit deeper into the corner. Somehow, this wasn't exactly what he had expected when he decided he would finish out his career rescuing a civilization from eradication. Not, he told himself quickly, that he was opposed to a little messing around on the job; it came with the territory whenever he got lucky. But as his gaze wandered over the chintz, the tassels, the silk, the velvet, the satin, the crystal, the candles, and the stuffed dog on the hearth, he wasn't sure all this was what he would call luck.

Dawn turned to show him her profile, placing the open fan delicately across her bosom with a shy though brazen flutter. "I gather," she said in a voice sultry and slow, "that you understand why you are here?"

"I am not naive, Miss Eglantine, but—"

"Fine. Shall I call the girls down one by one, or do you prefer the ensemble presentation?"

A swift wave of warmth began to encircle his neck. "Really, Miss Eglantine, I'm not—"

She smiled at him. "Ah me, you're a stranger. I had forgotten. A little shy perhaps?"

"Broke," he admitted.

"I see," she said.

"Your brother was insistent."

"I see," she said.

"And I see by the elegance of your home," he said with a wave to the room, "that you are not entirely dependent upon the kindness of strangers."

She shrugged. "I do all right."

"I also notice that you are not a shadow."

Her eyes widened.

He felt confused. "Does that surprise you?"

The fan danced in agitation over her face, her bosom, the mantel, the stuffed dog, and she walked with dainty, tiny steps from one end of the hearth to the other. When her pacing was done, she was red of face and puffing.

"Are you all right?" he asked, getting to his feet.

"Fine," she answered, waving him back down. "It's the dress, that's all." And she ran a hand along her side to her thigh to prove that the material and the sequins were so closely bound and so tightly knit that walking proved to be a major skill. "But that's of no importance. It keeps my weight down."

Jerico rose. "Would you like to sit?"

She waved him down with the fan. "No. What I would like is to know what you saw out there." And she pointed at the bay window.

"Shadows," he told her.

"Nothing more?"

"Your brother."

"And . . . and I am not a shadow to you?"

"No, should you be?"

She paced again, more quickly, and the rotation of waist, rump, and ankles was almost too much for the weave she wore.

"Please," he said. "I don't understand."

She stopped, tucked her fan into the snug valley of her breasts, and clasped her hands in front of her. "Do you know where you are?"

He frowned. "Your brother said this was called Fadfy."

"Yes. And do you know what that means?"

His frown deepened. "That I'm in a town called Fadfy."

She nodded so vigorously that a curl dropped over her left eye. She blew it away. It returned. She licked a palm and slapped the curl back into place.

"And do you know what that means?" she asked.

"Sure," he said. "It means I'm not anyplace else."

"Stranger," she said in an odd voice, "are you always so literal?"

"I do not look for meaning where none exists," he replied stiffly. "That is the province of philosophers and politicians."

Dawn stretched her arms outward, looked to the mirrored ceiling, and said, "Fadfy means The City Where The Dead Walk At Night And Strangers Are In Danger."

"Ah," he said.

Dawn lowered her arms. "Ah?"

"Ah."

She shook her head, stepped carefully down off the hearth, and kicked aside enough bric-a-brac and foot-stools to enable her to stand in front of him. "You don't get it, do you?"

"I told you, I'm broke."

"Me," she said angrily, thumping a fist against her chest. "I live in Fadfy."

"Yes . . ."

"I am not a stranger."

"Yes . . ."

She leaned over until her nose was less than a hand's breadth from his. "*You* are the stranger."

He almost nodded, caught himself before colliding with her bosom, and suddenly snapped his fingers. "God!"

"Finally."

"But you can't be dead!" he protested.

And whispered it again when she winked, whistled, and disappeared.

10 Jerico could barely credit what his senses insisted was true—that the woman named Dawn had actually vanished before his very eyes. But when at last the realization struck him, he leapt to his feet, checked behind all the furniture he could, then ran into the hallway, calling for Gramlet.

There was no response.

He started for the door, changed his mind, and raced toward the back of the house. He knew it had to be a trick, something to do with the mirrors, or the empty glass of wine or the way she kept looking at him over the top of her fan. Perhaps the fan itself was some sort of hypnotic device, and his fascination with it and the way she had used it had temporarily put him into a trance during which she had simply walked out of the room.

A single door in the lefthand wall was unlocked. He opened it, plunged in, and found himself in a kitchen as cluttered as the front room had been. But there was no sign of Dawn or her brother. Nor was there any other exit save the one he'd just used as an entrance.

He ran back to the foyer, looked up the stairs, and suggested strongly to himself that if it wasn't a trick and she was really dead, he didn't want to know what was up there.

Ten steps up, he came to a landing and told himself in the sternest possible terms that he should find himself a nice park bench somewhere and get a little sleep, that the morning would be plenty of time to reinvestigate if he had to, or to continue searching for the Plackers and the means of carrying out his assignment.

Ten steps later he was at the top, looking down a short corridor at the end of which was a closed door. Flanking the door were two tall candlesticks in which had been placed two short candles. Lighted. Casting shadows on the paneled walls. Doubling their images in the dozen triangular mirrors inlaid in the ceiling.

"Gramlet!" he called.

Again there was no answer.

He adjusted his jacket, polished his boots on the backs of his trouser legs, and strode to the door. A glance behind him produced no miracles. He pushed back his hair. A polite knock produced no bid to enter. A test of the crystal knob told him the thing was unlocked.

Jerico, he told himself, you are an idiot if you do this.

He agreed, turned around and started back for the stairs, paused midway along the corridor and looked over his shoulder.

Suppose, he thought, the answer to the puzzle is in there; and wondered which puzzle he was thinking about—the one about the heroes, the artifacts, his task, or the dead woman. Not that it mattered.

Answering any one of them would put him a long way ahead of where he was now, which was in a hall in a brothel that, if things were to be taken at face value, catered primarily to ghosts.

He hoped he wouldn't meet one who got excited about chains.

"The hell with it," he said; returned to the door and opened it. Stepped inside. Closed the door softly behind him. Put his hands over his eyes and counted to ten, then put down his hands and opened his eyes.

It was a bedroom.

The windows on the left were covered with heavy, red velvet draperies. The carpet was of Oriental design—red dragons, black flowers, and white trim. On the gold-and-black walls were a half dozen mirrors framed in silver. In an elephant's foot umbrella stand stood a score of peacock feathers. A crystal chandelier hung from the ceiling on a chain of glimmering gold.

And in the center of the room, on a platform, was a bed.

And lying on the red sheets and red pillows was Dawn Eglantine, her hands folded on her stomach, her eyes closed, her dark hair fanned out behind her head.

"Miss Eglantine?" he said as he tiptoed across the carpet.

She did not stir.

"Dawn?" he said as he stepped onto the platform and leaned over her.

Her eyelids did not flutter.

His cheeks puffed, his instincts told him to get the hell out, and his right hand reached for her wrist—there was no pulse. He leaned over and placed his ear against her chest, wincing at the cold firm flesh and telling himself he was sick to be even thinking about thinking about what he was thinking—there was no heartbeat. Then, in a moment's inspiration, he snatched one of the smaller mirrors from the wall and held it in front of her mouth—it did not fog over.

"Well," he said, "I guess you're dead."

"No shit," she said, and sat up.

When Jerico next opened his eyes, he was on the bed and Dawn was sitting anxiously on the edge of the mattress. As soon as he realized where he was, and what she was, he tried to back away, but she took hold of his hand and forced him to remain still.

"You've had a shock," she said.

"Tell me about it," he muttered.

"You fainted."

"No. I merely suffered a temporary displacement of blood from my brain. Elevating my feet as you did brought me back to my present condition." He frowned at her expression. "It's a family thing. Nothing I can do about it."

But when she smiled, he couldn't help smiling back. Dead or not, she was one hell of a handsome woman. She also seemed to care, because she withdrew her hand as soon as she understood the discomfort her touch caused him. The sorrow in her eyes, however, made him feel like a shit.

"I think," he said, fluffing the pillows behind him and sitting up, "we ought to exchange explanations."

"I agree. But first, would you mind telling me your name? I can't keep calling you stranger, now can I?"

He told her.

She grinned. "Nice. Very nice. And I bet you hate it when people call you Jerry."

"Why . . . yes! How did you know?"

She winked broadly at him. "Please. A little mystery, all right? For now, let's just say that I'm a good guesser and leave it at that."

Jerico had no choice but to agree, though he hoped that her secret didn't involve reading his mind. If it did, he was going to be slapped silly before the next five minutes had passed.

"Explanations," he reminded her. "Ladies first."

Dawn nodded, rose, and started off the platform. The snug condition of her dress caused her to stumble, however, and she swore loudly while reaching down to grip the hem and tear the skirt up along the seam until virtually her entire leg was exposed.

She's dead, Jerico reminded himself.

"Do you know," she said as she massaged her calf, her knee, and her thigh, "that the man who created dresses like this is now down in Hell wearing a jockstrap three sizes to small?"

"Fascinating," he muttered as he crossed his legs.

"They should've used bricks on him."

His smile was strained.

Her smile was radiant, one might even say alive, and she walked around the room gracefully, her long legs taking strides that winked various parts of gorgeous dead flesh at him to such a feverish degree that he was forced to turn away and remind her somewhat reluctantly that she was going to explain whatever it was she had agreed to explain.

"Sorry," she said, returning to the bed and sitting beside him. "I got carried away."

"No problem."

She patted his hand. "You're cute."

"You're dead, no offense."

She laughed. "None taken." She patted his hand again. "And so, for that matter, is the entire town."

"Fadfy?"

"Exactly."

"But . . . but I saw . . ."

"Shades," she said, leaning back against the ornate headboard and crossing her legs. "God, if only I were alive again, this bed would feel great, you know what I mean?" She sighed deeply and tugged at her bodice. "Shades are shadows of the not-really-dead. Which is not to say that we're not dead, because we are, but we aren't, not really, which is why I can feel this damned dress but not this damned bed. What we are is dead enough to produce shades, but not dead enough to be ghosts. Because if we were ghosts then we'd really be dead and there'd be no chance of our ever being alive again."

Jerico nodded thoughtfully at each point made, nodded when she looked at him to see if he understood, and nodded when she asked him if he always looked that way or if he only seemed stupid.

"That is," he added hastily, "I understand some of it, but I admit to being stupid about part of it."

"Which part?"

"The part about being dead."

She turned slightly on her hip and took hold of his hand. "A long time ago," she said, "a man came to town. He didn't look anything like you, but he was still big and strong and promised everyone he'd make life easier if only we'd listen to him. He talked a good line, believe me, and there were only a few who didn't buy it. Well, obviously he was lying. And when he was done, some of us were really dead and the rest of us were only dead enough to hang around and wish we were either dead or alive and not this horrid in-between."

"A magician?" he asked, well aware that her forefinger was doing some fancy tracing around the mounds of his knuckles.

"No," she said. "A hero."

He sat up so abruptly she dropped his hand and clasped a palm to the flat of her chest. "What's the matter?"

"A hero," he said with undisguised disgust.

"That's right. Do you know him?"

He shook his head. "No. But I know of him. Or rather, I've heard of someone . . . a few, actually, who were like him. As I understand it, he, or they, acting in concert or alone, made off with some religious artifacts. But I . . ." He rubbed his forehead with his fingertips until the skin began to burn, then slid off the bed and paced the length and width of the room. "I had no idea this was more than a simple theft."

Dawn's expression was one of wonderment. "I love the way you talk," she said breathily.

"Thank you."

"But how did you know about the hero?"

"Some people told me."

"Anyone I know?"

"I don't know."

Using an empty smile to cover her perplexity, she pushed herself to her hands and knees, following him as he continued his pacing. "Jerico, does your being here have something to do with the man who did this to us?"

He stopped at the foot of the bed and looked at her. "Until this minute, I wasn't sure of anything. But now I am. Sure, that is."

She crawled toward him. "Sure of what?"

"That I was brought here to help you. At least in part."

When she reached the end of the mattress, she sat back and loosened her bodice again. "Why do I have the feeling you're stumbling around in the dark?"

"Because I am," he admitted ruefully. "I was told only about the heroes and the artifact things, but there was no chance to learn more because those who brought me to Robswerran are gone now."

"Oh, dear," she said, and took his hand in sympathy.

He sat on the footboard. "They deserted me."

"Oh, my dear," she said, and laid her cheek on his arm.

He looked down at the top of her head. "Are you sure you're dead? In the partial sense, I mean?"

She looked up at him and smiled. "Dead I am, but not as dead as I thought I was, since you don't see me as either shade or shadow."

He gazed into those delicious black eyes and blinked. "I must know more," he told her. "If I am to help, I must know more."

Her fingers skated over the course of his lapels. "It's not a pleasant story, Jerico."

"I'm used to that."

"You probably won't want to do anything about it once you know all about it."

Her hand found the buttons of his shirt, lingered there and tumbled into his lap. Tenderly he removed the hand to her own lap, where it fluttered and slipped to the mattress.

"Tell me," he insisted.

She looked at him, at his lap, at her lap, and sighed as she crawled off the mattress and hurried to a wardrobe beside the window. From the top shelf she lifted a large red book whose pages were edged in gold. She handed it to him. He was amazed at the weight, and the thickness, and the soft give of the leather covers. There was no title that he could see.

"What is this?" he asked as he opened it to the first page. "*The Book of Ralph*? Who's Ralph?"

She stood in front of him, eyes lowered, hands folded prayerfully. "It's a long story."

"I have the time."

"All right," she said decisively. "All right. Ralph Yama was the Sorcerer of Robswerran. He had seven spears which bound all his magic together. They were placed in several cities around the country. He died. His brother and two cousins brought in some men from the Outside. They broke into the impregnable places where the spears were kept and stole them. The magic faded. We are as you see us now. Here. In other places other terrible things happened."

He looked at the number of the last page of the book, looked at her and said, "That's it?"

"Well, someone wrote a song about it, but I don't know if you want to hear it."

He shook his head.

She agreed with a smile. "Anyway, I guess you're supposed to get the spears back to their rightful places and save Robswerran from complete desolation."

Jerico rose, placed the book on the bed, and turned to face the not-quite-dead woman. "It won't be easy," he said.

"I know that. Others have tried."

"Oh, really? A lot?"

"We lost count last year." She frowned in concentration. "Twenty or thirty, I should think. They died."

He glanced at the book, glanced around the room, and asked her if she had any idea where the seven sacred spears had been taken.

She paled. "Yes."

"You must tell me."

She gripped his hands and pressed them against her chest. "In Kyroppig. Ralph's brother has a castle there. That's where he has them, and that's where he's trying to learn to use them so that, when Robswerran is destroyed and the Outside comes inside, he'll be able to use their power to rule the world."

Jerico thought of Nevada.

Dawn released his hands and walked to the window, glanced out, looked back.

"Jerico?"

I don't want to know, he thought.

"There's something else."

Damn.

"What?"

"There's a band of Nessars outside in the street, and I think they want to kill you."

11 At Dawn's urgent gesturing, Jerico moved warily to one side of the window while she stood at the other. Together they pulled aside the fringed edges of the draperies and looked down into the street.

He scowled; she was right.

A band of at least a dozen of the noxious creatures was milling about on the cobblestones, muttering to each other, pointing ominously at the houses, racing off in one direction or another and returning again, to mutter and point. To Jerico's trained eye it was evident they had no leader, but he was not assured by his observation; all that meant was that they would spend another five minutes or so milling about and arguing before finally deciding to begin a house-to-house search.

And since Dawn's residence was the only place that had any lights on, he had no doubts as to which would be first.

After a second check just in case the creatures had

changed their minds and were moving on, which they weren't, he moved away from the window and rubbed his palms anxiously. "As I understand it," he said, "those things cannot separate into their component parts."

Dawn nodded.

"They are large, though, so I don't see how they could get through the door."

"Hell, they don't worry much about doors," she said. "They pick a spot and move in. There isn't much in Fadfy that can keep them out."

He nodded.

"Jerico," she said then, crossing to him and grasping his hands, "you must leave immediately."

"I gathered that," he told her gently. "But what about you?"

"I'll be safe enough," she assured him. "I'm dead, remember?"

God knows he had tried, but there were moments when his resolve and imagination conspired to overwhelm him.

"Then I must go," he said sternly. "There are spears to be taken and lives to be saved."

She smiled dreamily.

He put his hands on her dead, though tender, waist. "I would like to see you again," he whispered.

"Me too."

"I . . . I don't suppose there's a chance you'll be able to go with me?"

Her eyes, so large and round and clear and lifeless, filled with regretful tears. "No, I can't. It is said that once a shade leaves the limits of Fadfy, the shade becomes a ghost, if you catch my drift."

He caught it, examined it, saw no flaw in its logic, and sighed as she replaced the sacred book in the wardrobe, closed and locked it, and led him quickly into the hallway. Below, he could hear a fearful pounding on the door and, a second later, the harsh shattering of glass in the front room, followed by what could only be Gramlet's shriek of terror. Dawn gasped and, as he watched in amazement, began frantically tapping the wall near the top of the stairs. A tap here, a curse, a tap there, an obscenity, on up near the ceiling as high as she could reach and Jerico looked away, and one down by the baseboard, and within moments a panel slid open, revealing a stairwell which led into unrelieved blackness.

"That's awfully complicated," he said. "It must be hard to get out of here fast."

"Oh, it's really very easy," she told him as she grabbed one of the candles from the wall. "I just keep forgetting which way it goes, that's all."

She pressed the candle into his hand.

"Dawn," he said huskily.

Gramlet shrieked again, immediately followed by the roar of a Nessar still working on the entrance.

"Hurry!" she urged. "There's no time to lose."

The front door splintered, and the bellowing beasts poured into the house.

He looked at her, swallowed, then swept her into a one-armed embrace and kissed her. Before she could recover, he gave her a bravado smile and vanished with a flourish that would have worked better had he worn a cloak into the secret passage, the door sliding silently shut behind him and leaving him alone, with only the memory of her refreshingly cool lips pressed to his.

You're mad, he told himself as he made his way down; you're completely out of your tiny little mind.

His boots struck the narrow wooden steps softly.

His shadow filled the narrow stairwell like the cloud before a storm.

You, sir, are an idiot.

He didn't care.

Despite his present situation, he believed fairly strongly that his lustful feelings for the beautiful Dawn were rapidly being replaced by deeper and more meaningful affections of a sort he hadn't experienced since he'd fallen for the second cheerleader from the end at college. Whether this was true or not, however, he did not know because their time together had been so short; nevertheless, though the second cheerleader from the end had proved herself false by splitting at midterm with the physics professor, her mere presence had been sufficient to change his heart forever.

Thus, he suspected, would it be with Dawn.

But in order to explore the possibilities, he first had to get out of the house. Which was proving more difficult than he thought because the stairs continued downward without providing him with an exit. He could, he imagined, tap the walls as Dawn had done, but the muffled sounds of the rampaging Nessars made him think twice.

He had no choice.

Downward it was, and when he reached the last step some fifteen minutes later, he found himself in a large room whose accumulations of cartons, rags, and stacks of broken furniture told him he was in a basement.

And once off the last step, another door closed behind him, eliminating any thought he might have had of returning to the top to escape the dust that made him sneeze and wheeze.

"Well," he said, and began a rapid search for a second exit.

It was difficult.

There was, on the one hand, a lot of junk to be avoided, while, on the other, candle wax dripped in

stinging droplets to such a degree that he feared his
hand would soon pucker into one unsightly scar.

Yet impetus was provided when he heard thundering footsteps overhead, the crash of shattered furniture, the shower of broken glass.

Dawn, he thought painfully.

Then he found a door, found it unlocked, and
opened it.

The way beyond was darker than the room he was
in, dank, floored with slimy brick, walled with dripping stone, ceilinged with cobwebs and shadows that
indicated a number of crawly things just waiting to
drop into his hair.

He shuddered.

He backed away with the decision to hunt for some
other way to escape; and threw himself headlong into
the tunnel when part of the ceiling collapsed not ten
feet from where he had been standing and through the
resultant hole came the head of a Nessar, snapping at
the air while it struggled to bring the rest of its body
through.

Jerico ran, heedless of the candle's flickering flame
in the feeble cup of his hand, heedless of the crawly
things that were dropping into his hair, heedless of the
echoes of his footsteps filling the way ahead and
behind with a mockery of flight. He didn't care that it
would sound as if he were afraid, because he was; and
he didn't much care that the noises popping from his
throat sounded like whimpers, because they were. He
was, after all, a mere mortal man somewhat elevated
above the others, and his father before he ran off with
the chauffeur's daughter had always taught him that it
was better to retreat in the face of lousy odds than
stick around and make the odds worse.

Another door, another basement.

And no stairs up.

He shoved as much junk in front of the tunnel as he

could to forestall the soon-to-be-pursuing Nessars, and ran on, through a door on the far end and into another tunnel.

And again.

And again.

Junk and block, junk and block, eight or nine times until he concluded by the amount of wax building across his left wrist, and the absence of another door, that he had reached the end of the block or the house of someone extremely distrustful of his neighbors.

Hurriedly he searched for some means to get to the upper floors, for surely the people who lived—or had lived, he corrected himself grimly—in this house had to have used the basement for something and so had to have a means to enter it.

The problem as he saw it, however, was that the basement was perfectly clean. A little dust here and there, cobwebs on the beams, shadows in the corners, but otherwise nothing. As if the owners didn't even know it was here.

There wasn't even the courtesy of a boarded window.

Holding the candle stub over his head, he peered back down the tunnel, straining to catch signals of the Nessars' approach. He was not heartened when he heard and saw nothing; all that meant was that they were somewhat slower than he, and probably a lot more confident because they probably knew he was at a dead end.

"Well, damn," he said in disgust, putting his hands on his hips and exinguishing the candle.

"Well, damn," he said again.

He waited for a minute, hoping his eyes would adjust; and at the end of that minute realized they wouldn't because there was nothing to adjust to. The dark was so complete that he began to feel as if he were floating; without reference points, his equilibrium was thrown out of whack, and his training at Yale, not to mention his postgraduate work at Cleveland, warned him that he would soon be falling without even knowing he was falling and most likely crack open his skull on the hard earthen floor.

Gingerly he lowered himself to his hands and knees, kept one arm stretched in front of him and made his way to the nearest wall. Then he worked his way around the room's perimeter, testing the stone for signs of hidden manipulation; when that failed, he began the perilous journey across the room itself, testing the floor for signs of a trapdoor; when that failed, he crawled to the door that led back into the tunnel and sat there, panting and shaking his head.

Well, Jerico, he said to himself, it looks as if brute running isn't going to do it. You're going to have to be clever.

Easy for you to say, he answered wearily; how am I supposed to be clever without a weapon, a tool, or a light, in the pitch dark, in a cellar, at the end of a tunnel on the other end of which lies death and madness and not necessarily in that order?

Sighing, he reached into his jacket, pulled out a cigarette, lighted it, and took five or six puffs before slapping himself soundly on both cheeks.

This world was driving him crazy, so confusing his mind that he had completely forgotten that not only had he given up smoking some three years ago, but also that he continued to carry around the habit's accouterments to remind him of what he had done to his body. Contemptuously, he tossed the cigarette away. Then he scrambled through his pockets to see what else he brought with him from the Outside. Since, however, it was dark, he couldn't see much, and working by feel only brought him a brief moment of illicit pleasure before his fingers closed again on the lighter.

Holding it overhead like a weak but sturdy torch, he glanced around that portion of the basement he could see, sighing when he realized that his previous blind expedition had been thorough. He was still trapped.

Trapped, he thought then.

"Jesus!" he yelped when a Nessar screamed at him from the other end of the tunnel, in the next basement.

The little bastards had snuck up on him, and all he had was his lighter.

But what, he thought as he backed away from tunnel's mouth, had he just thought which had given him that flash of relief? He had thought . . . trapped. Trapped. Trap.

The mental exercise in vocabulary and previous exclamation retention made him look up at the beamed ceiling; then he moved swiftly over the floor, shuddering each time the Nessar rammed its bulk against the tunnel's sides to widen them. Dust fell in sheets over his face. Bits of rotted beam showered onto his shoulders. His gaze finally stopped focusing on eternity and traced the outline of a trapdoor in the bare wood above.

The Nessar grunted as it crunched its way toward him.

He looked up again and estimated two jumps—one to open the door, the second to grab the edges and haul himself through. There would be no time for more. And there was no sense speculating on what would happen if the door was locked or opened downward instead of upward, aside from a broken wrist at contact from the force of his blow, and the probable loss of his lighter when he fell back again and faced the end of his retirement in the dark.

A deep breath.

A fragment of extemporaneous mantra to give him calm.

The Nessar shattered the frame of the doorway and rammed head and shoulders into the basement. Out of the minor wounds of its passage dripped a hideous black essence that hissed and boiled on the floor. Of the creature that rode it there was yet no sign.

In his mind's slightly glazed eye Jerico marked the place of the trapdoor and, telling himself it was easy and he really wasn't giving himself a line, he extinguished the lighter, flexed his knees, and jumped.

The Nessar complained as its midsection barged in.

The trap door shuddered under Jerico's open-palm blow and flew up and back on its hinges.

He landed awkwardly and fell onto his knees, hissed at the pain as the Nessar hissed at the pain of wriggling its haunches into the basement.

Another creature followed immediately.

Jerico stood, flexed again, jumped again, and swore as he'd never sworn before when his hands took hold of the edge of the opening, and began to slip away because the floor above had just been waxed.

12 | If I die now, Jerico promised whoever was listening, I'm not going to be happy.

His legs flailed wildly in a futile effort to drive himself upward, while he simultaneously attempted to move his hands to different spots along the slippery opening. Nothing worked. He dangled, and continued to lose his tenuous grip, and the roars of the Nessars were only partially comforting since they were as blind as he.

Until they found him.

Unless, he realized with a certain clarity that comes with imminent dying, he should find them first; and with that began to flail his legs all the more, steeling himself when a foot struck one of the beasts, turning his resolve to iron when the other one did as well.

The creature was angry; he could tell that.

The creature was also puzzled, and in that moment before it discovered what was afoot, Jerico used the bulk of the beast to propel himself up and through the gap, roll over, and slam the trapdoor down.

He sat on it and sought the air his lungs needed to clear his brain, grateful that whoever the owner was, he had not done something stupid like put a chair or carpet over the door to conceal it.

The room was sparsely furnished, and lighted only by the streetlamps whose glow fell weakly through the multipaned bay window. Since no one came to find out what was going on in the sitting room, he assumed the house was empty; since there was the distinct odor of must and dry rot, not to mention something that had died in the kitchen too long ago to bear thinking about, he assumed the place was deserted.

But he was not granted, though god knows he prayed hard enough, the time to ponder or give thanks.

Suddenly the trapdoor bumped upward, rolling him over to his hands and knees, and when it rose halfway before he was able to bring reason to bear and drop something on it, he scrambled to his feet and made for the front door.

He listened.

He opened it a crack and looked out.

The street was empty save for a single Nessar milling about to his left, down in the vicinity of the Eglantine house. To his right there was nothing, and he slipped outside, dropped off the steps into the wilderness of the tiny front yard, and forged his way to the end.

He was at a corner.

Ahead were more houses, up and down was the same, and it was a matter of tossing a mental coin and praying it wouldn't land on its edge.

But at least now he knew where he had to go— Kyroppig, where the spears of the former sorcerer Ralph were now being held by the man who had, in some evil way, corrupted Jerico's fellow heroes and had bound them to his side.

He would not let that go unpunished.

Stealthily he slipped out of the garden jungle and hurried down the street to his right, crossed over and moved back up to the corner, keeping to the shadows and making sure the shadows weren't simply shades hanging around with nothing better to do. Although he supposed his destination might more easily be reached by returning to the crossroads on the plain, he was not foolish enough to believe that one or more of the Nessars wouldn't be waiting out there for just such an appearance.

He was also now of the belief that the Nessars were not after him simply for revenge on the abortive attack at the parking lot; someone, and probably the nefarious brother of Sorcerous Ralph, knew he was in Robswerran and was out to stop him from completing his quest.

Therefore, it was only good tactics to get out of Fadfy another way, confound the enemy, and take them by surprise.

He hurried around the corner, looked back and saw Nessars piling out of the houses along the block he had just left. They were confounded. They were annoyed. He used the distraction to race to the next corner, cross the street, and pausing only long enough to blow a kiss and good thoughts to Dawn and her pimp brother, sprint straight ahead, not lessening his speed in the slightest despite his weariness.

He pursued a zig-zag route, not daring to run more than one block in a row before cutting into another street.

And as he ran, then trotted, then moved along at a brisk walking pace, he noted that the houses themselves were changing. Their triangular natures were subtly altered, the apexes blunted, the bases more frilled, most of the outer trim more inclined to gingerbread ornate than whole wheat spartan. They were also farther apart, and their front yards deeper than those he'd just left.

The privileged, he supposed, and suffered a brief pang of nostalgia before giving his head a vigorous shake to keep his mind on the problem at hand.

Twenty minutes later the buildings changed again: larger, richer, even more land separating each from its neighbor. The triangles were completely gone now, replaced by squares whose corners had been rounded.

The only thing that didn't change was their lifelessness—in not a single structure over the past hour or so had he seen a light, a sign of occupation, a hint of inhabitants. It was as if he were walking through an elaborate pagan graveyard. There weren't even any shadows save for the one that sprung from the soles of his feet.

He slowed to conserve energy. His throat complained, his stomach was annoyed, and his legs weren't feeling exactly up to par. Breathing came less easily, and several times he was tempted to seat himself on one of the benches that began to appear at the low curbing. They were of wood and backless, but their siren call to his muscles and his lungs was coming through all too clearly for his peace of mind.

He sat.

He could do no other.

And when he heard the unmistakable rattle of a cart coming his way, he barely found the strength to lift his head and pray it was the miracle he was seeking.

The vehicle, if such he could call it outside his last class in refinements of medieval torture, was little more than a long open box suspended between four high, irregular wheels. It was pulled by a creature that would have been a shaggy palomino if it hadn't been for the fangs, and the driver looked only straight ahead until Jerico rose and waved a hand.

The man pulled on the single rein which was attached to the horselike beast's barbed tail, issued an order, and waited until the animal had, some twenty yards later, come to a halt. Then he looked over his shoulder.

"Need a ride, do you, my son?" he said in a melodiously deep voice.

Jerico hurried to catch up with him, limping as his legs protested the abrupt end of their rest. "I do indeed, sir," he said.

The man, Jerico saw now, was dressed in dark blue monk's robes girdled with a silver braided rope. His face was ruddy, his eyes set widely apart, and through what was left of his nose was a hat pin topped with a tasteful red stone.

The driver looked him over, from tweed jacket to raw leather boots, and raised a hairless eyebrow that nearly knocked his tonsure askew. "Stranger?"

"Yes. And a weary one, I might add."

"Well, this old nag here hasn't had a decent pull all day. I don't see any reason why you shouldn't come along, long as you don't mind perching in the balcony."

Jerico thanked him and sat at the box's rear, open end, his feet dangling just shy of the cobbles as the driver snapped the rein and the palomino thing grunted and started forward. It was a few, bone-jolting yards before it was up to speed, and in all that time the man kept up a stream of commands the gist of which, Jerico gathered, was to keep the creature from sitting on one of the benches.

"Where you headed, stranger?" the man asked.

"Out of town," Jerico replied.

"Ah. Well, you're headed in the right direction."

He nodded, and nodded more slowly as the rocking

of the cart began to work on his fatigue. Though he desperately wanted to continue the conversation, to surreptitiously learn more about Robswerran and the troubles it suffered, he was unable to keep his eyes open for more than a few seconds at a time.

"Excuse me, my son."

Jerico smiled.

"You appear not only weary to these expert eyes, but also in need of sustenance."

Jerico's stomach agreed in a frenzy. "Well," he said, "I wouldn't say no to a hamburger."

The driver scowled. "I don't understand. But perhaps . . ." and he reached into his voluminous robe and pulled out something he tossed over his shoulder. Jerico caught it, looked at it, looked at the driver, and decided not to ask as he bit hungrily, though cautiously, into the hamburger bun.

It wasn't a feast, but his stomach didn't complain. And when he was finished, his eyes settled again.

Then the driver asked him a question that jolted him awake: "Tell me, my son, are you a Ralphite, or a pre-Ralphite?"

My god, he thought; what a horrid thing to say to someone you barely know.

The answer, he knew, would have to be carefully phrased. If he were to claim adherence to the former, the driver, who was clearly a member of a religious order, might be one of the latter, which might lead to some difficulties; and it might also be vice versa. Or the man might be of another group entirely, in which case Jerico's neck might be firmly and irretrievably extended on the block. He wished he had asked Dawn more questions; he wished he had refused to move from the parking lot until the Plackers had given him an entire history of that which he was walking into; he wished the misbegotten palomino would stop racing across each intersection as though anticipating a collision, even though they hadn't encountered a single other vehicle since he'd been picked up.

Then the driver clucked at the beast. "Sorry, friend," he said. "I didn't mean to pry."

"That's all right," Jerico said in relief. He waved a devil-may-care hand. "I don't mind. We strangers have to stick together, I suppose."

The man looked sharply over his shoulder. "How did you know I was a stranger?"

"How did you know I was?"

"You're not a shadow."

"I could be a shade."

"Shades don't sit on benches," the man informed him. "They get drunk, they hang around on street corners, but they don't sit on benches."

"And neither," Jerico said smugly, "do they ride in carts."

"I see," was the thoughtful reply.

"So did I," he muttered miserably. "That's what got me into this in the first place."

With the rein entwined snugly about his hand, the man turned on his seat and seemed to be involved in a fierce internal debate. His eyes squinted, his lips popped in and out from between his teeth, and his free hand fussed with the friz of his hair. Finally, he nodded once, sharply.

"I don't know who you are," he said carefully.

"Jerico Dove," was the equally careful reply, all muscles tensed to leap from the fast-moving cart should danger suddenly spring at him unawares.

"I see."

Jerico waited.

"Have you ever heard of me?" the monk asked then.

Jerico lifted an apologetic shoulder. "I don't know. I don't think so. What's your name?"

"Is this a trick?" the man snapped, one eye closing in suspicion.

"What?"

"Is this a trick, stranger?"

"How can it be a trick?"

The monk swung one end of his heavily knotted girdle thoughtfully and *hmmmmed* to himself for a moment. "You wanted to know my name."

Almost immediately Jerico surmised there might be some sort of social ritual involved here, but he was too tired and confused to try to figure it out. "You wanted to know if I'd heard of you," he said.

"This is true."

"Well, I don't know. What's your name?"

"See?" the monk said. "There you go again!"

"But if I don't know your name, how do I know if I've ever heard of you?"

The monk twirled his tassel for a moment more, looked at the back of the quasi-palomino, and scratched at the side of his neck in deep thought. "I see."

God, Jerico thought, I wish he'd stop saying that.

"Buck," the monk said.

"I beg your pardon?" Jerico said.

"I am Buck Fye," the monk announced. "Innkeeper of the Fadfy Tabernacle of the Most Holy W'dch'ck. At your service, if you're not going to trick me."

Jerico frowned briefly. Whatever devious trick the man was afraid of was, for the moment, beside the point. "The most holy what?"

Fye raised himself as high as he could without actually standing up and tipping the uncomfortable cart over. "W'dch'ck," he said haughtily.

"I'm sorry," Jerico said. "I'm a bit tired, and I've been crawling through basements and things so my mind is not as its most efficient. If it wouldn't be too much to ask, would you mind spelling that?"

"Which? That?"

"Please."

"T. H. A. T."

Jerico smiled weakly. "I'm sorry. I put that badly. What I meant was, would you please spell whatever it was you're the most holy innkeeper of."

"I am not holy, sir," Fye said angrily. "I strive, but I cannot permit myself to believe, if you understand me. The W'dch'ck is the Most Holy. I am merely its humble servant and devoted innkeeper."

"That," said Jerico quickly, "is what I want you to spell."

"Innkeeper?"

"No, the part about the holy thing."

"W'dch'ck?"

"Right."

Fye did.

Jerico frowned again and ran a hand over his chin. "Lots of glottal stops, aren't there?"

"It takes years to perfect," Fye answered proudly. "Not everyone can do it."

Jerico didn't doubt it, but he said nothing for fear of antagonizing the one man—other than Dawn, who didn't count at the moment because she wasn't a man, much less alive—who wasn't trying to involve him in dying.

"Does this . . ." He stopped. He weighed his words. He said, "Does this Most Holy have anything to do with spears?"

Fye did stand this time, and his height was impressive, especially from the considerably lower vantage point of sitting at the edge of the cart, which was now rounding a corner and entering a vast plaza.

"Spears?" Fye said loudly.

"Jesus," Jerico said, ducking in anticipation of an assault from somewhere.

"Spears?" Fye shouted, one fist brandished high over his quaking head.

"I think there's seven," Jerico ventured.

"Seven? Spears?"

The ridiculous palomino stopped with a snorting, Fye swayed, and Jerico scrambled hastily from the cart into a defensive position he wished he'd been able to remember when faced by the old man and the German shepherd. Then he saw where they were and all thought of defense, offense, and continuing to breathe on a natural basis faded.

The plaza, he now realized, was flanked on three sides by redstone buildings all a single story high. At the east end, however, was a vast greenstone structure in the shape of a sphere sliced across its diameter and jammed into the ground. At its apex was an immense version of the crossed-spears medallions he had seen throughout the city; to either side of twenty-foot wooden doors were ten-foot arched, stained-glass windows; approaching the doors were seven wide steps, and on each of the steps, after having poured out of the twenty-foot doors, were a score or more of men in monks' robes.

The urge to genuflect was swamped by the sight of their weaponry—spears, crossbows, and here and there a staff with a knobbed end as large as a man's head.

Ominous as it was, Jerico could not help but be awed by the cathedral and its attendants.

On the other hand, it was ominous, and he had only to take the one step backward, which he did, when Fye pointed at him and said, "Seize the booted dandy! He's a hero!"

13 "So you can see," Jerico said calmly, "it's all a mistake which, in other cultures such as the one I have just journeyed from, might be called tragic. Or perhaps blackly humorous. Or even, depending upon your philosophy, inevitable."

Fye grunted. He was working busily at a waist-high rusted brazier in whose soot-encrusted iron bowl glowed the angry eyes of a multitude of white-hot coals."

"As it is," Jerico continued, "I was merely trying to find my way out of town—which I told you earlier I was doing, by the way, so that should count for something—in order to get to the city of Kyroppig and do my best to retrieve the artifacts which you refuse to permit me to mention."

Fye grunted again, pulled what looked like a branding iron from the coals, spat on it, ducked away from the steam, and shoved it back again, gave his hat pin a twirl, and grunted a third time.

Jerico watched the monk's deliberate preparations with the fascination of one who knows that miracles that come equipped with stupid-looking horses are indeed a double-edged sword. He would have begun pacing, to better marshal his thoughts for yet another presentation of innocence, but the leg irons held him close to the damp stone wall; he would also have used one of those several branding irons in the coals to beat some sense into the monk, but the iron cuffs attached to the chain which was attached to the wall kept his wrists and arms fairly close to home.

"Nice place you have here," he said finally.

"Simple but effective," the monk replied without looking around.

And it was.

A large stone room not unlike a dungeon cell, with no other occupants save Jerico and the blue-robed monk, no furniture, no light except what was cast by the monotonous seven bracketed torches set high on the walls, and no exit save a single, iron-bar door which was on the far side. Though Jerico was relieved that he could see no vermin, spiders, or creatures for which he had yet to learn names, he wondered if perhaps he was just grasping for straws.

"You come here often?"

"No," Fye muttered, checking another device which was apparently not vicious enough heated for his satisfaction. "I'm a stranger here, too, remember, my son?"

"But . . ." Jerico took a moment to corral the proper words. "But I thought you were the . . . the Innkeeper of the Fadfy Tabernacle?"

"And so I am."

"Well. Okay, isn't this the Fadfy Tabernacle of the Most Holy Whatever?"

Fye turned an iron over and shook his head in

disappointment at its evident lack of progress from red- to white-hot. "It is."

"So how can you be a stranger?" he asked, desperate to comprehend the nuances of such an exotically odd, yet totally familiar, language.

"Ah," the monk said with a thoughtful snap of his fingers. "I do see your problem. I am in truth the Innkeeper, but my Most Holy Obligations lie elsewhere."

"So why don't we go there?" he suggested, and smiled when the monk looked sourly in his direction.

Footsteps sounded in the corridor outside the huge room, echoing, solemn.

Fye ignored them.

Jerico hoped they didn't belong to the monks who had, outside, immediately surrounded him with fierce gazes and brandished weapons, then hustled him through the twenty-foot doors so fast his feet didn't have time to touch the ground until the last of the chains had been locked on him. But at least, after one of them had clouted him with a club, he'd been able to get some sleep. Not that the headache he felt now was worth the price of the rest; on the other hand, without the rest, who knew what sort of condition his once weary mind would be in now?

He frowned.

He wondered if he was making any sense.

"Now look," he said a few moments later, his patience wearing as thin as the dungeon's stale air, "I don't know what you hope to accomplish by all that torture stuff there. I'm telling you the truth."

Fye dusted his hands on his robe and walked over, just out of reach of Jerico's feinted lunge. "I could believe you, my son, I really could. But something in here," and he tapped his temple with one finger, "tells me you're not telling me all you know."

"But I am," he protested. "My god, I even told you about my bathtub!"

"True," the monk admitted. "Such personal revelations are a sure sign of truthfulness."

"Well then?"

"The Plackers."

"What about them?"

"You say it was they who brought you to Robswerran."

"They did. In a truck. With an elephant."

"An old man," the monk said, "a woman, and a fellow about your age."

Jerico nodded quickly.

"Dressed in red."

Another quick nod.

"Deserting you on the Temlark Plain when an armacon tried to attack you."

Another nod that wrenched his neck and made him dizzy; but he would persevere because the monk was driving at something, that much was obvious. Otherwise, why distill three hours of breathless narrative into a few stunted sentences that lacked all the drama and pathos of the original?

Fye twirled his tassel pensively.

But before he could say anything, the iron door swung open with a shuddering crash, and a woman stepped in. Jerico knew he was nearly beaten when his heart didn't even bother; it just lurched on, though she was lovely in a slender and boyish sense, her dark blue gown edged in silver trailing on the ground and oddly complementing the close-cropped red hair that framed her harsh young face.

"Father," she said by way of greeting as she crossed the stone floor and stood beside the monk.

"Jini."

"This the man?"

Jerico did not move. He would give neither of them

the satisfaction of seeing the cringing that was rampant within him.

"He is."

"Tall."

"Strong."

"Handsome in an Outsider sort of way."

"Plackers."

She gasped. "Him?"

"No. Brought him."

"Yes," Jerico insisted.

"Hero."

"Yes," Fye said.

Scorn twisted her features. "Damn."

"Sorry."

"Me too."

"And I, goddamnit," Jerico declared heatedly. "I'm sorry this man won't believe me, I'm sorry you think so badly of heroes, though I can understand why, and I'm sorry I ever left Dawn. At least she—"

The woman stepped closer. "Dawn?"

He nodded, puzzled but hopeful. "Why, yes. Miss Eglantine, of Fadfy."

The woman grabbed the monk's arm, and they stepped away to the other side of the brazier in sudden hushed conference. Jerico wondered what he'd said now, and didn't much care for the way the woman toyed with one of the branding irons while she spoke low and quickly to Fye.

They looked at him; they looked away.

He looked at them, keeping his chin up, his chest out, and his stomach in as best he could manage. And it was, without doubt, a difficult management—on the one hand, he was depressed because of his situation, and he didn't blame himself for that because he was, after all, only human; but on the other hand, he was elated because nothing, not even the German shepherd, had even come close to giving him the excitement he'd looked for when first he'd embarked on his chosen profession. If he were to be honest, though, he probably could have done with a somewhat different sort of excitement; if he were going to be even more honest, he probably would have preferred his excitement in the real world as he knew it; and if he were going to be brutally honest, he probably would have passed on the excitement altogether.

But what the hell, he thought, and waited anxiously for the results of the consultation.

Which came almost as soon as he started waiting, when the woman and the monk approached him, one to either side, each with a branding iron in hand.

"Dawn," the woman said.

"Yes," he said bravely, chin high and rigid. "She protected me against the Nessars."

"I see."

Shit.

"She seemed all right to you?" Fye asked.

"A little pale, but otherwise, fine."

"Dead," she said.

"In a way," he answered.

"But you saw her?" Fye asked.

"Well, of course I did. And Gramlet."

"Little shit," the woman muttered.

"I would say," Jerico said judiciously, "that as a shade, he takes what work he can find."

"Jini," Fye said.

"What?" the woman replied.

"Has a point."

Jini turned away in absolute feminine disgust, turned back and held the iron close to Jerico's chest without a single hint of wavering. The intense radiated heat almost instantly took the wrinkles out of the tweed, but at the same time threatened to scorch the silk.

Jerico squirmed.

"She didn't kill you," Jini said.

"You see me," he answered.

"I do."

"Me too," said the monk.

"Then I am not dead."

"Dawn."

"That's different and you know it," he said quickly, wishing the hell she'd either brand him or spare the shirt, which he was sure he wouldn't be able to replace anytime soon, and definitely not around here.

"Has a point," Fye said.

The woman called Jini spat her disgust, and faced Jerico squarely, the iron swinging at her side and growing no cooler for it. "We trust her," she said grimly. "She is one of us, and if she didn't kill you, there must be a good reason."

"She didn't kill me because she believed me," he said, overwhelmed by her verbosity.

"And what about the Plackers?"

"What about them?" he said, trying hard not to yell. "They were the ones who brought me here to help."

Her smile was one-sided. "They brought the others, you know."

"The . . ."

"Yes."

"But the others stole . . ."

"Yes."

His mouth widened. "Ah!"

Fye said, "I hate perfect teeth."

"You . . . you think I'm here to join the others!" Jerico exclaimed, panting with the stress of revelation.

"It's the obvious conclusion," Jini told him.

"But why, if they already have the spears?"

"Because Joquinn Yama still needs an army," she explained none too patiently. "An elite guard that will protect him until he's mastered all the convoluted spells and castings which bind the Most Holy Spears together. Once he accomplishes that, this branding iron will seem like a pleasant breeze compared to what's going to happen."

"That branding iron's going to ruin my shirt, if you don't mind," he said stiffly. And inwardly sighed his relief when she tossed it blithely over her shoulder. "And who," he added, "is Joquinn Yama?"

"The Most Sorcerous Ralph's younger, fathead brother," she said, her contempt as ill-disguised as her distrust for him. "The one who is right now preparing to destroy one world in order to rule another."

Fye, meanwhile, having chased after the discarded branding iron, jammed it back into the brazier with his own, and folded his arms across his chest.

A gong sounded somewhere in the tabernacle.

Jini shivered.

The gong sounded a second, more insistent time.

"The problem, my son," Fye said when the noise died down, "is that we have a problem—whether to trust you or not."

"Dawn did," he reminded them. "And it's apparent that that must carry some weight with you or you'd have me screaming for mercy by now. Although I must warn you—or I would have if you had started the torture stuff—that I have a fairly high threshold of excruciating pain. It would have taken a hell of a long time to get the truth from me, which truth I have already told you so it would have been a waste of time anyway. And I think I'm not far from wrong in saying that I don't think you have a lot of time left."

"He's right, Father," Jini said.

"I know, Daughter," Fye said.

"Then maybe we ought to get on with it. If he turns out to be a traitor, we can always torture him someplace else."

The gong, echoing.

Fye rubbed his chin, frizzed his tonsure, and nodded. "All right, Daughter. Whatever you say. But he must be your sacred responsibility. I've never really trusted the Eglantines, not since that afternoon in Yoteoc when she broke the mirror over my head."

"You know you deserved it," she said with a bright laugh that filled the dismal cell with the sound of finely tuned crystal. "Now let's get going before Joquinn finds out we're still here."

Jerico grinned, squirmed, lost the grin to a frown, and said with as much authority as he could muster under the circumstances, "Hey, damnit!"

Jini stopped, one hand on the door. "Yes? You cursed?"

"That gong," he said. "What does it mean?"

"A call to arms, I would imagine."

"Whose arms?"

"Not ours."

"A bit of danger then?"

"Yes."

"Death, and all that?"

"If we get caught."

"Well," he said, shaking his shackles, "I will be if you don't get me out of these things."

And though they did free him, for which he was very grateful, he wasn't sure how to take the two or three minutes they used to make up their minds. Nor was he sure what to do when, as soon as they stepped into the corridor, a wave of blue-robed monks swept down upon them from the stairs at the far end.

14 "You can tell me if I'm wrong," Jerico said, gamely trying to maintain a belated air of confidence in his tone, "but as I see it, while you, Buck, are in fact the esteemed, and striving to be Most Holy, Innkeeper of this tabernacle, those who are in your employ, so to speak and meaning no sacrilegious intent, have evidently defected to the side of this Joquinn person, who is obviously a very persuasive fellow, since they were clearly on your side when this entire affair began."

Buck, yanking for the hundredth time in as many seconds on the chains which bound him to the wall, grunted his agreement, though not with much enthusiasm.

"And that, if I may be so bold at such a trying time, tells my instincts that there is, perhaps, a spy in your midst, since that Joquinn person could hardly have known about this in the time since we decided to leave."

Jini kept her thoughts to herself.

Well, Jerico thought, this is another job for Superman, and he wished to hell he'd stop thinking like that because it was going to get him nowhere in their present situation—which was back in the cell they'd just left, the branding irons simmering on the fire, and the crowd of blue-robed monks gathered in the corridor, while one of their number played a curious wind instrument made of wood and bone.

It, and the tune, were unnerving.

It smacked of sacrifice in all its pernicious forms.

Though fully aware that he was being watched closely, he tested his metal bonds by sagging slowly and permitting his arms to bear most of his weight. The flat-head iron bolts which held the chains to the walls quivered a little and shook loose a little promising dust, but they did not give. He tried it a second time, with no better results save a faint strain of his left wrist and dust that made him sneeze.

Nuts, he thought. Now it would have to be something more dramatic, but at the moment he could think of nothing that would fit the bill without bringing the entire building down on their heads. He couldn't do it. Especially when there were all those monks out there. It would do none of them any good if he were to break free in a spectacular fashion, only to be captured yet again by the local clergy and placed in a place from which he would not be able to escape a second time.

An hour passed during which Jini breathed a lot and Buck gave up on the chains and tried kicking the wall instead. Jerico wanted badly to offer them both some small modicum of comfort, some sip of solace which would not only lift their spirits but also prove himself worthy of their trust; but his mind was a frustrating blank when it came to administering balm.

All he could do was sneeze, and that only gave him the start of a headache.

He thought of Dawn; he thought of Rhonda; he thought of the predicament he was in and decided to think about Dawn instead.

The wind instrument played on, passed now from hand to hand and becoming increasingly melancholy.

A second hour calmed the monks in the corridor, shut the instrument up, put Fye to sleep standing up, and improved Jini's vocabulary as she speculated on the genealogy of those who were guarding them.

Finally, just as Jerico had come to believe that Jini was no lady and he, for lack of substantial nourishment, was about to join the spectral Dawn in a way he hadn't exactly counted on, a diminutive berobed figure entered the cell, his cowl giving his face a veil of deep shadow.

Buck awakened, saw he was still chained, and recommenced grunting and groaning.

Jini glared at the newcomer, widened her eyes in fearsome recognition, and spat toward him with a defiant sneer.

Jerico merely waited.

"So," the monk said, placing himself in front of Fye and silently commanding attention.

Fye refused to look at him.

"So," the monk said, moving down the line to Jini, and neatly sidestepping another rain of indignant saliva.

"So," the monk persisted, standing now in front of Jerico and eyeing him from that darkness nesting beneath his cowl.

"Yes," Jerico said, narrowing his eyes slightly.

"You are who?" the inquisitor demanded, his voice somewhat higher than average, though no less filled with the expectation of obeisance.

"I am who I am," Jerico replied.

"Which is?"

"Myself, and none other."

"You speak well for a stranger," the little monk said with an approving nod.

Jerico bowed as best he could at the compliment, taking them where he could since he wasn't getting any from his so-called new friends.

The little monk waited, hands swallowed by his voluminous sleeves.

Jerico was patient; his time would come.

The little monk stirred, glanced at the expectant mob in the corridor, looked back, and said, "You do not have a name?"

"My name," he answered, "is for those who respect or fear me, not for those who would use a cowardly army to subdue a stranger, a woman, and an old man."

Jini gasped.

Fye froze.

But the little monk laughed, as deeply as his voice would allow, and shook his head, waggled his finger. "No, stranger, you are not going to trap me into unreasoning anger, after which I dismiss my men and attempt to take care of you on my own so that you may escape and have me look the fool. No, no, no. I am not that stupid."

Live and learn, Jerico thought.

"Oh, for Ralph's sake, Ham," Buck snapped, "what the hell do you think you're doing?"

The monk turned to the monk and threw back his cowl, and Jerico was amazed that so short a person could have all that hair growing out of the center of his scalp. Which was, as far as he could tell, the only hair growing out of the center of his scalp. Which was, as far as he could tell, the only hair the man had on his head at all, and dyed the most unflattering shade of blue he'd ever seen outside a convention of retired

English teachers. His eyes were fair and huge, his puny lips virtually bloodless, and when he strode back down the line to Fye, it was clear that he suffered an impediment of the left leg.

"What I do here is my business," the little monk said disdainfully.

"Wrong!" Fye bellowed, forcing the little monk back a step. "*I* am the Innkeeper!" He glared at the mob in the corridor. "*I am the Innkeeper*, and you'd damned well better remember it when I get out of here, you little shits!"

Several of the outstanding monks vanished almost instantly, and the others milled about like Nessars, uncertain in which moral direction their greatest haven lay.

The little monk held up a palm and merely laughed. "But you are not getting out of here, Buckie, haven't you figured that out by now? You and your silly friends are going to rot here until you die." As soon as the little monk spun away from Fye, Jini spat again, this time catching him on the shoulder.

The little monk froze.

Jerico suggested in a whisper that perhaps she ought not to provoke him that way.

"What?" she said incredulously. "You don't know who this is, hero. You have no idea who we're dealing with here."

"Well," he admitted, "that's true enough. But I don't think, to be frank, we're dealing with anyone at this point."

Jini's laugh was harsh. "So let me introduce you. This is Ham Attadon, formally fourth in command at the Fadfy Tabernacle, formerly a good friend of Father Buck, and the lousiest lay this side of Peplow."

Attadon whirled and pointed a blue-tipped finger. "You are a liar, harlot! You could not possibly know such a thing."

"Why not? I saw your mother yesterday," she said smugly. "She told me all about it."

Oh boy, Jerico thought; this is going to get ugly.

Attadon, puckered face red and lips trembling violently, sputtered, murmured, gasped, stuttered, and finally walked up to her, glared for several long seconds, drew back his hand and slapped her. Hard. Rocking her head back against the wall and bringing tears to her eyes.

"Bitch," he said.

"Bastard," she managed through her daze.

Ugly, ugly, Jerico thought.

He slapped her again, and again her head slammed against the stone, the hollow sound of the collision making even the other monks wince.

"Sir," Jerico said.

"Cram it," the monk told him, and punched Jini quite callously in the stomach.

Fye roared, and yanked furiously at his chains.

The monks, using their finely honed tabernacical training, sensed danger in the air; half of them fled, and the other half milled more rapidly.

Jini slumped, not yet unconscious, yet without the strength to defy Attadon again. He grabbed her hair and yanked her face up. He leaned close and grinned.

"Attadon," Jerico warned.

The little monk looked over, half-closed one eye, looked back at his prisoner, and released her with an exaggerated shrug. Stepped away. Scratched lightly at his cheek. Stepped forward, and slapped her as hard as he could across the mouth, instantly bringing blood and a moan to her lips.

Well, Jerico decided, that tears it.

He flexed. He strained. He concentrated so hard he successfully split his shirt, and at the same time pulled from the stone the chains that bound his arms. Then, while kicking his legs free, he used the chain of his

right arm as a whip, snaking it expertly around
Attadon's neck, and yanking.

Attadon, taken unaware, gurgled as he left his feet
and crashed to the stone floor. He thrashed and
gasped for help, but Jerico stood over him and planted
a heavy foot on his chest. The man's face was turning
as blue as his hair, but Jerico felt no compunction to
give him a breather.

Meanwhile, the monks, though milled and muttered to a frenzy, were not about to permit their leader
to be treated in such a manner, and after a swift
inventory of their weapons, they charged into the cell
under cover of a war cry, only to be met by a windmill
of blurred chain Jerico set before them.

They screamed.

He screamed back.

Several of them were immediately dispatched to
meet their god with necks and chests crushed as Jerico
pushed off Attadon and waded into their midst,
ignoring their spears and pikes and swords in his rage
and determination; several others, who attempted to
surround and outflank him, were dispatched across
the room to the brazier, which set their robes afire
and them shrieking out of the cell; and the rest had all
they could do to get out without being crushed in the
rush.

Jerico, still swinging the chain, followed, panting
his exertion, making sure the corridor was cleared of
the monkish rabble before returning. He was exhausted. He also discovered that he was bleeding
where a few of the enemy had, albeit weakly, made
their point; the wounds were not serious, but he knew
that the night was not yet done.

It never is, he thought sourly, and slammed his
chafing wrist cuffs against the wall until they split,
then used leverage and a little metallurgic luck to
release his ankles.

Attadon remained unconscious, his face still a pale shade of unflattering blue.

The gong began sounding frantically.

"I don't goddamn believe it," Fye said, and repeated his assertion as Jerico freed him by a simple yank-and-twist. "How'd you do that?"

"I pulled the chains from the wall," he answered modestly, busily following brag with deed and deftly catching the comatose Jini in his trembling, waiting arms. "Now lead the way again, Buck, before the little devil monk here comes around and regathers his forces."

Fye looked at the fallen fourth in command. "Aren't you going to kill him?"

"There is no need," Jerico said as he headed for the exit. "He isn't going to bother anyone for a long time. And by that time, we ought to be far away from this diabolical place."

Fye nodded wisely at the judgment, kicked Attadon in the ribs, and hurried after the man carrying his daughter. "Will she be all right?"

Jerico sincerely hoped she would. Fortunately, there seemed to be no blood damp or dry in her hair, which indicated that no skin or skull had been shattered by her ordeal. He did not care for her continued injured sleep, however; despite what was depicted in film and theater, one who remains thus for more than a few seconds is in danger of remaining thus for a hell of a lot longer. And she was, lithe or not, one hell of a heavy lady.

They moved swiftly along the darkened corridor, away from the direction the fleeing monks had taken, up a long flight of wide stairs which eventually brought them to a landing lit by a single torch. Fye turned left, and Jerico followed, through a series of gaily painted doorways, through what looked to be an extensive library, through a dining hall, and at last to a closed door whose surface was a bas-relief of a ship at sea.

"When we go through here," Fye whispered, his hand already on the latch, "we have to run."

Jerico shifted Jini, puffed his cheeks, and blew.

"It's a field."

He nodded.

"On the other side is the River Nunby."

He nodded, and shifted Jini again.

"When we get there, there ought to be a bridge."

He nodded. Shifted. Said, "Ought to be?"

"I'm a stranger here myself, remember?" the monk reminded him. "I can't always speak for the customs of every town I find myself in."

"Okay. Open the door."

"Of course," Fye said, glancing back the way they'd come, "if there is no bridge, we'll have to swim."

The ringing gong was joined by another.

"Okay. Let's go."

"Can you swim?"

He nodded.

"You'll have to help me. I can't."

"Fine. Let's go."

"And watch out for the armacons. It's their breeding ground."

Jerico put Jini on the floor, covered Fye's hand with his, and said, "If you don't open this goddamned door, Buckie, this tabernacle's going to be a day short and a monk shy."

He smiled.

Fye smiled back.

Jerico picked up Jini, sighed in lost hope of receiving a little Ralphian charity, and sighed again when Buck opened the door and pointed to the vast, probably verdant field that lay in complete darkness ahead of them.

"That way," he said, and immediately raced into the night.

Jerico, who had studied tactical instances like this in his Nevada bathtub, waited for sounds of pursuit, capture, or battle; when he heard nothing but Fye's pounding feet, and the two gongs joined by a third, he charged over the threshold, into what danger he did not know, knowing only that there'd better be a bridge or someone he didn't know very well was going to learn to swim awfully damned fast.

Destiny, he thought as the night and the field took him, is not what it's cracked up to be.

15 It wasn't so much the running that annoyed him—a healthy sense of speed was, after all, part of his stock in trade and expected of him in cases like this, when walking would be disastrous; what bothered him was the fact that he was unable, with the comatose woman so carefully cradled in his arms, to run as fast as he would have liked, which was pretty damned fast and not a stride slower. It rather soured the otherwise heroic effect of plunging dramatically through waist-high sharp grass beneath brilliantly twinkling stars, the enemy in hot vocal pursuit, his only escape lying just ahead if only he did not trip, stumble, or fall.

Nevertheless, opting for substance over form, he persisted, since to do otherwise clearly would have meant not only his and Jini's capture, but also their probable and certainly final torture and death.

A moon, if indeed that's what it was, rose bleakly above the horizon, bloated, a sullied white, and casting its sickly light across the broad field, which only served to make it seem larger, and set shadows moving that he would just as soon not have to deal with just now.

Fye was nowhere to be seen.

The river, however, could easily be heard over Jerico's increasingly harsh panting. It sounded quite large, and it did not sound, as rivers go, as if it were merely rambling along its flowered banks toward some unknown pastoral destination; it sounded just like a depressingly large body of water does when that depressingly large body of water is impeded in its progress by equally large boulders.

He prayed that Fye had not neglected to feed him certain information.

He shifted Jini and ran on.

Behind him the alarm gongs were vibrating at a pitch certain to wake the dead, and more than certain to disturb the sleeping armacons whose tunnels extended below his feet. Though he was not afraid of the former, he had no desire to interrupt the latter in the procreation and continuation of their species. He had a feeling it would be disgusting. And dangerous.

Therefore, he strove to remain as silent as he could, but the attempt was futile. The coarse grass was stiff, and it rattled as he plowed through it; the gongs were, if anything, louder than they had been, and would surely bring the entire community down upon him; and once, when he paused for a breath and checked to be sure Jini was still living, he thought he detected the clamor of monks racing after him.

Jini moaned but did not waken.

The river grumbled.

Jerico plunged on, after several minutes resorting to a zigzagging maneuver he hoped would confuse those following while, at the same time, taking him closer to the water.

He stumbled.

Jini groaned.

He blinked away perspiration that poured from his brow and stung his eyes.

A faint shout from the direction of the tabernacle told him that his trail had been discovered.

The gongs fairly rang off their stands.

We'll make it, he swore silently to the unconscious woman; don't worry, we're going to make it.

Then the land began to slant upward, not distressingly so, but sufficiently steep to make progress more difficult. The grass began to thicken, become shorter, stab at his shins and poke at his boots. The ache in his arms grew to a constant sullen burning. His legs, if they were still down there, and he wouldn't have taken any odds on it, had apparently been replaced by limbs made of uncooperative lead. Yet he did not falter, reminding himself with every painful step that the woman who was his burden depended on him for her life, not to mention the guy who was doing all the running in the first place.

The slope ended.

He stopped, and swayed as his pants became gasps.

Behind him were the imposing towers and walls of the Tabernacle Square, the dim glow of a few streetlamps, the ragged outlines of the nearest Fadfy houses against the starbright sky.

And ahead, only a few yards down a slope far more steep and barren than the one he'd just climbed, was the River Nunby.

"Fiddle," he said.

It was less like those waterways he'd become used to in the East, much more like those that transversed the wild and still somewhat unsettled West—it was wide. Damned wide. So goddamned wide he couldn't see the other side. Which immediately became the least of his problems since the span between one bank and the other was quite clearly marked by huge gouts and slides and boilings and whirlpools of foamy, raging white. Which meant, even to his untutored eye, that the rapids here were going to be a bitch to get across.

Hastily he glanced up and downstream, searching for Fye and the crossing he must have used, but there was no sign of the man who claimed no knowledge of swimming. He glanced back, over the field, and spotted a myriad of bobbing lights heading in his direction —torches and lanterns, perhaps half a hundred, which he estimated would arrive at the rise's summit within the quarter hour.

Of Fye, still no sign.

Jini shifted, and moaned.

The armacons, he thought then; despite the monk's hasty warning, racing headlong through the dark might well have caused him to stumble accidentally into one of the nuptial burrows. If that was so, there was no hope. And since he could think of no other solution, he decided that he was, at the last, on his own.

And in so thinking, he slung Jini unceremoniously over his shoulder, rubbed his arms briskly to bring the circulation back, and began a rapid, sideways descent to the bank below. And once at the bottom, the moonlight allowed him to see a narrow path, not much wider than a man's casual stride but well worn and smooth. He took it without question, heading south, walking rapidly to preserve his strength, though the temptation to run again was hard within him, and it took all his will to maintain the steady, but excruciatingly slow pace.

Jini woke up.

The river roared.

"Where?" she muttered, her head bobbing against his chest.

"The trail along the river," he answered.

"I feel . . . terrible."

"It's all right," he said, stopping and lowering her gently to her feet. "Attadon won't touch you again."

"Swine," she spat, and rubbed her hands over her face.

"We're away now," he said. "All we have to do is run for our lives."

It was several precious seconds before she was able to understand, several more to realize that Father Fye was nowhere to be seen. She glared at him. He refused the intimidation by indicating that their pursuit was nearing the rise and they really didn't have much time to linger.

"You were heading south?" she asked incredulously, throwing back her cowl and planting her hands on her hips.

"It was either that or north," he explained.

"You should have gone north. There was a bridge."

He felt his temper rising. "Fye said there wasn't one."

"He's a stranger, here, remember?"

"He said that too."

"Nuts," she said heatedly, and rubbed her face again. "We could have used that bridge."

He pointed again at the brightening glow of the bobbing torches. "Too late now."

"This," she said, "is ridiculous."

He didn't understand.

She didn't stand still long enough to explain. Instead, she began to run, swiftly, without looking back to see if he was following; and without her weight Jerico, once he shook off his surprise and got moving, was able to match her pace for nearly a hundred yards before he faltered once more, a breath hard to come by, his legs once again protesting.

The torches reached the rise, banded, finally split into two sections and flowed down to the bank.

The river roared.

"We must go across!" Jerico called to the woman.

She nodded, and kept running.

"Buck said we'd have to swim!" he called, vainly trying to close the widening gap between them.

She nodded, and kept running.

A ford, he concluded; she must know of a place where we can safely ford the river, which is what Buck must have done. Unless he went north and used the bridge, the sonofabitch.

She waved frantically over her shoulder.

He called that he was still here.

She spun about, waved again, and headed on, holding up the robe with one hand now in order that her legs, which he noted were rather charmingly enhanced by the moonlight, could take greater unimpeded strides.

He gasped, he tracked his second wind, and he pushed on, puzzled by her mimed directions, but willing to follow her lead because he had none of his own to propose.

The riverbank began to curve to the left.

Trees appeared on its bank, small and leafless though thick about the bole and possessing many branches which would, if he only had the time, make excellent clubs in case he had to stop and fight in order that Jini might go free.

Then he glanced over his shoulder. The monks had split their forces a second time—some running north toward the unseen bridge, too many chasing him because the moonlight obviously made him a clear goal. There were shouts. There were cries. There was a shriek and a scream when one of the monks fell into the river. And there was a subtle but definite change of direction when he spotted a huge shadow appear suddenly on the rise.

Immediately, some of the monks retreated, some of

them ran faster, and the rest of them plunged instantly into the water.

An armacon, he realized; raccoonus interruptus, and God save them all.

He redoubled his efforts.

Jini kept running.

He refused to look back when he heard several screams and a distinctly triumphant bellow.

He stumbled and nearly fell.

Jini looked back, and kept on running.

Panting, his arms dangling weakly at his sides, he looked to his left and realized that the land had flattened and spread without a noticeable break to the invisible black horizon; the river, however, was no less formidable, the rapids, if anything, wilder and more dangerous. There was no sign of a fording place. No sign at all.

Stop, he begged the woman; for god's sake, stop and give me a break.

Jini continued to run, as if all the monks of Hell were at her back.

Realizing that there was something inherently unfair about all this, he staggered onward, refusing to give her the satisfaction of his imminent failure. But there was, he knew, only so much strength to be had in a man, only so much reserve for him to draw on in his hour of heroic need. And it wasn't *she* who carried *him*, was it? Hell no, of course not. It was *he* who carried *her*. And while he certainly couldn't expect her to reciprocate exactly, the least she could do was pull him along or something.

Damn, he thought, and stepped over a rock that threatened to trip him; damn.

The monks continued to follow; he could tell by their shouts, though the noise wasn't as energetic as before.

The armacon he didn't know about, didn't want to

know about, and could only hope that he'd never learn about, at least not in this lifetime.

The riverbank grew more congested as it and Jerico continued their gentle westward swing—with taller trees, prickly shrubs, smooth arching roots that poked trippingly out of the ground. The path was virtually gone, and though the moon's light enabled him to avoid most of the obstacles, there was still the occasional twig to pink his cheek, the obstinate root to catch his ankle. He thrashed through and around it all, and nearly stumbled to a halt when the vegetation abruptly fell away.

The river was smooth, no white water visible.

The riverbank was empty, Jini vanished in the dark.

Snapping his fingers with impatience, he looked left; the field had been replaced by an exceedingly dense forest which began some fifty yards from the bank.

Well, he thought.

And, with a sudden frown, he whirled about and realized that the path behind him was empty. The monks and their torches were gone. The pursuit was over.

Well, he thought again, this time with a smile.

Which faded the moment an armacon rose out of the shadows.

Jerico backed away slowly, searching side to side for something to use as a weapon.

The armacon, its ringtail twitching, its fangs gleaming, its masked pink eyes glittering, followed him.

"You," Jerico said then.

The armacon paused, its head tilted to listen.

"Aren't you the one I saved back there on the road?"

The tail stopped its twitching, the mouth closed, the claws on its center paws partially retracted.

Jerico grinned. "Sure you are! Hey, sure you are!"

If he'd read it in a book, he'd never have believed it, but he would have sworn on his mansion bathtub that this was indeed the very creature that had been stuck in the hole. The very beast he had rescued.

He laughed his delight.

The armacon bobbed its head.

He slapped his thigh.

The armacon reared, and raised a clawed paw.

And Jerico guessed from the peeved expression on its face that the creature had never in its life heard of Androcles and the lion.

Oh pshaw! he thought, turned to flee, and fell into darkness as those claws came down across his back.

16 Someone was screaming.

Jerico knew it wasn't him because he was positive the dead, in their terminal condition, didn't know how. Or if they did, they weren't able to. Or if they were able to, they didn't bother because it wouldn't have done them any good. And since he was undeniably dead, cruelly clawed and mangled into nameless oblivion by an ungrateful, six-legged raccoon for Christ's sake, it couldn't be him. Not that he didn't feel like it. He did. His clothes were ruined, his retirement was a bust, and it was apparent that he wasn't even going to be able to come back as a shade, thus denying him even the platonic company of Dawn Eglantine and her brother.

The screaming continued.

Of course, Gramlet was no real loss, so there was a dubious blessing to be counted there, but Dawn . . .

This was, he decided glumly, even worse than the time he'd become hopelessly lost, the first time he'd tried to drive solo across the country. He knew he should have taken a left at Albuquerque, but the map he'd picked up in Fargo had instructed him otherwise, and he finally ended up stranded on a dusty road in Oklahoma, ambushed and mugged by a group of Tulsa toughs and left with only one pair of shoes, one shirt, and thirteen socks, none of which matched.

It had been hell.

But at least he'd been alive.

On the other hand, the dead seemed to have any number of faculties unlost in the transition—they could hear, if that damned screaming was any indication; they could feel, because his back burned fiercely from the passage of the deadly swift clawed paw; and they could sneeze like a sonofabitch when their noses were tickled, which he did when it was, which explosion gave him an instant splitting headache and snapped his eyes open just in time to see the armacon rear onto its tail in fright, spin about with scales flapping, and charge back into the night from which it had come.

Jerico watched the sky.

The screaming ended.

He watched the center of a cloud turn grey as it passed over the moon.

Footsteps hastened toward him.

He felt a stone dig into the base of his spine, and he reached beneath him, pulled it out and weakly threw it away.

"Are you all right?"

He sighed. "I'm dead."

"Oh lord."

"I'm sorry." He tried to turn his head, but his neck wouldn't move. "I did my best, though."

The cloud moved away.

Hands slipped under his shoulders and brought him

gently to a sitting position. He heard a hissing intake of breath, felt his shirt being lifted in flaps and strips.

"Wow."

"I really do think I would have made it, you know," he said. "If I had had the foresight to leap into the river when I had the chance, I could have avoided that creature. It would have been hell on the silk, but I would have survived."

"Don't move."

His laugh was brittle. Strange instructions for someone who was dead, but then, this was a foreign country and who knew what customs were rampant when it came to rites and—"Jesus!" A fierce blast of cold slammed into his back, nearly knocking him to his feet.

"Don't move!"

"How the hell can I?"

"Just—"

"Christ!" He rocked forward at another blast, his forehead brushing his knees before he rocked back again. "What in god's name are you—"

"You're lucky," the voice told him. A soft but strong voice, and one he recognized when his head was clear again. "If you were anywhere else but the breeding grounds, that 'con would have shredded you and had you for a snack."

The burning seeped through the cold, and he winced. "You mean I wasn't?"

"Well . . . only a little." Another touch of cold, not quite as strong. "The claws dull when they breed. It wouldn't be much fun otherwise."

He tested his neck again, massaged it with his left hand, and looked over his shoulder into Jini Fye's narrowed, concerned eyes. "You came back."

She grinned briefly at him. "You needed help."

"But you ran away."

"The armacon," she said, ducking out of his vision and bringing that cold to bear once again, "was a male."

He considered the erotic implications. He shuddered. He asked what she was doing, and she explained that she was applying a Most Holy Balm to his injuries which ought, if she were doing it correctly, to bind him long enough for the body's natural but now sped up processes to take over. Within hours he would be as good as new.

"Your clothes are a dead loss, though," she added when she was finished.

And for the first time since leaving Nevada for the big city, Jerico didn't care.

He was, when all was said and done, alive. And that, in the scheme of such things where necrophilia took last place, counted for a bit more than a simple shredded silk shirt shipped by hand from Singapore to the desert. He hated silk anyway; in winter it froze his nipples.

"Can you stand?"

Although he wasn't sure of anything after the battering he'd taken, he managed with her help only one stagger before gaining his balance. He took a deep breath for the sheer joy of it. Then he shook himself gingerly limb by limb to prove that he was indeed still functioning. A little bone weary, more than a little sore, but able, he assured the blue-robed monk's daughter, to continue if they had to.

She smiled up at him brightly. "Great." She looked at the trees east of them, at the river, and north along the path their flight had followed. A thoughtful frown disturbed her delicate features. "Those idiots will be back soon, once the 'cons are settled again. I think we'd better take the forest road. It isn't any faster, but it'll give us more places to hide in case they pick up the trail."

"Are they that good?"

"Attadon is," she replied flatly, and wasted no time, but immediately left the riverside path and ducked into the trees.

Warily Jerico checked the bank and the river for pursuit before following her. And though he saw no sign of the aforementioned road, he had no choice but to trust her. She had, after all, saved his life. And despite her prowess with a branding iron, she was obviously as committed as he to the recovery of the Seven Spears.

The question was: was she in fact committed, or was she working for the other side?

His doubt nearly shamed him, but he couldn't help but wonder at the way Attadon had so quickly, and conveniently, appeared in the Tabernacle. Despite his own assertion to the contrary, he couldn't believe that Joquinn was able to convert the Most Holy monks so swiftly. In a matter of minutes.

It was, to say the least, suspicious.

The forest was as dense as it appeared from the river.

The trees were high and their boles slick, their foliage thick, blocking out all moonlight save for a stray wavering beam; though there was scant underbrush, the way was difficult because he couldn't see a foot in front of his face until he tripped over it and nearly brought Jini down with him.

Underfoot the ground was soft, cushioned, it seemed, by a thick carpet of low grass that adequately muffled their passing to an occasional squish when the way grew damp; otherwise, they were too much like ghosts for Jerico's recent close call to be comforting.

And there were noises. Lots of them. Rustlings in the branches overhead, stirrings in the shadows to either side, slips of rolling rock, snaps of twigs, crunches of dead leaves. Yet he said nothing, made no sound of caution. He had no idea what sort of nocturnal creatures lived within the woods, had no idea if they were hostile or not, and did not want to alarm Jini to possible danger in case, as before, she took off and left him to wander into the arms of something unpleasantly big.

An hour passed.

They climbed a low hill.

He tried in a whisper to ask her if they were heading straight for Kyroppig, and she hushed him.

They crossed a shallow stream on slippery rocks and climbed another low hill.

His back began to stiffen; a good sign that healing was in progress, but it made walking uphill all that more difficult. He suggested, quietly, they take a short rest, but she refused with a scowl, and told him with a gesture to reconsider in her favor.

A large bird shrieked as it glided over the trees.

To his left, deep in the shadows, something muttered a growl, and a bush sounded as if it had been crushed by a single monstrous foot.

Jerico remembered the xazulla, rolled his eyes, and hurried on.

Another stream, no rocks this time, and the water was swift enough to penetrate the boots the Plackers had given him. His toes froze.

The trees grew higher, the dark darker, but at last the noises began to fade as they trudged up a third slope much steeper than the others.

At the summit she stopped, took his hand, and whispered, "We'll spend the night here. The moon's going down and it'll be too dark to move."

Right, he thought, and dropped immediately to the ground.

Jini lowered herself beside him and leaned back

against a smooth-bark bole. "Try to sleep," she said. "We have a long way to go."

"Time?" he asked.

"Not much."

"Joquinn?"

She shrugged. "Hard to say."

"Smart?"

"So-so."

"Magic?"

"Any fool."

He puffed his cheeks in frustration, as much for his unthinking collapse into her abdominable shorthand language as for the grim realization that he wasn't only going to have to fight traitorous heroes somewhere down the line, but also was now up against a time limit of some sort. Weeks. Perhaps only days. There was no telling because Jini was snoring, but instinct told him the luxury of casual rescue was not going to be his.

His back hurt.

His legs hurt.

The night grew cool and he shivered.

If I were clever, he thought, and before I went any farther, I would go back to the river, follow it back to Fadfy, find the road out of town, follow it to the intersection, turn left, and go back to the parking lot. Then, if I were still clever, I would walk straight through that goddamned golden wall, find a cow, and ride it back to New York. Then I would go to the airport, get on a plane, and haul it back to Nevada.

I really would.

I want my bathtub.

Jini rolled over in her sleep and curled against him.

You are an idiot, he told himself; Mother was right.

Jini sighed.

Jerico sighed.

And with a great deal of difficulty, he managed a basic fetal position and dozed, dreaming of bathtubs made of green Italian marble set in a floor of turquoise Mexican tile, of a bed ten by ten and more blankets than he could shake a pillow at, of tailors having nightmares about customers sleeping on forest floors.

He rolled over once, and woke up nearly screaming at the agony of his spine.

He woke up a second time and discovered he was alone.

17 | When Jerico was a young boy, not yet fully cognizant of the fruits of his family's wealth, his least favorite game was charades. It wasn't because he wasn't good at it; his play was, as a matter of established fact, awfully close to professional quality. What distressed him were the messages he usually deciphered when his mother was doing the pantomime. It was as if, on some less than subliminal level, she was trying to give him a subtle warning to get out of town before sundown. Not that he ever did. And not that he ever fully believed that she was trying to get rid of him.

Nevertheless, the feeling persisted that maybe, just maybe, he wasn't wanted at home.

That feeling returned.

Here he was, standing in the middle of a clearing on the top of a hill in the middle of a forest, and the only one who knew how to get him where he was going, or where he had been, was gone. Without a word.

Without a sign. Without even a hint that she would be back at any moment and don't start without her.

"You know," he said to his shadow, "a guy could get ideas."

But there was no sense crying over split monk. Instead, he began a short series of exercises to limber up his sleep-stiffened joints, in the middle of which he paused just long enough to realize that his back no longer hurt him.

He tried to examine it, twisting this way and that, and succeeded only in catching glimpses of flaps and ragged ends of armacon-sliced riverbank-soiled silk. Which led him quite naturally to notice how thread-poor his trousers were, and how scraped and tattered were the boots given to him by the Plackers.

God, he thought, what a mess.

The exercises ended.

His stomach grumbled.

The idea of eating rose optimistically as he scanned the forest around him for something to break his fast, and fell when his botanical education left him bereft of the skills needed to decide which grass or leaf was worth taking a chance on.

Hell, he thought, I wasn't hungry anyway.

And to keep his mind on not being hungry, he walked around the large clearing, studying the trees so remarkably similar to those he'd left behind that he was almost forced to call them oak and elm and maple and fir; yet they were none of those. Their leaves were much larger and of a circular nature, their boles were smooth and gleaming, and their roots rose like the knotty brown spokes of a warped wheel above the thick and weedless grass. They were also so close together that only in two or three spots was he able to find room enough to squeeze through.

Which he didn't, because once through there was no assurance he'd be able to return.

"Jini!"

Her name carried on the gentle morning breeze, but was not returned with the promise of her reappearance.

He checked the sky and found it blue and beautiful and devoid of clouds.

"Yo, Jini!"

A butterfly fluttered gaily out of the foliage, darted toward him, away, and vanished back into the forest.

When he judged an hour had passed and the Fye woman hadn't yet returned, he sat cross-legged in the clearing's center and pulled off what was left of his shirt. It wasn't a pretty sight, and he quickly wadded up the foul cloth and tossed it over his shoulder. A quick scan of his chest and arms showed him no lasting damage, and he attempted again to get a look at his back, trying to understand just how Jini had been able to rid him of those potentially lethal claw strokes.

A twig snapped.

He froze.

Another twig snapped.

Silently he rose to his feet and backed into the shade of a tree somewhat taller than those around it. Someone was coming, and though it might well be Fye's daughter returning to fetch him, it might also be one of Attadon's thugs.

He waited.

The breeze blew and a songbird warbled to its mate.

Then, at the south end of the clearing, a shadow moved in the forest.

Jerico searched in vain for something to use as a weapon, cursed his failure, and pressed closer to the bole. Though he knew there was no way he'd be able to blend into the crimson bark, there was a faint chance the traveler, or bandit, might be so preoccupied that he'd see nothing out of the ordinary.

What the hell, he thought; it's a shot.

And five minutes later a man eased between the trees and stepped boldly into the clearing.

Jerico almost called out.

The stranger was not terribly tall, reaching no higher than Jerico's chest, and the way he walked suggested something amiss with his right hip. Yet he was sturdily constructed, as though from equal-sized building blocks which consequently made him nearly as wide as he was tall. He was dressed in the scaled skins of a now-naked armacon—loose shirt, baggy trousers, ragged cloak thrown about his shoulders. On his feet were rough and stiff boots, around his ample waist a wide silver belt, and on his head a tall black cap pointed fore and aft.

Jerico held his breath.

The man scanned the clearing with a squinting gaze until he looked straight at the red tree.

Be clever, Jerico told himself, and stepped out of the shade into the sunlight.

"Hello," he said, smiling, nodding, extending a hand in universal greeting.

"You don't have a shirt on," the man said, as calmly as if he were announcing that the sun was still shining. "You're almost naked."

Jerico didn't know what to say. The man didn't have a visible weapon, his stance was such that he felt no intimidation, and judging by those clothes, he certainly wasn't a tailor; so why, then, did he insist on measuring him that way? Could he be a luckless cannibal hunting for brunch? A thief wondering if what was left of Jerico's clothes was worth the effort. Something worse?

Jerico smiled again, albeit wanly, and slipped his hands into his pockets.

The man reached behind him then into the cloak and pulled a large feathery sack to him. He rummaged in it for a while, muttering and whistling soundlessly before finally yanking out some cloth he tossed at Jerico's feet.

"It gets cold," the man said, tucking the sack away.

Seeing no harm in at least looking at the man's wares, Jerico grabbed the bundle up, held it to the sun, and realized he was holding a pair of exquisitely handsewn trousers—they were dark green, sinfully soft to the touch, and, when he slipped them on, a perfect fit.

"They fit," he said in amazement.

"Now you're talking," the man told him, and tossed over a matching shirt and cloak, the latter evidently fashioned from the scales of a now-freezing armacon.

As he finished dressing, and sat to pull on a pair of marvelously cobbled green feather boots, he said, "I don't know how to thank you enough."

The man shrugged.

"I wish I could repay you in some way."

The man lifted one shoulder.

The urge to ask about Jini was strong, but he restrained himself, knowing that a simple wrong word could very well mean his life. He stood, smoothed his new ensemble with his palms, and nodded his approval. Then he asked the odd man where they were.

Cautiously, the block-shaped man inched closer, and his face was revealed to be that of someone close to Jerico's own age, though the mass of bloodhound wrinkles and sunken colorless eyes managed to camouflage the fact. His nose, what there was of it, was red as if from drink, and his mouth, what there was of it, was evidently toothless, and marked by lips which were a stunning shade of corpse.

"You," the man said, "are on my hill."

"Ah. Yes. And where is that?"

Don't say it, he begged silently.

"Here."

Nuts.

He put his hands on his hips and turned in a circle, praying like hell that Jini was nearby. "My name is Jerico Dove."

"Winngg Indo," the man responded in kind.

He noted the clever use of feathers and was not surprised.

They were silent for several minutes.

The sun grew much warmer.

Jerico cleared his throat. "I am . . ." He hesitated then, struck with sudden doubt. Thus far everyone he had met in this backwater Oz had somehow managed, by either design or accident, to prevent him from getting where he was going. He cleared his throat a second time and decided he had nothing to lose now that the silk shirt was ruined. "Winngg, I am on a mission."

"Hill."

"What?"

Winngg tapped the ground with a knuckle. "Hill."

He grunted. He closed his eyes in a brief prayer he recalled his dear mother saying each night as she tucked him into the attic bed: *Why me?*

"Yes," he said, nodding. "Well, Winngg, I am . . . looking for something." He waited, and held his breath. "I don't know how to get to where this thing is." He waited, and crossed his fingers. "I need directions."

Indo nodded sagely.

Jerico tugged at an earlobe. "Will you tell me . . . no, never mind. Please tell me how to get to Kyroppig."

Winngg pulled the edges of his cloak close about him and stared for several minutes at the ground. Then he closed one eye and stared at Jerico.

"Jini."

"No you're not," Jerico reposted.

The man grinned. "Damn you're good."

"But you know her?"

"Sure."

"Do you know . . .?" Careful, lad, he thought; careful does it, or you're going to pop him. "You know her. You know where she is."

Indo nodded encouragement.

"So. You are here to take me where she is waiting, so we can join her and move on to Kyroppig."

Indo held out his hand and they shook, laughing, slapping each other's backs and shaking their heads. Then the man pointed southward. "Joquinn is a prick," he said.

"So," Jerico said, "I gathered."

"Follow me."

And Jerico did. Slipping and sliding through the boles as if coated with grease, once losing the cloak off one shoulder and nearly taking off all his skin. Indo laughed. Jerico smiled tightly and readjusted the garment. And they eventually made their way down the hill to where a creek flowed through an almost treeless hollow.

"Why did Jini leave?" he asked as Indo scooped some water into his mouth.

"I don't know."

"But she sent you back for me."

"Sure."

"Are there going to be others? That is, will it be just we three, or will there be more?"

Indo waded to the other side. "Yes. No. Yes."

Jerico followed, too tired to figure out how to ask the next question.

Another hill, smaller than the last, was easily climbed and easily descended.

"I'm a hero, you know," Jerico said, panting.

"Yes."

"I was retired."

"Sure."

"Are you . . . what do you . . . how do you . . .?"

Hell.

And a third hill, not much more than an ambitious bump, was accomplished in much the same way, save that here the crimson trees were taller still, and the boles so thick that Jerico guessed it would take a good dozen men holding hands to surround it.

"Is she much farther?" he asked, trying not to gasp in the heat that poured sweat into his eyes.

Indo leaned against a boulder and took a cup from his cloak, a canteen, and poured himself a drink.

Jerico gaped.

The man pointed.

Jerico reached into his own cloak and laughed aloud. There was a complete selection of foodstuffs in there, cleverly stored in pockets of all shapes and sizes, the manufacture of the cloak hiding all telltale bulges and somehow even managing to conceal the added weight.

"This is incredible," he said, gladly taking some of the clear cool water.

"Water," Indo corrected.

"Right."

"One hour."

"Okay."

Indo moved on.

Jerico capped the canteen, placed it back in the cloak, and followed, noting that the trees were farther apart and a clear path was now visible on the forest floor. Ahead, he could see a brilliant light, diffused and touched with gold, and he supposed it was a meadow which began where the trees ended.

Which it was.

A monstrous meadowlike table which Indo called the Fuddermel Plateau, many square miles of rich grassland and streams much of whose southern border formed the upper edge of a precipitous gorge carved by the relentless push of the River Nunby.

"Jini is here?" Jerico asked before he could slap himself to silence.

Indo shook his head, and pointed in a vague southwestern direction. "There," he said, and began walking.

There, Jerico repeated silently; now why didn't I think of that?

And several hours later, just past noon, as the sun nearly blinded him in its intensity, and the thickness of the grass, and the several dozen burrow mouths hidden therein, made travel unexpectedly hazardous, he spotted a cabin, a crimsonwood cabin with a roofed porch, and two hitching posts. It was a relief. He was beginning to think there wasn't anything on this plateau but horizon.

With a sigh of expectation he hurried to Indo's side, matching him stride for stride, swinging his arms, feeling his spirit renewed. It seemed, when he thought about it, that he was, in time-honored fashion, gathering a band together. A courageous and fear-naught band which would, in time and a bit of hard-earned luck, bring the vile enemy to its knees and Robswerran's religious heritage back to its people.

He felt good.

He saw a blue monk on the cabin's porch and said, "Is that Jini I see there?"

"Cabin."

He didn't even scowl. He only nodded and quickened his pace, waving to her, grinning shyly when she waved back, and running when she suddenly shrieked, whirled, and threw herself through the doorway and out of sight.

18 "I can't help it," she explained as she expertly muscled a large wooden ladle around a large iron pot set over a fire in a large fieldstone fireplace in the cabin's large main room. "I get that way sometimes. I think it's a spiritual thing."

Jerico, seated at a rough-hewn table with his cloak draped over the back of his simple chair, shook his head in bemusement. "About stew?"

"You haven't tasted mine. There are monks I could name who would kill for this stuff."

He waved the claim aside and shook a teasingly scolding finger at her. "You scared me to death, you know. I thought we were under attack."

She looked at him and winked. "You're never off duty, are you, hero?"

"Never," he declared proudly. "It's my job."

And it was. Just as standing guard in the doorway was apparently Indo's. He'd been there since they'd reached the cabin porch, explaining that the Fuddermel Plateau was no place to leave unwatched. Especially during the long daylight hours. When Jerico reminded him, rather testily, that they'd just run across it without a single weapon between them, the feather-bedecked man pulled a sword from his cloak, swished it expertly a few times, and laughed so hard at Jerico's expression that his wrinkles threatened to slap him to death.

Not only that, the stew smelled dreadful.

I persevere, he thought, I persevere.

He glanced around the room again, wondering who had built this cabin and why. There was a narrow window on either side of the door, one on each sidewall, and one in a tiny room just to the right of the fireplace. There were no shelves, no other furniture save the table and its five low-backed chairs, and the only source of water was a pump on a platform you had to reach through the rear window.

A way station, he imagined; an oasis for weary travelers on their way from one place to another. How nice.

"Why are we here?" he asked as Jini tested the stew with her elbow, then dropped three tin plates onto the table.

"Someone is coming."

Jerico leapt to his feet and fumbled in his cloak for the sword he prayed was there.

"Later," she said, staring at him oddly. "Not now. Later."

"I knew that," he told her. "I just need to keep my reflexes in sharp order. I also need to find out which of these stupid pockets has the stupid—shit!" He sucked his bleeding thumb. "Never mind."

Indo didn't move.

Jerico sat again and watched the way Jini's blue robes wrapped about her lithe figure as she scurried from pot to plate with the ladle, dishing out generous portions of the midday meal. When she was done she sat opposite him, drew a fork from her sleeve, and began to eat.

Jerico checked through the cloak and found his own utensil. Then he poised it over the steaming heap on his plate. It certainly looked like stew—all those chunks of meat, all those chunks of potatoes, all those chunks of vegetables—but he couldn't quite bring himself to overcome the olfactory reaction that rose with the steam.

Jini looked up without raising her head. "When was the last time you ate something?"

He opened his mouth, and closed it again. He couldn't remember, but he suspected at least a day, if not more.

"Dumb," she said.

He speared some of the meat.

"You'll get weak."

He brought it to his mouth.

"You won't be able to save anyone, including yourself, if you don't have something."

He put it between his teeth and nibbled.

She watched him with wry amusement.

After he had swallowed, and had frantically emptied his canteen to sluice the clinging spices from his mouth and throat, giving up all hope on his tongue and at least one molar, he gasped, "How often do the monks eat around here?"

"They are there," Indo said without turning around.

Jerico twisted in his chair. "Who?"

"They." And the block-man pointed.

Jerico lunged to his feet.

"Relax, relax," Jini told him. "It's company. Eat. Eat. Didn't your mother ever feed you?"

Since he didn't want to go into that, trying to explain how little there was to forage for in the desert when you found your mansion's back door locked, he gulped another spare forkful to keep her happy, then hastened to the door to look over Indo's shoulder.

"Well," he said.

Approaching the cabin from the west were two riders. He could not see them clearly, but their beasts were obviously first cousins to the elephant in Placker's truck. Though they were not the same tasteful puce—they were, as far as he could tell, a somewhat offbeat deep green—they had the height and bulk, the forward-aiming horns, the furry tail, the curious topknot between the humps of their heads, and the feet that could stomp a vineyard into bankruptcy.

"What are they?" he wondered.

"Company," Indo replied.

"No," he said. "What I meant was, do those creatures have a name?"

"Not mine. Wouldn't know."

"Horses," Jini called over the sound of her picking up plates and forks.

He looked again. "No, they're not. Horses aren't nearly that big, they have hairy tails, and they have big teeth. Those things are elephants."

"Whatever you say," she said, "but they aren't going to come when you call them."

Horses, he thought, and with a shrug decided that there was no sense arguing; sooner or later the language would make sense. Maybe. Meanwhile, what the hell—horses.

The beasts in question were now less than a hundred yards away, and Indo stepped boldly into the open, hands on his hips, cloak flung boldly back to show the riders he had a sword in his belt. Jerico remained in the shadow of the doorway. He wanted to study these newcomers first before committing himself.

One was dressed as Indo was, in armacon scale, though without the block-man's pointed high hat. His hair was long and pale blond, braided into a ponytail long enough to reach his horse's rolling haunches. His face was dark and handsome, and the patch that covered his left eye seemed to be made of a single, gleaming black stone. The other could quite easily have been his sartorial and physical twin, except that his patch was on the right eye, and its glittering stone was purple. He also had a superb mustache, the ends of which the wind swept back over his shoulders, and his own hair was cut so short that from a distance he appeared to be bald.

"Not bad, huh?" Jini said, shouldering him aside so she could step over the threshold. "Giles Xamoncroft and George Jambo. Brothers."

"Are they of your order?" he asked, impressed by the way they steered their mounts to the cabin without so much as a single rein as guidance.

"Monks?"

"Yes."

"No. Giles is a cook. George is a gardener."

Jerico frowned. "But you said they were brothers."

"Of course."

"Yet they do not have the same last name."

She waved; they waved back. "You think that's odd?"

"Naturally."

"You have stew on your chin."

He sputtered, but had no swift retort, and could do nothing but cleanse the offensive spot while the brothers reached the cabin, tethered their mounts to the hitching posts, and jumped to the ground. There was an immediate round of convivial huggings and backslappings, Indo chucking one of the horses under the chin while Jini fed the other a hunk of her stew.

Then the brothers noticed Jerico, and there was an abrupt, suspicious silence.

Two dark eyes stared at him, looked away to Jini, and looked back. They were reserved, neither hostile nor friendly, until she took each man by the hand and brought them to the porch.

"This is Jerico Dove," she said. "Buck found him in Fadfy. Dawn likes him."

They nodded to him sharply.

He nodded back.

George of the purplestone flung the ends of his mustache out of the way, reached into his cloak, and pulled out a thorn at least four feet long. "In your honor, I shall fight at your side until our land is free." Then he swept into a bow and backed quickly away.

Jerico just managed not to gape.

Giles of the blackstone reached into his cloak and pulled out a small pellet he pressed into Jerico's hand. "Chew on this, sire," he said, sweeping into a bow and backing quickly away. "Her stew'll do it every time."

So surprised was he that Jerico did as he was bidden, and before he'd swallowed the last piece, they were on him again, this time including him in the huggings and backslappings and the generally boisterous jovial greetings which carried them all into the cabin, where Giles immediately lidded the pot and opened all the windows. Then they sat at the table.

"Your plan, sire," Giles said, laying a bejeweled dagger before him.

"Yes. How shall we devour the cretinous wretches who have despoiled our homeland and besmirched our afterlife?" George wanted to know, stroking his thorn and polishing it with his mustache.

Jerico lay a thoughtful finger on his cheek. "Well, I must first—"

"I suggest," Giles suggested with an apologetic smile, "a night maneuver. Joquinn will not expect us to come at night."

"Well, I believe—"

"I disagree," George argued politely. "He will expect it, which is why we should attack during the day. He will not expect that. After all, only a fool shows his cards in sunlight."

"I think—"

"Which is why he'll be expecting it," Giles countered. "Which is why the night attack, which he was expecting and then changed his mind about, will not be expected."

"I—"

"Indeed," George agreed. "It's a point. But suppose he expects, doesn't, and then does again? We're doomed if we go in at night, don't you see?"

"How about high noon?" Jerico asked sourly.

"Tacky," the brothers said in tolerant disapproval. "Very tacky, sire." They looked to Jini for agreement, found none, and agreed with each other. "A man has to eat, you know. Even the enemies of the Most Holy."

"Exactly," Jerico exclaimed, slapping his palm on the table and making Indo jump at his position in the doorway. "Catch them off-guard in their coffee, decimate them, scatter them, and we'll have the Spears before you can say Jack Robinson."

"Jack Robinson," Indo said.

Jerico got up, walked across the room, closed the door, walked back, and sat down. "How," he asked Jini, "do you stand him?"

"He's the Most Holy Innkeeper of Indo Mountain Tabernacle," she replied smugly. "Very strict."

The brothers agreed.

Jerico stared at the door. "I see."

"No, you don't," Indo called.

"Which is getting us absolutely nowhere," Jini said from the table's head.

And she proceeded to explain that Buck, even though he wasn't exactly here, was with them on this one. He had sent word to those tabernacles not yet infected by Joquinn's madness to prepare for a holy war if it came to that. No one, however, really wanted a war. Especially when it was evident to all that should a holy war break out, one side was going to have an advantage, what with the magic and all on the side of the usurpers. Therefore, it was vital that Jerico get into Kyroppig unseen, discover exactly how far Ralph's brother had gotten in his studies of the W'dch'ck spells, and find out precisely where the Seven Spears were being kept. Once that was done, Jerico would get out of the city, return to his loyal band, and lead them back into the city on a foray that should, with luck and Ralph's blessing, end this potential terror once and for all. And if he killed a few heroes along the way, who was to know?

"I would," Jerico said sadly. "Alas, I will have to live with that for the rest of my life."

"A burden," said Giles sympathetically.

"A cross," said George with a sad shake of his head.

"A crock," Jini said angrily. "They're not heroes anymore. They're goddamned murderers and thieves!"

"They are here," Indo announced through an open window.

Jerico didn't move. While it was true that the patch brothers seemed competent enough despite their nonmilitary vocations, he wondered just how many more Jini had invited to this war party. It was going to be difficult enough for five to remain out of Joquinn's way; more would make their infiltration virtually impossible. Especially if they were all riding those big green horses.

Jini, however, jumped to her feet so hastily she knocked her chair over.

"Trouble?" he asked.

"No more."

"Indo."

"No more!"

"Indo!"

"Jesus H, Dove, can't you understand English? I didn't ask anybody else to meet us here!"

With an angry cry George flung himself out of his chair, stepped on his mustache, and slammed his head against the wall. He sagged limply to the floor, eye closed, stone dull. Giles grabbed up thorn and dagger, raced to the door, tangled a leg in his braid, and hit the lower hinge with a crack that made the cabin shudder.

"Swell," Jini said, searching her robes for an as yet unseen weapon. "Swell."

Jerico, on his way to his feet, gestured calmingly. "Excuse me, but isn't this what you wanted *me* here for?"

She paused. "Well . . ."

He found his sword, tested it, shrugged, and nudged Giles to one side before opening the door. "Don't worry," he told her. "After all, we took care of the monks, didn't I?"

Indo nearly knocked him over as he bolted inside.

Jerico sneered with benign tolerance at the behavior of well-meaning amateurs and stepped out to the porch. Flexed the blade, his muscles, and stared out over the Fuddermel Plateau.

"Hmmm," he said.

Then he stepped back inside, closed and latched the door, and said, "I don't suppose you have any tunnels here, do you?"

19 It had seemed at first glance as if the Plateau had become infested with a small herd of Robswerran horses.

Or worse—that the Nessars had finally caught up with him, determined to seek vengeance for the recent fiasco in the suburban tunnels beneath Fadfy.

His second look, however, confirmed his second-worse fears—that those pachydermic greenish horses had very tall riders on them, and the very tall riders, unsuitably dressed in nonreflective black from head to boot and most certainly frying their brains out in all that heat, were carrying weapons of a sort that did not bespeak well of their intention to take prisoners.

He bolted the door in a fit of prudence.

The brothers, having been revived by Indo and now trembling with fear and indignation, posted themselves at each of the side windows. Jini took the window to the door's left, Jerico the right, while the block-man scurried into the back room to guard the pump.

The attackers, perhaps three dozen of them, were well spread out across the Plateau. They moved slowly, even indolently, and they called to one another as they waved their swords and maces and one or two whips with glints of razors in the tails. The horses themselves were draped with flashing sheets of chain mail, their striped yellow horns were sharpened to a clumsy butcher's dream, and their articulated white trunks slapped the ground as if beating tympanic doom time.

Dust rose in their wake.

Startled meadowbirds darted from under their feet and fled toward the distant, hazed hills.

"You know, as much as I abhor open warfare and the criminal element," Jerico said quietly, leaning casually against the wall and watching the steady approach, "it certainly would be nice if we had a few guns."

"We do," said Jini idly.

"We . . . what?"

"But of course," Giles said with a disdainful sniff. "Do you think my brother and I would dare to embark on such a perilous journey without the most contemporary weapons available to us at the time?"

"Well said," George told him.

"It is nothing."

"Nevertheless."

Jerico waited impatiently, but neither man made a move to burrow into their cloaks. "Well?"

Jini wiped her brow with a sleeve. "Well what?"

"Well get out the damned guns!"

"Oh, we can't do that, sire," Giles said, and made a swift and elegant apologetic bow. "No. I fear not. No."

Ignoring parts of his brain that seemed suddenly to

have gone numb, Jerico demanded an explanation on the one hand, while on the other, more silent and less charitable, one, he wondered why Joquinn hadn't taken this place over the morning he started. Could he really be that inept?

"They're at Kyroppig," explained George as he polished his thorn. "The guns, that is."

"Kyroppig."

"Protected in a secret cache ready for our use when we move in on the evil Joquinn."

"We're surrounded!" Indo called from his pump station.

"It was all Buck's idea," Jini said with a brief feeble smile. "Put the stuff there and it won't be lost in case we're captured along the way. We don't have very many—it has something to do with Robswerran physics—so what we do have we have to take care to protect."

Jerico saw the wisdom, if not the practicality. "So how long has that cache existed?"

Jini looked at Giles, who looked to George, who said, "Night before last, I think. Wasn't that when we were there, brother? Night before last?"

"I do think so," Giles answered. "Though I'm sure it was after midnight, so more properly it would be—" He frowned and stared at his fingers. "Yesterday?"

"No . . . no, I don't think so, brother."

Jerico kicked the wall.

The room fell silent.

"You were there yesterday?"

"I believe so," Giles said with a mild frown. "It was after midnight, as I said, so I can't really be sure. But . . . yes. Give or take."

One of the black riders cracked his whip three times, and three times more. There was applause, and a few of the horses trumpeted.

"You were at Kyroppig? With guns?"

"Naturally. That was the order given, sire, and we obey. It is our nature!"

A rock landed on the roof.

Jerico felt his throat begin to close. "You were at the city, and you didn't check the place out? You didn't try for the Spears? You didn't—"

"Sire!" George snapped in daring reproof. "Sire, please! You must remember we are not heroes, after all. We are not trained! We are as mere peasants in the dust storm of time, bowed against the wind and humbled in your presence. Do the deed ourselves? We dared not. We . . . dared not."

"It was tempting, though," Giles admitted.

"Well, yes it was, brother."

"Would have knocked Buck right out of his girdle."

George laughed.

Giles laughed.

Another rock hit the roof.

Jerico put a hand to his throat and wondered what it would be like to strangle himself. Then he looked outside and saw that the attackers had stopped and were strung in a wide circle around the cabin, some fifty yards away. The brothers' horses were champing at their chain bits, and their horns were rubbing restlessly against the hitching posts.

Jini looked a question at him.

He looked an answer back.

She scowled.

He shrugged.

She stomped over and grabbed his arm. "You're the hero!"

"I'm not Superman!"

"Save!"

"Ha!"

She slapped him.

He raised his hand to slap her back.

Her mouth opened, her eyes widened, and the cheek where he had aimed to strike her began to tremble as she backed fearfully away.

Jerico knew instantly what frightened her—his dark blue eyes were growing unpleasantly darker, his face had hardened into sharp, and one might say arrogant, planes, and a set came to his mouth that not even a mother would want to kiss. Not his mother, anyway. And when he frowned, his eyebrows virtually obscured everything to the middle of his nose.

He could feel it then—he was losing his temper.

He turned to Xamoncroft. "How fast are your horses?"

Giles fingered his blackstone patch nervously. "Rather. Wouldn't you say rather, George?"

Jambo twisted one mustache around his wrist. "More than that, I should think. Much more. They get excited and . . . well, you know . . . whooooosh! As it were."

Jerico closed one eye in thought. "Can they carry more than one person and still whooooosh?"

"Oh indeed," Giles answered hastily. "Indeed."

"Jerico," Jini said, "you can't mean—"

"I can, and I do."

"But they outnumber us six to one!"

His visage softened enough to prevent her from screaming when he took her by the arms. "In here we are trapped, Sister Fye. Out there we have a chance. In here they could wait until we starve to death. Out there we have a chance. They could burn us out, pull the place down around our heads, or charge and kill us all. Out there we have a chance. We have no choice. We either make a run for it, or we die."

"We could die out there too," she answered.

He nodded. "Yes. Yes, we could. But out there one of us may break through. One of us may be able to get a message to Buck, warning him new plans have to be made if we are to succeed. One of us may take the bull by the horns and face the Most Holy's brother one-on-one. One of us, in other words, out there is one more than we might have in here if we don't do something about it soon." He put a finger under her chin and lifted her face tenderly. "It's our only chance, Sister. It's the only chance we have."

"Oh God," Xamoncroft wept. "Oh God, sire, lead on!"

"Yes!" Jambo agreed tearfully, thorn at port arms. "Yes!"

Indo ran into the room, sword poised, gaze searching for the intruder.

Jerico laughed heartily. "No, friend Winngg, we are not yet under attack. We are making a run for it."

Instantly Indo charged for the door and would have gone through it had not Jini tripped him. "Idiot," she scolded. "Pay attention for a change."

Quickly Jerico divided his meager force—he and Indo would ride behind George, while Jini rode with Giles. They would head southwest toward Kyroppig and, at Jini's breathless and eager suggestion, meet outside the village of Gubs, which was, she assured them, still loyal to Ralph.

They held hands.

Jini donned her cowl and muttered a Most Holy blessing that took the better part of an hour and a lot of rocks on the roof; and then, with Winngg and a prayer Jerico adjusted his scaled cloak, flung open the door, and sprinted across the porch, shouting a battle cry from his warrior bathtub days, brandishing his sword, and leaping nimbly to the hitching post and thence to the back of Jambo's astonished mount.

Before the beast could react, he was joined by the others, and after a scramble for position on the horse's broad back, George slammed a fist between the humps of its massive head. It reared, it trumpeted, and it whirled with filed horns at the ready, charging straight for the nearest black rider with such a fierce bellow that the menacing circle was breached more by astonishment than by fear.

The enemy bellowed its collective enraged shock.

A well-aimed razorwhip hummed over Jerico's head, and he ducked just in time to avoid an unwanted tonsure; a wild sword attempted to skewer Indo, who slashed wildly at the blade and shattered it to glittering pieces.

There was shouting.

There was screaming.

There was Jerico trying to find a way to hold on, finding himself facing backward and finally having to grip a strap of white leather which wound snugly about the horse's hindquarters. He had no idea what the device was for, but he refused to release it, employing it as an anchor while he lashed out at one of the black riders who had foolishly drawn too near. The sword sang, the rider fell, and its horse dropped away and turned, just in time to collide with two others which immediately reared in panic, throwing their riders into the path of several more.

Confusion filled the sky with lament and choler.

Dust filled the air and momentarily dimmed the sun.

With all the confusion Jerico was unable to see how Giles and Jini were faring in their own escape, but by the way the opposing force was splitting up and struggling for some semblance of attacking order, it was apparent that they too were in the clear and running like hell.

He laughed with joy.

Indo slapped his shoulder in congratulation.

George's mustache wrapped around his neck and nearly throttled him.

But they were away, widening the already impressive gap, the thunder of the horse's great flat feet cheerfully deafening, the frustrated cries of the black riders fading with distance. All in all, it was a sensation so marvelous that he didn't even bother to become seasick. He only urged the marvelous beast onward, ever onward, grinning like an idiot while keeping a wary eye on the dogged pursuit. They might be behind, he knew, but they weren't going to give up; they had been humiliated and weren't going to let that go without exacting a price.

The problem was, he noted shortly afterward, they didn't have to stay close at all; the horse's passage through the Plateau's lush grassland left a trampled trail a blind man could follow.

That, he realized, could be serious.

But for the time being it was something he was willing to shunt aside for the sheer exuberance of having been bold and gotten away with it.

Take *that*, he thought to the goddamned toothless German shepherd.

20 Despite the rush of air across the horse's back, Jerico soon felt the heat again. There were no clouds to ease the sun, no haze to soften the glare of the sky, and within minutes George's mount had slowed from its headlong rush to a more leisurely, though no less anxious, trot. Jerico wondered at the tactic, but he said nothing. He was, after all, no trainer of animals, and perhaps this was merely a clever subterfuge the purpose of which eluded him completely.

An hour passed.

The black riders remained a goodly distance behind.

And the Plateau rolled on. Knolls and rises, troughs and depressions; stands of crimsonbark trees, swaths of brilliant flowers, the occasional rotting log that proved that all was not paradise here on the Fuddermel.

Another hour.

Leather-wrapped flasks were drawn from cloaks, the cool liquid within quenching parched throats.

George remained silent, only once in a while muttering directions to his charge, the horse once in a while thumping its trunk on the ground; Indo kept shifting, facing right, facing left, swinging his sword in hostile intent, daring the black riders to stop fooling around and get on with it; and Jerico couldn't help wondering what kept the enemy at bay. It certainly wasn't Indo, nor was it the horse's horns, and modesty even suggested they weren't much afraid of him.

They only stayed back there, carelessly fanned out, a dozen or more, easily matching the trio's unusual pace without closing the distance.

Of Jini and Giles there was no sign.

Indo Mountain had long ago dropped below the horizon.

At the third hour, as Jerico's legs were aching close to splitting, Jambo finally turned around and said, "It will be dark soon, sire."

Jerico glanced at the sun, lowering in the west. "I think you're right, George."

"We'd best find a place to camp."

"But—." He pointed at the black riders.

"Well," George said, "there is that. I mean, we can't just decamp and camp, now can we? They'd see us."

Jerico nodded.

"Which means . . . oh drat, they're doing it again." He uttered an order to the horse, who snorted, thumped its trunk, and altered its direction to a more southerly one.

Jerico, on the other hand, stared at the riders and could not see what they had done that had caused the gardener-cum-warrior such mild consternation. They were still there, though perhaps a bit more to his right than they had been previously.

He frowned.

He took another drink.

He slipped his hand out from under the white belt and flexed his fingers until feeling returned.

"Winngg," he said then, not looking around.

Indo grunted.

"What can you tell me about Gubs?"

"A lot."

He glanced over his shoulder at Jambo. "George?"

"I hear and obey, sire. What your wish is, so is my command, virtually to the death if it means the freedom of my country."

"This village."

"Plateau," Indo said.

"What?" George said, loudly because the horse had picked up a bit of speed.

"The village," Jerico called.

"Gubs!"

"Yes!"

"Right!"

Another glance that took in both his companions, and he decided there was probably a certain amount of inbreeding here; maybe it had something to do with the water. Or the fruit. Then he realized, so slowly it was as though he were watching himself in a dream, that his view of the Plateau had grown somewhat askew, one confirmed when Indo grabbed his arm and yanked him upright before he toppled off the rambling mount. His left hand slipped back under the belt and gripped it tightly.

"Damn!" George exclaimed. Then, "Pardon, sire, but those vile creatures refuse to make up their minds!" Another order, and the horse bobbed its great head before turning slightly again.

Suddenly Jerico straightened.

"Indo," he said, twisting about and taking the man's arm, "didn't you say something about—?"

The black riders charged, yelling and screaming and waving their whips madly.

The horse, at George's urging, began to accelerate until it was once more at full speed, trunk high in the air, head lowered, feet thumping and pumping and creating such a thunderous racket that Jerico was unable to gain its master's attention.

Wrong, he thought as he simultaneously strove to reduce the panic he felt; Jesus, this is about as wrong as it can get.

Indo yelled, though whether in fear or exultation it was impossible to tell.

The black riders drew nearer.

"George!" he shouted.

No use; there was too much noise, and he was being thrown about like a fallen saltcellar on a revolving table.

"Indo!"

No use there either; the block-man was too busy threatening the black riders and trying to stay on the horse's back without looking extraordinarily stupid.

"Cliff!" Indo shrieked in the midst of his troubles.

"What?" Jerico yelled back.

"Cliff, sire!" George bellowed.

"Cliff!" Indo wailed.

And Jerico cursed when Indo cried out again. He cursed because his rather basic geological training at the university should have warned him hours ago that a plateau, of its very nature, was merely a step on the land's aspiring way to higher elevation. Sometimes, he recalled, the passing eons wore that step down to a mere pleasant slope; and sometimes it was . . . a step. A fairly high one, in many cases. One might even call part of it a cliff.

Which Indo did, a third time.

And which cry also explained why the black riders had been chasing them as they had, and were now slowing down, arms waving in triumph, heads thrown back in delight—it had all been a simple herding operation, cleverly designed to kill three birds and a horse with one stone.

He looked over his shoulder.

In the near distance, and too damned close for his taste, the sky had become hazed with a glittering, multicolored mist. A mist that seemed to rise from the very earth itself, until he remembered with a shudder Indo's idle mention of a gorge at the Plateau's southern end; a gorge no doubt formed by the timeless savage flow of the River Nunby, which even now must be in an aquatic turmoil unseen since the formation of the planet which he was now poised to fall off of.

George flogged the horse with one of his mustaches, and some minutes later the beast began to turn.

Slowly.

The black riders cheered.

Too slowly.

The beast's speed and bulk, its momentum, and its excitement, all conspired to prevent the miraculous turn on a dime Jerico had fervently been praying for. And Indo, he noticed without much enthusiasm, was kicking the creature fiercely while at the same time pointing to the drop ahead as if the horse had better make up its mind soon.

And still the animal continued to veer, in a great wide arc Jerico saw instantly was not going to be sufficient unto the saving thereof.

George had evidently come to the same conclusion, about the time the first droplets of the mist began falling on their shoulders. He patted his beast lovingly on the head, gathered his mustache, and jumped, rolled, and came to his feet in a battle-ready position.

Indo did the same, though he fell once or twice trying to get out of the tangles of his cloak.

Jerico watched them dwindle, braced himself,

jumped, and was yanked back onto the horse because his hand was caught in the white belt.

"Hey!" he called, pointing to his predicament, and cursing his charisma when both men, openly weeping, saluted his courage for going down with the horse.

Great, he thought, and tried to slice the belt apart with his sword, a desperate move that, combined with the rolling and bunching of the animal's back muscles, served only to nick its hide, make it squeal, and make it run even faster.

It didn't, however, part the belt or shorten the arc.

The gorge grew nearer, and he heard, over the thundering feet, even more thunder. Water thunder. A tumbling, battering thunder that suggested all too clearly the prevailing odds against simply leaping into the river and swimming away.

The mist fell more heavily.

The horse grunted in its desperation, slamming the ground with its trunk in an apparent attempt to knock its path more safely eastward.

Jerico slapped himself in frustration, and again when he saw the black riders reach and surround his two compadres, whips high for killing blows. He looked away. He looked back, but the mist had formed a foglike curtain before him, and all he could see was one rider still coming after him.

To make sure I'm dead, he thought bitterly.

The horse turned a bit more.

Jerico looked to his left and saw, with more clarity than he believed a man of his decent nature had a right to, the edge of the gorge. It was a ragged rock-strewn brown scar that jutted indecently away from the Plateau, and beyond, completely obscuring the opposite side, billowing roiling clouds of prismatic mist, dispensing rainbows within rainbows, glinting and winking and altogether so beautiful that he decided that maybe this wasn't going to be all that bad.

Oh, the dying would be terrible, no question about it, but it was better than being raked by an armacon or branded by a blue monk with fire in her eyes.

Falling to one's death in the very place that gave birth to colors like that would be, he thought, as a valiant Viking being taken by a Valkyrie to the crystal halls of Valhalla—when you have no choice, what the hell.

He braced himself.

The horse thumped its trunk.

The black rider came abreast of him, not ten yards away.

Jerico checked the edge again, saw over it, into nothing.

Oh, he thought.

The horse shuddered.

The rider waved.

And Jerico realized that the edge, instead of vanishing beneath the horse's feet, was running alongside. No nearer, no farther, and he yelled his relief as the animal ran full-tilt along the gorge's lip, avoiding the rocks and partially buried boulders which might, at any time, send it and its rider plunging into oblivion.

Jerico wanted to kiss it, but he wasn't sure of the protocol in situations like this. Rather, he turned, drew his sword, and mockingly saluted the black rider, who rose in his saddle in visible fury, drew a bow from his side, nocked an arrow, and shot the horse in the rump.

The left rump.

Which made the horse leap away from the stinging, just far enough to plant its hind foot on a slippery rock. It skidded. Jerico grabbed the belt with his free hand, which he realized wasn't free at all but had the sword in it, which nicked the device just enough to permit the horse's frantic scramblings to split it even more.

Suddenly the horse lunged to the left.

The belt parted.

Jerico grabbed for it and missed, then tried to grab some of the animal's hide, but the mist had made it slick, and when the creature lunged again, Jerico fell, hit the ground, and rolled into the gorge.

21 Reviewing his life thus far was not something Jerico was eager to make a habit of, especially when said review kept cropping up at times when, in the normal course of events, he should be dying. And there had been, for him, far too many such instances of late, which was making his thus-far life less dramatic and uplifting than a stultifying bore.

Nevertheless, as he clung unexaggeratedly precariously to the edge of the ledge lying just below the gorge's ragged lip, his feet struggling for purchase, his arms bulging in their effort to keep him from falling, he supposed he shouldn't search too hard for cause to complain. Especially when he dared a look down and saw nothing but an unnerving thick mist. Somewhere below that rainbow enticement was the River Nunby. That river was either disrupted by an awesome waterfall, or by rapids which made those outside Fadfy look like ripples.

There were most certainly a lot of rocks.

There most definitely was no net.

And oddly, the thunder he'd heard on the Plateau had now muted to a soft, almost weeping sound, like a tone-deaf wind hunting a recognizable melody in wind chimes on a back porch in summer.

It was driving him up the wall.

And so thinking, and when his grip began to slip and his muscles began to tire, he grabbed, snatched, grunted, and finally flopped onto the ledge, rolled onto his back, and gulped for the air his lungs demanded.

Mist beaded on his brow and matted his hair to his scalp; the clothing so generously given him by Winngg Indo was dark with dampness; and the scaled armacon cloak was sodden despite its usual rejective properties.

He sneezed.

He shifted to his side and winced at a twinge of pain that reminded him that falling onto a ledge, however incredible and life-saving, was hurtful.

Alive, he reminded himself as he struggled to his hands and knees; you're alive, and it's up to you now to get on with it.

Easier, he thought five minutes later, said than done.

His preliminary exploration proved that the ledge was undeniably large enough—a good fifteen or twenty feet long by eight or nine feet wide—to prevent him from falling again if he were cautious and didn't step over the side; a long part of it cut deeply into the cliff face itself, thus offering him a modicum of mistless comfort; and it was, by his estimation, less than ten feet from the top, an easy climb for those with the proper equipment and the frame of mind to ignore the fact that the rock wall was dripping wet and as slippery as a bar of soap in a fourteen-foot bathtub.

It was, without question, a situation.

By lying on his stomach then and inching himself to the gorgeward edge, he noted that there were, as well, any number of convenient outcroppings and sodden brush branches that would make climbing in the opposite direction not exactly an effortless task, but a possible one, if he ignored all common sense and the prospect of falling, plummeting, and eventually dashing himself to death on the unseen terrain below.

"Well, Dove," he said as he stood and wiped the water from his face, "it definitely looks as if you have a situation here."

His eyes widened.

He blinked away the droplets clinging to his lashes.

Someone stood at the top.

"I'll be," he said.

It was a black rider, who at that moment chose to whip off his black hood, revealing beneath it a surprise that nearly knocked Jerico off his feet.

"You!" he cried, unsure yet if he should be angry or pleased.

"You said it," replied Rhonda Placker. "How the hell did you do that?"

He looked around him. "I fell on the ledge."

"Yes, but why didn't you fall all the way down?"

"Because I fell on the ledge."

"Well, how the hell did it get there?"

He was beginning to suspect that her tone was not as bantering and well-meant as he'd first imagined. "Geologically, I suppose it was created by—"

"Hell," she said.

Considering the circumstances, he wasn't inclined to argue.

With an expression of what obviously couldn't have been disgust, she balled up her black hood and tossed it over the side, past the ledge, into the mist. "Jerico," she said flatly, and apparently could say no more beyond a mute shake of her head.

None too soon it occurred to him that she had somehow managed to ingratiate herself with the black rider leader, pretending to be one of them in order to effect his rescue—without realizing that he needed no rescue except off this ledge. This quite naturally put the lie to Buck Fye's assertion that the Placker family was in league with Joquinn, and so he waited several impatient minutes for her to throw him a rope.

She didn't.

She only shook her head again and walked away, returned, looked down, and when he waved, walked away a second time.

He began to wonder if this was the man with the white cane all over again.

"Hey!" he shouted, hands cupped around his mouth.

Rhonda peered over the edge.

"A rope!" he called, and pantomimed climbing to safety.

She disappeared.

Not to mention, he added to that previous thought, the German shepherd.

Yet he refused to allow despair to color his shifting comprehension of her inexplicable behavior. She had, after all, made a certifiably dangerous journey into the real world as he knew it in order to locate him, had fought beside him against the Nessars, and had even behaved tenderly toward him at some point or other. Didn't that mean there was, beneath that seemingly cold exterior, the beating of a human and humane heart?

"Help me, Rhonda," he cried then. "Help! Help me, Rhonda, for the love of Ralph!" Or whatever.

A rock landed at his feet, bounced, and vanished into the mist.

He frowned.

Another rock landed on the ledge, and this time bounced under the overhang.

Since it was apparent she had no rope, it was quite possible she was dropping the rocks to him, not at him, so that he might somehow build himself his own way to scramble to the grass above.

Her face appeared without warning. "You still there?"

He gave her a fist of victory and called, "Get me out of this—"

The third rock was considerably bigger than the others, so much so that he had to dodge it in order not to be struck; and he reminded himself glumly that the German shepherd had been toothless, a fact that did not, at the moment, seem germane to his situation, but nevertheless sent him scrambling under the overhang when she threw two down in the next volley.

There was no doubt now that it was going to be a long night.

I'll say this for her, he thought later, hands wrapped about his knees, knees drawn to his brooding chin; she's certainly persistent.

The ledge was as littered as if a high school picnic had passed through, the rocks growing smaller with time, then larger again as she found her second wind.

The sun had set some while ago, and though he had no means to provide himself with light, Rhonda had somehow jammed into the ground a row of torches which burned with such preternatural intensity that their glow made it seem as if he were spotlighted on a stage.

Her arms must be killing her.

He considered the possibility of reinforcements, and dismissed it when she called down with a raucous laugh not to go away, she was taking a break and would be right back. She gave him no opportunity for negotiation, pleading, or some extemporaneous groveling; one moment she was there, the next moment she was gone, and he was left to listen to the chimes of the gorge soften even further as the stars he couldn't see rose in the sky above the mist.

And with no place to go, he decided that sleep would probably be the best thing for the nonce; it would invigorate him, clear his mind, and regain the strength lost in the flight, the fall, and the subsequent bombardment.

Thus, drawing his cloak snugly about him, he pressed hard against the wall, closed his eyes, and used his heroic will to gather his dreams into an interlude of soporific peace.

Jerico.
He moaned.
Jerico, it is I, your beloved.
His hand brushed across his cheek.
Jerico, you must listen to me. It is I, your darling Eglantine.
He groaned.
Jerico, please wake up!
His left leg kicked out, struck rock, pulled back.
Jerico, please, for your sake, please wake up!
He shifted his shoulder.
Jerico!
He snored.
Nuts.

A stone bounced off his knee. He shifted without fully waking and silently told his mother he was getting tired of this game; and besides, he didn't really believe her claim that Poe always practiced what he wrote before he wrote it.

* * *

The ledge collapsed under the weight of all the rocks, and he plunged into a Stygian hell, buffeted, belted, battered by the unknown that tore off his flesh and ruined his good shoes. When a part of him recalled that he no longer had his shoes, he wept for the loss of a cobbler's dream, given tongue by a man who turned out to have no soul.

He dreamed the same thing again and told himself he was sick.

Jerrrriccccoooooo
His left arm covered his eyes; his right arm held the cloak.
Jerrrriccccooooooo, I'm naaaaaaaked.
He groaned.
Jerr—
He moaned.
Jerico, please—
He swallowed hard and . . .

. . . his eyelids snapped open, his hands clutched at his chest, and his mouth felt as if someone had swabbed it with reconditioned cotton.

"Lord, what a nightmare," he muttered as he rubbed the sleep from his eyes. Bad enough he was stuck on a ledge being pelted by a vengeful woman; now he was given to adolescent dreams about his mother, and the luscious, if currently insubstantial, Dawn. It was a torture he was not willing to repeat, and once he had come fully awake, he sat up, hit his head on the overhang, sat back, and examined his surroundings for signs of improvement.

The ledge was covered with rocks; the glow of the torches was still reflected off the mist; and the mist was still in the gorge.

He was still on the ledge.

And so was Rhonda Placker.

As quickly as his tangled cloak would permit, he scrambled to his feet, arms loose, fingers flexing. "So," he said.

"You're a hard man to pin down," she told him, and drew a dagger from her waistband.

"You lied to me," he said, sidling to his left.

She pouted. "I most certainly did not."

He continued his stealthy move. "By not telling me the truth, you have committed a sin of omission, which is no less damning than a sin of commission."

The dagger turned slowly in her hand, its edge more than adequately bragging how sharp it was. "And how do you know," she asked, "that it is I who am lying? How do you really know that those Ralphites are the ones telling you the truth?"

He paused. "Because I have an instinct for these things."

She laughed.

"And," he added, "because I have heard the truth from the lips of one who would not tell me falsehoods."

She laughed again, and the dagger spun this time.

He leaned forward. "Dawn."

She looked up.

"Eglantine," he expanded.

She stared. "You're kidding." Her cheeks swelled as she blew out a slow breath. "Well, I guess you know I lied then."

"Which means?" he asked, on the move again and forcing her to turn with him, her back now to the rock wall.

"That I didn't tell the truth."

"No," he said, a swift check showing him the dangling rope down which she had climbed while he'd been dreaming. "I meant, what are you going to do now?"

Her face, dampened by the mist and set a golden glow by the torches, saddened. "Death, I suppose."

Which was precisely as he'd suspected. The problem now was whether to simply disarm and capture her, or dispatch her so that she would never be able to bother him again. It was a difficult choice. He flipped a mental coin, and grimaced when it dropped into the river.

Rhonda, meanwhile, took hold of the rope, gave it a yank, and smiled. "I was going to use this, you know," she said, pointing the dagger at him, "but I think I'll let you do the honorable thing instead."

"I shall never!" he declared, shocked by the suggestion.

The rope began to shorten, and Rhonda began to rise. "Is that so?"

"Good heavens, woman, do you take me for a fool?"

She sighed, wiped the blade on her hip, which gave him a moment's unseemly palpitation, then drew back and threw it.

His reflexes ducked Jerico easily out of the way of the spinning, humming dagger, and reacted again when his feet slipped out from under him and he felt himself falling. It wasn't until he realized that his hands would probably have been better in gripping the ledge's edge that he knew that he was once again embarking upon an adventure, the multiplicity of which in this damnable land was beginning to get him down.

22 It wasn't the falling so much as it was the not knowing where he was going to land that let him decide it was all right for a hero to scream his lungs out. Which he did until those same reflexes which had betrayed him before now flung his arms over his head, which was now aimed downward; he gasped as he plunged into water considerably lower in temperature than the mist it created.

Immediately, he turned the dive into a slow, upward glide, hoping that the bottom was not too close at hand. If it was, he was dead; if it wasn't, he had a chance to reach the surface and take one more sweet breath before deciding what to do next.

The bottom cooperated, but when his head broke the surface, he barely had time to fill his lungs before he was under again. Struggling against the current he battled his way up once more, toward what he hoped was the shore, because the light was too faint for him to see anything besides the river and his stroking arms.

It was; and it was also steep enough to prevent him from climbing out.

Struggling again, and battling.

Until, with his arms weakened and his legs severely bruised by constant batterings against submerged rocks, he discovered a small pebbled beach onto which he gratefully crawled. And collapsed. And passed out.

When he awoke, he gagged, retched, and passed out again.

When he awoke, he shivered, quaked, pulled his feet out of the water and sat against what felt like a sheer wall of rock. It was impossible to say, for the light at the bottom had grown no brighter. There were only dim shapes and dimmer shadows; even the mist was only felt as it collected on his brow.

And the thunder was gone; the chimes were gone; there was only the gentle burbling like unto a small country stream, a sound that belied the fearsome power that had nearly killed him minutes before. He did not question it; it would have made no sense to do so. He wished instead for warmth; what he got was a clammy reminder that his clothes were soaked, and his hair wasn't so dry either. So he rose, swung off the cloak, checked for something he might use to provide heat, and found only a small paddle.

Why, he wondered, am I not surprised?

He searched next for a collapsible boat, or even something the maker of the garment thought was a boat. But there was nothing. Not even a scrap of paper he could origami into shape.

"Well," he said, "shit."

And slammed the cloak against the rock in frustration, strode to the river's edge, and glared at it. "I am," he announced suddenly and loudly, "getting annoyed!"

There was no echo.

The river swept past without so much as a sidelong splash.

He frowned and decided he was tired. Rest, then, because in the morning he was going to have to figure a way to ride the river out of the gorge. For surely, even in this misbegotten place, a gorge couldn't last forever.

He stomped back to the cloak, which was a bitch to unfold to refold into bedding because the scales had somehow managed to lock themselves into a shape that would have made him feel as if he were sleeping in the bottom of a supremely uncomfortable canoe.

By the time he was settled, he was puffing and swearing; by the time his eyes finally closed, he was reasonably calm; and by the time he sat bolt upright and nearly strangled himself when the cloak didn't shift fast enough, it was too late to do anything because he was already exhausted.

In the morning, he told himself; I'll kick myself in the morning.

Which he did when his feet tangled at the hem as he forgot where he was and tried to bound out of bed. He fell. He cursed. He grabbed up the goddamned cloak and made to throw it against the wall to teach it a lesson.

Then a slow and sly smile parted his lips, and he settled himself again, sifting through the myriad pockets for a bite of this and a sip of whatever the hell that godawful stuff was. And once breakfast was over, he made a careful examination of his immediate surroundings.

The paddle still lay on the pebbles, and when he examined it closely, he saw that it had been manufactured in a telescopic way so that when he pulled it gently, it grew longer, and would evidently continue to do so until it was the proper length for his arms and stroke.

And the light was at last in his favor. Though the mist still hid sky and sun, there was sufficient mistglow to see that, upriver, the river flowed so rapidly it appeared not to move, and so powerfully that it had smoothed the gorge's dark walls to glassine perfection.

Directly opposite his pebbled beach, a good quarter mile across, the walls settled directly into the water. There was no beach that he could see.

But downriver the height of the gorge seemed measurably lower, and a bend was less than two hundred yards away. He shuddered at the thought of being swept around that curve; the water appeared to sweep up against the far wall before setting back into its banks. The current would have brought him there. The rock would have smashed him, or scoured him so raw that his tailor would have thrown up his hands at getting a good line.

"All right," he said then. "All right, hit the road."

He stood, performed a few brief exercises to chase the kinks from his limbs, and picked up the cloak. He turned it over in his hands, looked at the wall, and prayed as he never had before that his previous angry act hadn't resulted in a fluke.

He threw the cloak.

The cloak fell to the beach.

"Hmm," he said.

It still looked like a cloak lying on the beach.

By the sixth throw he had worked up a fairly decent sweat, a few new words that made his ears burn with shame, and the idea that flukes were things that ought to damned well stay on fish.

It was when he kicked it that he spotted the outlines of the canoe; it was when he picked it up and made a few adjustments that he realized that the scales that had slid and slipped him down Indo Mountain could indeed slide and slip him over the Nunby.

"O Lord," he prayed as he carried it to the water's edge, "let not Thy heroic servant screw it up again."

He placed the canoe on the surface, placed the paddle on the bottom, and suggested to his trembling hands that this was no time to get the shakes. He eased one foot inside. He leaned over and saw that the craft barely sank below the surface; a swallow, a longing glance at dry land, and he swung the other foot in, settled instantly on his knees, and gasped when the current took the canoe and sped it away.

A moment of panic as the dark walls blurred past and he thought the boat was tipping; and another to blow on his palms, snatch up the paddle and spear it into the river, where it was almost wrenched from his grip before he remembered the current's awesome power.

After that, he found both stroke and steering that kept him up with the Nunby's speed without losing control. It was almost too easy, and he reminded himself to stay as close as he could to the righthand shore—there were no beaches, but it was better than the boulders that were popping up along the left.

The bend made him whimper—as the river flowed up the gorge wall, he paddled furiously to avoid the higher elevation, knowing that failure would result in a centrifugal thrust that would have him out of the water and into the hereafter before his feet got wet again.

But once that was behind him, the river slowed, the gorge lowered, and the walls became more rough and ragged, spotted here and there with tenacious shrubs and courageous flowers that alleviated the dark with welcome splashes of color.

He relaxed without relaxing vigilance.

And he wondered, as the mist cleared and he held his face up to the sun, what in god's name he was going to do now.

As the walls continued to diminish and sprout vegetation, the day brightened, the sun warmed, and he was soon overwhelmed by a not unpleasant feeling of lassitude. The pace of the river had slowed to a virtual dog paddle. Birds of indeterminate nature soared and glided overhead. Reeds began to clog the shallows. Fish splashed. Insects buzzed. And it became no effort at all to steer the canoe, since the current was now only just strong enough to carry him along, to permit him to rest the paddle and his arms, and simply watch the scenery.

He yawned.

The Nunby widened, becoming placid, smooth, and deep. Cool, clear, and refreshing. Stretching on for many gentle, meandering miles, and no sign of anyone or anything in determined pursuit.

Lunch was some pepperoni stuff he pulled from the canoe's side, and several quick palmfuls of fresh water.

The sun was high when he finally trusted the river not to sneak up on him unawares and belt him with rapids; and with a sigh he stretched out as best he could in the canoe's bottom, head cradled comfortably on one arm, the other hand gripping the paddle lest he need leap to his knees and steer himself from danger of a sort he didn't want to think about since he doubted he'd be able to vanquish a foe simply by yawning again and stunning him with his teeth.

He dozed.

The Nunby rocked and soothed him.

He considered his next move, and dozed again. The hell; there wasn't a next move. Or even one after that. He hadn't the slightest idea where he was, where he was going, or where Kyroppig lay in the geographical scheme of this remarkable land. It was as if his heroship had been discarded like an old snakeskin, and he was little more than a tourist without a bus or guide, map or brochure; it made him feel naked.

And when an eager voice hailed him from the lefthand bank, it was several seconds before he could rouse himself from his depression, lift his head, and see a figure dancing excitedly in the low grass. He squinted. He sat up. He shaded his eyes. He grabbed the paddle and aimed for the shallows.

It was George Jambo, and he was alive.

"You're alive!" he said happily once he'd plowed through the reeds and leapt to solid ground.

"Your boat," George said, and Jerico plowed back through the reeds and dragged it back. Once there, he kicked it a few times, shrugged at the sound of breaking glass, and swept the cloak around his shoulders, where it settled with a form-fitting ripple.

"You're alive!"

George smiled and shook his hand warmly. "Only through your magnificent sacrifice, sire."

Jerico was puzzled.

"Which is to say," the gardener explained, "that when you charged off like that on my one and only and awfully valuable horse, those Joquinnites who had cleverly surrounded Indo and myself realized quite quickly that we were not the designated target of their ire."

"You weren't?"

George lowered his head. "I'm sorry, sire. And ashamed at not being the designated target of their ire, which surely would have drawn them from your trail and thus permitted you to live."

Jerico put a hand on the other man's shoulder. "George," he said, "if you were a designated target, you would be dead by now."

George fussed with his mustache for several seconds. "I would, wouldn't I?"

"And I was not chased."

George tucked one end of his mustache thoughtfully into his mouth. "Oh," he said. "So where's my horse?"

"I don't know. I fell off a cliff."

The two men moved on, George explaining with much spirited gesticulation and woeing how he and Indo had slipped away from their slipshod captors during the night, each in his own direction. He had heard nothing about the riders' plans, nor did he dare venture a guess.

And once gone, George had decided that the best thing would be to head straight for Gubs in the faint hope that Jerico might have somehow survived. Of his brother and Jini he had no knowledge. Of Indo he would only say that the block-man had a mind of his own.

"I see," Jerico said. "So where is Gubs?"

"Straight ahead," George said ominously. "Beyond the shores of the Miteyose Mas."

When Jerico asked, inwardly wincing, he was told that Miteyose was a name, and Mas was a Robswerran designation which meant, in rough translation, either pretty big lake or damned small inland sea. It was, in fact, the body of water into which the Nunby flowed when the rains that usually fell quite heavily at this time of the year kept the river filled; otherwise, it was the body of water which had a long dirt road leading to it. In addition, the Mas was surrounded by the dense Miteyose Forest, through which travelers had been traveling, and vanishing, for as long as George could remember. Most people used the river. Those who didn't walked around.

"Monsters?" Jerico asked.

"No one knows. You go in, you don't come out."

23 Monsters, Jerico thought, and considered his options: walk through the Forest and save time, and maybe not survive; walk around, which would take several days and nights no matter what direction was taken; or go across Miteyose Mas, which meant that one had to have first the transportation, and second the stomach.

Jerico checked the position of the sun, which was still in the sky and rather close to the horizon back in the gorge's direction. "Let me see . . . if we start off in the canoe now, will we make it to the Mas before dark?"

"I doubt it, sire. It will take several hours even with strong paddling."

"All right." He pointed to a grove of white-leaved, green-barked trees on a rise far off to their left. "Then we'll camp there for the night and start out in the morning."

"But—"

"But me no buts, George," he said emphatically. "We'll camp, rest, and be fresh as daisies for the challenge on the morrow."

So saying, he marched confidently away from the river, smiling as George followed, humming.

The grove was dense, its white foliage casting such shade as to prevent the growth of a single blade of grass within its uneven perimeter. And, as Jerico neared it, the overall sensation was one of being closely watched; he wondered if perhaps he'd missed something in George's reluctance to spend the night here.

Nevertheless, he did not stop until the gardener cut himself off in midhum. When he looked around, George was staring past him. When he turned back and looked at the nearest tree, he could see nothing but tubular leaves, scaly bark, and branches that jutted at right angles from the trunk.

"Sire," George said, his tone apprehensive, "I am not from these parts, but they say that those who deliberately provoke the whitetrees are asking for more trouble than they can handle."

"Is that so?"

One of the trees moved.

"I believe so, yes."

"Are you trying to tell me that these . . ." He glared at the trees; none of them moved. "That these trees are *alive*?

"More than you know," George replied, hastily backing down the slope.

"Nonsense."

A tree moved.

Jerico snapped his head around, eyes narrow, lips taut. Then he turned his gaze slowly toward the river.

A tree moved.

His head whipped around again, and he saw the

roots poking out of the ground—large, brown, and knobby. They hadn't been there before.

"Sire?" George said, backing away, "can you kill a tree?"

"Only by quoting Joyce Kilmer, I think," he answered, drawing his sword and backing up himself. But not as rapidly; he didn't want whatever lived up there to think he was afraid.

"Sire!"

"Oh, for god's sake," he snapped, "what the hell is it now? Are we being attacked by hungry weeds? Voracious acorns? Seditious seeds?"

"No, sire. Black riders."

The enemy swept out of the north, a dozen of them, their razor-whips cracking and slashing, swords flaring red as the sun touched the horizon. Their approach had been on the far side of the grove, and their silence indicated they had walked their mounts as close as they dared before beginning the charge.

It was clever.

Jerico saluted their ingenuity, whirled, grabbed Jambo's arm, and raced to the river. It was their only hope—if the riders could be made to dismount their distressingly large beasts, he was sure he and the thorn-wielding gardener could make good account of themselves; if, however, they were encircled, they would probably have just as much chance of being squished as skewered.

The idea gave him a headache.

The riders spurred their mounts to greater speed, shrieking their battle cries and demanding that the fleeing men stop, be counted, and be taken prisoner without harm.

Right, Jerico thought, and abruptly angled to his left, heading for a large bush only a few feet from the river. A stand there might be feasible.

George saw his intention and changed direction too.

The riders saw their intention and kicked their mounts with their heels, many of them standing and nocking arrows into bows they'd pulled from their cloaks.

The bush moved.

Jerico ran harder.

An arrow thunked just behind him and made him jump.

The bush moved.

George faltered but did not stop.

The bush moved a third time just as Jerico caught up with it, and skidded to a halt when Giles leapt to his feet with a yell and a brandished dagger.

"Jesus!" Jerico yelled as he fell back.

"You do me too much credit, sire," the cook said, blushing, then whirling to face the oncoming horde.

In turn, Jerico held his sword ready as he sidled toward the river, explaining quickly what had happened, what was happening, and what was about to happen if those riders had their way.

Giles laughed, and his blackstone flared.

George laughed, and his purplestone flashed.

Jerico braced himself and, as the riders divided their force, darted between the two assigned to him, pinking one man's leg, the other's thigh, and raking his blade along the meaty haunch of a horse. The animal reared, and its rider fell, bounced, and lay still. The third man turned sharply and charged again. Jerico wiped the sweat from his eyes and eyed the white trunks that were now beating a death march on the ground. He wondered if the appendages were vulnerable to attack; when the enemy reached him, he darted between the beasts again, ducking under the razor-whips just after slashing at the trunks. One horse screamed and kept on running; the other one simply turned on a radius Jerico had thought previously impossible, and charged again.

There was no chance of avoidance now.

The rider laughed and twirled his whip over his head.

Jerico waited, but not for long. The animal thundered on, Jerico threw himself to one side, and felt a painful burning on his leg just before he fell.

The horse turned again.

Jerico saw blood on his calf, and the mess it made of his Indo-given trousers.

He limped to his feet.

The rider snapped out his whip, and Jerico was just able to part it with his blade before one horse-knee cracked into his side. The air in his lungs vanished; the pain in his leg was as nothing to the pain that erupted across his chest; and when the single-minded horse spun around again, he pushed to one knee and waited. Bleary-eyed. Gasping. Watching the beast turn again. And again. Four and five times before he realized that the trunk, far from being a biological breathing apparatus, appeared to be in fact a directional one.

The elephantine creature ran itself dizzy.

The black rider atop it finally jumped clear and ran away.

Jerico wanted to give chase, but he could barely move. And was glad of it when the rider raced up the rise, was grabbed by a whitetree's prehensile root and tossed into the upper reaches of its branches. A leaf or two fell. A few seconds later, a boot, a whip, and what he hoped was only the man's patent leather belt.

Well, he thought. Well.

Then he pivoted on his knee and saw the brothers sitting by a campfire next to the river. Something boiled in a small pot while George strummed his mustache and hummed.

"Hey," Jerico called.

Giles looked up and waved.

"Hey!"

George stopped his strumming.

"Hey, goddamnit!"

He was pleased when their respective eyes widened at the sight of him—the blood, the ravaged clothing, the sweat, the untidy hair—and allowed himself to sag when they ran to him with self-deprecatory anguish.

And when they reached his side, he smiled, told them what he thought of their support, and passed out because, all things considered, it was better than listening to them discuss removing one shinbone to replace what was evidently a broken rib.

He dreamed he was drowning until he woke up in the rain.

"We thought you knew the horses were blind," Giles said as he stirred a sweet-smelling broth in his pot.

"Of course we did," George protested. "Do you think we would have let you take on three of them if we didn't?"

"How would I know?" Jerico asked from the half-tent he'd kicked his cloak into. He groaned. His rib ached; his leg was bound with the same cloth as the trousers; his head throbbed; and his hip was in Manitoba.

"That's why you always go for the trunk," Giles said, leaning over the steaming liquid and sniffing, closing his eye, picking up a pinch of grassroot and dropping it in. "Always the trunk."

"Jini," Jerico said then.

Giles lowered his head and wiped a tear from his cheek.

Jerico put a hand to his forehead. "She's dead?"

"No," the cook replied. "It is . . . much worse."

Jerico waited for the explanation, and when it didn't come, he dug a stone from the ground and threw it, pleased when it struck the long-haired man square on the shoulder. "She's wounded? Captured? Tortured? What?"

George patted his brother's back. "It seems, sire, that Giles, who is too overcome to do anything but cook, led our leader from the cabin. But not far enough. The Joquinnites caught up with them and engaged them in fierce battle. Several riders were killed. Several more fled, but there were too many of them."

"I see," Jerico said. "So she was captured, and you managed to escape in order to continue the fight."

Giles lifted his shoulders. "If you say so."

Jerico frowned. "But isn't that right?"

"Some of it is."

"Which part?"

"The captured part," Giles snapped. "Are you happy now? Are you happy you've browbeaten the truth from me?" He jumped to his feet and shook off his brother's arm. "Are you happy that you've forced me into revealing me for the bounder, the cad, that I am? Are you happy, sire, that I am exposed to the entire—"

George yanked him back down. "But that's what you told me."

"Well . . ."

"You lied?"

Giles' lips trembled. "I was so ashamed."

Jerico yawned.

"The truth is, they let me go. To find you and tell you that if we don't desist in our attempts to regain the Most Holy Spears, they'll . . . Oh, sire, they're going to kill her!"

George placed a spoon in his brother's trembling hand. "You did the best you could, Giles. No man could have done better."

"I could have hit one of them maybe."

"Well, that's true, but they were mean."

"Oh, they were horrid!"

"Where are they keeping her?" Jerico asked.

"And they were," George continued, "probably really rotten."

"Where," Jerico asked, "are they keeping her?"

Giles looked over and swallowed, hard. "I'm not sure. But if we show ourselves within ten miles of wherever it is, they're going to rip her face off."

Jerico nodded, and to prevent Giles from feeling any more badly, he explained that it was an empty threat, because he knew that they knew that he knew it was an empty one because they knew he would not stop simply to save face. He knew, too, that they knew that he knew, because by taking Jini to Kyroppig, which he assumed logically was their destination, meant that he would have to go there to save her. Which was where he was going in the first place, so nothing had changed.

And then, caught in the tangles of his own superb logic, he fell back onto his bed and decided to pass on dinner, especially when Giles said, "Here, taste this," to his brother.

George did, and frowned. "It needs something. Dirt. A soupçon. Perhaps mud."

Jerico closed his eyes.

"I wish we had some armacon tail," the cook muttered.

"Show-off," the gardener said.

Jerico slept.

And woke to a gentle rain that spattered on the river

and the roof of the tent, creating a soothing melodic sound that almost made up for the burning in his leg. He grimaced and looked to the fire, saw it was out and the darkness complete. He didn't wonder about the brothers—he could hear snoring nearby; and he didn't wonder about the black riders—if they were out there, with Rhonda, then they were out there with Rhonda and there was nothing he could do about it.

He shifted as best he could toward the back of the tent, away from the rain, and closed his eyes again.

The pain remained.

He shivered and wished the sun would hurry up.

He fell asleep.

He woke up to the aromatic signals of a steaming warm breakfast, and saw three men squatting by the fire. Two were his fellow freedom fighters; the third was dressed in a monk's blue robe, and Jerico eased his hand toward his sword, ready to spring into limping action in case the tableau had been planned for his benefit, and the brothers were actually being held prisoner.

Then the monk turned and grinned at him, and Jerico rolled out of the tent, held the sword in front of him, and said, "You, sir, are doomed. Defend yourself! Defend, I say, so that honor will triumph even if we shall fail!"

24 | "Don't worry about it, my sons," said Buck Fye when Giles and George leapt to their feet anxiously. "He always talks that way when he's excited."

Jerico ignored the slur. After taking a deep breath to bring himself under control, he stomped across the grass until he stood in front of the tall monk, glaring at the ruddy face, the redstone hat pin gleaming so arrogantly through his nose, the eyes that glittered with great good humor until, a moment later, they realized he was serious.

"Now, Jerico," he said, a palm up to calm him.

"You ran away!"

"So did you."

"But you went across the bridge that wasn't supposed to be there!"

Buck's smile became strained. "I got lucky."

"You, an Innkeeper, left Jini and I to die hopelessly among the armacon and the monks!"

The monk fingered his silver girdle. "I . . . I didn't realize . . . I didn't know . . . I—"

"Christ," Jerico muttered in alternate blasphemy, and stomped away again, to stand at the river's edge and stare with supreme pique at the opposite bank. The sky was still blanketed with clouds, but the air was clear and growing warm; a soft wind danced among the reeds and tousled his hair; an unseemly growling in his stomach suggested that eating, at this time, was probably more profitable than posing.

Damn, he thought; and it was the first good pose he'd been able to work up since coming here.

He turned; they were watching him.

"We must get to Kyroppig," he told them sternly. "Our differences must be put aside for the nonce, for the good of the Spears. And of the helpless Jini."

Buck bowed his head.

Giles and George wept.

And within three hours he was once again on the River Nunby, this time in a cleverly designed conveyance constructed not of kicked cloak, but of hundreds of supple reeds cleverly woven and tied by Fye's deft hands. It was large enough to hold the four of them comfortably as long as nobody tried to move, and its broad keel and arrowlike prow served to stabilize the craft as it rode the current and a few halfhearted rapids. Fore and aft were a number of large red sheets which, he assumed, were patches in case the boat collided with something that managed to pierce the hull. Steering was provided by a stripped sapling which Buck manned willingly; in penance, he insisted, for his desertion in Fadfy. No one argued; the sapling was a bitch to hold onto and had more splinters than an Italian government.

Jerico stood in the center, cloak taking the wind becomingly, hair swept back from his forehead, while the brothers remained in front, kneeling as they scanned the banks for signs of impending, if not potential, assault.

They traveled silently.

"I am worried," Buck said at last, shortly past midday.

"You should be," George muttered. "This thing's leaking."

Giles bailed with his pot.

Jerico put his hands on his hips in what he hoped was a more heroic stance.

"We're going to the wrong place," the monk continued.

Jerico snorted. "Kyroppig is where, as the young of my country say, the action is."

"So is Las Vegas, but Jini isn't there either."

He turned and stared. "What are you talking about?"

"The riders have her."

"Right."

"Then I must tell you that they won't take her to the Tabernacle in Kyroppig."

"Oh, really?" Jerico said, barely containing a disdainful laugh. "And where would they go then?"

Buck twiddled his nasal hat pin. "Gubs."

"You're kidding."

The monk shook his head solemnly. "No. And I would explain more, foreign hero, but I think you ought to see what I mean first. She's there. You'll have to trust me."

"Like with the bridge?"

Buck looked shamefaced, but something in his otherwise somber demeanor suggested to Jerico that, being a stranger here, he might not know everything there was to know, especially when he was only guessing half the time anyway.

"All right," he said, though his tone also said, *One more stunt like you pulled in Fadfy and you'll have to deal with me.*

Buck nodded to both messages, then cleared his throat as Jerico posed again.

"Now what?"

"These riders," the monk said. "They seem to be always one step ahead of us."

Jerico nodded curtly. That disturbing fact had not escaped his attention, but he had not yet been able to ascertain exactly how his movements had been so accurately telegraphed. There were no telephones in this land, no desertions from the ranks save one, and until the attack on the cabin, he hadn't been followed by anything except a ridiculous horny raccoon. It was a puzzle. They didn't teach puzzles at Yale. They didn't teach them at Princeton either, but since he hadn't gone there it didn't matter; for that matter, puzzles weren't taught at Harvard, but nobody cared anyway.

All signs pointed to a traitor in his midst.

He stiffened, and narrowed his eyes thoughtfully.

Unless, of course, he considered the possibility that Joquinn, some time ago, already knew he was coming because of the Plackers and quite naturally decided that he would head for Kyroppig and the source of Kyroppig's 's irritation. The only irritation. The only problem then would be discovering the route, which, he admitted glumly, he hadn't been all that ingenious in concealing. Perhaps he should have taken on some sort of disguise.

Jerico shrugged. Good ideas were a dime a dozen when you didn't need them. Besides, at the moment he was more interested in the trees that had begun to fill up the spaces between the blades of grass. It seemed that a forest was in the making, a rather extensive one if the spiked horizon was any judge and the fact that George was so nervous he was mindlessly braiding his mustache.

Yet there was still one question Jerico needed answering. "Buck," he said flatly, without looking back, "how did you find us?"

Buck cleared his throat.

"I have to know. I need to know if you are truly on my side. If I know that, then I know that I can count on you not to run away again."

Buck steered the boat away from a boulder in the center of the river.

"Buck?"

"I am praying for understanding."

"As well you should. For forgiveness, however, I trust." He squared his shoulders. "Now answer my question."

A minute passed.

George unbraided his mustache when it pulled his nose to one side and loosened a molar.

Giles hummed and rocked and sharpened his dagger on his patch.

Jerico's voice deepened. "Buck, I'm waiting."

"Your trail," Fye said quickly.

Jerico looked over his shoulder, eyes without expression.

"When I crossed the bridge I swear to Ralph I didn't know was there no matter what Jini told you, I made a boat such as this and took the river route. I knew about the cabin. I knew you wouldn't be there when I got there because I couldn't get there in time, so I kept on until I saw signs of fighting. I figured it was you or Jini, so I kept on until I got to the fire Giles had made in the middle of the night, which probably told every rider within a hundred miles where you were whenever you got to where you were going. So when I got there, to the fire, you were there, and I was there, so I figured there was no sense going any farther."

"Thank you."

"You're most welcome."

"You get to live."

From the sigh he heard, he knew the monk believed him.

The Nunby narrowed, and the reeds and shallows were slowly replaced by trees and high weedy banks, and the already gloomy day was darkened by the long thin leaves that twined from their branches and twigs like nebulous clouds of green mist. The river itself grew less deep, and various streams forked off from it, sliding into the forest in almost every direction. Every so often a bird flashed in front of them, and Jerico wondered how they managed it with feathers instead of raincoats.

"Disgusting," George said, brandishing his thorn at an obese pink one who managed to hover as it taunted them. "A little closer, you fiend, and you can be lunch."

The pink bird fled.

The only sound then was the voice of the river, and the creak of the sapling as Fye guided them under the overhanging limbs.

An hour as the mint tint deepened and pure sunlight seemed a desirous thing of the past.

Then Jerico wrinkled his nose at a stench briefly carried to him on the wind. He looked a question when Giles looked back, and the cook mouthed *Miteyose*, exaggerated a shudder, and held his dagger so tightly his knuckles paled.

Buck hummed a hymn.

The creak of the sapling; the lapping of water against the boat's stout hull.

Jerico drew his sword and examined it for faults. He

was pleased with it, though it appeared to be nothing special except for the extraordinary sharpness of the cutting edge and the beveled hilt that so perfectly fit into his grip; and he was amazed that he had been able to use it so dexterously. He'd never had one before. The wooden one his mother had made when he was nine didn't count since the hilt was sharp too and he'd almost lost his fingers before he switched it for a boomerang. Which, upon reflection, wasn't all that hot either because it never came back when he threw it, except for the time his mother showed him how, and ducked.

Nevertheless, he was gratified with its performance, and he leaned on it now and peered through the green gloom for the first sign of the lake.

"Jerico," Buck whispered, for such silence as the forest engendered seemed to dictate a soft tone.

He cocked his head to indicate he was listening.

"Don't do that."

"Do what?"

"That."

"I'm not doing anything."

"Yes, you are."

He frowned. He looked down. He saw the point piercing the deck and yanked the blade out, saw the water gushing in, and stamped his foot on it. The water slowed to a trickle, and he knew this was going to restrict agile movement should his prowess and strength be required.

"A cork would be better," the monk advised.

"What?"

"For Ralph's sake, put a cork in it!"

"But I didn't say anything!"

"Jesus," Buck muttered, and Jerico felt something strike his back. He turned slowly in order not to increase the disaster that his, not to put too fine a point on it, stupidity had created, and saw a cork floating at his heel.

He picked it up and jammed it into the hole and flexed his leg, which had begun to threaten cramp. Then he looked forward again, and saw the brothers on their feet, shoulder to shoulder, their attitude suggesting that Miteyose was soon upon them.

"The rudder," Fye said.

Jerico nodded and took the monk's place, and watched in silent amazement as the man swiftly wove together what he had thought were the reed patches, then wove their ends onto the gunwales, thus providing a low roof of sorts, a miniature open-ended cabin in the craft's center.

"Rain?" he asked when Fye was done.

"Vantolas," was the answer.

"Which are?"

"Pray," the monk said solemnly, "you never have to find out."

Jerico tightened his grip on the sapling rudder, and watched as the brothers backed slowly under the makeshift shelter. He watched further as the three men checked their weapons, said a few prayers, and did some efficacious bailing.

He checked the sky, but there was no sky to see.

He checked the river, and saw only the clear water, the rocky bottom far below, and an occasional flash of silver as tiny fish swam past in the opposite direction.

"Buck," he said.

"Sire," said Giles, "don't you think you ought to come in here with us?"

"I would if I could, but then there'd be no one to steer."

"Damn," Fye said. "There's always something, isn't there?"

"Not to worry," George told him. "You can't be expected to think of everything.

"But I'm an Innkeeper! It's my job!"

Jerico said nothing while the remonstrations and consolations continued; he could see, through the cabin, his first glimpse of the Miteyose Mas, and his breath was taken away.

25 The wind still blew, but the surface of the Mas was completely unruffled; and the forest grew right to the edge of the shore, but there were no reflections in the water of either flora or cloudy sky.

It was black; a featureless plain of utterly black water several miles wide, the only sign they were moving at all was the falling away of the river's mouth and the trees alongside it.

Jerico looked away before the hypnotic nothingness of the Mas drove his mind to seek shelter elsewhere. Yet he could not prevent his gaze from returning—to the stillness, the unbroken surface, the way the sapling seemed to be swallowed by something that in no way resembled a monster's mouth, but it was as good a way as any to describe what he was looking at, unless he likened it to an abyss over which had been stretched a sheet of microthin plastic across which they were floating toward the opposite shore.

He didn't much care for that one either.

"Sire."

A lone bird rode the warm currents high above him, its cry faint and rasping and instantly swallowed so that he wondered if he had even heard it at all.

"Sire?"

In fact, the more he studied the Mas, the more he was convinced they weren't on water at all. It could not be simply nothing, black or not, reflections or no, and it occurred to him suddenly that he was thirsty. And the Mas, being water, was probably a good source for the quenching he felt he needed.

"Sire!"

He leaned over the gunwale and examined the passing liquid, which wasn't passing at all or else there'd at least be the suggestion of a wake, which meant they were stopped, becalmed, stuck in this hideous place for the rest of time.

Trapped, in a desert of black water.

Forever.

So what was the use? Why bother? Why go on?

He hummed.

And somebody slapped him.

He whirled, sword at the ready, and was slapped again, this time so hard that he stumbled backward, was grabbed and slapped a third time and dragged under the shelter.

"Sire!" Giles said uneasily.

Jerico blinked, looked out to the Mas and the receding shore, and hugged himself as a surge of cold made his teeth chatter.

"I . . . I . . . I wanted to *die*!"

"Indeed," said Buck solemnly. "It is the Miteyose, my son. The spell it casts is powerful and seductive."

"You didn't warn me," he said, aware of how weak he sounded and humbled for the realization.

"You would have dared it," was the response.

He nodded. He supposed he would have. It was his nature not to pass up a challenge. And yet . . . had he dared the Miteyose to do its worst, he would have died. Trapped. Forever. Lost on a desert of black water. Begging to be killed in order that he might die without having to live a living death without dying. Eternity had nothing on the Miteyose and its effects, and he—

—was slapped again.

"Do that again," he said, pushing himself to a sitting position, "and I'll tear your arm off."

"Oh Lord, sire!" George cried in relief.

His smile was embarrassed, and he readily accepted a potion from Fye which he quaffed without investigating the ingredients thereof. Within minutes he was on his feet, hunched over because the roof was so low, but ready to take on anything.

"Insidious," he said. "Are we to be subjected to this the entire way over?"

"Every second," he was told. "We must be strong, Jerico. We must be ready to slap each other into next week if necessary, for it is the only way one can defeat the miasma which attacks from the very heart of the darkness you see all around you."

"How long?"

"Until dawn."

"That long?"

"You could have walked."

"I was told it was dangerous."

"That's true. In the forest you would have found yourself jumping out of trees, eating gold berries, digging for roots, crying out like a wolf in the night for a mate you can no longer have because infirmity and age force you to hunt alone, always alone, always— Jesus Christ! What the hell did you slap me for?"

Jerico grinned. "I've just saved your life."

"The hell. I was only telling you what would happen."

But Jerico only winked broadly at the brothers, who winked broadly back and cheerfully slapped the monk again.

Buck raised his fists.

Jerico interposed himself and ordered them sternly to get hold and get with it and get the hell out of his face.

They slapped him.

He slapped them back.

They decided it was best not to separate and so managed, with much slapping and pinching, to tie one of George's mustaches to the rudder in order to maintain their course while, at the same time, maintaining their equilibrium, even though Giles protested there weren't enough drugs to go around.

Hours passed.

When they began traveling in circles, it was decided just to pinch George so his head wouldn't jerk.

When night fell, they sat facing each other and told jokes, none of which Jerico understood, which was all right with him because they didn't get his either, but the least they could do was laugh politely and not deprive him of an alternate profession in case this one didn't work out, which it wasn't, so why bother going on, explaining intellectual repartee when—

—they slapped him.

Shortly after midnight, Buck was knocked out.

"Slap," Jerico scolded as George blew on his knuckles. "You're supposed to slap, you idiot."

"Sire, I am abashed."

"Not yet," he muttered.

They exchanged George's mustache for Giles' hair, and Giles wailed and threatened to get a haircut.

When the sky lightened, they exchanged Giles'

braid for George's mustache, a temporary measure since Jerico volunteered to hold the rudder once he could see well enough to keep them on course.

Giles protested.

George shook his head, and suddenly cried, "There! There! Yonder!"

Jerico followed his pointing thorn and closed his eyes in a brief thank-you to whatever gods there were in this land.

The forest was visible less than a mile ahead, clearly split by the Miteyose as it emptied into the southern reach of the Nunby. Which meant they were only a two-day journey from Gubs.

Buck roused himself from his morning devotions just long enough to suggest that they prepare themselves for action.

"My god," Jerico said, "what more can there be? Haven't we suffered enough? Haven't we been through our own personal hells for nearly—slap me, monk, and I'll girdle your loins."

Buck retreated hastily, yet continued to warn them that the forest on this side was not as innocent as its opposite number. Beasts roamed the area, and if they didn't remain alert, their unprecedented journey might well be for naught.

George agreed and took up a position at the bow.

Giles was ambivalent and so stayed near middeck.

Jerico wanted to know what the monk meant by unprecedented, and shook his head when Fye began to explain. "Forget it. I shall revel in my ignorance and not regret it in the morning."

And as they slipped off the Miteyose Mas into the river again, he looked behind him, looked ahead, and realized that soon enough, and probably too soon for his peace of mind, he and his friends would be grappling with Joquinn.

Soon enough some of them were going to die.

Soon enough the future of Kyroppig would be at last decided.

Jesus, he thought, and thought nothing more when the first monster appeared.

Actually, he decided as he prepared to brandish his sword with his free hand, it wasn't so much a monster as it was a damned ugly bird. A red-winged creature had bolted out of the trees and flew directly at the boat. Its head was grotesquely parrotlike, its three eyes obscenely wide and flaring green, its beak as long and as sharp as a well-thrust lance. It made no sound other than the thrum of its massive arched wings, which kept hitting the branches reaching over the river and knocking the bird askew, forcing it to retreat, regroup, and restart its charge.

"If it ever gets here," Fye remarked, "we're going to have a hell of a fight."

Jerico tightened his hold on the sapling, since the river had begun to flow much more rapidly, tripling the boat's speed.

The reedy banks flew by, the river widened abruptly, and the bird was no longer hindered by the trees on either side. It screamed, and charged, and with a tremendous leap, George slashed its bulbous yellow breast with the tip of his deadly thorn.

It screamed, turned, and turned again and kept on going, diving into the forest with a defiant vengeful cry that was cut off by, Jerico assumed, a chance meeting with a trunk.

Blood dripped thickly from the shelter roof. George sat on the deck, moaning, gingerly rubbing his arm, numbed by the shock of the impact. Buck quieted him with a clear balm, then joined Jerico at the stern, tucking the rudder under his arm.

"We're almost there, my son," he said, steering the boat into the center current.

Jerico breathed deeply. "I worry about Jini."

"She'll be fine, have no fear. She's a strong woman, that one, and those who have her have their hands full."

He supposed that was true. But for the first time in many days he remembered the army of heroes Joquinn had gathered, and pointed out to the monk that only four men and a captured woman opposed them. Five, if they counted Winngg. But five against several dozen wasn't much better odds.

"And then," he added, "there's the magic of the Spears."

"Agreed," Buck said, nodding. "But there is one consolation, if you will permit me, my son."

Jerico waited.

"If Joquinn had learned how to use them, he would have already. He's that kind of man. He leaves little to chance."

"You know him?" Jerico asked in surprise.

The monk grunted his disgust. "I have had the dubious pleasure. When his brother was the Most Holy." Buck lowered his head, then placed a fist to his chest. "Smarmy little bastard. Joquinn, I mean. Has an attitude problem. And if I'm any judge of character, he most likely suffers from an intense Wilfred complex."

"A what?"

"Like a Napoleon complex, only shorter."

"Ah. And when Ralph . . ."

The boat drifted on.

At midafternoon George, at the rudder, told them they were being followed. When Jerico left his place at the bow and returned aft, he saw a curved motley fin break the surface just beyond the last ripple of their wake. From the size of it, he estimated the creature below at least as large as the boat itself.

"Buck," he said. "What is it?"

"Could be a fish," the monk said. He was lying on the deck under the shelter, hands cupped behind his head, eyes resolutely closed.

The fin rose higher, and he could see a sleek grey form attached to it. He revised his estimate; the thing was twice as long as the boat and half again as wide.

"Buck," he called again, unable to conceal his nervousness.

"What!" the monk snapped.

George refused to look. His gaze was steady, though his knees were somewhat tremulous.

"It's big!" Jerico said, pulling out his sword.

"What color is it?"

"Grey. Gold stripes. With a circular fin." Suddenly its tail rose from the river and slammed down again, drenching the banks and George, who still wouldn't look. "And it's got a tail you wouldn't believe."

Buck groaned, rolled to his feet, and strolled to the stern. He glanced at the water, the fin, the tail that rose again, fell again, and sent the boat surging forward. "Oh shit, it's a peplor."

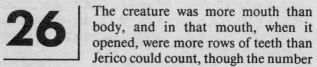**26** The creature was more mouth than body, and in that mouth, when it opened, were more rows of teeth than Jerico could count, though the number he did reach was sufficient to make him judge the distance between the boat and the nearest shore.

He didn't want to know what had once belonged to the flesh that hung in red strips from a few of the back molars.

Then Buck pulled a loaf of bread from his robe and tossed it overboard. The peplor snapped it up and swerved sharply away.

Jerico took the monk's arm as he headed back for his nap and demanded to know how a loaf of bread could satisfy such a monster.

"Hey," Buck said, brushing the hand away, "it's a fish. What the hell does it know?"

"But what if it hadn't worked?"

"If," the man said, lying down, stretching out, "it

hadn't worked, you wouldn't be asking me that question."

I am confused, he thought, but said no more until Buck relieved him at the rudder, just before dinner.

"What," Jerico asked then, "exactly happened to Ralph?"

"It's a long story," Buck said sadly.

"So?"

"He died."

Jerico sighed.

Evening fell shortly after sunset, and they tied the boat to a convenient bankside tree stump and slept on land.

The next morning they set off at dawn, the river twisting now and turning and sometimes almost doubling back on itself.

A road soon appeared on the left bank. When Jerico commented on it, Buck told him it was the Gubs road; when he suggested taking it, Giles told him that it was fraught with highwaymen; when he reminded them that they had little time to lose, George told him that since the road followed the river exactly, all the way to village, why walk when they could ride?

"I get the feeling," he said, his tone mildly disapproving, "that you are in no hurry to reach Gubs."

"Me?" said George, looking with shock at his brother.

Jerico praised himself for not throttling him and took his turn at the rudder, immediately aiming for a trio of aged windbent trees that hung over the river at the next bend.

"Sire!" Giles protested.

"Son of a bitch," Jerico said.

"Sire!" Giles complained.

But Jerico only pointed. The trees had disappeared, and part of the bank, and there were singed leaves floating to the ground and water, remnants of a silent explosion.

Instantly he changed direction while the brothers dove for the protection of the reed shelter. As the boat retook the center current, Buck stood beside him, staring southward as he scowled and fingered his hat pin. The red tip began to glow, and Fye, somewhat cross-eyed, stared at it until, at last, he looked up again and sighed.

"It is as I feared," he said.

"The Spears," Jerico guessed. "How bad is it?"

"I don't know. He missed."

"True enough. But he knew enough to do it anyway."

"Aye, he did. But we must never forget that the people of the land are with us. To a man. We do have that on our side. One more day," he added quietly. "All we need is one more day."

Another tree exploded in silence not fifty yards to their right.

"He's getting the range," Buck commented as he strode none too hastily toward the shelter.

Giles asked if anyone wanted dinner.

George remained loyally at Jerico's side, hands boldly on his hips, gaze and purplestone defiantly square on that section of the sky from which he believed the invisible bolt had originated.

A third bolt came less than fifteen minutes later, knocking a brown flying thing from the sky on its way to splitting a boulder in three pieces, quite a distance behind the boat.

A fourth bolt sent George checking after dinner.

A fifth blasted a daisy.

And when a sixth, an hour after the fifth, fizzled on a leaf of what George called a hemospice shrub, Jerico suggested that the decreased power of the last attack might well mean that Joquinn had shot his last bolt, so to speak. For the moment, at any rate.

Buck agreed, though he didn't leave the shelter.

"And it may come as a surprise to you," Jerico continued, "but none of those magical assaults came directly on the river."

He put a finger to the side of his nose. "That may be significant."

"In what way, sire?" Giles asked.

"Well, if the Nunby, being by nature water, is somehow serving as protection, then we have nothing to fear."

"But that's wonderful," the cook said. "We'll be able to get to Gubs in one piece! Oh sire, what a relief you have taken from my shoulders." He frowned. "I think."

Jerico, his modesty lifting a blush to his cheeks, only shrugged, scuffed a boot along the deck, and reminded them all that the danger was only just beginning. "We must be ever alert and on our toes. We cannot let our temporary invincibility lull us into danger."

"Right," said Buck, who lay down and fell asleep.

Jerico stared, beckoned Giles away from the pot, gave him the rudder, and walked over to the monk. He looked down. He brushed his palms over his chest and kicked the man soundly in the ribs.

Fye leapt to his feet, snorting, red-faced, hands fisted and at the ready.

But Jerico grabbed a handful of robe and yanked the man down to his size. "Look," he said tightly, "we have a long night ahead of us, Brother Fye, and I'll be goddamned if you're going to sleep it away while we stay out here and count the damned stars." He released Buck with a push. "Now get your blue ass over there and steer us to a place just upriver from Gubs. A place with a lot of trees, someplace where we can hide until morning."

"You talk big for a little man," Buck said at last.

Jerico glowered.

"And besides," the monk continued, "why land now? Why not wait until we're at the village?"

Jerico sighed. "Forgive me, Brother, or Father, or whatever it is we're supposed to call you, but hasn't it occurred to you that Joquinn knows where we are?"

"I should think that was obvious."

"And has it not occurred to you that perhaps Joquinn knows where we're going?"

"He might suspect, yes."

"And has it not occurred to you, in your Most Holy slumbers, that Joquinn suspects we will keep to the river because it offers us the only protection we have against his burgeoning powers?"

Buck thought for a moment. "It just did, yes."

"Then if we leave the river, he'll think we're still on it."

"Excuse me, sire," Giles said then. "But suppose one of those bolts hits us while we're ashore?"

"We won't be close enough," he answered. "He's hit the bank and whatever's on it every damned time. So we go inland a little way. Out of range. Out of reach. Out of sight. Out of mind."

"No kidding," Buck growled, "but it just might work."

Jerico clapped his hands. "Then let's be on with it! Fye, man the rudder! George, watch the skies! Giles, clean up that godawful stew and be ready to abandon ship at my signal! We'll tie the rudder to its current course so the boat will remain on the river—long enough, I hope, to give us time to get away. Once on land, we'll head for the protection of the nearest grove."

Jerico grinned as the men leapt to action. Adrenaline drove swiftly through his system, blood raced rapidly through his veins, thoughts tumbled chaotically through his mind, and all of it felt wonderful! He was at last in charge. He was at last doing what he was supposed to be doing. He was at last no longer playing the heroic role, but living it.

Then George said, "But what about the peplor?"

The plan, once one evolved, was so simple Jerico tended to distrust it, and would have were it not his own and so forcefully presented that the others soon agreed it was their only chance—when the time came to leave the boat, each would find something in his cloak to offer the riverbeast as an alternate sacrifice. Meat was preferable, but bread seemed to work well, and once a check had been made, all discovered that they at least had something to toss into the drink.

The bread or meat to one side, the swimmer to the other, and the remaining travelers would pound the water and such in order to cover the sounds of splashing and kicking feet.

"Sire," Giles said deferentially, "what happens to the last man? Who will cover for him?"

Jerico gripped his shoulder firmly. "My dear friend, you are not to worry. I shall be the last man. I will trust in Ralph and your genius to think of something before I'm swallowed."

Giles lowered his eyes. "That is too much, sire. I can't allow it."

"You could, you know," George told him. "He is the hero, remember, and he'd be insulted if you offered to take his place."

"Well I wasn't going that far," Giles snapped.

Try, Jerico thought.

"Nevertheless, you could have at least made the offer. It's the only proper thing to do."

Giles wavered, torn between the right thing and the smart thing; Jerico steadfastly held his smile, though a rather unsettled feeling in his stomach told him Xamoncroft wasn't going to do anything but dither around until it was too late.

"I'll stay," the cook whispered at last.

"No," Jerico told him. "I can't let you."

"Okay." He walked to the bow and stood by his brother, shrugging at the hero's bravery, while the hero wanted to grab his throat and explain that the idea was to offer three times, so that on the last the offer could be accepted without losing face.

"Well!" Fye said from the rudder. "Well, that about takes care of everything, wouldn't you say, my son?"

Jerico glared at him.

Buck winked back.

And less than an hour later, as the sun slipped from its zenith, the boat rounded a gentle bend and on the left bank, some thousand yards distant, was the grove they'd been looking for.

It huddled against the river, stretched back to the first rise, and seemed to be thick enough to offer adequate protection against the elements, magical or not. The trees were high, their crowns round and multicolored, and the birds flying through and around it indicated that there was nothing threatening nearby.

Not to birds, anyway, and Jerico sounded the call.

George was the first—he stood on the starboard side of the reed boat with his brother and Jerico beside him. He grinned wanly, took up a magnificent steak large enough to feed the four of them for three days, and took a deep breath.

Then a slap on the shoulder, a hug for Giles, and he tossed the steak into the water, spun around, and dove over the opposite side. As he did, Jerico and Giles punched and slashed the river with sword and dagger, yelled, screamed, and watched the steak sink without so much as a ripple.

"He made it," Buck announced five minutes later. "I'll be damned, the dope made it."

Giles was next, another steak his offering, and Jerico did the honors of beating the hell out of the water.

"Amazing," said the monk when the cook dragged himself dripping to the bank and waved his success. "Amazing."

Quickly he bound the rudder in place, tossed a third steak overboard, and flew from a standing position into a dive that would have wiped out a swan and six or seven goslings.

Jerico was alone.

The grove approached rapidly.

And a bolt of invisible death blasted a boulder and four chickens on the lip of the right bank.

While the fin of a peplor broke the surface at the stern, and within seconds the rudder swung wildly side to side.

Jerico didn't have to look—the sapling was rootless, the boat without steering, and Joquinn had evidently gotten his second wind.

Buck shouted encouragement from the shore, the brothers exhorted him, yet he was frozen with indecision. His men were safe, and if they didn't move soon, another one of Joquinn's messages would boil their blood. But still they refused to take cover; they stood there and waved and jumped up and down and the peplor worked on the keel with one row of its teeth.

Think! Jerico ordered himself; goddamnit, either think or swim, but don't stand there like a jerk.

He reached into his cloak and pulled out a meat loaf.

"Swell," he said.

A bolt demolished a tree.

"All right then. All right. Hit the road, Jack. Get your ass in gear."

The boat shuddered.

A bolt struck the ground not ten feet from his men, and they scattered instantly without so much as a by-your-leave, good luck, write when you get work.

Gathering the force of his cloak around him, Jerico shook himself vigorously, tossed the meat loaf at the riverbeast, and leapt into the water. Diving low, swimming hard, surfacing and shaking the water from his eyes. Then he reached out, kicked out, and looked down to see the riverbeast swimming lazily below him.

27 While hope, Jerico recalled, often springs eternal in the human breast, he himself felt nothing but a sinking sensation as the peplor slid darkly and slowly beneath him, turned, and swam back without, he suspected, even looking up. The thing's eyes being where they were, where he couldn't see them, it was hard to tell, but he had no doubts that the riverbeast knew exactly what it was doing.

He could do nothing but swim.

His arms reached, his legs slashed the water powerfully, and during his infrequent glimpses of the shore, he spotted his three companions watching him anxiously.

Fifty yards, he told himself; fifty yards more and the river will be too shallow for the thing to get you.

He stroked. He kicked. He tried to figure out how the others had reached safety so rapidly. It must have something to do with the properties of the armacon cloak, but right now it wasn't doing anything but weighing him down.

And the Nunby was cold. His fear had masked the initial shock of the water's temperature, but now it seeped into his clothes, laced his skin, belied the heat of the sun on the back of his head.

The peplor swam past him left to right, not quite as deep as it had been before.

He stroked. He kicked. He saw Buck yelling something, but the noise of his less than Olympic-class passage prevented him from hearing anything but his own labored breathing. Breathing that soon became a gasping as his arms tired and he could barely lift his legs out of the water.

Cold.

It was cold.

Forty yards.

The peplor swam past him right to left, so closely now that Jerico had to suck in his stomach to prevent the dorsal fin from tickling his navel. And then it was gone at a flick of its mighty tail, and Jerico heaved himself up, gulped for air, and settled into a calmer, smoother, but not less fatiguing variation of the Australian crawl. His right leg, however, was giving out, slowing down, and he cursed when he checked the bottom and saw that it was still too deep for him to let his feet down.

Fye yelled.

Jerico didn't bother to wave.

Giles threw a rock that nearly caught his shoulder.

Jerico swam.

Thirty yards.

George began sprinting inland, stopped, ran back, grabbed his brother's arm, and they both fled inland, angling toward the grove.

Jerico didn't need to know that another bolt was coming, and so wasn't surprised when a gout of dirt and grass exploded into the air not ten feet from where Buck was standing. What did surprise him, almost as much as the fact that he could notice all this while preparing to drown, was that the monk didn't flinch. He ducked a little, but he didn't join the others in their dash for safety.

He didn't understand.

Not until, a mere twenty yards from the bank, just as the bottom was within a few feet of his soles, he felt a slight change in the water, a surging, a gentle shove forward as though he were riding a low wave.

Oh, he thought, shit.

Though he knew he would regret it, he looked over his shoulder and saw it—the peplor had breached the surface and was speeding straight for him, mouth agape, hundreds of teeth dotted with bits of meat loaf, its dead red eyes focused directly on him. Were this another time and another place, he would have got up and left the theater, leaving his 3-D glasses behind; as it was, he stopped.

Just . . . stopped.

There was nothing else to do.

And in treading water, drifting backward as the river nudged him gently, and watching the riverbeast accelerate and ride higher, so much so that it was virtually balancing on its tail, his first final thought was of his precious Dawn, his second of his retirement now shot all to hell, and his third a swift puzzlement why he was wasting time thinking when all he had to do was dive under the creature, then swim over it to the shore before it knew what had happened.

Madness, he thought then, is the handmaiden of imminent death.

His feet touched the rocky bottom.

He swallowed and stood as tall as he could, chin high, nostrils flaring, hands gripping the edges of the cloak. Using the sword was out of the question; he wouldn't even be able to get in one good slash before he was smashed. Which left him only his dignity, his memories, and the sound of Buck bellowing hysterically on the bank.

And when the peplor's shadow at last covered him and its pitiless dive began its lethal descent, he did the only thing he could think of—he filled his lungs with as much air as they could hold, snapped up his legs, let himself sink, and in the sinking, curled himself into the tightest ball he could manage. The cloak folded over him as if it had been made for such a maneuver, and he was tumbled end over end by the force of both the dive and the thrust forward.

And he nearly screamed when he felt the first teeth close upon him.

He was shaken violently side to side.

He was squashed to a size that nearly popped his legs out from beneath the cloak's protection.

He was rolled, and battered, and rapidly losing his breath no matter how hard he tried to keep his lips together.

His head ached, his arms ached, his chest ached, his heart ached; and there were red eyes and red stars and a tight red dress and a snug red blanket and green stars and yellow stars and a mournful bubbling cry when his lungs finally released the last of his air.

In blackness there was light.

In light there was darkness.

In darkness there was noise and he wished he could sleep the endless sleep of the dead.

In the noise there was a voice, and the voice called his name, and his name sounded unfamiliar so he paid it no heed.

His name again. Louder.

The noise again. Much louder.

And the darkness gave way to the blackness which gave way to the light which stung his eyes and made them water, and burned his lips and made them chapped, and parched his throat and made him thirsty, and dried his clothes and made them dry.

"Jesus," he gasped hoarsely.

"That's the second time he's done that," Giles said in a soft wondering voice. "Does he know something I don't?"

"Perhaps," George answered, "but let's not get carried away."

"It might come in handy."

"Only if you intend to take over from Ralph."

"*Bite* your *tongue*!"

"Gentlemen." It was Buck. "Gentlemen, some restraint."

Jerico threw a trembling arm over his eyes, and there was an excited muttering. Someone placed a cup of water to his lips, and he sipped the cool liquid cautiously; someone else placed a morsel of meat in his mouth, and he chewed without tasting; someone else, unless it was the first one, gave him more water and bathed his face tenderly, crooned a rutabaga lullaby, and finally, when he shifted to ease the pain in his back, someone assisted him in sitting up.

He lowered his arm.

He blinked.

He said, "I was dead."

The clearing he found himself in was a small one, the foliage permitting just enough light for him to see the monk and the two brothers sitting cross-legged before him. Their faces were pale with relief. Their expressions were concerned. Their skin oddly flecked by the colors reflected off and filtered through the rainbow hues of the leaves. It was like peering through a stained-glass window, and the effect, while startling, was not unpleasant.

"I was dead," he said again, looking at his legs, his chest, examining his arms and touching his face. "But I don't have a single scratch."

"You did," George told him solemnly. "Tooth marks all over the place."

"Dents, actually," Giles corrected with a shy smile. "The cloak protected you."

Jerico put a palm to his forehead and rubbed it carefully. "I was in the thing's mouth." He pinched himself. "I was actually in that thing's mouth."

"Pretty much," Giles agreed.

"Close enough to call it," George said, nodding.

"But then . . ." He looked at the tree he was propped against, the grassy ground, the prismatic air. "But then . . . how?"

And he looked at Buck clearly for the first time.

And gasped silently.

The monk was bruised over every inch of his ugly face, and his right arm, its sleeve severely tattered, was nestled in a sling fashioned from his left sleeve, which left his left arm open to the air—a left arm Popeye would have sold Sweetpea for if it hadn't been for the bandages, the dried blood, and the huge yellowed tooth that protruded from his elbow. Jerico stared as Buck yanked out the tooth and calmly bandaged his arm.

Buck grinned and shrugged. "I heard once," he said, "that all you have to do is bop the sonsofbitches on the nose and they'll swim away. He doesn't hang out in the same Tabernacles I do, I guess." He shrugged again. "He was, nonliturgically, pissed."

"You saved my life," Jerico whispered.

A tree blew up near the river.

Giles glanced apprehensively over his shoulder.

"You were so close," the monk said, "I couldn't let you have all the fun, now could I?" He laughed.

Jerico laughed.

And they continued laughing until George suggested they stop their merriment, have their dinner, and get some sleep. After all, tomorrow morning they would be in Gubs, and they needed their strength for the last push for the Spears.

A tree blew up by the river.

"Tomorrow," Jerico repeated quietly.

Buck nodded. "It begins at dawn."

"Then this could be our last night together."

Giles averted his face and hurried to serve the meal; George took out a square of satin and polished his purplestone; and Buck Fye, after murmuring a prayer of grace and deliverance, walked out of the clearing, cowl up, head down.

Tomorrow, Jerico thought. Oh . . . my . . . god.

And a tree blew up, down by the river.

28 They lay on the flat summit of a low, sparsely wooded hill. Its southern slope was, Jerico noted quickly, more of a precipitous drop than a slope, something just this side of a cliff; yet its northern slope was so gentle, so unostentatious, that he hadn't known they were climbing until they reached the top. It had been an arduous journey, since he still felt as if he'd been turned into a bruise, and Buck still kept his right arm cradled in its sling. They moaned with every step. They cursed the Nunby and everything that lived in it. They tried to explain how each was more injured than the other until, at the last, they began giggling, then guffawing, then stifling their laughter with bits of meat from their cloaks.

Noon came and went.

It was, at the last, nearly the middle of the afternoon before Jerico dropped to the soft grass and looked out at the panorama of the Lower Nunby Valley. Which was, he corrected with a scholar's critical eye, not really a valley. It was more a series of foothills, some heavily forested, some lightly, which climbed one behind the other until they merged into two massive mountains whose peaks punctured the distant horizon. At the base of the western one lay the city of Kyroppig, too distant to be seen.

But closer, where the Nunby curved east toward them as it wound through the foothills, was a collection of half a hundred buildings he knew could only be Gubs. Roads led away from it in all directions; several bridges spanned the river; smoke rose from chimneys in spite of the day's heat, and he could see tiny figures in the handful of convoluted streets, tiny figures in the fields, tiny figures swimming in the water while tiny figures watched them.

"How lovely," he said.

And it was. The houses, Buck narrated, were constructed of stone quarried on the other side of the river, which explained why they weren't set in any particular pattern. Carrying all that weight was a chore-and-a-half, and most builders simply carted their share along until they were too tired to take another step. When they dropped, the house was built, the neighbors and symmetry be damned. And because the quarry was unpredictable in its supply, some of the homes were mostly green, some red, a few yellow, one or two a pretentious dark brown. The roofs were sharply peaked. The windows he could see were round. And in front of each was a wide patch of green where, he was told, each family ate its meals, played with its children, and buried its dead.

"Intriguing," he said, resting his chin on a forearm. "But with all that wood, why use the stone?"

"With all that stone?" Buck answered, "why use the wood?"

"The wood is lighter."

"Stone lasts longer."

"The wood is easier to shape."

"Stone lasts longer."

"Wood—"

"—burns."

He watched the village for nearly an hour, studying the intricacies of its patternless design. He assumed one never met a friend on a corner because there were none; he further assumed that at least some of those buildings held shops, entertainment emporia, and perhaps an inn or two where weary travelers might rest their equally weary bones, have a good meal, tickle the barmaid, and sleep in a decent bed.

It was, in fact, so perfectly peaceful that he soon grew suspicious. For a land in religious turmoil, there didn't seem to be a hell of a lot of agitation.

Where, then, was Jini?

Eventually he focused his attention on two particular buildings: the first, and nearest to them, was set apart from the others by a good hundred yards. It was also twice as big, of a gleaming dark green stone, and had several impressive square towers from which flew white-and-green banners.

"The Tabernacle of Gubs," Buck informed him. "One of the most powerful in Robswerran."

Which explained, Jerico thought, why there wasn't any visible unrest. The monks evidently had everything in hand, despite the fact that Kyroppig lay only three days' journey away.

So what about Jini?

The second building was to their left, to the east, again set apart, and notable not for its size, which wasn't very large, nor for its elaborate construction, because it was a simple unadorned square, but because it didn't have a single window that he could see, nor door or entrance or exit of any kind at all. It was a dull white with a dull red, jaggedly peaked roof. And while tiny figures occasionally passed the Tabernacle, stood before it and conversed, or went in and out, no one went near the white one.

And the ground around it was completely bare, the exposed earth a foul and most odious sort of yellow.

"Ghorfon Ghorlen," the monk said flatly.

"Rather ominous," Jerico said, "despite its pristine outer shell."

"Ominous isn't the word for it," said Giles with an uncharacteristic bite in his tone.

"It looks ominous to me."

"The word is *prison*," the cook snapped, grabbed a handful of grass and threw it angrily over the edge.

For a change, George said nothing.

Jerico did not pry. He sensed a bitterness in Xamoncroft and his brother which he did not wish to exacerbate on this most important of days. Buck leaned his head close to Jerico's and whispered, "The lad has had several members of his family in Ghorfon Ghorlen, and once you go in, you never come out."

Jerico glanced at the cook and looked away. "What did they do?"

"Nothing."

"But how could that be?"

Buck stared at the ground. "Actually, it wasn't nothing. It was something."

"It was *nothing*!" Giles insisted heatedly. "Framed, that's what they were, sire. Framed and imprisoned because they dared be their own men!"

Immediately, Jerico placed a restraining hand on the man's arm, smiled his commiseration, and suggested that they postpone further discussion of Giles' family's predicament until another, more pleasant time. At the moment, and no offense to anyone, they had more important things to worry about.

"Such as?" Giles asked, clearly insulted.

"Such as getting to Kyroppig, finding the guns, getting Jini out of wherever she's being held, taking care of Joquinn, and getting the Seven Spears back into the right hands."

"Well, if you're going to put it that way . . ."

"I am."

"You would."

"Giles!" George snapped. "Please! Remember to whom you are speaking!"

The cook sputtered, and subsided into a hair-braiding pout.

Then Jerico turned to the monk. "Jini is in there," he said without making it a question.

"Yes."

"How do you know?"

"The Ghorlen is one of their strongholds. You may have thought that all is peaceful down there. Don't believe it. Those people—*my* people—are in mortal terror."

"Damn right," Giles muttered.

So, Jerico thought, and examined the building as closely as he could from this distance. The few questions he had brought depressingly few answers—no, Buck didn't know the secret of getting in or out; no, Buck didn't know who knew; no, neither of the brothers knew either; no, Buck didn't know if any of the monks knew.

Swell, he thought.

Finally, just as it seemed that the very sight of the prison was going to send the sullen Xamoncroft into a cantankerous fit, Jerico suggested that they slip into the village at night, find a place to stay, and perhaps speak to a few of the locals. They might, if they were talkative, tell them the latest news of Joquinn and his army of heroes. They might even be so roused at the prospect of being freed from the prospect of a bitter and prolonged war which might end several of their lives that some might even join them on their crusade against the enemy, and perhaps, even provide them with a clue or two about entering the Ghorlen. Getting a key or a free pass was probably too much to hope for.

Buck immediately nodded his approval.

Giles pouted, and George slugged his shoulder.

"Then it's settled," Jerico said. And before anyone could speak further, he pushed away from the edge until he was positive he couldn't be seen. Then he sat up, brushed the grass and dirt from his clothes, and reached into his cloak to be sure his sword was still there.

"Damn!"

He sucked his finger.

Buck joined him, and soon the others as well, and they decided that the best way to infiltrate the village was to slip in one at a time. Buck would go straight to the Tabernacle and see what support he could muster from his blue-robed brothers; Giles and George would take the first tavern they came to, buy a round or two of drinks, and generally pretend to be innocents on the road, eager for news, ready to pay.

"And you, sire?" George asked.

Jerico gazed at the horizon, at the two malevolent peaks, and sighed. "I shall simply wander. A pedestrian here, a vagabond there—who knows what I may turn up?"

"Sire?" Giles said timidly.

Jerico smiled at him. "Yes?"

"I thought, and please don't think ill of me for I am only your humble and loyal servant who wants nothing more than to fight at your side for the freedom of his home and hearth—"

"Jesus," Buck muttered, "the damned thing's catching."

"—but wasn't the plan—that is to say, the plan Jini expounded to us in that ill-fated cabin—wasn't the plan for you to slip into Kyroppig alone, learn what you could, then return to us so that we may storm the citadel of evil together?"

"Well put," George said, hugging his brother and slapping his back. "Well done indeed."

"I was only trying to keep things straight."

"And you did it well. Superbly. I might even say, top notch, if I knew what it meant."

"Look," Jerico said, "I know what Jini said, but—"

"Super," said Giles. "It means super. I think."

"Well, then . . . super!"

Giles blushed.

"I really do think that my new plan, in which we are all involved to some extent, is far more efficient—"

"You know, Giles, sometimes I'm so proud to be your brother that I could just bust."

"Oh . . . silly."

"No, really. Don't you think so, Brother Fye?"

Buck rolled his eyes.

"A Most Holly response," the gardener said.

"Shut up," Jerico said.

"A truly—huh?"

Slowly Jerico reached for George's arm, pulled him slowly close, slowly wrapped his hands around the man's neck, and said, slowly, "Where I come from, Jambo boy, it is customary for the hero to do most of the talking. It is also customary for the hero's side-kicks, which is you, to keep their goddamned mouths shut when they don't have anything to say. Which you haven't had for at least a goddamned week, and if you open your yap one more time I'm going to fill it with a knuckle sandwich."

"Yap," Giles whispered to his brother, "means mouth."

Jerico lowered his arms. He stood. He gathered his cloak around him. He looked down at the monk, who looked back and grinned.

"Not a word," Jerico warned him. "Not a god-damned word."

29 | I am adrift on a sea of tremulous uncertainty, Jerico waxed; I have at last launched what ought to be the final steps of my last hurrah, stalking the lion outside his den, striding boldly through the enemy camp with no fear save that I will not accomplish that which I have set out to do, and I don't know what the hell I'm doing.

A sigh; a shrug; a slow shake of his head.

After scrambling down a less perilous quadrant of the hill's southern slope, the four men had split up as arranged; it was done so rapidly, however, that Jerico was left alone on the outskirts of Gubs with nothing more than a touch of dust in his eyes and a powerful, rousing speech chapping his lips. It didn't seem fair. Nor was it fair that no one had bothered to inform him of whatever peculiar customs the populace might adhere to. It made his position hazardous in the mortal extreme, and as he started along the road, he prayed that whoever he met would take into consideration his foreign extraction and not, willy-nilly, raise an alarm.

That it was also still daylight disturbed him.

None of the others had wanted to waste any more time waiting for nightfall. Fye reminded him of the various impending dooms and deadlines hanging thereon, the brothers reminded him of the exploding trees, and he himself had to admit that if he was going to stumble around in the dark, he might as well do it while the sun was still up.

Still, it would have been a hell of a speech.

But in truth, he wasn't terribly nervous except for the part about the alarm, and the potential for death, and the other things that threatened his body, his mind, and the hope that someday he might get another pair of English shoes.

Gubs, from ground level, seemed less chaotic and therefore less intimidating. The colorful buildings were certainly taller—most of them two stories, excluding the roof; the villagers were not nearly as short—indeed, many were at least his height, if not taller; and the curious street system was not as haphazard as it had appeared from on high. Each street was hard-packed earth, unless of course it was just one very long and winding street, along which settled the quaint homes, the green lawns, and, every few feet, stiff colored ribbons attached to waist-high poles which, he assumed, were guides to the various establishments about town. But since he had no idea which ribbon was attached to which reputation or lack thereof, he simply walked.

For over an hour he walked. And without a particular destination in mind, he settled for closely examining his new environs in order to garner as much information as he could. Once done, he could then assimilate it, sort it, and digest what he had learned.

Other than asking anyone outright if they had seen any black riders with a redheaded blue monk, it was, undoubtedly, his wisest course.

Luckily his native dress and armacon cloak seemed not to attract undue attention. Those villagers he passed also wore the occasional cloak, the once-in-a-while cape, the bulging burlap sack casually tossed over one shoulder. The men were prone to low boots, snug leggings, billowing shirts, and carrot-shaped ties loosely knotted about the throat; the women favored slipperlike shoes, kiltlike skirts, blouselike tops, and varying degrees of cleavage which adequately attested to the vitality and vigor of their diet.

One or two of them, in fact, dared a wink as he passed. His response was a neutral smile, a slight nod, and the hope that he hadn't just promised to marry anyone.

Finally, as he passed before a bronze-stone house in front of which sat a large family at a darkwood table having what he gathered was their evening meal, he decided he wasn't going to learn any more by acute observation. Now was the time to get acquainted with the natives. Besides, his feet hurt and he was bored.

So he stepped off the street, expression arranged to exhibit candid friendliness, with just a touch of lost helplessness, and approached the diners, hands well away from his sides to prove he carried no visible weapon.

But before he had moved six paces a bearded and heavily jowled man leapt from his chair, pointed, and screamed, "What the bloody hell do you think you're doing?"

Jerico stopped, confused. "I—"

"Christ," the man said to his assembled relatives, "if this don't beat all? I mean, for Ralph's sake, look at him!"

And they did. Four blandly inquisitive male faces,

all younger than the screamer, all bearded, and all deeply tanned; four intensely curious female faces, only one of them bearded, two of them tanned, one of them so deeply lined that where her mouth was was a mystery whose solution was known only to her stomach and dentures.

"I . . . I'm sorry if I offended you," Jerico stammered, taking a quick step back.

"Jesus, there he goes again!" the man shouted, thus prompting several nearby doors to fly open and neighbors to file out onto their front or back stoops.

"Shoot him, Perce," the old woman said, tugging her reed shawl more snugly about her neck.

"I'll do better than that, Mother," Perce replied. "I'll plant the sonofabitch."

"Now wait just a minute," Jerico said. Quickly he looked around him, vainly searching for some clue as to the origin of his trespass.

A comely woman seated opposite the jowly man turned around, smiled apologetically, and touched Perce's arm. "Calm down, dear. Can't you see he's a stranger in town?"

"Stranger my ass!" Perce said, shaking her hand away. "What the hell is Father Obbin going to say?"

"Father Obbin will say nothing."

Perce glared at her. "Anita, you just keep out of this."

"Shoot him," Mother said.

With a sigh loud enough to ruffle the curtains, Anita stood, and Jerico willed himself not to gape at the woman's extraordinary figure, which surely must be the object of every man's unclean though not necessarily unhealthy desire in this rural community. It certainly defied her clothing's attempt to disguise it as ordinary; and it certainly fit her like a glove the thumb of which he desperately wanted to be before he died.

"I'm very sorry, stranger," she said gently. "Perce isn't usually like this."

The others, except for the old woman, nodded vigorously and continued to eat. Heartily, he noticed, as if there were no tomorrow. Or even this evening's twilight.

"And for my part, I apologize for whatever discourtesy I may have visited upon your lovely family," he answered with a smile. "It was not my intention to disrupt your repast but simply to ask a few directional questions."

"Shit," Mother said, pushed herself to a somewhat wobbly stance, and pulled a long-barreled revolver from one of her sleeves.

Jerico sensed the danger instantly and dove for the ground, clipping his chin on an elbow as he simultaneously burrowed in his cloak for something to use as a deterrent. Anita, meanwhile, idly and without turning around swatted the gun away; and Perce began screaming that Father Obbin was definitely going to be pissed when he found out.

"He's not going to find out!" Anita snapped.

Jerico came to his hands and knees.

"How can he not?" Perce snapped back. "The stupid bastard's kneeling on his head!"

Jerico looked down at the grass, looked up at Anita and Perce, and scrambled backward yet again, having just remembered the Gubsian tradition of burying the deceased family under the front lawn.

"My god!" Perce screamed at his wife. "Now he's doing it to Cousin Ida!"

"Shoot him," said Mother.

"I think," Anita said, "you'd better leave, stranger."

Nodding and swallowing, Jerico sprang to his feet, leapt to the street, and hurried off, though he refused to demean himself by running; the speedy walk, however, was close enough for jazz, and he put several turns and houses between him and the Obbin residence before believing it safe enough to slow down and catch his breath.

Then he noticed that the street ended rather abruptly just an inch from his toes. And when he looked up, he blinked once, very slowly, for he found himself on the fringe of the area marked off for Ghorfon Ghorlen.

It could be fate, he told himself as he hunkered down, hands draped over his knees; blind chance has brought me here because this place and no other is where Brother Fye's daughter Jini is incarcerated.

The earth here was indeed a sickly yellow, without a single blade of grass or shoot of shrub growing anywhere on it. The few stones he spotted were sharp-edged and placed in such a manner as to prevent anyone from striding boldly up to the door. If there had been a door, which there wasn't, which explained to him why there were no tracks leading directly or otherwise to the waterstained white walls.

He didn't move.

He stared.

And he knew without question that he was being watched. From somewhere deep within the walls of that hideous place, someone was watching him. Taking his measure. Deciding whether or not this heroic stranger posed a threat or not.

Jerico smiled, looked quickly side to side, and lifted his left hand in a brief mocking wave.

There was no response.

He took a deep breath and scuttled an inch closer, reached down and poked a finger at the ground. It felt like dirt. It had the consistency of dirt. It moved around like dirt when he moved it around. Yet there was the unmistakable presence of either powerful magic or virulent poison—when he plucked a handful of grass from the roadside and tossed it onto the

ragged circle, it shriveled instantly, turned brown,
turned yellow, became one with the earth from which
it had once grown, though in a different, more hospit-
able place.

He wondered what it would do to humans.

"Fry your ass off," a voice said behind him.

He was on his feet in a trice, trying not to appear
defensive for fear of appearing offensive, and did not
relax when he saw that the speaker was Perce Obbin,
his rugged face flushed from either anger or embarrassment from the blunt of his nose to the hang of his
jowls.

The man pointed a knobby finger. "Cousin of mine
tried it once, two, maybe three years ago. Got maybe
halfway there before he turned to stone." He shook his
head and spat to one side. "Mother wanted to blow
the place up."

Jerico nodded his understanding.

Then Obbin extended his hand. "Sorry about before," he said gruffly. "Just my farmer's natural instinct to protect his family."

Jerico shook the hand willingly. "No need to apologize. It was my doing. I had been advised about your
funereal customs, and they unforgivably slipped my
mind."

"Don't worry about it."

"Thank you."

Obbin sniffed, looked at the prison, and beckoned
to Jerico to follow him.

They walked then for several silent minutes, nodding to neighbors out for early evening strolls, grunting to each other at the sight of a particularly lovely
woman or adorable child framed in a window itself
framed in flowers.

Then Obbin said, "You're a hero, ain't you?"

Jerico stopped.

The farmer moved on, looked back, and without expression said, "Don't worry. I won't tell Mother."

Thank god for small favors and feeble women, Jerico thought as he rejoined Obbin.

"But you are a hero, right?"

He admitted it warily.

"Good. I could tell. Always could. It's your way with words. Ornate, you might say. Could tell the ones what the Plackers recruited too." His laugh was unpleasant. "Mother potted two of them before that bitch, Rhonda, hit her with a flat iron. Took a week before her face popped out again."

Rhonda, Jerico thought then, with a twinge of regret at his own gullibility; ah, Rhonda, Rhonda.

"I take it," he said, "you have something to tell me?"

Obbin hesitated before nodding. "They'll do me in, you know, if they find out."

"The black riders?"

"That's right. More and more of them every day, coming around here, scaring the women and children, trampling the hell out of our crops. Bold as brass and twice as stupid. Ain't been the same since the you-know-whats were nipped."

"Yes. I can imagine."

Obbin's look told him he doubted it. Nevertheless, he said with a certain relish, "Wouldn't mind doing a few of them myself, if you know what I mean."

"Yes," Jerico replied cautiously. "Yes."

They walked on.

The sun drifted toward the far glitter of the river.

"We have a saying here," Obbin told him, leaning over to pet a stray dog, who wagged his spiked tail happily, yelped with joy, and bounded away to club a butterfly to death.

"I see," Jerico said.

"You know it?"

"I don't think so."

Obbin nodded.

Jerico sidestepped a cart pulled by one of those ridiculous palominos. A young man and woman were riding inside, laughing and giggling, and they waved enthusiastically as they passed. If this be mortal terror, he wondered what it was like around here when somebody had a nightmare.

Obbin massaged his jowls thoughtfully. "If the W'dch'ck wills it, don't go for holes in the ground because you ain't gonna fit anyway, and besides you'll get dirty."

Jerico grunted.

"Me dad always said that."

"Wise man."

"You know what it means?"

You're out of your mind, he thought.

He shrugged. "Leaves room for a lot of interpretation, I would suspect."

Obbin grinned and nodded. "Me dad always said that too. You know him?"

Jerico eyed him cryptically.

"Damned good with flowers," Obbin said gravely. "The best." He sniffed, wiped his face with a sleeve, and waved to a young mother and her fourteen children frolicking on the lawn. "'Course what I'm getting at is, you need a bit of help, you can come to me, hero. I'd love to see this place back to normal."

Jerico bit his tongue.

"Damned Joquinnites ruining the whole country. Something needs to be done. Anita says I ought to offer you some advice." The farmer stopped, glanced around them, and pulled Jerico close. "I can do better than that. How'd you like to meet the local revolution?"

30 There was something about the simple rustic charm of Perce Obbin that gradually disarmed Jerico's highly trained natural suspicion of revolutionaries walking calmly down the middle of the street. If what the farmer said was true, this was a superb opportunity to muster a force behind him which was considerably larger than the one he had when he started this business. Though, he reminded himself, when he started he was the only one, not counting the Plackers, who turned out not to be on his side after all, especially when Rhonda tried to stone him off the cliff. And he couldn't count Dawn and Gramlet because they were almost dead. And the brothers were getting drunk in some tavern while the monk was in the Tabernacle doing Ralph knew what with the other monks who supposedly held Gubs against the black riders and weren't, on the face of it and to listen to Obbin, doing a very good job of it.

A group of laughing children raced down the street, and Obbin drew Jerico aside to let them pass.

"Tragic," the farmer said, a catch in his voice. "To think they'll grow up never knowing a bit of peace." He gripped Jerico's arm firmly. "Let's be on with it, hero. I know the boys'll be pleased as hell to meet you."

For a moment Jerico resisted, thinking that he ought to try to contact Giles and George, to let them know where he was going. Their expertise in matters Gubsian would be invaluable, and they were, after all, part of his company. On the other hand, he didn't know where he was going, and Obbin was obviously impressed by his confidence and Anita's assessment of his basically sterling character; to balk now might prove disastrous.

"All right," he said decisively. "Lead on, MacDuff, and the devil take the hindmost."

"Right," the farmer said, then ducked his head and cleared his throat. "It's 'lay.'"

"What?"

"It's 'Lay on, MacDuff.' Not 'Lead on.'" A common error of misquotation. Nothing to be ashamed of."

Jerico gasped at the gap in his university education. "Are you sure?"

"Sure. No need for shame when shame isn't to blame."

Why, Jerico wondered in dismay, do I get the feeling we're not in step here?

And groaned when Obbin strode off at a speed that took him by surprise. He had to trot to catch up, lengthen his stride to keep up, and refrain from speech in order to give himself enough wind to keep him from falling flat or sideways on his heroic face.

Ten minutes passed.

And another ten.

Fifteen, and he stopped counting.

Finally Obbin looked at him and smiled crookedly. "You have a question?"

"Well," he said, not wanting to appear more stupid than he felt, "it does seem to me that those fourteen children frolicking on that lawn over there are awfully familiar."

"Ah." Obbin smiled approvingly and placed a finger alongside his nose. "You noticed."

"How could I not? They're naked."

The farmer winked. "Very good," he said quietly. "Very good indeed. Much better than that other lot, the bastard ones, who couldn't recognize a piss in a windstorm. Not very clever, if I do say so myself."

Jerico's answering grin was feeble at best, but he managed to recover by continuing to walk. "Let's keep at it, Obbin," he said in his best no-nonsense voice. "No time to waste. An hour could mean all the difference in situations like this."

"Just trying to throw off the enemy," the man said. "Can't let them know where we're going."

Jerico felt his head begin to turn, and he grunted with the effort not to look around. Whereupon his neck cramped, his jaw clenched, and his eyes glazed for a second before he was able to regain his former casual stride. They might not have been walking around in circles for nearly three-quarters of an hour, but they had come damned close to it, and any enemy worth his salt would have taken a seat somewhere and waited for them to make up their minds.

"They watch, you know," Obbin whispered, one hand to the side of his mouth.

"Oh?"

"Oh yes. From the Ghorlen. Don't know how they do it, but they do it. I say witchcraft. Anita says telescopes in the windows."

"But there aren't any windows."

Obbin looked at him strangely as they hustled past a

picnic complete with aunts keeping an eye on the food while the parents and children played a crude form of rugby that somehow involved a net and four fish. "Of course there are," the farmer said. "How the hell do you think they look out?"

"You suggested witchcraft."

"Ain't no witches here. Only the Most Holy Spears, and that sonofabitch's got them."

"But I didn't see—"

"'Course you didn't. They're painted white."

Jerico ducked a rooster-shaped kite that fluttered down across the road, patted a freckled girl child on her pigtailed blonde head, and swept around the street's next bend before he said, "Doors?"

"Now hold on just a minute," Obbin said, his attitude changing from one of trust to niggling doubt. "I thought you was a hero."

"I am!"

"Then how come you didn't see the doors?"

"But I was told there weren't any."

"Then how the hell do you figure people got in and out, eh? You want to tell me that?"

"No, not really," Jerico said, and was saved from further humiliation when they took yet another bend, the taking of which made him slightly seasick, and he found himself staring at the plaza of the Gubs Tabernacle of the Most Holy W'dch'ck.

It was truly a most remarkable place. The ground was covered with dark green octagonal tiles, polished to a sheen that reflected the sky like water, and in the center of which were inlaid sparkling gold representations of the Seven Spears. Here and there were booths in which merchants sold everything from horse teeth to prayer handkerchiefs, while among them children ran and laughed and played to the lyrical music of several musicians, whose music was, out of respect to the Tabernacle, quiet yet merry.

A true centerpiece for a village.

As was the Tabernacle itself, which he could see was much like the one visited in Fadfy, from the half-dome main structure to the huge crossed-spear medallion at the top; the stained-glass windows still flanked the twenty-foot doors, and there were the seven steps that led to the threshold.

"Oh, whoa!" he said, remembering what happened the last time.

But Obbin grabbed his arm and yanked him along. "Don't stop, you fool! You want them to think we're going in?"

"Who?"

"Them!" the farmer said, jerking a thumb over his shoulder.

"But we are!"

"Of course we are! But we have to look as if we're not, don't you see?"

Please, Jerico prayed, get me out of this now and I swear that I'll never leave Nevada again. I'll never leave my bathtub again. The next time I see a mugging I'll look the other way and read about it in the newspapers. Honest. I won't even flex, okay? Please? Huh?

There was no answer.

Jerico knew a sign when he didn't see one.

"All right," he said. "How do you propose we get in without looking as if we're going in? And don't," he added, shaking a finger at the farmer's ready open mouth, "tell me we're going to walk backwards so it'll look like we're just leaving."

"Well pipe me home and call me Stanley," Obbin said in open admiration. "I never thought of that."

That's right, Jerico thought; and if I have anything to say about it, you never will.

Despite all the activity, there were not many people in the plaza at the moment, and the closer he and

Obbin drew to the steps, the more exposed he felt. His shoulders itched. The feathers on his boots trembled. The urge to run made his eyes water, and it was as he was wiping away one droplet of the salty liquid that he saw the lefthand door begin to creak open.

"They know we're here," Obbin said with a grin.

"Who?"

"Them!" he said, pointed to the Tabernacle.

"And your friends?"

"Inside."

"And the monks?"

But Obbin merely put a cautionary finger to his lips. "Just do as I do," he whispered, "and soon enough you'll see what the men of Gubs are made of."

Jerico supposed it would be cruel not to tell the eager farmer about his own contact within the gleaming greenstone walls, but as the opportunity hadn't yet arisen, he saw no harm in allowing the man to show off a little. After all, he thought, what could it hurt?

They took the steps casually, every few seconds stopping to turn and admire the view. Obbin exclaimed loudly about the preponderance of the fair sex abroad in the plaza this pleasant evening, and Jerico marveled at the skills of the jugglers and the sword-swallowers, one of whom was having a hell of time getting a blade past his neck brace.

The sky darkened.

A pair of clouds fired by the setting sun drifted over the valley.

Obbin reached the top, dug into a pocket, and pulled out a stone which he stared at, then stared at the sky, then stared at the shadows drifting away from the booths. "Well, I'll be," he declared at the top of his voice. "Will you look at the time?"

Jerico tsked and shook his head.

"Guess we should say our ablutions, don't you think, Cousin?"

"Of course," he agreed. "I wouldn't want Mother to think I'm all wet."

Obbin winked his satisfaction at the exhibition of a hero's quick and cunning wit, put the stone away, and strolled through the open door. Jerico followed, his left hand buried in the inner folds of his cloak, his right hand held lightly where his belt buckle would have been if he had a belt and a buckle to go with it. It was, he'd decided, the best way to make a convincing entrance without being entirely pompous about his station.

And once inside he knew he'd been right.

They were in a vast antechamber lighted by smoking torches. Ahead was another pair of doors he surmised led to the sanctum of the Tabernacle where the services were held. Two blue-robed monks stood there with silver platters in their hands, speaking softly to a quartet of villagers, who were turning out their pockets to prove they had no donations tonight, but surely Ralph wouldn't mind since he wasn't around anyway. The monks shook their heads. The quartet produced a common pouch they emptied onto the platters.

"Heathen," Obbin whispered when he saw Jerico's interest. "They think they can just walk right in without so much as a by-your-leave and a buck in the bucket." He sneered. "How the hell do they think the Innkeepers clothe and feed their men—spiritual parthenogenesis or something?"

Jerico said nothing; religion was not his forte, bathtubs were.

Then, as Obbin feigned brushing plaza dust from his chest, he noted that to the right was a much smaller door covered with chains and locks; and to the left a similar one, but without the chains and locks—a cowled monk sat there instead, perched on a stool and reading a cumbersome tome bound in green leather.

The monk wasn't Buck, and Obbin walked over to him without hesitation.

The monk looked up, saw the farmer, saw Jerico, and closed the book, his finger inside to mark his page.

"Yes, my son?"

Obbin narrowed his eyes slightly and glanced side to side before lowering his voice and saying, "As the W'dch'ck truly says, we are all flattened in the eyes of Ralph."

The monk started. His free hand adjusted his cowl so that his face remained in shadow, and after glancing side to side, he squinted and rose, put the book aside, bent down and retrieved his finger and straightened again. "And those who are flattened shall be puffed up in his sight."

"And those who are puffed shall be wheat among the chaff."

"And the chaff shall be taken by the wind of Ralph's laughter."

"And the laughter shall be heard from unto generation to whoever so shall hear the cottonwood whistling above."

Obbin began to sweat, and Jerico touched the small of his back to indicate his support in the ritual he couldn't make heads nor tails of, but who cared as long as it worked?

"The old hooty owl," Obbin replied, "hooty whoos to the dove."

"And the dove shall respond with a clicking of his tongue."

As which point the two men clasped forearms, embraced, clasped hands, embraced, turned to Jerico and pulled him into a three-way embrace before he could explain that he didn't dance, don't ask him.

And in the middle of that embrace the monk whispered, "Is he the one?"

"Aye," Obbin answered.

"Oh boy," the monk said. He stepped back and opened the door, ushered the two men through, and closed it behind them.

31 The passageway beyond the guarded door was narrow, dank, and weakly lighted by a series of torches the butts of which had been rammed into whatever cracks in the walls were large enough to hold them. The stone floor was slippery with moisture that gleamed in the flickering flamelight; the ceiling was cobwebbed. And there were sounds that had nothing to do with Jerico's footsteps—vigorous chanting in the Gregorian mode, the infrequent tonal aspirations of a gong, stone slowly grinding upon stone, and the flat clank of metal striking hot metal.

Obbin hastened on, mumbling to himself and frequently holding up one hand to tick off something on his fingers.

For his part, Jerico stayed as close to the farmer as he could without actually riding on his back. He didn't like the fact that the monk watching the door hadn't gone with them; he didn't like the fact that the passageway led gently downward because it reminded him of the last time he went down in a Tabernacle; he didn't like the cobwebs; he didn't like the water slipping and sliding and dripping from the walls.

And he didn't like the odors that wrinkled his nose, odors that reminded him of his mother's cooking on those days when the chef went to get married in Reno.

He had a feeling he was being led into a trap.

His only consolation was the knowledge that somewhere in this building Buck Fye was even now marshalling his own anti-Joquinnite forces, and he wondered with a half-smile if Obbin's revolutionaries knew about Buck's. If they did, then the farmer was in for a most pleasant surprise; if they didn't, Obbin was in for one hell of a shock.

Downward; and around turns in such a senseless pattern that he stopped trying to remember them. If they were separated, he'd never get out. Trapped forever between walls of stone. Beneath the earth of a country that had no right existing anywhere on the planet, much less in New Jersey.

"Perce," he whispered, tapping the man on the shoulder.

Obbin only grunted and gestured for his silence.

Downward.

The passage opening once to the size of a small room, closing again and diving even more steeply, the footing more treacherous, the absence of steps more puzzling than ever.

The chanting grew louder, then softer.

The gong was coupled with a chime.

Something scratched at the wall just at his shoulder, but when he whirled and dropped into a crouch, he saw nothing but stone, and rivulets of water, and a shadow that vanished as soon as he saw it.

The floor leveled.

The gong and chime fell silent.

Obbin came to an intersection and took the righthand turn without a moment's indecision; the floor canted upward.

Another turn, and upward again.

Jerico tapped Obbin on the shoulder.

"Hush," the farmer ordered.

A small brown naked thing with a furry tail squealed out of a hole bored into the rock, attacked Jerico's boot and ran away with a feather in its mouth.

The stench of rotting vegetation and dank unhealthy swamps filled the passage in an almost visible mist, and Jerico covered his nose with one hand and breathed through his mouth.

A third turn, ever upward, now in an indisputable wide spiral, while the torches became more infrequent, always seeming to be just around the next bend, yet when the bend was rounded, the torch was gone.

Just before the next intersection Jerico grabbed Obbin's shoulder and turned him around. "You're lost, aren't you?" he said.

Obbin glared at him. "Don't be daft, hero," he said disdainfully. "I'm only trying to throw them off our scent."

"Who?"

"Them!"

"Them," Jerico said with exaggerated patience, "are outside somewhere. We, on the other hand, are down here, and the only one who knows it is that monk at the door. And besides it stinks down here, so how the hell could they follow us or our scent?"

"They have ways," the farmer answered darkly.

"Damn," Jerico said, more to himself than the other. "Damn, we're lost."

Obbin's belligerence faded. "Well, it has been a long time, you know. I don't come here every day."

"Great."

"But I have the general idea, so—"

Jerico stopped him before he walked off again, checked their surroundings, and saw nothing different in the walls, the bends, the cobwebs, the floor, the dripping water, the stench, the naked things with the furry tails, or the absence of steps. Then he told Obbin with a look to stay where he was and walked up to the intersection, his boots slipping on the floor, his hands recoiling when they grabbed at the walls for support.

He stood with hands on his hips and looked in both directions, shaking his head, puffing his cheeks and blowing out a sigh that rippled the cobwebs.

"There's a door here," he said.

"I knew that," Obbin told him.

"Where does it lead?"

"Open it and find out."

Jerico turned. "What?"

Obbin cringed at the way Jerico's eyes darkened and his brows came together in a disapproving frown. "I . . . I said, perhaps you could open it and see what's on the other side."

Jerico smiled.

Obbin cowered.

Jerico beckoned.

Obbin took his sweet time getting to the intersection, and yelped when his shoulders were grabbed from behind and he was propelled to the left, to the door, where his hands were then seized and clamped onto the latch.

"You are the revolutionary," Jerico whispered harshly in his ear. "You open it."

"But I'm a farmer!"

Jerico squeezed and cracked the man's knuckles. Obbin received the message, acknowledged it, lifted the latch, and swung the door open. But before he could move away, Jerico shoved him over the threshold, drew his own sword, which he finally located at the cloak's hem, and leapt in after him.

And stopped.

And sniffed.

And said, "Well."

The room he found himself in was exemplary of its kind, the name of which momentarily escaped him. There was no water on the walls, which were covered with intricate tapestries of a pastoral nature; there was no water on the floor, which was covered by a carpet a solid and glittering silver; there were no cobwebs on the ceiling, which was covered by a mural portraying a huge brown and furry creature smiling benevolently through sunlit clouds upon those gathered below it; and on the far wall was a ten-foot bronze door in the center of which was a bas-relief of the same divine creature depicted in the overhead mural.

In the center was a refectory table large enough to seat three dozen overweight men in full battle gear. The chairs were carved from black stone, simple, without ornamentation. On the table's mirrorlike surface were silver platters laden with food, chandeliers with silver candles burning steadily without smoke, silver chalices filled with wine, and a four-foot-tall hourglass in a mahogany frame.

The sands of the hourglass were mostly at the bottom.

"Well," Jerico said again.

Each one of the chairs was occupied—by men in blue robes, cowls thrown back, silver girdles and tassels about their ample waists. But only one of them had a ruby-tipped hat pin in his nose, and he was sitting at the table's head.

"Oops," said Buck Fye.

"Oops?" Jerico echoed, marching the length of the table, dragging Obbin behind him. "Oops?"

Fye rose. The others rose. Fye bade them be seated. They sat. Jerico reached him and placed the tip of his sword none too gently against the general area of his heart.

"Oops?"

Fye, to his credit, neither flinched nor blanched nor motioned to anyone to rescue him. He merely gazed benignly down at Jerico and said, "Only in the sense that you were not expected so soon."

Jerico looked at the feast, at the other monks, and nodded. "I can see that." Then he yanked Obbin around to stand beside him. "And I suppose that Obbin here is not, as I had been led to believe, completely innocent in this attempt to deceive, distract, and otherwise throw me off my plotted course?"

Obbin smiled as one does to a flu-ridden dentist with a drill in his hand.

"I see."

"No," Buck said. "No, my son, you do not see. Not at all."

"I can make a pretty good guess." But he released the farmer, who scurried away to a chair set against the wall. Then he glanced around the table, and was not at all surprised to see Innkeeper Winngg Indo seated halfway down on the left side. He nodded. Indo nodded back. "A fair guess."

"Not even close."

Jerico's eyes narrowed, and the Innkeepers at the table began to stir. "I can see," he said to Buck without shifting his gaze, "that you have what is probably all the loyal Innkeepers remaining in Robswerran here under one roof. I can imagine that you are discussing ways of rescuing the Seven Spears from Kyroppig and Joquinn without the entire country breaking into open and possibly genocidal warfare. I would suppose," he continued, his voice rising, "that the bumpkin over there—"

"Here now, watch it!"

"—was deliberately set upon my tail so that he could lead me around in circles in order to kill time so that you all here could come to a conclusion concerning what you would have me do in order to achieve our mutual goals. I would further surmise," he continued, just about shouting now and not giving a damn because his feet still hurt and he smelled like a sewer, "that you still don't trust me well enough to include me in these awesome deliberations because I am a hero—yes, goddamnit, and proud of it!—and therefore hoped to present me with a *fait accompli* once I had arrived!"

"Not bad," Fye admitted, one finger nervously at his hat pin.

"No!" Jerico yelled when one or two Innkeepers made feeble protest. "No, do not demean yourselves by denying what I have said! It is clear to me, who was recruited for this task by those who were, in fact, the enemies you hope to defeat, that trust is in pitifully short supply in this Most Holy Tabernacle. Trust which I have more than once placed in your kind, and more than once had thrown back in my face like a wet glove! *Trust I freely gave out of the goodness of my heart and the nobility of my goddamned profession!*"

"No!" he shouted over the shouts rising from the table. "No, it is no use! I've been battered, bruised, betrayed, and besmirched, and I'll be goddamned if I'm going to be shit on as well."

Trembling with rage, he turned to Fye. "You want to get the Spears? You want to prevent murder and mayhem? You want to save the women and children from a life of abject misery and relentless poverty?"

He nodded once, sharply. "Fine! Go ahead! But you'll have to do it without Jerico Dove."

Whereupon, with a flourish that had his sword back in his cloak without so much as a pinked shin, he strode to the bronze door, shoved it open, and stalked out. Then he turned and glared at Fye, who had stepped around his chair to gape in dismayed astonishment.

"Jerico—we did what we thought was best!" the Inkeeper pleaded.

"Screw it!" Jerico retorted.

"But think of the children!"

"I was when this started," he snapped, "and look where it got me."

"But you can't!"

"I can."

"Jini!"

"I feel more sorry for her captors."

"Robswerran!"

"Think good thoughts," he sneered. "Maybe you can conjure up Tinkerbell or something."

He grabbed the door's edge and made to slam it shut.

Fye looked at his colleagues desperately, but they were so taken aback by the hero's outburst that they could do nothing but twiddle their tassels and crumple their cowls. Then Fye dropped to his knees and clasped his hands.

"One minute!" he begged. "Please, hero! One minute of your time before you desert us in our hour of need."

Jerico closed his eyes and breathed deeply several times. He was not ashamed of his temper, nor did he retract anything he'd said, but he supposed he could be magnanimous before he headed home. What could it hurt? Besides, if that hourglass was any indication, an hour was about all they had anyway.

He nodded.

Someone at the table sobbed with relief.

Obbin applauded.

Fye groaned to his feet and hurried to Jerico's side, took his arm, and led him down a short tapestried corridor to another door. Saying nothing, he opened it, ushered Jerico in, and closed the door behind them.

"This better be good," Jerico warned.

Fye only nodded, and wiped a wash of perspiration from his face with his sleeve. Then he walked to the far wall and stood before a dazzling white cloth affixed to a silver rod. He looked over his shoulder.

Jerico tapped an impatient foot.

"Patience," the monk pleaded.

"Right," Jerico said.

The cloth was drawn aside to reveal a large oval mirror framed with rubies, diamonds, and heart-shaped zircons. The face itself was cloudy, and Jerico had to blink to be sure that there were indeed clouds boiling and spinning there.

I think, he thought, I'm about to be snookered.

Fye reached into his robe and pulled out a Spear medallion attached to a long, delicate, silver chain. He pressed it to his forehead, mumbled something Jerico couldn't catch, and lifted his gaze to the ceiling, then the mirror, then lowered it to the medallion.

Jerico took a reluctant step forward, told himself to leave, and walked across the room.

Fye lifted a hand and snapped the mirror with his thumb, then lifted a hinged flap of diamonds and pressed several buttons which had been concealed therein.

"You must stay," the monk said as the clouds shredded and reformed.

"Sure," Jerico said sourly. "I love being stabbed in the back. It takes my mind off being clubbed."

Fye whimpered, punched the buttons again, prayed,

lifted the medallion, prayed, stared at the mirror, and finally, with a relieved gasp, asked Jerico for one more minute.

"I'll count," he said.

Fye nodded, stepped closer to the mirror and drew the white cloth around him. Jerico wondered if this was some sort of voting machine, unless the monk wanted four lousy snapshots of himself; he was about to stomp back to the corridor when the cloth parted again, and Buck stepped aside, in one smooth move tossing the medallion to him and sweeping his arm toward the mirror.

"You must stay, Jerico Dove!"

"Forget it," Jerico told him.

"Nay, stay!" And the monk tossed him the medallion.

"Damnit, Buck—"

Then he looked in the mirror, saw the face looking back, looked at Fye, who was already on his way out of the room, looked back at the mirror and muttered, "Oh hell."

32 She was as he had seen her last, though under considerably more tragic circumstances, and she was still so ethereally beautiful that his lungs begged for a jump start: her long silky eyelashes fairly fluttered her off the floor of her scarlet-and-gold bedroom, the delightful dimple in her delicate chin quivered with anticipation, and her lustrous dark curls framed perfectly the ebony of her concerned and lusty eyes.

"Dawn," he breathed.

"Jerico," she sighed.

"Dirty trick," he muttered, glancing back at the closed door.

"We don't have much time," she said.

"I know."

"Brother Fye tells me that you are . . ." She turned away, and her fan came into view, working overtime to calm her. "He tells me that you are leaving Robswerran forever."

He felt like an idiot.

"It had crossed my mind, yes," he said with a touch of regretful sorrow.

"But why? Why?"

He told her. Every step of the way from Fadfy to Gubs was narrated in uncompromising detail—his successes, his failures, his encounters, his tribulations —he left nothing out, and though it tore at his breast when she flushed at the mention of Jini and Anita, it wracked his conscience even more when he spoke of his temper and its fraying at the hands of those who led him around like a puppy dog learning not to soil the good carpet in the living room. Or even the linoleum in the kitchen.

And when he was finished, his voice soft, his manner contrite, he dared not look upon her visage for fear of being struck by the reproach he knew he'd find there.

But all she said was, gently, "I understand."

He flinched. He groaned silently. He raised a fist to his lips to prevent a cry of defeat from escaping his quivering lips.

Oh *god*, how he hated it when someone said that! The two most potent words in the language which, when wielded at the proper time, could reduce a saint to begging forgiveness for eating a fig instead of a peach. They were the trigger words for crushing guilt, the execution of decent intentions, the mass murder of good deeds and kind thoughts delivered with a vengeance to prove how noble and good was the doer and the thinker.

"Hell," he said, and walked several paces away. "Oh hell, I don't deserve you, Dawn."

Her expression was beatific. "You are wrong, Jerico."

"No," he said, a hand up to silence her. "No! I have behaved selfishly, cruelly, and most shamefully against all the credos of my profession." He turned, his face a mask of anguish. "How could I call myself a hero and then desert these people in their hour of need? How can I call myself a savior—which I don't, but they might—when all I think of saving is my own worthless skin!"

"Jerico," she said. "Jerico, don't do this to yourself."

He lowered his gaze. "I'm a failure."

"Oh no!"

"I am a disaster in feathered boots."

"Jerico!" she cried, a pearllike tear glistening on her sumptuous cheek. "Jerico, please!"

He waved her silent again. "I am . . . garbage." He looked up. "Yes. Yes, my love—and there! There, I've said it!—yes, I am garbage, not fit for a plastic bag or a gutter or the bottom of a man's shoes!"

"Oh my darling!" she wailed.

"No!" he said, and waved his hand again. "It's no good. It's no good."

"Jerico," she said, leaning closer to whatever magical device projected her image from her shady purgatory in Fadfy. "Jerico, if we are to be together again, in a form much more conducive to our mutual desires and all the implications you can handle, you must continue your battle for the forces of good and what's right!"

"I . . ."

Her eyes grew limpid, and his knees grew weak.

"For me, Jerico," she whispered. "Do it for me."

"Oh god," he said. "For you? But I don't deserve you!"

"You said that already."

"But I don't! I . . ." He turned his back bravely. "No. Dawn, go away. I'm no good for you."

"Jerico?"

He tried to make an exit, to walk forlornly to the door and out of her life forever.

"Jerico? My . . . love?"

He stiffened as if goosed.

"Jerico . . . turn around. Tell me to my face that you will not do this thing. Tell me to my face that you do not love me and do not want to see me ever again."

Don't do it, he ordered as he watched his legs begin to move; don't do it, Dove, or you'll slit your throat in the morning and ruin a perfectly decent day.

Slowly he turned.

"Jerico, come to me."

Step by step.

"Jerico. Oh my Jerico."

He looked up and saw her face, and was a believer.

"Okay," he said, his grin so wide he felt as if his ears had fallen off. "You win. You . . . win."

Dawn's joy was so radiant, so naked, so unadulterated, that he could not stop himself from stepping to the mirror and planting a kiss on the place where her lips quavered. Then he stepped back and drew himself up, squared his shoulders, and made rugged his chin.

"I've been a fool."

"Oh Jerico," she said in a near swoon.

"And it took you, my beauty, to direct me away from the second retirement I nearly fell into because I was, and no question about it, a fool, a dope, a jerk, a vain and silly man. But I am, and always will be, a hero! And hero I stand, I can do no other!"

Dawn's eyes widened, and for the most erotic and impossible of moments, he was convinced that she was going to come straight through that gaudy mirror and throw herself into his arms.

Instead she grew a beard.

"What?" he said, suddenly aware that things were not all that they seemed to be.

"Jerico!" Dawn cried then. "Jerico, I'm . . . losing
. . . you!"

"Dawn!" he shouted.

"Shove it," the face behind the beard said, and
laughed maniacally when Dawn vanished, and Jerico
was left alone with a vision from Hell.

The face that had somehow driven his beloved
Dawn from the mirror was one he was positive he
would never forget, not even on those long boring
evenings when nightmares were the furthest thing
from his mind.

It was long and narrow, its bone structure clear and
sharp-edged, which gave it a routine but effective
satanic look. Its hair was black and parted in the
center, falling straight to the shoulders barely visible
at the bottom; its brow was high and ridged; its eyes
peaked at top and bottom as if they were on sideways,
and they were of a pale green color that reminded him
of something his mother used to put on his salad and
tell him it was healthy, don't bother to pluck it off; the
nose was a dull blade set on edge; its mouth was wide,
its lips barely there, and its teeth merely ragged black
stumps with dots of leftover silver fillings glinting in
the light.

"Joquinn," Jerico said.

"Ah! You recognize me, you fathead hero!"

"No," he admitted, "but I'd know you anywhere."

Joquinn laughed again, his hair dancing as though
touched by electricity.

"What do you want?" Jerico demanded.

"Nothing," the man replied. "I just wanted to see
what you looked like, that's all. I've heard so much
about you that I couldn't let this moment pass."

Jerico attempted to see behind the man's head, to
see the room he was in, but there was nothing there
but what looked like tumbling black clouds.

Then a finger appeared to scratch Joquinn's nose. A long finger with a single simple band of copper around it. "You've been very lucky, hero," Joquinn said, his tone indicating precisely what he thought of both the luck and the hero. "Very lucky indeed."

"It isn't luck that has carried me this far," Jerico declared. "It is purpose."

"Ha!"

"Yes!"

"Ha!"

Jerico glared. "You laugh, yet you have a purpose yourself."

"That's true," the usurper admitted. "But my purpose will prevail because I have all the cards."

Jerico smiled. "You wish."

"I know."

"You pretend great confidence, but I can tell from the subtext of your pronouncements that you are worried about me." He thrust out a pointing finger. "And well you should, you vile and crass miscreant! Since you know who I am, then you know what I am, and if you know what I am, then you know what I can do. And what I will do. To you. As soon as I leave this place and meet you face to face."

Joquinn closed one eye. "You're threatening me, little man."

"No. I merely promise."

"And now you lie!" The other eye closed. There was a moment of silence. Then both eyes opened, and Jerico saw the rage and fear battling within them. "You will have to die!"

"You've already tried."

"I'll try again."

Jerico shook his head. "It's too late, you poor hapless fool. Don't you know that the sands of time have already run out on you? Don't you realize that the entire country is ready to rise and crush you?"

"Do I care?" Joquinn said, picking at a foodstuff caught between his front teeth.

"You'd better if you want to live."

The man snorted derision. "Oh please! Let's be realistic, okay? You have you, a cook, a gardener, a monk, and a monkette—who even as we joust happens to be in prison. I, on the other hand, have an army of heroes, the Seven Spears, the magic, and all that goes with them. You have no chance against me, Dove. No chance at all."

Jerico threw back his head and laughed.

Joquinn ignored him. "So I'll give you one chance to stop screwing up my plans—leave now, go back to New Jersey, and I'll see to it that you don't die."

Jerico laughed again.

Joquinn's face flushed with annoyance. "Stop it!" he commanded. "Stop it at once!"

Jerico did, but not without a stray giggle or two. "Oh, you *are* an imbecile."

Joquinn raised a fist and shook it.

"You think that's all I have going for me?"

"But of course, you misguided foreigner, of course."

"No!" Jerico said. He reached into his cloak and pulled out the trinket Buck Fye had tossed to him before he'd left the room. "I have *this*! I have the W'dch'ck on my side!" And he held up his hand to show the miscreant the Seven Spears medallion cradled in his palm.

"The what?" Joquinn said.

"What do you mean, the what? The W'dch'ck!"

"What?"

"Jesus, man, the goddamned W'dch'ck!"

Joquinn closed one eye again. "Spell it."

"Oh for Christ's sake," Jerico snapped, and thrust his hand out to show the man the medallion.

"Oh!" Joquinn said. "That!"

And with that, he flung himself back, cringing, shrieking, throwing his arms up to cover his face while Jerico damned all those damned glottal stops. But he pressed his advantage, advancing on the mirror, holding the medallion up to keep the man at bay. Until he stopped when he realized that the man wasn't here, he was in Kyroppig, and as soon as he hit the mirror his attack was over.

"You'll pay!" Joquinn screamed. "You'll pay, you toad!"

And the mirror shimmered, there was thunder, and before Jerico could reach the door, the entire wall exploded.

"When I was a little boy," said Jerico from the reed cot in the tiny room he had been carried to after the explosion, "I used to play in the backyard of my family's mansion. Actually, it was Wyoming. At least that's what my mother told me. Anyway, one of the games I played was—ouch! Watch it!"

"Sorry, sire," mumbled the bald swarthy monk who had been summoned to tend his wounds.

"That's all right," he said magnanimously. And looked to the others clustered around him—Indo and Fye and Obbin, plus a delegation of Innkeepers who had been praying feverishly over him for the better part of an hour. "But this game, gentlemen, consisted of taking large clumps of dried mud, a few toy soldiers, and—Jesus!"

"Sorry again," the medic said. "But, sire, you do keep moving around. I can't work if you keep moving around."

Although the one-legged monk's ministrations produced periodic burning and a twinge or two, Jerico took the calm rebuke in good spirits. After all, he wasn't dead despite the tons of rubble that had crashed onto his back when the wall blew up in a fit of Joquinn's pique. In fact, the only thing that pained him was the back of his left knee and thigh where the armacon cloak had ridden up when he'd been blown off his feet. Shards of mirror had lodged there, and the monk was anxious to pluck them out before the trousers healed themselves and imprisoned the glass in the flesh.

One sliver at a time, then, with a pair of tweezers the man obviously also used to keep his eyebrows well arched, while Buck interrupted his explanation of the game by informing him that great progress had been made in locating Jini.

"I *know* where Jini is," Jerico said. "She's in Ghorlen."

"Yes, but where in Ghorlen?"

"How should I know? I've never been—watch it, Brother, don't let your reach exceed your grasp."

The medic blushed.

Buck scowled. "Jerico, will you please keep your mind on what's going on around here?"

"I am," he insisted with one eye on the medic.

"Not that! This!"

"What?"

"The prison!"

"What about it?"

"Jini is there!"

Jerico closed his eyes, hoping they might think he had either passed away from the excruciating pain or had fallen asleep. When he opened them again, however, the room was still crowded and Buck was still at the foot of the cot, but the medic was gathering the tools of his trade into a soft leather pouch.

"You'll be all right now, sire."

"Thank you, . . . ah . . . ah . . ."

"Fanno," the monk answered shyly. "Brother Fanno Zay."

Jerico grasped his hand and shook it warmly. "My thanks, Brother Zay. And I apologize for being such a lousy patient."

"I've had worse."

"Perhaps."

"Hey," the monk said, turning neatly on his wooden leg, "no perhaps about it. The time Twiddles here got clobbered in Yoteoc, you'd have thought it was the end of the world, for crying out Ralph."

"Brother," Buck cautioned.

"Right," Zay groused. "It's always 'Brother' this and 'Brother' that, isn't it, and never a kind thought for the inside of the man, is there? Never a thought or thank-you for a job well done." He pegged to the door, opened it, and pouted over his shoulder. "Try and speak your peace around here, hero, they sit on you 'til you're squashed." He spat on the corridor floor. "And if you keep twiddling that goddamned thing, Fye, you're going to unscrew your stupid nose."

The door slammed.

The Innkeeper chorus sent a prayer to the ceiling for the forgiveness of Brother Zay.

And Indo, after consulting with Buck, suggested to Obbin that this might be the time to get things moving since it was very nearly midnight, and all must be ready for the hero's heroic deed.

"Deed?" Jerico said, sitting up.

"In a minute," Buck told him, pushing him back down onto his pillow.

Indo and the farmer bowed and hurried out.

The Innkeeper chorus sent a prayer in their wake.

"Deed?"

"You're wounded, Jerico," Fye reminded him as he sat on the edge of the cot. "Don't strain yourself."

Jerico eyed him suspiciously. "What strain is there in asking about what you're talking about?"

"Well, you might get excited, for one."

"Excited? About Jini?"

"No. About breaking into the Ghorlen and breaking Jini out."

That's not a bad reason, he thought, shoved the monk to the floor with his good leg, and jumped to his feet. His trousers adjusted beautifully, and he soon had the chorus herded together and out into the corridor before they could think of a quick prayer for his complete recovery. Then he stood with his back to the door and waited until Buck had climbed back to the cot, red-faced and somewhat annoyed.

"Now," Jerico said, folding his arms across his chest, "tell me all about it."

During the next thirty minutes, Jerico decided that he had died and had gone to whatever equivalent of Hell there was in North Dakota. In spite of the fact that it wasn't Philadelphia, he still didn't like it, said so several times, and almost crossed his eyes in rage when Buck insisted on explaining yet again what the rescue plan was. He didn't care what the rescue plan was. He didn't care that he was the only man in Robswerran who could pull it off and not be made dead in the process. He didn't care that Buck was on the verge of pleading again.

What he did care about, eventually, when Buck got around to explaining it, was the fact that Jini was evidently the only one who knew exactly how to get into the Holiest Supreme Tabernacle of the Most Holy W'dch'ck, which just happened to be where Joquinn had broadcasted from, and where the Seven Spears were kept.

He also cared about the fact that, while he had been unconscious, a house near the river had mysteriously blown up.

"All right," he said. "Tell me again. Slowly."

"No," he said. "You're out of your mind."

"Absolutely and positively out of the question. I've decided to retire again. To Fadfy. With Dawn. If I get nervous, I can always beat up on the kid."

"Uh-uh."

"Are you *crazy*? Are you out of your tonsured little mind? Perce told me what happens when you cross that yellow stuff! I saw what happens to a lousy piece of grass! You're *nuts*! You're a goddamned coconut tree!"

"The hell with this, Bucko. Warm up the shower, Mother, I'm coming home."

"A what? A slingshot? *You* want *me* to get in a slingshot? A big slingshot? *You* want to shoot *me* onto that *roof*? In a slingshot? Jesus Christ, who the hell do you think I am, Superman?"

"Shit," he muttered. "I wish I hadn't said that."

Once it was clear that he was able to travel—willing having nothing whatsoever to do with it—Buck led him through a maze of corridors and hallways, each with its own distinctive personality, each devoted to a different segment of the Ralphian ideal as embodied in the teachings of the Most Holy W'dch'ck. Were there more time, Jerico would have loved to study each of the facets of this curious and uplifting spiritual force; and though, several times along the way, he tried to make that very time in the interest of learning still more about how things worked on this side of the golden wall, he was frustrated by the way Buck refused to listen.

Still, he thought as they went through yet another door and into the main antechamber on the ground level, they have at last admitted that I, and only I, am the one to lead them from the desert of bondage to the promised land of freedom, justice, and the W'dch'ckian way.

Jesus, he thought then; what a crock.

But he managed a smile when he saw the others waiting for him at the doors.

"Well," he said, palm against the flat of his chest, "I'm flattered."

Indo stepped up to him, clasped his hand, and placed a piece of metallic crimson cloth into it. "This is a piece of cloth."

"Yes."

"Use it."

Jerico considered carefully before asking, "How?"

Indo took the cloth back, pulled a dagger from his cloak, and rubbed the cloth energetically over it.

"I see," Jerico said. And then he did see—the blade was now gleaming as if new, and its edge would cut a stone to the quick. "My," he said, reaccepted the cloth and folded it safely away. "Thank you, Innkeeper Indo. I shall—"

"You will," Indo said, and took his place among the others.

Next was Obbin, who fingered his jowls for a moment before saying, "Keep off the yellow stuff, hero. Remember my cousin the swine."

"I will," Jerico said solemnly, and accepted a handshake that nearly broke his thumb and two fingers.

Brother Zay gave him a compact but complete first aid kit, with all the instructions written on the inside of the lid, and all the medications necessary to heal everything but the most grievous of mortal wounds. Not realizing there were degrees of mortal wounds, Jerico began a series of intensive, vaguely hysterical questions which were cut off when the medic blessed him and stepped away.

The four exchanged silent farewells.

Buck then took his elbow and led him outside.

The night was complete. Stars, moon, a gentle breeze, the reassuring and melancholy sounds of music and laughter and little children playing far past their bedtimes; the booths in the plaza closed now, perhaps forever; lamps burning in windows all over Gubs; a mournful gong ringing back in the Tabernacle.

It was more than Jerico could stand.

"Jesus," he said, "do you have orphans to give me flowers?"

Buck stared at him, mouth open, eyes wide, then burst into laughter and slapped him heartily on the back. "By Ralph, you're a hard little shit, aren't you?"

"No, but I know when I'm being manipulated, Brother."

"Ah, do you?"

"Sure. For example," he said, leading the monk down the seven holy steps, "right now you're waiting for me to ask about our mutual friends, the brothers."

"Well, I'll be," Buck said, clearly impressed.

"And when I do ask, you're going to tell me that they too are a part of this fatheaded plan of yours. And while I was inside, they were busily preparing the slingshot which will, if they've done their job right, land me on the roof of the Ghorlen without so much as a dent in my tush."

Buck shook his head. "Am I so transparent, Jerico?"

"No, not really. You could just as easily tell me they're in a bar somewhere, drunk as lords and having more fun than I am."

Buck laughed again, and this time Jerico joined him, and the two men extended their strides into a leisurely trot. As they ran, Jerico said that he didn't want to seem pushy, or even ungrateful, but was there also a plan for getting him out again once he had managed, miraculously, to rescue Jini from her captors?

"Well," Buck said, "there's a problem with that one."

"Really?"

"It's actually rather hard to say."

"Really?"

"The problem is, you see, no one has ever gotten out of there alive. Or dead, for that matter."

Jerico took it in stride. "I already know that much, Buck. Everybody in town seems to want to tell me. But what I want to know is, now that you've figured out how I should get in, how do I get out?"

They passed a house in which a birthday celebration was still going strong, long past the witching hour. Not five minutes later its lawn blew up.

"That," Buck said, slightly panting and brushing burning grass from his shoulders, "tends to want to bring up yet another problem, my friend."

Jerico wanted to stop. He didn't. "Which problem is that, Brother Fye? Getting into the Ghorlen, or Joquinn zeroing in on Gubs?"

"The getting in part."

"But I *am* getting in. You're shooting me, for god's sake, onto the damned roof."

"Yes. Well."

"Oh."

"You see the problem then."

He did.

Getting onto the prison roof was about as far as the monk's plan had gotten. Once on that roof, alone and heroic, Jerico would be on his own, left to find his own way through to the cells beneath, or spend the rest of his life hunting for food in the eaves, which he didn't think the prison had but he wasn't going to spoil what fun there was left in what was left of his misbegotten life's profession.

Somewhere on the outskirts of town a house exploded.

"I was going to retire, you know," he said, dodging a smoking piece of wall.

"So I heard."

"The Plackers talked me out of it."

"You told me."

"I think I'll wring their fucking necks."

"Good plan. Now what about the roof?"

He shook his head and chopped the air with his hand, an indication that he wished silence, and they traveled hastily through the village for another twenty minutes before rounding a gentle bend, passing a darkened house, and spotting Xamoncroft and Jambo sitting cross-legged on the side of the street. The brothers leapt to their feet immediately when Jerico called their names, and there was a brisk round of hugging, vaguely ribald masculine pleasantries, and silent greetings before Buck hushed them with a look.

"It's time," he said, keeping his voice low.

"Yes," Jerico said. "Before I lose my nerve, show me this contraption you're using to get me on the roof."

Giles looked at George, who looked at Giles, who reached into his cloak and pulled out a slingshot.

"Buck," Jerico said, "I don't want to get you excited, but I don't think I'm going to fit."

34| Giles threw the slingshot angrily onto the ground. "I *told* you he didn't mean a slingshot slingshot."

George puffed his chest. "Well then you didn't ask the right questions!"

"I asked him if he really meant a slingshot, and he said that Brother Fye said a slingshot."

"Well, you did do that."

"So I made a slingshot."

"Brother Indo," Jerico said, revelation dawning. "Wonderful. So now what the hell do we do?"

Buck, who had plucked the slingshot from the ground and was examining it closely, shrugged. "Well, I guess we have no choice but to go on without her."

"But if she's the only one who knows—"

The prison blew up.

One minute Jerico was trying to decide if ending his life would have any meaning in this world as he was coming to know it, and the next, he was lying flat on his back, watching the stars, the moon, and hundreds of tiny pieces of blackened white and red stone soar over him. He was dazed. But now so dazed that he didn't automatically curl up in his cloak when the tiny pieces began falling to the ground. It sounded like hail. It felt like hell. And when it was over he was on his feet, dusting himself off, and coughing as a thinning cloud of smoke billowed around him.

"Giles! Buck!" he called.

"What about me, huh?" George demanded.

"I was coming to you."

"Well, I think you always liked my brother best."

Stunned is what Jerico decided when Jambo stumbled into him, his face covered with dirt, his mustache singed to half its length. He grabbed the man by the shoulders and eased him to the ground, rose again and looked around him.

All visible sections of the street were filling rapidly with villagers, some loudly proclaiming the end of the world, some carrying lamps and torches, others simply wandering silently about, picking up shards of stone block and roof tile and stuffing them into bulging sacks. A woman was crying. A man was cursing. A black-and-white dog used its spiked tail to make gravel for its gloating master.

Buck, his robe tattered and his tonsure frizzed, ran up and knelt beside George. "Are you all right, my son?"

"He likes my brother better than me."

"Not to worry. We all do that on occasion."

Jerico found Giles a few minutes later, standing at the end of the yellow patch, arms limp at his sides.

"They're in there," the cook was saying in a monotone. "They're in there. They're in there."

"Who is?" Jerico asked gently.

But Giles only shook his head, then suddenly covered his face with his hands and began to weep.

Jerico, remembering then that several members of Giles' family had been imprisoned in that hellish place, held him tightly and looked over his shoulder at what was left of the Ghorfon Ghorlen. Which wasn't very much. Little more, in fact, that one or two portions of the back wall and a slab of the red roof. The rest was rubble, or that part of it which hadn't scattered over Guba and the countryside, and flames sprouted weakly where splintered beams had been exposed, casting a sickly wavering light over the earth.

Of any survivors there was no sign.

Jini, he thought.

Buck and George came up behind him, soon joined by Indo and a handful of Innkeepers, as the villagers themselves began to gather around the yellow, calling out names, wailing names, calling down curses upon whoever had caused this monumental tragedy.

"She might still be there," Buck said then, into Jerico's ear.

"Impossible, Brother. Just look at it. An ant couldn't have lived through that explosion."

Buck touched his shoulder. "Look again, my son. Do you see any evidence of cells or offices or guards' quarters?"

"How can I? It's all blown up. Besides, it's dark."

Giles raised his head, wiped the tears from his cheeks. "Underground," he whispered hoarsely.

"Yes," Buck said.

And Jerico seized upon the faint hope offered by the monk by shouting at the assembled crowd until it had quieted down. Then, with gestures and all the public speaking skills he had at his command, he told them to surround the yellow patch with high-burning torches while the rest threw their stones back. When they stared at him as if he were out of his mind, he told them why, told them what he planned to do, and watched with great satisfaction as they followed his instructions with a mighty cheer and hurrah.

Buck shook his head. "It's madness, my son."

Part of the plaza blew up.

"But go!" the monk added hastily. "Go with Ralph, and may the W'dch'ch be with you!"

Without so much as a pose or a speech, Jerico whirled, and leapt upon the first rock large enough to hold him. Then, balancing perfectly without being smug about it, he stripped off his cloak, intending to use it to land on should his feet not land where his mind willed them.

Stone by rock, then, to the exhortations of the crowd, thinking that Eliza on her best day never had a day like this.

Stone by rock.

Slipping once as the dancing shadows caused a misstep, hearing the villagers hold their collective breath.

Nearer, ever nearer, while a series of explosions out in the fields eventually showered him with budding ears of popped orange corn.

He could hear Buck praying at the top of his voice, he could hear Giles begging him to find them and bring them home; he could hear the Tabernacle gong sounding encouragement from afar; and he could hear someone following in his stonesteps, but he didn't dare turn around.

This, he thought when he nearly fell again, is the second dumbest thing you've ever done in your life.

Bud he did reach the still-smoking foundations of the Ghorlen without serious mishap, and when he turned, Giles fell into his arms.

"Sorry," the cook said, instantly disengaging. "Tripped."

He was followed almost immediately by George,

then by Perce Obbin and a handful of other villagers, who had taken their lives in hand in order to search the smoking ruins for their loved ones, their lost ones. And once there, they wasted no time clearing what was left between what was left of the walls, tossing the debris onto the yellow, exposing more and more of the floor, and not a thing more.

"I don't know," Jerico muttered as he lobbed a massive chair seat over his head. "I don't know."

Then: "Here, hero! Over here!"

Obbin stood over a large door cleverly built into the floor. Actually, there were two of them, but he was standing on one while pointing to the other. He was also jogging in place, a curious reaction, until Jerico realized that someone beneath the door was trying to get out.

Obbin realized it too and jumped to one side.

The door slammed up.

A head poked out. "Is this Albuquerque?" a voice asked, and Jerico laughed as he reached down and caught Daughter Jini under her arms, pulled her out, and spun her around, hugged her, kissed her, danced away with her as others poured out of the Ghorlen proper into the night's free air.

There were cheers.

A band began to play.

Jini wiped the dust and soot from her eyes and stared at him in amazement. "Incredible," she said.

"Hero," he explained.

"I'll be damned," she answered, and fainted.

With no time to waste, Jerico once again carried the unconscious Jini Fye in his arms, across the field of stones which had replaced the yellow patch. And once at Buck's side, they instructed Indo to be sure to let the brothers know where they were, then pushed their way through the crowd and ran as fast as they could to the Tabernacle. Brother Zay was busily working in the antechamber, which was filled to crowding with hospital cots bearing wounded monks and groaning villagers. When he spotted the woman cradled in Jerico's arms, he cried out piteously, beat his breast, then grabbed her still form into his own grasp and gently placed her on the floor.

"Likes her, does he?" Jerico asked when Buck pulled him aside.

"You could say that. She's his daughter."

"What? But I thought she was your daughter."

"Only in a spiritual sense," Buck replied with a sigh. "A Daughter, not a daughter, if you catch the drift and I think that you do."

Jerico shook his head at all the complications he was expected to keep up with, then knelt beside Brother Zay and asked if she would be all right.

"Just a knock on the head," he said with relief. "And exhaustion. Give her a few minutes and you can go out and save the world."

"A few minutes?"

"But of course, hero." The monk held up his hands. "These are, if I do say so myself, pretty good at what they do. A few minutes, and you can go."

Jerico doubted.

But a few minutes later Jini was indeed with him on the Tabernacle steps, sitting, watching the glow of the torchlight over what had once been the Ghorfon Ghorlen. Butck had hurried off to find out what was keeping the brothers, instructing them not to leave until he returned.

Part of the river blew up.

"Was it bad in there?" Jerico finally asked.

Jini shuddered. "They wanted to ravage me, the beasts."

He moaned in sympathy. "You fought them off?"

"I kicked their balls in is what I did," she answered

savagely. "They were going to fry me in the morning."
She looked off to the southwest, across the dark hills
to the twin mountains unseen at the unseen horizon.
"To think I have that son of a bitch to thank."

"A miracle," Jerico agreed.

"Lousy aim," she corrected.

"A miracle of lousy aim," he compromised, and
was pleased to hear her laugh, softly, finally leaning
her head against his shoulder and sighing.

"It's going to be tough out there tomorrow."

"I know. He knows we're coming."

"He's going to throw everything he has at us."

"I know. He knows it's the end of his nefarious and
evil reign."

She shifted. "You're pretty hung up on this dead
woman, aren't you?"

He shrugged. "It happens."

"We could die."

"She already is."

"You wanna get laid?"

He looked at her, shocked. "But you're a monk!"

"Right," she said, "but I ain't no nun."

Whereupon she grabbed his head, pulled it down,
and kissed him so passionately and desperately that
he could not help but recall that he was indeed a hero,
and as a hero had a moral obligation to shield from
distress and harm all who asked; and while Jini Zay
was not, in the strictest sense of the word, in danger of
being harmed in the next few hours or so, she was
most certainly in a distinct kind of distress, even
though it looked like a blue robe.

What the hell, he decided; indecision causes wars
and social unrest. Decisive action, on the other hand,
makes things happen, and heroes, if nothing else,
make things happen.

He kissed her back.

Buck thumped him on the head.

"Jesus," he said, breaking Jini's embrace and rubbing his skull.

"Third time's the charm," Giles giggled from the plaza, "but George says I have no ambition."

Flustered, embarrassed, and headachy, Jerico pushed himself to his feet, was about to tell Buck that what he saw wasn't what he thought he saw, changed his mind because it was, and suggested that they head 'em up and move 'em out before Joquinn finally figured out what he was doing.

Buck glowered.

The brothers swept on their cloaks and announced their readiness for whatever lay ahead.

Jini ducked into the Tabernacle to say goodbye to her father, and returned just as Buck had decided, much too vocally for Jerico's peace of mind, to use his Innkeeper's powers to cut a hero down to size. She forestalled him by kissing him on the cheek; then she slapped him when he decided to use his powers for something else.

"Children, children," Jerico said with a touch of sanctimony that sent his conscience into a tailspin, "let us not squabble. After all, we have an enemy to defeat."

"He's right," Buck said, though he begrudged every word. "And if I'm not mistaken, Indo is bringing the horses up even as I speak."

Jerico frowned. "Horses?"

"You know, the big things."

"But they're blind!"

"So it's dark."

He looked to Jini. "Why not the river?"

"Horses can't swim," she said, taking his arm and leading him down the steps. "Besides, the Nunby winds too much this close to Kyroppig. It'll be quicker to take the hill route."

He shook his head doubtfully, and shook it again

when he was told that each of them would have their own mount. His complaint that he couldn't drive was countered with the point that they couldn't see; when he said that was like the blind leading the blind, they told him he'd hit it right on the nose so what was the problem? And when he told them that the last time he'd hit one of them on the nose, the horse had stopped dead in its tracks until it had been frightened, they told him to shut up and get his horse in gear.

Heroes, he thought glumly, don't get no respect.

Then he climbed onto his magnificent white beast, made its acquaintance by whispering into the tiny ears placed just behind its horns, and, with a look at the dark deserted plaza, wondered aloud if they ought to wait for daylight so they could move a bit faster.

When the steps blew up, he said, "Never mind."

35 Gubs was far behind and below him before Jerico realized that somehow he'd acquired the skill of steering his horse without having to shriek in its ear every time a boulder popped up in the road. It was, he discovered, a simple matter of discreet thigh and knee pressure, combined with the rhythmic thump of the beast's trunk, which, Buck informed him, was less like the tap of a white cane than the dispersing of subterranean and barely terranean sonic waves which eventually returned to the horse's extraordinarily sensitive feet, which in turn translated those waves into images that enabled the animal to detour around just about anything but a chicken. For some reason unknown to even the greatest Robswerran minds, fowl were an enigma to the elephantine horses, but that didn't matter because there weren't many chickens left in the country these days.

Wonderful, he thought.

But however all of it worked, it worked, and within

hours he was able to pay more attention to the
countryside than not falling off, and had even accustomed himself to the beast's rolling, sometimes stumbling, gait. It reminded him of the time he'd ridden
through rural Sussex County on such a creature, the
good times he had, the seasickness his memory had
until now successfully suppressed. And were it not for
the somber and sober nature of his journey, he would
have laughed aloud at the joy of feeling so close, give
or take, to Robswerran nature.

By dawn they had reached the crest of the first hill.
The line of thump was single-file, the best to avoid the
invisible bolts that still ripped through the sky now
and then. Jerico, as befitted his stature, was first,
followed by Buck, Jini, and the brothers. So it was he
who saw the wide valley first, the verdant fields, the
glorious flowers, the groves and small woods of trees
so tall the closest branches to the ground could only be
reached by daring birds. As far as he could tell, there
were no villages here, nor single dwellings to suggest
folk living the solitary life. And to his right, far enough
to be little more than a silvery glint, was the Nunby.

Wow, he thought as the horse wended its way along
the winding road; what a lovely place to set up a
homestead, raise a family and a few chickens, and
grow old with dignity.

A snake slithered across the road a few yards ahead.
It was a rather large snake, broad as well as long, and
the way it suddenly curled into a coil and lifted its
black-banded head suggested a good reason nobody
lived here.

He froze as the horse neared it, hoping the animal
wouldn't panic once its feet had picked up the peculiar sound of the snake's hissing, which was more like
someone whistling a tune he didn't know, with notes
yet undiscovered. His mount thumped on. The snake
reared back, exposing three fangs and raising a crest of

horns along the top of its flat skull. Jerico looked over his shoulder, and Buck simply waved him on with a not-to-worry gesture and a smile, which he took to mean that the snake's whistle was worse than its bite. A concept he doubted when the horse began to tremble, nearly throwing him off before he could grab hold of a fistful of the bristlelike lavendar topknot that grew between the humps of its sturdy skull.

He drew his sword.

The snake rose to the level of his chin.

Suddenly the horse snapped its trunk around the serpent, body-slammed it twice without breaking stride, and threw it a good quarter mile toward the river.

"Bless you," Jerico said.

The horse snorted and thumped, and wagged its furry tail.

By nightfall they had reached the base of the second range of hills. Though the band had stopped twice to feed and let the horses graze, Jerico was more than happy to slide to the ground and stand there, swaying slightly, his legs bent into a bow that suggested a lifelong affection for barrels. And once he had regained his land legs, he brought his mount to an area of high grass and succulent flowers, tethered it with a chain Buck had given him when they'd left, and stroked its flank, patted its cheek, and walked over to the others, who were seated around a campfire Giles had started in a shallow pit George had dug with his thorn.

As he sat, groaning, stretching his neck, rummaging in his cloak for a flask of water, Jini knelt in front of him and said, "Why did you do that?"

"Because I'm sore," he answered.

"No. I mean, why did you do all those things to your horse?"

He was puzzled. "Why not? He's a good horse. He saved my life. He worked hard today. Why not show him how grateful I am for his efforts, especially since his handicap forces him to labor much harder than others who do not suffer as he."

Jini looked over to Buck. "He's still talking like that."

"He's a hero," Buck explained, and returned to his explanation of how a proper stew of snake meat and rosebuds ought to be seasoned.

Giles merely harumphed and ignored him. Buck didn't take the hint.

"You know," Jerico said, "I'm getting a little tired of people telling me that I talk funny."

"Well, you do."

"No. I perhaps speak differently than you and the rest in both syntax and symbolic interludes, but basically we speak the same language."

"You couldn't tell it by me," she said, and crawled over to her cloak, which she had kicked into her evening's bed.

He was too tired to argue. Instead he laid back and cupped his hands behind her head, listening to a flock of birds wheeling in toward a distant grove for their night's nesting, to Buck trying not to lose his temper when Giles slapped a handful of common dirt from his hand, to George humming a marching song as he combed his mustache, to the horses snorting and thumping as they sought comfort for the night.

The campfire crackling.

His own breathing steadying.

What a life, he thought, oddly and suddenly content; what a life this is. What a life.

He dozed for an hour and had no dreams. He awakened when the stew's delicious aroma proved too much for his stomach. He stretched, he yawned, he crawled over to the fire and accepted a plate of dinner from Giles, who warned him not to eat too much before going into the water.

"Water?"

"Yes. As in swimming, sire."

"But I'm not going swimming."

"I told you," George said, reclining beyond the pit with a meal of his own.

"But Mother always said that before we ate," Giles complained.

"Yes, but—"

"It's all right," Jerico said hastily, before the brothers came to blows. "I understand that it is a tradition in your family. A caution to savor rather than gulp down one's meal lest one lose the pleasure of its digestive company."

"Exactly, sire!" Giles said with a big grin. Then he glared at his brother. "Shows what you know, creep."

"I know it needs more mud," George said, and turned his back.

Jerico smiled tolerantly and returned to his place, ate, drank some water, and was about to ask Buck what he could expect the following day, when he yawned, looked surprised, and thus surprised, fell asleep just as a tree blew up less than a mile away.

"I can't imagine what came over me," he said the next morning as the party climbed the second hill. He was third in line today, ahead of George, behind Giles. "One minute there I was, and the next minute, there I wasn't. Incredible."

"It's the air," Giles said, speaking loudly because of the distance between them. "All that fresh air and good food just works miracles on you after a hard day's ride."

"I suppose." But he felt as good as he ever had. His legs were getting used to the odd spread on the horse's head; his spine was getting used to swaying with the horse's sway; and he found that he was no longer jumping whenever a tree or a stump blew up without any warning. Joquinn was still at it. More so, it seemed, since there weren't many trees left between the travelers and the next hill.

He smiled without much humor. The man was afraid, that much was clear; his increasing attempts to reduce them to cinders only proved that he was frantic, that he was desperate, that he was still not able to work the Seven Spears.

Yet Jerico was bothered, and could not bring himself to mention it to the others.

Bothered because he had remembered upon walking that Joquinn had more at his disposal than a simple armory of powerful and terrifying magic—he had the heroes. An army of them. Just waiting to do his bidding. Unless they already were doing his bidding, biding their time until the lone band of Ralphian freedom fighters were lulled by mere exploding trees into false security. Waiting until, with a cry, with a shout, they would sweep down upon them and hack them to shreds, or take them prisoner after beating them all to hell and returning them to Kyroppig and the presence of their master, there to be tortured, then killed, and planted in someone's yard.

Heroes.

His colleagues.

Men who, like him had sworn to uphold justice and truth and the rights of those who are downtrodden by others.

It was enough to turn his stomach, which it did, which made him belch, which made his mount skitter sideways a few feet until he was able to bring it back under control.

"A problem, sire?" George asked solicitously.

"Just thinking about what lies ahead," he answered truthfully.

"The way of heroes," Giles said in admiration. "Would that I could do such a thing."

"But everyone," Jerico told him, "can think about what lies ahead. It's only natural."

"Oh, natural for you, maybe," the cook replied. "That's because you're a hero. I just boil water. I can't think more than three or four hours beyond where I am."

Jerico looked at him, but the man was serious, and he could only smile encouragement and ask, as a change of subject, if he'd been able to locate any of his captive relatives in the ruins of Ghorfon Ghorlen.

"Alas," said Giles, "though we freed two hundred and some, none belonged to me."

"Damned good thing," George muttered loud enough for the whole country to hear.

"George!"

"Well, it's true, brother. They were a disgrace to the family names."

"They were freedom fighters, just like us!"

"They cut off the head of the Innkeeper of Sanzogel Tabernacle, that's what they did!"

Jerico's eyes widened in astonishment. "They did what?"

George twisted around on his mount. "They lopped, sliced, and otherwise removed the head of an Innkeeper, the one in Sanzogel." He made a chopping motion with his head. "And all he did was refuse to marry our sister."

"He deserved what he got!" Giles insisted. "Our cousins were well within their rights to enforce the marital contract."

"Well, not really," George said. "There wasn't a contract, if you remember."

"But there would have been if the Innkeeper had asked her to marry him."

"Yes, that's true."

"So when he refused, they had no choice." Giles then displayed a remarkable talent for decapitation-and-mangling mime. "And for that, they were thrown in the worst prison in Robswerran. Now I ask you."

Jerico faced front. This was no time to get embroiled in familial politics which had themselves become entangled with the laws of this land. He would grant both men their positions and try not to bring it up again; later, when he was alone with Buck, he would ask about the ramifications of beheading where proposals actual and intimated were concerned.

Finally the hill was topped, and the valley on this side was twice as wide, twice as beautiful, twice as serene as they one they'd just left. He was entranced, and didn't mind at all when Buck's mount took care of a party of serpents lying in ambush behind a thorny hedgerow. In fact, the thuds of snakeskin slapped against the road quickly became lulling, and he dozed for a long time, straight through lunch and well into the afternoon. He awoke only when a section of the road behind them blew up.

"He's getting better," Giles said nervously.

"Better all the time," George admitted.

Buck apparently thought so as well, for he increased the speed of the thump until they were galloping, taking the turns on two legs, storming along the straightaways, shrieking over a slight rise and trampling a family of serpents snacking on what looked to Jerico like the carcass of a buffalo, and not slowing down until they were safely under the canopy of a belt of woodland which, he noted, reached all the way to the Nunby.

The last hill loomed above them when they broke into the open again.

Buck stopped and gestured for the others to gather around him.

"We have two choices," he said when the horses

were all facing the center of a ragged circle. "We can slip over the hill now and be in Kyroppig shortly after midnight. Or we can wait here until dawn, thus bringing us into the city around noon."

"Noon," voted Giles. "They won't be expecting us at noon."

"Midnight," contravoted his brother. "They'll be asleep."

"They're already expecting us," Jini said, "and they won't be sleeping as long as they are, so it's really six of one and half a dozen of the other. I don't care."

Buck looked at Jerico.

Jerico stroked his mount's lavender topknot thoughtfully before clearing his throat and saying, "I think we should wait until tomorrow, my friends. It will," he continued forcefully over George's moans of disgust, "give us a chance to see the enemy when they attack."

"Not necessary, my son," Buck said. "For Joquinn to see us, I mean. He's doing all right as it is."

"I wasn't talking about Joquinn," he said, and pulled his mount out of the circle and rode on, slowly, wondering if he would be able to actually engage in combat with other heroes. And no matter how often he told himself that they weren't heroes if they were engaged in unheroic activities, he still couldn't get the distasteful prospect out of his mind.

Jini rode up beside him. "Buck remembered," she said.

"I figured he would."

"He thinks you'll have a hard time of it."

"I do too."

Though she was unable to reach him, she held her hand out anyway. "You do have friends, you know. You won't be alone."

He smiled, a bit sadly. "I will and I won't," he told her. "I will and I won't."

"Then I guess . . . it's tomorrow."

He raised an eyebrow, a shoulder, and when she asked him why he was twitching, he stuck out his tongue, laughed, and decided he might as well stop now and rest, because from tomorrow at dawn he wasn't going to be able to stop until either the Seven Spears were freed, or he and the others were dead.

"God," she said, shuddering.

"It's a living," he said, and belched.

36 They rode midway up the slope and pitched camp under the shade of a fir tree whose crown was fully fifty feet wide. No one remarked on it. No one said a word when Jerico clambered up it as far as he could go, to be sure no ambush had been laid for their demise.

Evening arrived much too fast.

All of them were jittery once the decision had been made, and at the same time they were glad that something was about to happen which they could control. That knowledge helped pass the hours after the last meal of the day, those hours when, try as they might, they were unable to sit still. They walked. They paced. They climbed the tree and swung from branch to branch until the birds got fed up and drove them down again.

Weariness set in.

No one expected to sleep, but each knew it had to be if he was to be effective in the morning.

A rotation of watch had been set up at Jerico's behest, and once the brothers had stopped arguing about who should go first, the others laid on their cloak-beds and closed their eyes, opened them, closed them, finally got up and sat staring into the dying flames of the fire.

One by one they came to the pit. One by one they looked at each other and looked away, afraid they might see fear in someone else's eyes, a fear that would transfer itself to them and make them panic.

George tried singing a few cheerful songs he had learned as a child at his mother's knee, but when Buck tried to accompany him on the humming hat pin, the gardener volunteered for the early watch, gathered his equipment glumly, and trudged up the hill to the summit.

Jerico sat apart from the others. In his hand he held the medallion Buck had given him so long ago, and his finger traced the exquisitely etched Spears of the W'dch'ck. What power lay within the actual objects? he wondered; how had a simple man named Ralph been able to imbue such simple things with so much devotion, so much magic, so much utter faith that an entire, or most of an entire, country was willing to lay down its life to simply to preserve it? Or them.

He supposed, as he tucked the medallion away beneath his shirt, that it was the same belief in the innate goodness of life that had propelled him on his own odyssey of heroism—and while he was not, he added quickly, comparing himself in any way to the divine attributes of Ralph, he could see the similarities, except for the bathtub in Nevada.

At the moment it was small comfort; Ralph was dead, and there was no sense carrying that stupid analogy too far.

Finally he laid back and closed his eyes, hoping against hope that Dawn would find the magical means to come to him once again, as she had that horrible night on the ledge above the gorge. But all he saw were the sideways mocking eyes of the evil Joquinn, that hideous nose, that disgusting hank of hair. The sorcerer laughed silently, pointing a bony finger at him and cackling, turning around and looking over his shoulder and sneering, opening his mouth so wide that the stubs of his blackened teeth wiggled and danced.

He woke with a start, sitting up, listening, afraid that somehow the enemy had snuck past the watch. But the campsite was silent except for a lot of snoring, and he yawned, stretched, and dragged his gear up the hill.

Buck was there, seated, not moving.

"It's me," Jerico said, sitting down beside him.

"I know. I could hear you coming." The monk rose and pulled his cowl over his head. "In the morning," he said.

"In the morning," Jerico said, and looked out at the valley where his destiny waited.

As the second valley was twice as large as the first, so was this twice as large as the second. And at the far end, at the base of the southernmost of the two mountains, he could see the lights of Kyroppig. From here they formed a solid mass of gold and white and flickering blues and reds; it was impossible to judge how large the area was, but he knew that even Fadfy would seem small by comparison.

And in that sea of light was the man he sought, no doubt sleeping the sleep of the unjust and having a damned good time at it too, the sonofabitch.

Then a tree blew up behind him and he thought, oh hell.

And thought it again when someone shook his shoulder and he rubbed at his eyes as he stood. He was under the tree again, having been relieved by Jini, and he ate the breakfast Giles prepared without tasting a thing.

The truth was, and he was not ashamed to admit it, he was excited. Somewhere in the land of his dreams he had resolved the question of his doubts about the army he was about to face, assuming Joquinn wasn't stupid enough to keep it in the city. They were, no matter what they had been before, the bad guys; he was the good guy. It was as simple as that.

"Jerico!"

He looked up the hill and saw Buck waving to him. Swiftly he mounted his horse and urged it onto the road, waited for the others to fall in behind, then took his time moving up. He wanted to see the valley unfold, not sweep over him; being overwhelmed would do him no good.

First, then, were the mountains, several miles away, yet seeming only inches from the tip of his nose so great was their height, so magnificent was their bulk. Peaks and canyons and forests and rock faces all were as clear as if he were standing on their slopes; haze ringed them at several elevations; clouds mustered about each of their summits. He knew not their names, nor did he care to know—if they weren't unpronounceable, they would probably be scary.

The valley floor itself was virtually perfectly flat. One vast meadowland with the Nunby cutting through it just before the city. No trees. No ravines. No knolls or humps or mud flats or groves. A vivid mix of greens that made his eyes sting when he stared at it too long.

And Kyroppig.

"My," he said.

"Not bad," Buck agreed. "It has its good points."

A sprawl. A blanket. A congestion. A vision. A hell of a lot of buildings, some tall, some short, too far away still to be seen as edificial individuals, yet giving the impression that each one was unique. Glitters of mica, striations of granite, swirls of marble, verticals and horizontals of exotic harvested woods. There was no wall around it. It simply began just beyond the banks of the river.

"Joquinn," he said, his voice giving away nothing.

Buck pointed to a massive greenstone dome on the city's western edge. Even from here Jerico could see the ever present medallion, this one a bronze so highly polished that the sun had turned it into a gigantic blinding mirror.

He turned to Jini. "You stay with me."

"Am I supposed to be flattered?" she said, a poor attempt at jocularity.

"You know the way. I need to know."

"Sire?" Giles said.

He smiled. "Yes?"

"You said we shouldn't let any of them get around us unless all of them do."

"That is correct."

"Who?"

Jerico blinked.

"Well, who do you think, stew brain?" George said with a snort of disgust.

"I'm sure I don't know," his brother replied huffily. "I can't read his mind. Can you?"

"Of course not."

"Then who is he talking about?"

"How the hell should I know? I just follow orders."

"Gentlemen," Jerico said, "I'm talking about them."

"Who?" Giles asked shrilly.

Jerico held his breath, released it. "Do you see me pointing?"

"Certainly. I'm not blind."

"Do you see where I'm pointing?"

"Now, I do, yes. Before, I didn't, because I was talking to George."

"Talk to me."

"Sure. What about?"

"Shoot him," he whispered to Jini, eased his mount around hers, came up beside Giles, and somehow managed to lean over far enough to grab his arm. "Look out there!"

Giles did.

George did.

"Oh," the cook said. "Them."

At first it looked as if a caravan had just crossed the only bridge across the Nunby. Dust of all shades rose and drifted away, the distant sound of metal clanking against metal, the vaguely experienced thunder of many hooves and trunks thumping the ground. But as they came closer, they separated, and no one needed to ask who they were and why they were spreading out over the plain.

Carefully Jerico balanced his sword on his horse's head and rubbed his hands together, rubbed a forearm over his lips, wiped a palm across his brow and dried it on his thigh.

A tree exploded not fifty yards away.

"Well," he said, "this ought to be different."

And he urged his mount down the slope, not galloping, not cantering, not trotting, just . . . walking. He wanted them to know that he was not afraid; he wanted them to know that their abdication of hereoship had not rattled him at all. He also wanted a few thousand more supporters, but as long as he had what he had, he couldn't be too picky.

A high-pitched humming began on his left, and he saw George slowly spinning his thorn over his head.

An equally loud, but lower-pitched, humming on

his right, and Giles did such amazing things with his dagger that Jerico had to force himself to look away.

Jini had a sword in one hand, a club in the other, and on her mount's skull she had placed a coiled whip.

Buck drew a quiver from beneath his robes, slung it over his back for quick access, and assembled a prefabricated bow almost as tall as he. When he saw Jerico staring, he winked and nocked an arrow. "You ready?" he asked, cowl thrown back, gold medallion gleaming on his chest.

Jerico didn't answer.

He rode on, every so often gesturing to either separate or draw closer his tiny band.

The hero army finally saw them, just as Jerico had counted at least thirty of them, all on horseback. None seemed to be carrying guns, but that was something he couldn't count on.

"George," he called. "The weapons you hid."

"I'll be with you, sire, never fear. I'll show you."

"Where are they?"

He didn't answer.

"George!"

"Sire, don't you trust me?"

His smile wasn't pretty.

"There's a pawnshop just as you take that side road over there into the city." The man pointed; he saw it. "Behind it is a big mound of dirt. I put the guns in there."

"A big mound of dirt?"

"Who had time to dig a hole?"

"Actually," Giles called from the other side, "it's more like a compost heap than a mound of dirt."

"A compost heap?"

Giles grinned. "You think anyone's going to root around a compost heap just for the hell of it?"

Jerico almost laughed; the man had him there, and

the guns there, and he was here, and the heroes were beginning to move a little faster.

"They're going to charge, sire," George yelled, thorn a blur and screaming.

"Oh no they're not," Jerico said.

"They aren't?"

"No. I am."

And he did.

37 And this, Jerico thought, is the dumbest thing you've ever done in your life.

Fortunately for his reputation and unfortunately for his bodily comfort and one-piece survival, the sheer noise of his tiny band coupled with that of the approaching horde was too deafening for anyone to hear him question the legality, the morality, and the wisdom of what they were doing. He was stuck, and the only way out of it was either to ram through the heroes as he had done the black riders, or save his own hide by splitting open a few others.

Retreating never occurred to him; and when it did, he slapped his face.

I was retired, he thought; Jesus, what an idiot.

But he kept to the road, leaning over his horse's broad skull and directing it with subtle slams to its temples with his fist. Giles and George had already swept far out on the flanks and had drawn a number of the enemy to them, though precisely how many it was difficult to say because of all the dust and the fact that they kept moving around so much. Buck remained nearby, hoarding his precious arrows, though those he did loose found their marks with an accuracy that had Jerico shuddering, and wondering if the monk had a thing about noses.

Jini simply screamed, a banshee ululation of sheer hatred and revenge that caused a handful of Joquinn's men to slow up and exchange questioning glances.

Jerico was silent.

He rode onward, ever onward, his unwavering sights trained on the man heading straight for him—a flaming redhead, unhealthily bulky, wearing nothing above the waist but a band of studded leather across his massive chest; he carried a short sword in his right hand, a mace in his left, and when he realized that he was the first target, he grinned so broadly his teeth sparkled in the morning sunlight.

Dumb, Jerico thought. Dumb. Dumb. Dumb.

Luckily he noted, when only a hundred yards separated them, that all pachydermic horses in Robswerran were not created equal, or equally fast. While he and his people were able to maintain a reasonably straight line of attack, the assembled villainous heroes were beginning to grow a bit ragged, some charging far ahead of the others, many lagging behind as if their hearts weren't really in it. And the dust raised by them all, he hoped, just might work to his advantage.

Then, with an inevitability he'd never encountered at Yale, he closed with the toothy one, their respective mounts passing so closely he had to jerk up his leg so not to have it rubbed off. At the same time, he leaned over as far as he could, ducked under the other's sword stroke, and lashed out with one of his own, catching the man cleanly across the wrist. He shrieked and dropped his weapon, but Jerico was already gone.

Mugging, he thought; god, my kingdom for a mugging.

A pair of dark-skinned barbarians converged on him next, whooping and hollering, and he realized that leaning over as he'd done earlier was a stunt that only left him wide open for a spinal injection, a decapitation, a scalping, and several other humiliations he instantly shunted to a side track where he hoped they'd be forgotten.

So he whispered again to his steed and with a prayer to the W'dch'ck and an appeal to Ralph's mercy for thundering fools, he spread his arms and lurched unsteadily to his feet, swayed, nearly toppled, then planted his boots solidly on the skull's mounds. When the first barbarian reached him, so astonished at the tactic that he forgot to use his razor-whip, Jerico leapt onto his horse, slashed his nape in half, and leapt back to the white beast, who had slowed down to catch him.

The second one pulled up and gaped in admiration.

Whereupon Jerico clubbed him with the flat of his blade while his horse wrapped its trunk around the other one's tail and yanked, released, and got out of the way just in time. The collision of man and beast with the ground was horrendous, but the tripping of several others over the writhering pile was worth a second look, which Jerico gave it, and nearly lost his equilibrium when a dark-haired hero threw a boomerang at his knees.

He jumped.

He ducked.

The boomerang eventually found its home.

So did one of his mount's horns when a hero tried a sneak attack from underneath.

A horse shrieked.

A man screamed.

He saw Jini deftly razor-whip three salivating men

to the bone before they realized they were no longer mounted, and had no reason to be so.

A bald hero in a kilt and Eisenhower jacket charged him with an arrow buried in his leg; Jerico yanked it out, threw it over his shoulder, and was pleased at the resulting scream to note that he hadn't lost his flamboyant touch.

And still he rode on, never swerving from his objective—the bridge over the River Nunby.

Dust clogged his throat and blinded his eyes; a thrust from a hell of a long knife laid open his left forearm, so he tore a piece of the sleeve off with his teeth and used the length of self-mending cloth as a tourniquet to stanch the flow of blood; his horse stumbled with weariness, and he urged it on, gently yet forcefully, and its trunk thumped so rapidly it became a white blur.

Buck passed him, a makeshift blue bandage tied around his head.

A hero blew up; Joquinn had found the range.

Another hero leapt onto the back of Jerico's white horse and grabbed him from behind, an arm hooked around his throat. He thrashed and twisted wildly, and finally snared the other's wrist as it and the hand attached to it came around to slit his throat to the spine.

"Cad!" Jerico gasped, his face shocking red.

"Miscreant!" he accused, his hand growing weak.

"My god," the attacker said, then shouted. "My god, boys, it's Jerico Dove!"

Jerico flexed. Jerico bulked. In a single fluid motion Jerico dragged the man over his shoulder and handed him to his horse's trunk, which thumped him once, thumped him twice, then thumped him once again before slamming him like a battering ram into two others, driving them to the ground where their mounts, confused by the shouting and the screaming and the running, thumped them into steaks for migrant armacons to find.

Jerico aimed for the bridge.

Jini drew up beside him and shouted, "They know who you are!" She was laughing with delight, and when he followed the direction of her pointing whip, he saw that many of the remaining heroes were charging the others instead.

Or . . . and he had to clamp a hand to his breast to keep his heart from leaving . . . or they were actually, holy cow he didn't believe it . . . they were actually running away! Away from the fray, away from the city, away from their mounts whose thumping was erratic.

A geyser rose from the Nunby, steaming and boiling and subsiding with a hiss.

Buck came to his other side, his quiver empty, his hat pin glowing. He was grinning even though he was bleeding from a dozen wounds.

Riding hard. Riding straight.

The bridge directly ahead, and Giles and George none the worse for wear despite a few slashes and bruises soon joined them, staying behind in case one of the remaining heroes tried to be a hero for Joquinn.

A bird exploded in the sky; Jerico figured Joquinn was excited.

Before they reached the bridge, Jerico slowed them to a walk. There were scores of people lining the banks on the other side of the river, and though he could barely catch his breath, he knew his horse was completely winded. There would be no charge if they were unfriendly; there would be no fancy maneuvers or clever ruses.

"Jerico," Jini said, "why don't you sit down?"

He sat.

"Jerico," she said, "you'd better take a drink."

He did. He emptied the first two flasks he could find. He slowed his valiant beast even more and, after scanning the riverbank for hints and signs of treachery, took the first step onto the bridge—an amalgam of lashed spars and beams that trembled under the weight.

The crowd increased as hundreds of people ran from their houses and stared at the procession. Some made tentative waves after looking over their shoulders; others simply watched them solemnly, nodding perhaps, perhaps fingering medallions they kept hidden under their clothes.

Jerico did not look at them. He looked at Kyroppig instead, at the multitude of glowingly picturesque buildings, none of which resembled its equally picturesque neighbor, at the broad cobblestoned streets, at the gaudy flags and vivid banners flying from poles in front of huge white structures with only posts at their corners, at the bewildering signs hanging over shop doors and large glassless windows of establishments to which he could not put a name or function, at the forbidding mountain that rose behind it, and at the dome of the Tabernacle that could be seen from every quarter.

A peasant blew up.

The crowds scattered, screaming.

Jerico said to Jini, "I think we'd do better if we left our horses here."

"But why? We can go faster with them."

"Yes, but we also make better targets."

"The sire has a point," George said, immediately slipping to the ground.

"But I'm so tired, brother," Giles protested. "How can I fight if I'm tired?"

"Keen observation," George said, but he couldn't remount because someone had stolen his horse.

"Well, if you're going to walk, George," Giles told him magnanimously, "I'll walk too."

Jerico looked at Jini. Jini looked back at him.

"Well?" he asked as they rounded a corner just after Giles' horse took a bolt in the tail.

"It's farther than it looks," she said.

"So's death."

"Oh, Jesus."

He grinned and dismounted. When an urchin raced up to steal the blind beast, Jerico grabbed him by the shirtfront, lifted him off the ground, and growled, "Do you know who I am?"

The urchin nodded, eyes filled with fear.

"Did you see what I just did, out there, on the plain?"

Another nod, and a feeble kicking of his feet.

"Then you watch after this noble beast, little man, or I'll find you when this is over, and I'll show you what a human heart looks like when it's still beating."

The urchin gulped, promised ever to be faithful to the wonderful Jerico Dove, and, when Jerico released him, gathered a dozen friends around the white horse and vowed vigilance and loyalty and no tax on the watching fee.

Jerico glared at them all, turned on his heel, and marched off.

"They'll steal it, you know," Jini told him as they rounded another corner.

"Sure they will. But Jesus, won't they have a hard time sleeping for the next few weeks."

She looked at him dumfounded.

He laughed and drew her to his side, kissed her forehead, praised her fighting, and threw her into the litterless gutter when a bolt struck an Elizabethan tavern only a few yards away. For nearly a full minute they were showered with harmless debris, but when they regained their feet and started running, some of the townspeople decided that the hero and the lady monk were more a blessing on the plain than in their precarious but previously intact neighborhood.

They threw rocks.

They threw garbage.

They found themselves in a riot when those of the opposite opinion engaged them in a vociferous and oftimes physical debate that reminded Jerico of Times Square.

Then George came up, panting. "Sire," he said, and pointed toward the dome, off to their right.

"The guns first," he replied. "We can't go in there without them."

The gardener nodded, ducked a flowerpot, then grabbed his arm and yanked him into a narrow, dark alley. "A shortcut," he promised. "And he may not see us in here."

Jerico hesitated, then agreed, and slowed to a quick walk as George and Giles took the lead now, and led him deeper into the heart of the city he'd come to save.

38 So this, he thought in amazement, is the labyrinth of the underbelly of the city.

The alley they had plunged into cleverly connected with others, a veritable maze of them that avoided any contact with the main streets, a maze darkened by the overhang of thatched and tiled roofs and exposed-beamed second stories, smelling of garbage, pocked with puddles of rank water, infested with insects that would have put flies and gnats to shame; others used this off-route route as well, but none looked up at the two monks, the cook, the gardener, and the hero. As far as the underbelly was concerned, they were anonymous.

And thus should it be, Jerico thought as he stepped lightly over a ragged man sleeping on a ragged mat of sodden reeds and apple cores; if any one of those unsavory folk knew who he was, they would have made their fortunes selling the knowledge of his whereabouts to Joquinn, who was, evidently, still trying to ferret him out by taking potshots at buildings, streets, and the occasional luckless stranger.

"Trouble," Buck said quietly, nearly an hour after they'd left their steeds behind.

Jerico whirled, sword at the ready.

"No. Up there."

He looked up through the narrow gap between overhangs, but could see nothing but the bright blue sky. Until he saw an orange flash, then heard an enormous explosion. When he looked his confusion at the Innkeeper, Buck said, "He's stronger. You couldn't see them before. Now you can."

"The man is mad," Jerico declared. "He'll blow up the whole city just to find us?"

The monk nodded.

He shuddered and urged the others to move more quickly; but they could go only so fast through the shadows, across the slippery stones, around the sudden sharp turns, and up the suddenly steep inclines. Several times he checked behind them, hoping to fix a landmark in his mind, and each time he gave it up and wondered if he ought to be dropping bread crumbs instead.

A gang of thieves blocked their path as they skirted a particularly noxious pool of something liquid, and Jerico glowered at them, Buck snarled at them, and George spun his mustaches fast enough to make them hum. The gang sped away. George untangled Giles, and Jerico rushed on. A sense of dread had begun to settle on his shoulders, and no matter how hard he tried, he couldn't shake it off. It was not unlike those horrid hours on the Miteyose Mas, when despair was the rule and hope the miraculous exception.

"I don't like it," he said much later, tripping over a carton of something whose insides broke into runny pink liquid. "There's something wrong here."

Jini scoffed, but Giles dropped back and agreed. "I've heard it for a while," he said, glancing anxiously side to side, front to back, up and down.

"Heard what?"

"Listen."

He did, and heard nothing, and shrugged.

"But don't you hear it, sire?"

"I confess, Xamoncroft, that I don't hear a thing."

"That's right."

"It is?"

It was. The man was right. He had been so intent on keeping up the company's speed that he hadn't noticed how silent the city had become. No longer could he hear the roar and bustle of the streets they were avoiding; no longer could he hear, or feel for that matter, the destructive explosions that marked Joquinn's points of rage; no longer was he able to distinguish his footsteps from those of the others.

"My god," he whispered.

"The Spear of Eternal and Most Holy Peace," Buck said, his ruddy face pale, his hat pin fairly spinning. "Man, we are in deep and abiding shit."

Jerico asked him to explain.

The monk, dodging a falling pile of effluvia from a third-story window, told him that the Spear, which is but the Second of the Seven (the first being the Spear of Transitory and Most Holy Materialism, and the one that blew everything up), sends out an aura of serenity so strong that virtually everything within its sphere falls into such a fear of disruption that the very thought of making the slightest sound is tantamount to blasphemy against the Most Holy Ralph.

"But we're talking," Jerico said.

"Yes. And I could kill myself for it."

Jerico waited for the laugh; it didn't come. And when he looked at Buck to be sure the monk wouldn't do anything stupid, he collided with George, who was skulking at a corner.

Sorry, he mouthed, and the gardener nodded, then pointed across a fairly medium-sized plaza to a tiny shop jammed between a tavern whose wood facade was carved into the image of an open dragon's mouth, and a butcher shop, whose display window had been cleverly designed in the shape of a mature armacon whose body had been highlighted to show its choicest parts.

A narrow alley separated the pawnshop from the tavern.

The plaza was deserted.

And to the right, practically filling the immediate sky, was the Tabernacle's greenstone dome.

Night fell. Instantly.

"The Spear of the Most Holy Predawn Reverie," Buck whispered in his ear before begging forgiveness for disturbing his peace.

"How long will it last?"

"Depends on how well the little toad is doing. Oh my, I wish you wouldn't shout like that."

"What's the worst case? How long?"

"All night."

Dim lights burned in windows and over doors, but rather than dispelling the premature night, they only served to enhance it and give birth to its shadows. Add to this the silence, and the soundless detonation which mushroomed far to their left, and Jerico decided that maybe rock music wasn't so bad after all.

He motioned for the others to stay behind him, made sure there was no one in sight along the five streets which fed into the plaza, and ran for the alley. Once there, he realized with a curse that they would have to travel it sideways, and ducked in without hesitation, scooting along, kicking unseen junk out of the way, wincing every time his hands pressed against the dank wall that faced him.

At the far end, which was too damned far for his

taste, he eased around the corner and hunkered down against the pawnshop's back wall. A light from a small window on the second floor illuminated the yard weakly, making the single tree there seen twice as high, the well twice as round, the trampled grass a sickly brown.

There was no pile of dirt.

When Giles crouched beside him, he pointed and said, "Well?"

"No. It was in the dirt, sire. I swear, I put the cache in the dirt. Oh, Ralph! I wish I could stop shouting!"

"Compost heap," George whispered in correction as he popped out of the alley and didn't bother kneeling.

"There is no compost heap," Jini said, weeping for the noise she made, and slapping George mightily for even thinking about answering.

"No," agreed Buck, "but there's an awfully big garden, isn't there?" And tried a ritual self-strangulation before Jini knocked his hands away and kicked him in the shin.

Jerico nodded. Wonderful. Swell. Great. Fiddle.

All they had to do now was dig up every inch of a patch of ground rather tastefully bordered by white stones, a patch that was, at his swift and disheartening estimation, thirty feet wide by fifty feet deep. Little sticks with colorful drawings of obscene-looking plants were dotted over the freshly turned black earth. Tiny green sprouts were already growing at the left-hand border.

There was only one thing left to do.

He rose, dusted off his knees, and herded the others back through the alley, across the plaza, and into the opposite alley, which was just as dark, but wide enough for him to face them all without having to stand on a soap box. They watched him anxiously.

For a moment Jerico lowered his head, gathering his

thoughts, whipping them into shape, before raising his head again and lifting his hands, jerking them to instruct the others to read his lips, watch his gestures, to assimilate all that he had to tell them through sheer desire and clever translation.

Giles applauded without his palms meeting.

Friends, he said, or at least did his best to say, which was, he thought, all one could ask at a time like this, *before we embark on the only course open to us at this time, permit me, a complete stranger to your shores, to tell you how much your friendship and loyalty have meant. I am a hero. You have every reason to distrust men of my professional persuasion. Yet I believe I have allayed your fears in a way that should free you from all doubt and suspicion. Therefore, do not fear when I say that we must, without delay, storm the Kyroppig Tabernacle with only those weapons and that guile which we now possess. It will not be easy. Some of us may not return to our loved ones, dead or alive. Some of us may be captured and suffer the most extreme of tortures. But the rewards are well worth the risks, I say, and I say this great land of yours can be proud to have known, or have heard of, all of you.*

Onward, then, my dear, dear friends, and may the W'dch'ck be with you.

"What'd he say?" Giles asked his brother.

"Follow him."

"How mysterious," said the cook, "are the ways of the Outside."

But Jerico was already in the plaza, marching boldly across to the street he surmised led straight to the Tabernacle. He was, in truth, a little disappointed that his oratory had fallen on deaf ears, but he had made the gesture and that's what counted. All he had to do now was get out of this alive.

And then . . . *then* he was going to retire, and not a

goddamned thing in this world or the next was going to change his mind.

Period.

Exclamation point.

"Holy shit."

The plaza of the Kyroppig Tabernacle of the Most Holy W'dch'ck was easily as large as his backyard in Nevada. Larger if you counted the Tabernacle. And it was empty. Not a booth, not an animal, not a single human or otherwise being waited, stood, or lay dead anywhere on its gleaming surface. No one could. Because every square inch of that surface was covered in flames that reached ten feet high without a single waver, a single dance.

"The Spear of the Most Holy Hearth and Perpetual Campfire," Buck said from behind his left shoulder.

"What are we up to now?"

"Four," said Jini from behind his right.

Jerico walked to the plaza's edge. He could feel no heat from the uncanny, steady fire, yet when he pulled a stick of that pepperoni stuff from his cloak and held it in for a second and pulled it out, there was nothing left but foul-smelling ash. He returned to the others and slowly rubbed his chin.

"He's getting good," he said, jerking his thumb over his shoulder.

"Not that good," Buck answered, smiling. "You'll notice that I am talking, and I don't want to die."

"I don't either, but—ah! The Second Spear is out of commission."

"I doubt it," Jini said, squinting at that part of the dome she could see over the flames. "I think he can't use them all at the same time yet. He must be getting ready to use—"

She disappeared.

Giles disappeared.

George disappeared.

"The Spear of the Most Holy Incorporeal Bliss," Buck said, his voice trembling.

"So we run," Jerico said, grabbing for Buck's arm, missing it because it wasn't there any longer, and turning as he ran just in time to see the flames pop out, the sky turn blue, and the whole world suddenly disintegrate into a distressingly blinding white.

39 Feeling somewhat discombobulated was not high on Jerico's list of fun things to do while being magically transported from one place to another; yet he was willing to put up with it if that was indeed what was happening. If, however, he wasn't being transported, but was actually in a state of deadness without being numb, he thought that it would be a good thing, both emotionally and psychologically, if he screamed a little.

Preferably, a lot, with a little bemoaning of his fate thrown in for good theater.

Then the blinding whiteness began to fade, and he was able to note that he was no longer in the plaza, certainly not dead, and probably, if one could actually calculate the odds on such matters, deep inside the Tabernacle where Joquinn was, even now, preparing to use the Sixth and the Seventh Spears.

He needed no tutor to tell him what that meant.

The last of the white drifted away like a reluctant

fog before a determined breeze, and the room he was in solidified. He dropped to the floor in a startled heap, climbed out, calmed the heap down and sent it on its way to a hole in the corner. Then he looked around as he readjusted his cloak, smoothed his shirt and trousers more suitably about him, and brushed his hands back through his hair.

It was a bedroom.

It was a bedroom whose size suggested a lot of interesting things going on whenever whoever was home was home.

At the back wall was a large simple bed without posts to adorn it, though its headboard was exceedingly elaborate in its carved depiction of a big brown furry creature looking benignly down through fluffy clouds at a group of little brown furry creatures cavorting in a pasture. The footboard was a slab of pine that had notches in it, nothing more.

By the righthand wall was a large round table, around which were set several high-backed chairs whose alabaster cushions were easily six inches thick. The lefthand wall was hidden by a ten-foot wardrobe, an all-purpose vanity, a door, and a porcelain bathtub just large enough for one.

The wall behind him was characterless, except for the door, and for the fact that it, like its three fellows, was painted to look like brown furry hide.

The door was locked.

Both doors were locked.

There were no windows and the bathtub was empty, no sign of a spigot.

The wardrobe was empty as well, and so were all the drawers in the vanity. Its mirror, on the other hand, was too cloudy to see into, and he deduced that here is where the evil Joquinn would make his first appearance, probably to gloat over the capture of his enemy, then threaten him with death and torture, then demand that he, Jerico, spill his guts or the girl would die a slow and guaranteed painful death.

Well, he decided, he might as well be prepared, and be comfortable in the process; so he dragged one of the chairs over, dumped the cushion on the floor, and sat down, propped his heels on the vanity, folded his hands on his stomach, and waited.

And waited.

And fell asleep thinking of all the venomous and destructive retorts he would deliver when Joquinn made his demands.

He awoke he knew not how much later because someone knocked insistently on one of the doors. There was a instant of consternation, followed by one of puzzlement. It had been his limited experience that one's captor did not knock before entering the place of capture; however, this being Robswerran, perhaps custom dictated a more sophisticated approach, which was, in and of itself, a rather hopeful development.

The knocking continued.

He tried the door by the wardrobe and it was still locked, so he tried the other one, which was, this time, unlocked. He dithered a bit, not sure if he was up to a full-scale battle even though his clothes had done a reasonable job of healing him; then he decided that whoever it was out there was going to come in anyway, so why not at least be civilized about it and open the damned thing.

And after he had opened it, he looked, he narrowed his eyes, he damned civilization, and sprang back into the room, sword drawn and at the ready as Dolph Placker walked in, still dressed in red from boots to jaunty neckerchief, and still with a smug ruddy face beneath those unruly tangles of black curls.

"What the hell," Jerico said, "are you doing here?"

Dolph held up a placating hand. "Now, Jerry—

oops, Jerico, sorry, slip of the tongue. Don't be hasty
with that thing. You know how I feel about guns and
stuff."

"This is a sword."

"The principle's the same."

"So're the results."

Dolph never lost his smile. "Just . . . take it easy, all
right? For old times' sake?"

After a long minute of raging internal debate that
would have done his old alma mater proud had he
been on the debating team, which he wasn't because
his mother told him it was only an insidious form of
backtalk, Jerico admitted to himself that pleasures
being few and far between as they were these days, he
would have gladly indulged in a little stomach poking
or heart stopping in order to lighten a thus far pretty
miserable day; on the other hand, he might as well
listen to what the man had to say, just in case it was
either important or gave him enough time to over-
power him and thus make good his escape.

"All right," he said, making a great show of reluctance, and backed away until he reached the bed,
where he hitched himself over the footboard. It was
not the most advantageous of positions from which to
launch an attack if one was needed, but Placker didn't
know that.

He nodded.

Placker walked in, leaving the door ajar. "You'll
never get me that way," he said, turning the chair
around and sitting.

"Talk," Jerico ordered.

Placker grinned. "You know, hero, you've made
quite a lot of noise around here."

Jerico bobbed the sword's tip up and down.

"Rhonda thought you were dead."

"Not for her lack of trying."

Dolph laughed. "Cute kid. Lousy on the follow-
through, though. Father always told her she was—"

"Adolph," he said, his voice low and warning.

"Right." Dolph toyed with a curl, tapped a foot, watched the sword's tip weave a liver transplant, and said, "Fact is, hero, you've made a hell of a mess. Poor Joquinn's got his dander up, and he's so busy trying to get those damned Spears to work that he sent me down to find out what I'm supposed to do with you."

"What?" Jerico said.

Placker laughed and shook his head. "My god, didn't the big blue monk tell you the conditions of your capture?"

"How could he? He was captured."

"Ah."

"So?"

Placker waited expectantly.

"So?"

Placker shifted uncomfortably.

"For Christ's sake!" Jerico said, and hoisted himself forward until he was sitting on the footboard.

Placker momentarily covered his face with his hands, then dropped them into his lap. "Look," he said. "The way it goes, see, is that you're supposed to tell me how you want to be kept a prisoner. Then I'm supposed to tell you that it doesn't work _that_ way around here, and that you're a prisoner and in no position to make demands. Then you tell me to go to hell, I get up and tell you that you have a choice: you can either work for the Almost Holy Joquinn, or die. Okay? You got it?"

"Drop dead," Jerico said.

"Damn," Placker muttered. "Now I'll have to improvise. He didn't tell me about improvising. Damn."

Jerico leaned over and tapped his knee with the sword. "I'll make it easy for you, okay?"

"Oh, Christ, would you?"

"No problem."

"Thanks."

Jerico smiled. "The thing is, sir, that I have the sword and you do not. This makes it rather silly for you to ignore whatever demands I may make, especially since I'm in no mood to listen to any threats you may wish to impart. Therefore, as I see it, you will save your life and take me to Joquinn, or you will lose your life and never see the light of day again." He raised an eyebrow.

"I see your point," Placker said after a few seconds. "When do we get to the part about your working for the Almost Holy?"

"That," Jerico said as he stood, "is the beauty of it. We don't. It's much less confusing that way."

"Easy for you to say. You don't have to listen to you."

Jerico accepted the insult in good humor, placing the sword's tip against the man's throat, thereby causing him to rise majestically from the chair and back guardedly toward the door.

"I don't think you'll get away with this," Placker said as they stepped into the hall.

Jerico only grunted, turned him around, and placed the sword's tip into the small of his back.

"I mean, really, hero. How do you expect to defeat the Almost Holy? Right now, the man is working on the Spear of the Abject Misery and Geographical Rearrangement. How the hell can you beat that?"

Jerico didn't even know what it meant, though he had a fair and terrifying idea, so he said nothing. Instead he shoved the man along a wide, high, carpeted, paneled, chandeliered corridor off of which were many doors, each one of which he opened in the hopes of finding his friends. Placker would offer him no assistance, and indeed, Jerico would not ask it since he didn't believe the man was constitutionally capable of telling him the truth. Except maybe the bit about his dying if he didn't join Joquinn.

After the sixth door he said, "I suppose you know that you don't have an army anymore."

Placker shrugged. "They were a pain in the ass anyway. Besides, we don't need one."

"Oh? And may I ask why not?"

"Because once Joquinn takes over the Sixth Spear, which ought to be any day now, he'll move on to the Seventh, and that's all she wrote, Jack."

"Jerico."

"Whatever."

They came to a broad winding staircase that led both up and down. Placker started down; Jerico forced him up.

Fifteen doors later they came to another staircase. Placker started down; Jerico forced him up.

"I get nosebleeds," the man in red complained.

Only four doors on this floor, and the staircase only went down. Which they did as well, until Jerico figured he was on the floor below the one he started out on. Then he checked the doors here, the ones on the floor below that, and the ones on the floor below that one.

"Jesus," he said, "where the hell *is* everybody?"

"In the basement," Placker told him.

"Then why the hell didn't you tell me, and don't say it's because I didn't ask you because I know I didn't ask you, but I would have hoped that you would have volunteered the information and saved us a lot of time. Cripes!"

"Two 'would have's don't make a 'did,' hero," Placker sneered as he opened a massive wooden door heavily banded in bronze and intricately carved in the likeness of a youngish man so handsome and innocent-looking that Jerico knew it could only be the Most Holy Ralph.

On the other side was a stone staircase.

They went down.

Placker complained that his feet were killing him; Jerico explained that he should be so lucky if one hair on the heads of any of his friends was so much as kinked.

"Does that include mustaches?"

"Damn right."

"Shit."

Jerico counted fifty-eight steps before they reached the bottom and faced another large wooden door banded in bronze and carved in the shape of a large wooden door. Placker hesitated then, for from the other side came the muffled sounds of explosions, silence, and rants and wails of despair and injury.

"Dungeon," he said.

"I gathered. Open the door."

Placker wiped his hands on his trousers. "Mind if I stand back? He's gonna be pissed."

Jerico smiled without a shred of mirth, and clubbed the man in red with his fist. Placker groaned, staggered against the wall, and sagged to the stone floor, which, Jerico noted with a tiny twinge of alarm, had begun to develop some alarmingly wide cracks that led from the mysterious room. The result, no doubt, of Joquinn's experiments in conjuring.

Then he opened the door and stepped through, and did not move a muscle when the door slammed shut behind him and he heard the echoing triumphant laugh of a man who believed he had finally caged his nemesis and rendered him helpless.

"Well," he said, "ain't this the pits."

40 The room could be called a room only by the wildest stretch of the imagination and an interior decorator with dogged optimism. If one put up greenstone-block walls and a heavy-beam ceiling around and over a football field, popped in a few fifteen-foot windows that tapered to points at the top, added a dozen wagon wheel chandeliers that burned candles eighteen inches in circumference, and gathered up all the throw rugs in Detroit to scatter over the stone floor, one might have an idea of what this room looked like.

Jerico was there, and he still didn't believe it.

There were, by rough count, a baker's dozen laboratory tables scattered about his immediate area, each of them loaded with the bubbling, multicolored paraphernalia generally associated with scientists working in and about the nineteenth century; beside each one were tall metal drums that spat and foamed smoke so heavy it sank immediately to the floor and writhed in lugubrious clouds to the walls; there were also any number of tall leather-topped stools, which indicated to Jerico that the experimenter was not the tallest of men.

Beyond the tables was an empty area dominated by what appeared to be a large pit covered by a wooden cap. From the center of the cap to a great iron hook in the uppermost reaches of the ceiling was a chain whose links were the width of a corpulent man's waist. The floor around the cap was stained a sickly white, and the few rugs remaining near it were scorched and curled to the very essence of their threads.

On the other side of the cap was yet another series of laboratory tables, equipment arcane and yet oddly familiar, with the added fillip of an electrical gizmo or two, which sparked and sizzled and made all sorts of ominous noises.

What touched off Jerico's reaction, however, was the fact that much of the otherwise fascinating furnishings was either broken, covered with layers of pristine dust, or cracked to within a sneeze of shattering on the floor. It was messy. It proved to him that the operator was someone he did not wish to know on a continuing basis, even aside from the established truth that the operator was also trying to kill him.

With an expression of extreme disgust, he began to make his way along an aisle formed by the tables, approaching the pit cap warily while, at the same time, checking to be sure there were no traps, no ambushes, no enticements along the way to divert his attention from the moans and groans that rose from the room's far end.

He could make out Buck's voice well enough, and the brothers, and the one with the most venom was probably Jini.

At the pit he knelt to examine the cap, followed the chain with his eye, and saw that it was lashed around and spiked to a thick post not twenty feet away to the right.

He wondered what was down there.

He rose and walked around it, heading into the aisle formed by the second group of tables.

The moans subsided.

And now he could see beyond, to the far end of the room, to a rippling silver-winking black curtain that hung all the way from the ceiling. The noise he had heard came from behind there.

And he stopped at the last table, fifteen feet from the curtain, when a voice said:

"Hello, *toad*. Welcome to my home."

Jerico did not bother to look for the source of the delivered scorn. He would not give the Almost Holy Joquinn the satisfaction of a reaction. Besides, the windows, as he had already covertly discovered, looked out on nothing but dirt, since he was in the basement, and the sidelines of this room were so shadowed and dim that an army could have hidden there and he'd never be able to spot them.

"Hello, Yama," he said, deliberately keeping his voice neutral.

The voice laughed. "So, you know my name, do you?"

"It had been revealed to me as thus, yes."

"And do you know that I am now the ecclesiastical ruler of this land, toad?"

"I know," he said, this time with a hint of sly ridicule, "that you wish it were so, yet know it is not so, for if it were so, you would not waste your self-appointed valuable time on one such as I, who have defeated your every stratagem, not to mention your vile army."

A second time the voice laughed, but Jerico was pleased to discern a note of insecurity humming around the edges.

"And you," the voice taunted, "call yourself a hero?"

"I do. For it is my profession, and my life's blood, even though much of it has been spilled on the ground of your lovely land."

Now the laugh was but a single, derisive, "Ha! Quite a pretty speech from a man who wants to knock around with a dead woman."

"*Enough!*" Jerico roared. "I have had my fill of your petty insults and childish attempts to force my temper out of control. You had better prepare your worst, you Almost Holy weasel, because I am tired of this place, and I am weary of you!"

"Jesus," the voice said, "do you always talk that way?"

Jerico drew his sword.

"And I am not a weasel!"

He took a step forward, and a tiny vermilion explosion put a crack in the floor. Undaunted, he smiled and moved again, and again the floor was cracked. A shake of his head at the futility of villains everywhere to believe they could scare him off with a little display of petulant magic, and another step, another crack, and by the time he reached the curtain significant portions of the floor behind him were already falling into whatever lay below the basement.

"I wouldn't touch that if I were you, toad," the voice warned when Jerico reached out to lift the curtain from its fringed and weighted hem.

This time he obeyed. Who knew what spells Joquinn had placed on the cloth that glittered and starred with thousands of meticulously inlaid rhinestones? Electricity could fry him, cold could freeze him, heat could bake him—the possibilities were endless. Yet he could not just stand here, for his friends and the future of the entire planet lay in jeopardy only inches away. It was a predicament he'd not faced before in his career, and he wondered if there was some precedent which could guide him, at least long enough to keep him from getting killed.

Suddenly a trumpet sounded—a rococo fanfare for lost souls and vanquishing aspiring sorcerers.

An intricate drum roll thundered throughout the cavernous room.

The trumpet again, on a single sweet note that accompanied a loud, atonal but oddly appropriate ripping noise as the curtain began to split majestically down the center. From behind it, as the music swelled and ebbed and the drums faded, a slice of white light sheered into the room, a light so pure and bright that it made Jerico turn away and close his eyes lest he be blinded and rendered more useless than he already was.

And when the curtain parted to and through its hem and was drawn to either side, he opened his eyes, set his shoulders and chin, and saw revealed before him the place where all movie epic extras go when they die.

"Good god," he said, "who the hell is your tailor?"

In startling, and perhaps even eccentric, contrast to the rest of the basement, here, Jerico knew, was where all the money went.

Etched pillars of gold rose to the ceiling along the silver walls; the floor was covered with an extraordinary carpet of deepest royal blue, the center of which held a crimson design depicting the very medallion he wore about his neck and which adorned so many of the homes and hovels he had come across in his travels; beyond the medallion were four shorter pillars, these encrusted with gems the names for which momentarily escaped him but did not diminish his capacity for awe; and beyond those pillars were yet four more, even shorter, of iridescent ivory upon which had been scrimshawed in black scenes of pastoral elegance that brought a tear to his eyes; and still beyond those pillars was a line of gilded, lion-claw chairs whose backs were set with ebony thorns shaped like roses; and beyond the chairs were seven greenstone steps leading to a greenstone dais upon which had been set a throne so high and wide that all the kings of history could have sat upon it and had room for a mistress or two.

Arrayed before the throne were a dozen blue-robed monks, their cowls thrown defiantly back. Jerico recognized Ham Attadon instantly; he was the one kneeling, and evidently polishing a pair of black, simulated-leather boots with white tassels at the top. When Attadon saw him, he grinned, and saluted him with a gesture even the ancient Romans found offensive.

But in the center of the throne was Joquinn Yama. His robe was scarlet, his cowl phosphorescent green, his girdle sunlight yellow, and his sandals beige.

The monks, save for Attadon, began a low chanting, snapping their fingers to keep themselves in time.

The trumpet sounded again.

The drums beat a rhythm that threw the monks off until they found the beat and carried on.

Jerico looked behind him, at the disarray of the room's other two-thirds; he looked back at the throne, the monks, Yama, and the gilded chairs around which, he now saw, were thick ropes. He strode forward boldly, cloak billowing behind him, heels hard on the carpet, eyes narrowed and gaze steady on the Almost Holy, who rose with a flurry of arms and robes and smiled at him so broadly his black-stubbed teeth actually glittered.

Jerico was right.

When he came abreast of the chairs, which were but a few yards from the steps, he saw his companions lashed to them. They seemed none the worse for wear, but the despair on their faces was enough to wrench his heart.

"I am here," he told them.

"Sire!" cried George and Giles.

"Talk him to death," Buck suggested weakly.

And Jini only looked at him, her eyelids aflutter.

The monks continued their chant, shuffling now side to side, Attadon humming as he polished off a toe with a spit and a swipe.

Jerico moved to the first step without taking it, and glared. "Am I to be impressed?" he asked over the noise of the chant.

Joquinn sneered, his sideways eyes fairly radiating contempt. "I don't want to impress you, you toad. I don't have to impress you. And even if I did, I wouldn't. Would you?"

"I would not permit greed nor hunger for power nor loathing for my fellow man to rule me in such a way."

Yama shook his head. "You are pitiful, toad. You think you can defeat me? I, who have now harnessed all the powers of all the Spears? I, who have transformed the magic of Robswerran from a minor-league fantasy into the power to rule an entire world, and a few of the nearest planets? I, who—"

"Needs his hair washed," Jerico said.

Yama gaped.

The monks stopped chanting.

Attadon rose to his full height and threw one of the boots at Jerico's head.

Jerico did not move; the boot sailed over him and bounced along the carpet.

"Well done," Yama said. "You have passed the first test."

"What test?"

The Almost Holy paced before his throne. "The test, you toad, to determine whether or not I'll let you join me in my crusade."

"Ah," Jerico said, smiling at his friends, tapping the side of his nose with a finger. "Ah. So that is the ploy, eh? Well, save your breath, bud, because this man's not for you."

"Don't be too sure. I have my ways."

Jerico laughed, and took the first step up. "Say your prayers, greasy, because I'm tired of all this chatter."

Yama immediately leapt onto the throne and drew a long silver whip from beneath his robes. "Do you know what this is, toad?"

"A whip," Jerico answered, moving to the second step.

Yama grabbed Attadon by the scruff of the neck and shook him unmercifully. "You told!"

"I didn't!" the blue-haired monk yelped.

"Then how did he know?"

"He saw it, Almost Holy."

Yama looked at the whip, looked at Jerico, who was now on the third step and making resolutely for the fourth, and said, "This isn't going as I planned."

Jerico paused. His sixth sense and decent eyesight warned him that the monks, who had drawn swords from their robes, were not going to remain impartial for very long. And since Attadon had one boot left, he decided to make a temporary retreat. Slowly. Ever so slowly. Until he was at the bottom, watching with some bafflement as Yama began twiddling with some of the throne's designs. Then, thinking there was time for a quick maneuver or two, he raced behind the chairs and slashed apart the ropes which had so cruelly bound his friends.

They chafed their wrists, limbered their muscles, and headed for the exit.

"Wait!" Jerico said.

They stopped as one.

"Aren't you going to help me?"

Buck folded his hands into what was left of his sleeves, and after a sorrowful look at the others, came forward. "My son," he said, "surely you recall that this is what we hoped you would do for us. Were we able to do it ourselves, we would not have needed you. Yes, this is the destiny of the W'dch'ck warrior, Jerico Dove, and all we can do is but wish you Ralph speed and a good eye for the vital parts."

"How about a cheer?"

"And now," the Innkeeper said, "a blessing to protect you from mortal harm, death, disfigurement, dismemberment, and the ultimate translation into parts foreign to each other." He mumbled something hastily as he glanced over Jerico's shoulder. "Amen."

"You could applaud or something."

Buck took his hand and shook it. "Good luck, little stranger. We will be rooting for you."

The monks began chanting, snapping, and shuffling again.

Yama pulled from a secret compartment in the throne a sheath of glowing spears.

And Jerico watched as those who had fought the length, if not the breadth, of Robswerran walked sedately and hurriedly toward the now-closing curtain.

He whirled.

Yama was holding the Spears over his head.

The monks were working up a fairly decent sweat.

The throne was flashing strobe lights up to the ceiling, sending floodlights slicing through the air, catching the facets of the pillars as they began to revolve with a deep grinding sound, and from the

ceiling descended an incredible display of doves flying
in such close formation they seemed but a single cloud
of delicate white.

Yama laughed.

The monks reached the last verse.

And Jerico could only scream when he saw that the
doves had beaks from which gleamed belligerent
fangs.

41 It was truly a predicament for which Jerico had no training; yet he did not chastise himself for the apparent lack of foresight. While New York and the other cities where he plied his trade certainly had an abundance of the bizarre and the unusual, this particular instance was beyond anything any metropolis in the world could fashion. Therefore, he thought as he adroitly dropped to his knees and curled the cloak over his head and arranged it artfully until nothing of consequence was exposed, he could not be held accountable for either the scream or the wish that his mother were here.

The pillars ground on.

The music played on.

Jerico looked through a tiny gap in the cloak and noted with grim fascination and no surprise at all that the pillars had begun to sprout what looked like lashes from their centers, those lashes whipping around as the pillars spun, reminding him of a berserk car wash that could, should he attempt to pass through, flail him to the bone, alive, and swiftly.

To get to Joquinn Yama, he would have to first pass through that gauntlet.

Wrong, he told himself when the doves landed, but what the hell, if it isn't one thing it's another.

He huddled, intent on deciphering the white cloud's purpose other than taking his life.

The answer came soon enough, and he damned enough for even thinking the stupid question—all too clearly he could hear their heinous shrieks as they attempted to peck and fang their way through the overlaid armacon scales, and heard as well their avian frustration as tooth after fang broke off in the attempt. The noise within the makeshift tent was perforce horrendous—the explosive tintinnabulation of a hundred zealous cobbler's elves putting sole into their work. But he persevered even though his ears felt as if they were going to burst, his head as if it were going to explode, his nerves as if they were going to fray and drive him mad.

That such an innocuous display of birdlike coordination should turn into a nightmare was something he would remember the rest of his life, assuming the rest of his life extended beyond the next hour or so.

A beak poked through the gap.

Jerico grabbed its rough contours between two fingers and gave it a vicious twist that sent its owner dashing to the floor in a writhe of agony.

Another beak, another twist, and the word soon spread that there was a chink in the enemy's armor.

Beak and twist, then, beak and twist, and as one replaced another and the tapping continued without abating, he feared that unless something happened soon he would truly be trapped here, twisting the night away until his fingers cramped and bled and he was inexorably beaten to the floor where the *coup de grace* would probably be administered by a blood-lust robin or an armored sparrow with a grudge.

Beak. Twist.

The pillars lashing and grinding.

Above it all an exultant assured laugh that told him that while Joquinn was unable to get to him personally, the Almost Holy believed that the end was near and victory would soon be his.

And so it might be, Jerico thought as a dove wormed its way through the gap and was only just trapped under the crushing weight of his kneecap; and so it might be.

An image, then, of the luscious Dawn Eglantine—weeping and wailing over his remains, vowing chastity and spinsterhood, hugging her bereaved brother to her bosom as the Fadfy fathers tore down her home and sent her into the streets, into the night, never to return.

His heart strengthened, his muscles tensed for action, and he raised his head to cry out in silence: Never! I didn't come all this way just to be defeated by a bunch of undergrown chickens!

But he didn't move, because the vow, despite its heroic statue and dramatic premise, didn't bring with it an answer to his dilemma—until he realized that the reason Yama couldn't get to him to finish him off was the lashes. And if the lashes were as nasty as they sounded, they would certainly be the scourge of the doves as well.

Determination thus renewed, he took a deep breath, and another, twisted a beak in the opposite direction to keep the doves off balance, and crawled forward. Inch by inch. Staggering under the renewed blows of the swirling white cloud the moment its collective tiny brain realized what the hero was planning.

The cries became more frantic.

Yama's laugh became more uncertain.

And Jerico prayed that the sustaining cloak, thus far fairly impervious, would continue to be so once it encountered the terrible power of the pillars.

Another foot, another yard, and the cloud suddenly settled on his back, and shifted side to side in a last-minute attempt to tip him over and expose his all-too-mortal flesh to the rending of those fangs which had not yet been chipped off. He shifted in the other direction and lurched forward, stopped, lurched back, and forward again, smiling grimly as he heard the death cries of dozens of the profane birds as they were flung between the pillars and were soon flailed into parts that were flailed into bits that were flung out again and splattered against the walls.

His arms and shoulders began to burn with the strain, but he kept on, bracing himself when the first lash swept over the hump of his head. It was a glancing blow, yet it nearly toppled him, and he froze, taking a series of belts while he considered his options—of which, he decided, there were none. Once on the road to the final confrontation, there was no turning back.

Nuts.

And he crawled again, battered, clobbered, smacked, lashed, hearing with growing alarm, as he passed safely through the first four pillars, the unmistakable sound of scales being torn from their moorings.

Soon the high-pitched whirr of the lashes and the grind of the pillars and the clank of cloak meeting whip was joined by the sound of the scales hitting the floor. Hellish hail was the image that came to mind as he staggered to his left and was whipped to his right.

He stared at the floor that passed under and behind him, and saw deep gouges in the material, deeper gouges in the stone, and the wretched yet valiant remains of the scales jammed into the foundation.

They had served him well for many a day, and he could not bear to look at their sacrifice any longer. Unfortunately, being under the cloak as he was, there was no place else to look, and so he hardened his heart to the remnants of his protection, and clenched his teeth against the blows that came closer and closer to penetrating his protection.

When they stopped, abruptly, he was so startled and unprepared he fell over.

A silence greeted his attempts to roll back to his hands and knees; further silence, punctuated by the odd dropping scale, as he pushed himself wearily back onto his heels and let the cloak drop denuded to the floor; and more silence when he looked up and saw several Yamas gaping at him from a throne that seemed to have grown multiple edges.

He rubbed his eyes.

He looked again.

A single Yama looked back, the silver whip now in the hands of Ham Attadon while the Almost Holy took the first step down, shaking his head in amazement, bewilderment, and no little concern.

"How did you do that?" he asked.

"I did. That is all you need to know," was the reply.

"But no one's ever done that before. No one."

Jerico felt no pride, only pain, and a expanding sensation of consternation when he saw the Seven Spears arrayed behind Yama.

They extended from the throne's back like the rays of a diabolical sun, their shafts flawlessly fashioned from precious stones, their tips catching the candles' light and throwing it back in lances and arrows bright enough to blind should one be unfortunate enough to stare straight at them and at such an angle as to have them blind him.

He swayed to his feet, ignoring the threatening

monks, the whipcrack of Attadon's weapon, the sneer of the Almost Holy. He would not be caught dead kneeling before such a man.

He staggered forward then, swayed again, and felt a melancholy pain in his heart until he flicked away the stray beak that had penetrated his shirt.

After all this time, all the fighting, the loving, the living, the dying; after the adventures and the interludes, the promises and deceits; after the nights and days and dreams and fears and prayers and god-speeds—

The Seven Spears of the W'dch'ck were at last there before him.

Yama noted the direction of his dazed and awed gaze, and he glanced over his shoulder, and smiled back down at the hero.

"Tell me, toad," he said, tossing his greasy hair behind his ears, "how do you want to die, now that you have seen the source of my power?"

"Of old age," Jerico whispered.

"Clever."

"You asked."

The monks brandished their weapons and took the first step down in order to flank their master.

Yama sighed. "You are a fool, you know. This isn't going to do you any good."

"What isn't?"

"Stalling for time while your friends battle with their guilt, regain their senses and courage, and rush back to fight at your side."

Jerico smiled sadly. "I fear you are wrong again, Joquinn. They are gone."

"No, I don't think so," the Almost Holy said, and pointed.

Jerico turned.

And there they were, all four of them, hustling as dignified as they could back toward the throne.

He smiled.

He laughed.

He waited until they joined them and asked them what it was about the past few minutes which had made them see the light.

"The pit," Buck answered, glancing nervously behind him.

"The pit?"

"Yeah. The thing with the cover."

Jerico parted them with his hands and stared toward the room's center. He saw nothing. Nothing, that is, until Giles pointed upward and he was able to spot, swaying slightly on its chain, the impossible tonnage of the wooden cap.

"I see," he said.

Yama laughed, a trait that was rapidly beginning to annoy Jerico no end.

"And I suppose something or someone lives in that pit, has now been released by the forces set in motion by Yama's greed and need to destroy us?"

"Prunella!" George said hoarsely.

"Hey," Jerico cautioned. "Watch the mouth there, gardener."

"No, sire," Giles said anxiously, taking his arm and lowering his voice to a bare whisper. "The prunella is a beast which the Most Holy Ralph—"

"Hey, watch the mouth!" commanded Yama.

"—imprisoned there many decades ago. It is the antithesis of all the Spears stand for, and should it ever escape the confines of the pit, no one but Ralph himself will be able to prevent it from destroying our land."

Jerico scratched his cheek thoughtfully. "But the cap is up. Isn't it too late?"

"It's a deep pit," the cook explained.

"Well, not all that deep," his brother suggested.

"Deep enough," Giles countered.

"True. I'll give you that."

"But not that deep that we can stand around forever."

"No one," George reminded him, "lives forever."

Jerico turned to Jini. "This is a problem, yes?"

"Quick," she said. "You're quick, Dove. Jesus."

He understood perfectly her conflicting emotions and defensive reaction to the situation at hand. His smile told her that he did; her smile told him that he might well be wrong, but this was not the time to get into group dissection. He nodded his agreement and turned back to Yama.

"I think this is the end," he said.

Yama put his hands on his hips and stepped back to the throne level. "I couldn't have put it better, hero. A shame you can't be on my side."

Jerico's quick laugh was mocking, and before anyone could stop him, he charged up the steps.

42 The admission that he was just as surprised as anyone by his action almost stopped Jerico in his steps; but the incentive the also suddenly converging and overtly hostile monks presented him with was enough to override his natural good sense and send him into their midst with a horrifically shrill battle cry the essence of which was lost to all but those who bothered to listen.

As he lunged past one sword, ducked a bulbous club, and grabbed the thick wrist of a man who held something that looked like a barbecue fork, it occurred to him that he didn't have a weapon. Unfortunately, his battle with the doves and pillars left him with less than a full tank of gas, and he was unable to wrest the pointed object from the monk's tenacious grip. Instead he thrust the man aside and, leaping agilely away from a hard-swung mace, spun to the top step and allowed Attadon to snake rather weakly the silver whip around his waist. Then he grabbed it and yanked, and the diminutive monk stumbled forward, close enough for Jerico to take hold of his topknot and yank that as well.

Attadon bellowed as only a tiny man can.

One of the other monks bellowed too, and Jerico's keen hearing told him that at least the brothers, and probably Buck in addition, had finally overcome their astonishment and had launched themselves into the fray.

Attadon didn't care. His feet were dangling off the floor, his hair was coming apart at the scalp, and Jerico was bending his hand to such an abnormal degree that he gave up the whip's grip with a whimper.

Jerico tossed him down the steps and turned to face the Almost Holy Yama.

"Now," he said.

But Yama leapt onto the throne and, in a single blurred motion, pulled one of the Spears from its place.

"A step and you're dead," the man warned.

Jini cried, "My god, it's the Seventh!"

And as suddenly as the melee had begun, it ended, though Jerico for the life of him couldn't see why. Yama was there, he himself had the whip, and all he had to do was use a flick of his wrist, and the Spear would be snared and rendered harmless.

He looked around then, and saw that the others, the Joquinnite monks included, were backing fearfully down the steps, their gazes not once leaving the fearsome Spear.

I have not been told something again, he thought; this is getting to be monotonous.

"Surrender," he suggested, not really believing the Almost Holy would actually do it.

Yama shook his head.

You never know until you try, he thought, and

considered another tack. "It will go well with you in the courts," he told him.

"What courts?"

Jerico recognized a problem when he heard one. "Then it will go well with me," he believed he recovered nicely.

"I could care."

"Then do."

And Yama lifted the Spear above his head, causing Jini and Buck to scream prayers and imprecations together, and the monks to begin a complex series of cringings that soon brought them to relative safety behind the pillars with the others.

"One more step," Yama advised, "and I will use this. And don't think I won't. I have nothing left to lose. I will sooner take us all with me than surrender and let you decide my fate."

Well, Jerico thought, that answers all my questions.

"Joquinn!" Buck called. "This is silly!"

Yama's face darkened. "Easy for you to say, Fye. You want this Spear as much as I do."

"A lie!"

"You want the power!"

"A fabrication!"

"You want the money!"

Jerico waited.

Yama nodded knowingly. "You see, toad, the sort of people you are aligned with?"

Slowly and deliberately, Jerico coiled the whip in his hand, checked its weight and balance, then played it out just as slowly, listening to its braided length hiss across the stone. "I think," he said, "I can probably break your neck before you can do anything with that Spear."

"Try it."

"No!" Jini shouted.

Jerico chanced a look over his shoulder. "Why?"

"It's too dangerous!"

"I gathered that much. But why?"

"Well, for heaven's sake, it's the Spear of the Most Holy Ralph's Direct Historical Revision and W'd-ch'ck Redetermination."

Jerico frowned. "Jesus, do you always talk that way?"

Jini threw up her hands in exasperation.

But Jerico knew instinctively what the appalling appellation meant—that the use of the Seventh Spear would so alter the past that the present would become whatever the wielder wished, and those caught up in the spell wouldn't know the difference. Or they wouldn't care even if they did. Or they wouldn't know that they didn't know because the past, to them, was the past and not what it used to be.

And this, he realized with a frisson of horror, was the way Joquinn Yama was going to conquer not only this world, but the Outside as well.

And Dawn would be even more dead than she already was.

Shaking his head, he drew his whiphand back. "I can't let you do it, Joquinn," he said. "Besides, you remind me of a German shepherd I once knew. One that taught me a valuable lesson."

Yama's eyes widened side to side. "You . . . you're really going to try to stop me?"

He shrugged. "What's the difference if I die now or am already dead in the new present you're going to define with that Spear's power? For me it's six of one, half-dozen of the other."

"I'll be damned."

Jerico turned sideways.

Yama, after a promising hesitation, narrowed his eyes and aimed the Spear toward the ceiling.

And from the center of the room came a sustained

gurgling, a spouting of vile-smelling steam, and a harsh prolonged scrabbling that sounded exactly like something's unclippable claws were digging into and climbing up a long stone wall.

"The prunella," Giles gasped.

It was precisely the sort of unexpected distraction both opponents had hoped for, but Jerico's faster reflexes had his whip humming through the air before Yama was able to deliver the spell to work the Spear's awesome power. The silver braid, in less time than it took Jerico to aim and snap it, swiftly coiled itself around the exquisite jaded shaft, initiating a brief but fruitless tug of war.

Yama lost.

The Spear clattered to the floor and rolled down the steps.

Buck cheered.

Jini swore delightfully.

And Jerico allowed himself a satisfied grin, which lamentable lapse in heroic sportsmanship permitted the opportunistic Yama to leap off the throne and land squarely on his chest. After a fierce moment's grappling, they toppled, fell, and tumbled down the steps while the monk's hands tore at his throat, his hair, finally gripped his ears and slammed his head against the stone.

Jerico, stunned and unaware for a second exactly where he was, released him.

Yama instantly snatched up a spiked club and, daring the others to try to stop him, raced across the room. His monks followed tentatively, though without much heart and no enthusiasm at all; the brothers raced to Jerico's side and helped him up, slapped his face gently and otherwise managed to bring him around.

"Yama!" Jerico said.

"Gone," George told him.

"Almost," Giles corrected.

Jerico scanned the floor, found a sword, and with an order for the others to follow, ran after the fleeing monk, cursing himself for his stupidity, scolding himself for betraying pretty much every principle he had stood for until he'd been knocked down the steps, and determined to put to rights all that he had undone once and for all.

Then he reached the pit, and skidded to a halt.

Buck came up beside him, a redoubtable club in his hand; the brothers began to circle the pit, and stopped at Jerico's restraining gesture.

Yama was already halfway to the door, but he wasn't running anymore. Through the noxious mist that rose from the pit, Jerico could see him standing arrogantly beside one of the laboratory tables, his hands cupped around his mouth. "Choose, you toad!" the monk called, and giggled insanely. "You can chase me, hero, maybe even catch me if you're fast enough —but if you do, my darling pet prunella will escape and destroy you all. If you stay here and deal with the beast from the heart of the earth, I will escape and you will lose!" He threw back his head and laughed. "Choose, you miserable toad, *choose!*"

Instantly Jerico wheeled and sprinted to his left, grabbing Buck's arm and practically dragging him along. When he reached the post that held the chain, he pointed and said, "Can you do it, Innkeeper?"

Buck hefted the club and said, "What the hell."

He reared back and slammed it. The post quivered, the cap began to sway. Again. Again. Giles ran up and added his club as well. When George ran up and realized he had no club, he ran back and took one from one of Yama's indecisive monks, ran back, and began pounding the hell out of the post.

The steam became thicker, the stench more unbearable.

Jini ran up to Jerico and grabbed his arm. "You're not going after that bastard?"

"How can I?" he answered, his face dripping sweat. "I must stand guard, so if the beast starts to—"

"Yeah, yeah, I know all that. But what about him?"

"I haven't forgotten," he said solemnly. "But one thing at a time."

"Well, that thing," she told him, pointing back at the pit, "isn't going to wait much longer."

A grunting could be heard then, filling the vast room with abrupt and unwanted images of death, destruction, and torment beyond description. Claws worked at the stone. More steam rose and peeled the windows away from the walls. The Joquinnite monks made their decision, ran to the post and started climbing up the chain in the clear hope that the added weight would loosen the hook from its beam. A bold plan, Jerico thought in admiration, standing quickly to one side while they fell one by one whenever Buck or the brothers added another blow with their clubs.

A shimmering black claw appeared at the edge of the pit.

Jerico noted its size, extrapolated, and refused to believe that anything that large had the right to exist.

He despaired.

The post held.

He ran back to the pit, shaded his eyes and looked down, saw even thicker bilious steam and a shadow rising toward him, ran back to the post and wildly exhorted the others to hurry, what time was left was growing shorter by the second.

Buck's face was alarmingly red, but he continued his assault until his club finally and inevitably shattered. The brothers kept on, hammering away, grunting, swearing, redoubling their efforts when the post wobbled a bit more, though it refused to come free of its base.

Jini began to weep.

Joquinn's receding laughter rose above the booming.

And another claw appeared at the edge of the pit.

"Stop!" Jerico commanded, and tossed his sword aside.

The others, astounded by the order, did just that, and stared at him.

"Jerico," Jini said. "Jerico, we haven't time for one of your speeches."

He pushed her gently away and walked up to the battered post. It was foolish, what he meant to attempt, but they were out of time, miracles, and luck. There was only one thing left to do, and though it would likely mean the end of him, it would at least give the others a chance to escape, find Joquinn, and end his plans of conquest forever.

"Damnit," Jini said, slapping his arm hard, "I told you there was no time for a speech!"

He looked at her, laughed once, and stared at the post while he took in as deep a breath as he could take. Released it slowly. Took it back again.

"Oh . . . my," Giles said, backing away.

"Oh . . . wow," George said, following his brother.

Jerico flexed.

And the clothing Indo had given him, the clothing he had healed and held him together, began to part—not, at the seams, but wherever Jerico's muscles found the room to expand, which were pretty much everywhere.

He flexed.

He expanded.

His shirt fell away in rags, his trousers in strips, his back bulged, his chest bulged, his arms became sculptured iron that gleamed with perspiration and quivered with the tension that filled them, powered them, held them steady when he curled them around the post, leaned his brow against the wood . . . and lifted.

Heat filled his brain; his heart raced so rapidly the threat of passing out prior to massive cardiac stoppage became more real than the prunella's lethal appearance.

He lifted.

Buck prayed.

His grip began to slip, his knees to sag.

Giles and George urged him on, calling out his name, pleading with him, begging, without a single contradiction.

He shifted his hands and lifted.

Jini muttered to herself.

He lifted.

And with a sudden cry twisted and yanked the post from its mooring, held it, held it, and with another cry flung it from him to the floor, which it struck for but a second before the weight of the pit's cap pulled on the chain, lifted the post again, and after a long second's fateful hovering, the wooden plug dropped like a stone onto the mouth of the pit. And four of the five claws. And the prunella's unseen head.

Jerico collapsed, every muscle in his body screaming for the medics. He swallowed air, gulped for air, panted, then turned to the brothers and said, "Don't let him get away," before a red fog drifted over him and the world went on hiatus.

43 Once upon a lifetime ago, Jerico sat on the marbled back porch of his modest Nevada mansion and watched a movie on the thirty-foot screen he'd set up in the backyard. Yet, despite the grand size of the images and the sweep of the story, none of it seemed real against the backdrop of the snow-capped mountains that rose above them, or the hundred-foot trees that grew beside them. The magic was missing. That peculiar fascination with the lives of people who weren't real even in real life was absent. He had mused over his reaction for several bewildered hours, pacing the porch, the yard, the driveway, until he decided that if he made the screen bigger and brought it nearer to the house, he wouldn't see the mountains or the trees, and thus return reality to where it belonged.

He did.

It worked.

And he thought as he swam laboriously through the red haze, that it was probably one of the more class-A stupid things he had ever done in his life. But what the hell, he was rich, he could afford it, and if the neighbors complained he could always shoot them.

The haze began to shade to pink.

A woman's face, dimples and dark hair, flickered before him and vanished; a hideous face with sideways eyes and greasy hair popped up in front of him and vanished; a tall, burly monk in a blue robe and hat pin tried to slap his face and vanished; a horse that looked exactly like an elephant except for the horns, the hairy tail, the white trunk, and the clarinet, floated ahead of him, and vanished.

This, he thought, is getting weird, and when he began to feel the sundry aches and pains in his muscles and bones, though not nearly as badly as he had before he'd jumped into whatever red pool he'd been swimming in for god knew how long, he decided that the party was over, the film was done, the neighbors had moved out, and he might as well wake up.

Which he did. With a start. And discovered by various tentative means that he was lying on a bed in a sedately dark green room. He sat up, and groaned at the headache booming through the tunnels of his mind.

At the foot of the bed stood Buck and Jini, smiling kindly at him, at each other, at him again.

"Welcome back, hero," said Fye, coming around to his side. "You've been away for a while."

"How long?"

"A day."

"Joquinn," he said then, his voice rasping.

"The boys are after him, as you ordered," Jini said gently.

He tried to rise, but Fye held him down. "It's

enough, what you've done, my son. Joquinn won't get far."

"He will if he tries," Jerico said.

"A point," the monk conceded, "but there's nothing we can do about it."

"You need your rest," Jini said.

"No," he insisted, and politely demanded some clothes, which he noticed he wasn't wearing when he threw back the covers. Jini didn't complain. Buck took a large garment bag out of a wardrobe and placed it on the bed.

"We will be back," he said, "in ten minutes."

They left.

Jerico wobbled out of bed, pulled down the bag's zipper, and for a moment felt the sting of unaccustomed tears fill his eyes.

A tweed jacket. English shoes. Silk shirt. Tailored trousers. Underwear he wouldn't be caught dead in without his clothes on.

He dressed. He stood in front of a mirror and brushed his hair, realized that while he'd been asleep someone had shaved him, and he wondered. Then he opened the door and stepped into the corridor where Buck and Jini were waiting, along with what seemed to be a hundred or so other monks, including, he noted with delight, Winngg Indo and all the Innkeepers.

They applauded when he appeared.

He blushed.

Buck took his arm solemnly and led him through the crowd. "We have something for you," Fye said, a glint in his eye and hat pin.

"What?"

"Wouldn't you like to know?"

"Sure."

Buck squeezed. "You have done so much for us, hero, that we can never properly repay you."

"Joquinn is still alive."

"Well . . . we'll see."

Puzzled, and distracted by the monks who lined the walls, cheering him now, throwing rose petals at him, clapping, hugging each other, straining to touch him, Jerico allowed himself to be led into the main ante-chamber. Here there were still others, and they broke into tumultuous adulation the moment he appeared.

"Oh my," he said to Jini, who had taken his left hand.

"Be strong," she told him. "There's more."

A fanfare of reverent flutes rose from a band standing in the corner. More rose petals drifted down from the ceiling. And the great doors opened, spilling sunlight into the room, blinding him as Buck and Jini led him outside.

He blinked and passed a hand over his eyes, and looked out at the plaza and said, "Oh . . . my."

They were there—on the rooftops, in the plaza, on horses and silly palominos, on foot, on daddys' shoulders, on crates and cartons and stilts and barrels; hundreds upon hundreds of Robswerran citizens, all dressed in the traditional costumes of their particular sections of the country, many holding tiny flags, many playing instruments, many involved in impromptu joyous dancing.

And as soon as they saw him they cheered.

They screamed.

They surged toward the steps and stopped only when Buck lifted a piously restraining hand.

When Jerico smiled, half a hundred damsels swooned and pissed off their lovers; when he waved, a thousand children waved back at him shyly; when he tried to meet each one's gaze, return each adoring look, they cheered again, and would not stop.

"Well?" Jini said with a dumb grin on her face.

Jerico couldn't speak for a moment, and when he

did it was only after great effort. "Where I come from," he said quietly, "they never even said 'Thank you.'"

"There's more," she replied impishly.

"There can't be," he protested.

Buck waved his hand.

The multitude fell silent and, as if on signal, parted in the center. A minute passed, and then, from the farthest reach of the plaza two men walked side by side toward the steps, one's hair flowing and gleaming in the sunlight, the other's mustache rakishly tossed around his neck.

"Oh god," Jerico whispered, "oh god." And he raced down the steps to throw his arms around the brothers, unashamed of the emotion and pleased that they were flustered, though they returned his embrace fondly.

"Joquinn," he asked, looking from one to the other.

George touched his purplestone patch knowingly. "We chased him to the far side of the plain, sire."

"He was on an elephant," Giles added.

Jerico smiled at their attempts to make him feel at home. "You mean a horse, don't you?"

"Oh no," the cook said. "It was an elephant. Big sucker. He stole it from the Tabernacle stables. In fact—" and he pointed behind him, to a group of awfully nervous men leading a beast Jerico had to look at twice to believe. It was draped in gold cloth, a crown over its spiked head, garlands of flowers wrapped about its four trunks, and silver lamé striped around its massive, stumpy legs.

But what really caught Jerico's eye was the creature that walked in front of it—the white horse. Jerico's own white horse.

"Tell me," he said then.

"Well," George began, "there's not much we can say."

"We chased Joquinn furiously, sire," Giles said, speaking slowly so that those of the crowd nearest them could pass the word to those on the outer fringes. "For hours. Lots of hours."

"A horrible ride," George agreed. "But we knew that we had to do this for you, sire, for all that you have done for us."

The crowd cheered.

The music played.

"But the monk," Jerico said. "Joquinn?"

"Well, you know," Giles said, "it was the funniest thing, now that we look back on it."

"Black humor," George explained.

"Well . . . yes, I suppose."

"I mean, when you think about what—"

Jerico smiled at them, put his arms around their shoulders, and squeezed. "Talk," he said quietly, "or I'll pluck you silly."

George stiffened. "Sire, we chased him through farms, through meadows, through weeds I've never seen in my life."

"Neither had the elephant," Giles said with an apprehensive look at the beast. "It was panicked, and you can imagine what happened next."

"No," Jerico said. "I can't."

"Well," Giles said, "the elephant sneezed."

George nodded vigorously. "And fell on its knees."

They both shuddered expressively.

"But what became of the monk?" Jerico shouted.

"The monk?" the brothers asked.

"The monk!" he demanded.

For want of a better word, Giles clapped his palms together. Once.

And the crowd cheered. The music played. And

Jerico knew that his task was done, that Joquinn Yama would be nothing more than a blot on the history of this wonderful land. Soon forgotten. Never emulated.

It was over.

It was time to leave.

Slowly he took the steps to the top, and shook Buck's hand. "There's a lot of work to do," he said to the Innkeeper. "You will do it well, you biggaloot."

They embraced.

He hugged Jini and kissed her. "I think," he whispered, "Giles likes you." She recoiled. "Think of what he could do with that mustache."

She glanced down at the cook, who went momentarily blind when he winked.

Then he looked out over the crowd one last time, raised his hands, and let them vent their appreciation, their love, their gratitude, while he returned to the plaza and swung onto the back of his impatient white steed.

"Sire?" George said. "Are you . . . that is, will you . . . what I mean to say is, shall you ride to Fadfy now?"

"Perhaps," he said. "I have a lot of thinking to do, my friend."

Giles wiped a tear from his cheek. "Sire, do think of us now and then, won't you?"

Jerico grinned. "How could I not? You realize of course that you're all, all of you, a bunch of looney tunes?"

And the crowd cheered, and the music played, and Jerico Dove rode out of the plaza, out of Kyroppig, and across the bridge that spanned the River Nunby.

No one followed.

He did not mind.

Soon enough he would be among people again; soon enough he would see his lovely Dawn and know if the curse had been lifted and she could truly be his; soon enough he would know if he was ready to return to his own world, the world beyond the golden glow in the sky.

For now, though, it was enough that he ride alone across the plain, casting his shadow, accompanied only by the singing of the birds, the soft voice of the wind, and the thump of his faithful white horse, Bill.